Welcome back to Kentucky, home of the magnificent Buckhorn brothers—an irresistible quartet of men who happen to be family— each one more dazzlingly handsome and charming than the last. Two may have already found true love, but two are still up for grabs....

In this second of two special volumes, you'll fall for mischievous Gabe, the heartthrob of Buckhorn County, and gorgeous Jordan, the veterinarian. Enjoy your stay!

Dear Reader,

You remember the old song about the woman who can bring home the bacon and fry it up in a pan? Well, ladies, what about a *guy* who can do that? A guy who accepts housework as part of his responsibilities? Or a guy who refuses to believe that raising the kids is strictly the woman's job? This is a new millennium. Times have changed. The men I write about reflect the men of today, the men I admire and respect and, yes, many of the men I know.

I've always lived by priorities and for me, children (my own especially, but all children really) have to be a priority. My sentiments have often come through in my books, in the close-knit families I like to write about. Well, thanks to all the wonderful letters you've sent me, I know that so many of you feel the same. You've shared stories of your own families, your own lives and loves with me, and now more than ever I'm reassured that the world is a beautiful place—because you're in it.

From the bottom of my heart, thank you.

Lori

P.S. Watch for *Casey*, the long-awaited story of Casey Hudson, a Harlequin single title scheduled for January 2003.

P.O. Box 854
Ross, OH 45061
lorifoster1@juno.com
http://www.lorifoster.com

LORI FOSTER

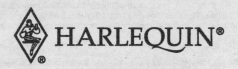

Forever
and Always

HARLEQUIN®

TORONTO • NEW YORK • LONDON
AMSTERDAM • PARIS • SYDNEY • HAMBURG
STOCKHOLM • ATHENS • TOKYO • MILAN • MADRID
PRAGUE • WARSAW • BUDAPEST • AUCKLAND

ISBN 0-373-83528-0

FOREVER AND ALWAYS—
THE BUCKHORN BROTHERS, VOL. 2

Copyright © 2002 by Harlequin Books S.A.

The publisher acknowledges the copyright holder
of the individual works as follows:

GABE
Copyright © 2000 by Lori Foster.

JORDAN
Copyright © 2000 by Lori Foster.

CONTENTS

Two very special dedications
for two very special men in my life:

First, for my son Mason
If we could bottle your endless energy,
we'd make a fortune! You are fearless,
always ready to shake things up, and you've never
met a stranger, because you make them all friends.
I hope the world is ready for you, because I know
you're ready for the world. I love you, Mason!

And to my husband, Allen
Thank you for giving me so much: unconditional love,
endless support, the closest of friendships and three
wonderful sons who are so much like you! There's
nothing more I need, nothing more I really want.
Everything else is just icing on the cake. Together, we
have been very, very blessed. I'll love you always!

GABE

CHAPTER ONE

"ISN'T HE JUST the absolute sexiest thing you've ever seen?"

"Hmm. And thank heavens for this heat wave. I love it when he leaves his shirt off." A wistful, feminine sigh. "I swear, I could sit here all day and look at him."

"We *have* been sitting here all day looking at him."

Gabe Kasper, pretending to be asleep, had to struggle with a small smile. Life was good. Here he was, sprawled in the warm sun, letting the waves from the weekend boaters gently rock the dock, with a fishing pole loosely held in one hand, a Van Halen hat pulled low over his eyes and a gaggle of good-lookin' women ogling him. He had not a care in the world. Man couldn't ask for much more satisfaction out of living.

"He is *so* gorgeous."

"And wicked lookin'. I dearly love those whiskers on his chin."

Aha. And here his brother Jordan had sworn the whiskers looked disreputable and tried to convince him to shave. Jordan could be such a stuffed shirt sometimes.

"I like that golden hair on his body, myself."

Gabe almost chuckled out loud. He couldn't wait to tell his brothers about this. Now that the two eldest were married and off-limits, Gabe and Jordan, the only two single ones left, got even more attention. Not that he was complaining. Female adoration was one of those things that couldn't really go to excess, at least, in his opinion.

"I don't mind tellin' you, Rosemary, it made me nervous when the first two brothers got married off. I cried for two days, and I was so afraid they'd all end up doing it. Heck, besides dying to have one of them to myself, those brothers were the biggest tourist draw we had here in Buckhorn."

Gabe bit the side of his lip. He'd just keep that little tidbit to himself when he did the retelling. Hell, his brothers' egos—Morgan's especially—were big enough as it was. No need adding to them. No, he'd just stick to sharing the compliments about himself.

"And Gabe is the biggest draw my boat dock has. With him sitting there, no one wants to get their gas or bait anywhere else. I keep thinkin' I ought to pay him or something."

"Ha! You're just hoping to get a little closer to him."

"No, I just wanna make sure he doesn't take his sexy self off to some other dock."

"Amen to that!"

Giggles erupted after such a heartfelt comment and Gabe sighed. He had no intention of switching loyalties. Hell, Rosemary's daddy had been letting him hang out on his docks since he was just a grasshopper and had first noticed what a pleasing thing it was to see females in bikinis. This place felt almost like a second home now. And since Rosemary's daddy had passed away, he felt honor bound to stick around and help out on occasion. The trick was to keep Rosemary from getting marriage minded, because that was one route his brothers could travel alone, thank you very much.

"It amazes me that those brothers aren't full related. They all look different—"

"But they're all gorgeous, I know. And they're all so...*strong*. My daddy used to say it took a hell of a woman to raise boys like that. I just wish they didn't live so far out on that land. Thinking up a good excuse to visit isn't easy. Not like accidentally running into the other men here in town.''

Gabe did smile at that, he couldn't help himself. He and his brothers—he refused to think of them as half brothers—had often joked about going into town to see who was looking for them. Usually some female or another was. But by living out a ways, they could always choose when and if they wanted to get friendly. It had been helpful, because once they'd hit their teens, the females had come on in droves. His mother used to claim to keep a broom by the front and back doors to beat the women away. Not that any of them minded overmuch, though his two new sisters-in-law were sure disgruntled over all the downcast female faces since the two weddings had taken place.

Gabe was just about to give up feigning sleep when a new female voice joined the others over by the gas pumps.

''Excuse me, but I was told Gabriel Kasper might be here.'' It was more a statement than anything else, and rather...strident to boot.

Female, but not at all local.

This new voice wasn't soft, Southern or sweet. She'd sounded almost impatient.

Gabe decided just to wait and see what the lady was up to. It wasn't unusual for someone female to be looking for him, and most everyone in these parts knew that in the summer, you could find him by the lake more often than not. He resisted the urge to peek at the owner of the voice and kept his body utterly relaxed.

''Whatdya want Gabe for?'' That suspicious tone was from Rosemary, bless her sweet little heart, and Gabe vowed to take her to dinner real soon.

There was a beat of silence, then, ''I have personal business to discuss with him.''

Oh, great, Gabe thought. That'll get the gossip going. What the hell kind of personal business could he have with a woman he didn't know? And he was certain he didn't know her. She didn't sound at all familiar.

"Well, he's right there, but he's relaxin', and he won't thank you none for disturbing him."

"I appreciate your warning."

Well used to the soft thud of sneakers or bare feet on the wooden planks of the dock, Gabe almost winced when the clack of hard-soled shoes rang over the water. He ignored it, and ignored the woman he could feel hesitating next to his lawn chair. The breeze stirred and he caught a light feminine scent, not really perfume, but maybe scented shampoo. He breathed deeply, but otherwise remained still.

He heard her clear her throat. "Uh...excuse me?"

She didn't sound so confident, and he waited, wondering if she'd shake him awake. He felt her hesitate, knew in his gut she was reaching for his naked shoulder...

And the fishing pole nearly leaped out of his hand.

"Son of a bi—" Gabe jolted upright, barely managing to hang on to his expensive rod and reel. His feet hit the dock and he deftly maneuvered the rod, going with the action of the fish. "Damn, it's a big one!"

Rosemary, Darlene and Ceily all ran over to his side.

"I'll grab the net!" Rosemary said.

Ceily, who usually worked the diner in town, squealed as the fish, a big ugly carp, flipped up out the water. Darlene pressed to his back, peering over his shoulder.

Gabe slid over the side of the dock to the smooth, slick, moss-covered concrete boat ramp, bracing his legs wide to keep his balance while he struggled with the fish. Rosemary, a fisherwoman of long standing, didn't hesitate to slip in beside him. She held the net at the ready. Just as Gabe got the carp close enough, she scooped him with the net. The fish looked to weigh a good fifteen pounds, and she struggled with it while Gabe tried to reach for the net and hold onto his pole.

But then Rosemary lost her footing and Gabe made a grab for her and they both went down, splashing and cursing and laughing, too. The rod jerked out of his hands and he dove forward to grab it, barely getting ahold and soaking himself thoroughly in the process. The other two women leaped in to help, all of them struggling to keep the fish and the rod while roaring with hilarity.

When the battle was over, Gabe had his fish, and a woman, in his lap. Rosemary had settled herself there while Darlene and Ceily hung on him, both struggling to control their raucous laughter. He'd known all three of them since grade school, so it wasn't the first time they'd played in the water; they felt totally familiar with each other and it showed. A long string of seaweed clung to the top of Gabe's head, and that started the women giggling again.

Gabe, enjoying himself, unhooked the big fish, kissed it—making the women smack at him—then tossed it back.

It was then they heard the tap, tap, tap of that damned hard-soled shoe.

Turning as one, they all peered at the woman who Gabe only then remembered. He had to shade his eyes against the hot sun to see, and it wasn't easy with three women draped over his body.

Silhouetted by the sunshine, her long hair looked like ruby fire. And he'd never in his life seen so many freckles on a woman before. She wore a crisp white blouse, a long jean skirt and black pumps with nylons. *Nylons in this heat?* Gabe blinked. "Can I help you with somethin', sugar?"

Her lips tightened and her arms crossed over her middle. "I don't think so. I was looking for Gabriel Kasper."

"That'd be me."

"But…I was looking for Gabriel, the town hero."

Darlene grinned hugely. "That's our Gabe!"

Ceily added, "The one and only."

Gabe rolled his eyes. "That's nonsense and you all know it."

The women all started in at once, Ceily, Rosemary and Darlene assuring him he was all that was heroic and wonderful and more.

Little Red merely stared in absolute disbelief. "You mean, *you* are the one who rescued those swimmers?"

He gently lifted Rosemary off his lap and cautiously stood on the slick concrete. The women had gone silent now, and Gabe could see why. While they looked downright sexy in their colorful bikinis, loose hair and golden tans, this woman looked like the stern, buttoned-up supervisor of a girls' prep school. And she was glaring at them all, as if she'd caught them having an orgy in the lake, rather than just romping.

Gabe, always the gentleman, boosted each woman to the dock, then deftly hauled himself out. He shook like a mongrel dog, sending lake water flying in cold droplets. The woman quickly backed up two steps.

Rosemary plucked the seaweed from his hair and he grinned at her. "Thanks, sweetie. Ah, would you gals mind if I talk to…" He lifted a brow at Red.

"Elizabeth Parks," she answered stiffly. She clutched a notepad and pencil and had a huge purselike bag slung over one shoulder, stuffed to overflowing with papers.

"Yeah, can I have a minute with Ms. Parks?" He had the sneaking suspicion Ms. Parks was another reporter, and he had no intention of chatting with her for more time than it took to say thanks but no thanks. "I won't be long."

"All right, Gabe, but you owe us for rescuing your fish."

"That I do. And I promise to think up some appropriate compensation."

Giggling again, the women started away, dragging their feet every step, sashaying their sexy behinds. But then two boats pulled in and he knew that would keep them busy selling gas and bait and whatever other supplies the vacationers wanted. He turned to Red.

"What can I do for you?"

Now, without the sun in his eyes, Gabe could see she had about the bluest blue eyes he'd ever seen. They stood out like beacons among all that bright red hair and those abundant freckles.

She flipped open her bag and dragged out a folded newspaper. Turning it toward him, she asked, still with a twinge of disbelief, "Is this you?"

She sounded suspicious, but Gabe didn't even have to glance at the paper. Buckhorn, Kentucky was a small town, and they looked for any excuse at all to celebrate. The town paper, *Buckhorn Press,* had used the changing of a traffic light for front-page news once, so it was no wonder they'd stuck him in there for a spell when he helped fish a few swimmers out of the path of an unmanned boat. It hadn't been even close to an act of heroism, but if changing traffic lights was important, human endangerment was outright momentous.

"Yeah, that's me." Gabe reached for his mirrored sunglasses and slipped them on, then dragged both hands, fingers spread, over his head to smooth his wet hair. He stuck his cap on backward then looked at the woman again. With the shades in place, he could check her over a little better without her knowing.

But the clothing she wore made seeing much impossible. She had to be roasting in that thick denim and starched cotton.

She cleared her throat. "Well, if it's really true, then I'd like to interview you."

Gabe leaned around her, which made her blue eyes widen, and fetched a can of cola from the cooler sitting beside his empty chair. "You want one?"

"Uh, no, thank you." She hastily stepped back, avoiding getting too close to him. That nettled.

After popping the tab on the can and downing half of it, Gabe asked, "What paper do you write for?"

"Oh. No, I don't—"

"Because I'm not interested in being interviewed again. Every damn paper for a hundred miles around picked up on that stupid story, and they blew it all out of proportion. Folks around here are finally about done razzing me, my damn brothers included, and I'm not at all interested in resurrecting that ridiculous business again."

She frowned at him, then snapped the paper open to peruse it. "Did you or did you not dive into the water to pull three people, a woman and her two children, out of the lake when a drunken man fell out of his boat, leaving the boat unmanned?"

Gabe made a face. "Yeah, but—"

"No one else did anything, they just sort of stood there dumbfounded while the boat, without a driver, began circling the hapless swimmers."

"Hapless swimmers?" He grunted at her word usage. "Any one of my brothers would have done the exact same thing, and in fact—"

"And did you or did you not then manage to get in the boat—" She glanced up. "I'd love for you to explain how you did that, by the way. How you took control and got inside a running boat without getting chewed to bits by the prop. Weren't you at all scared?"

Gabe stared at her. Even her lashes were reddish, sort of a deep auburn, and with the sun on them, the tips were turned to gold. She squinted against the glare of the sunshine, which made the freckles on her tipped-up nose more pronounced. Other than those sprinkled freckles, her skin was smooth and clear and...

He shook himself. "Look, sugar, I said I didn't want to do an interview."

She puckered up like someone had stuck a lemon between her lips. "My name is Ms. Parks, or Elizabeth, either will do, thank you." After that reprimand, she had the audacity to say, "All the others wanted to be interviewed. Why don't you?"

She stood there, slim brows raised, her pencil poised over that damn notepad as if she expected to write down his every profound word.

Gabe cursed. Profound words were not his forté. They took too much effort. "What others?"

"The other heroes."

He could see her long hair curling in the humidity even as they spoke. It hung almost to the top of her behind, except for the front which was pulled back with a huge barrette. Little wispy curls, dark with perspiration, clung to her temples. The longer hair was slowly pulling into corkscrew curls. It fascinated him.

The front of her white blouse was beginning to grow damp, too, and Gabe could detect a plain white bra beneath. Damn, it was too hot to be all trussed up like that. What the hell kind of rigid female wore so many clothes to a vacation lake during the most sweltering heat wave of the summer season?

He didn't care what kind of female. "All right, first things first. I'm not doing any interview, period. Two, I'll admit I'm curious as to what the hell you're talking about with this other heroes business. And three, would you be more comfortable in the shade? Your face is turning berry red."

If anything, her color intensified. It wasn't exactly a pretty blush, more like someone had set a fire beneath her skin. She looked downright blotchy. Gabe almost laughed.

"I, ah, I always turn red," she explained, somewhat flustered. "Sorry. Redheads have fair skin."

"And you sure as certain have redder hair than most."

"Yes, I'm aware of that."

She looked stiff, as if he'd insulted her. It wasn't like her red hair was a state secret! A body could see that hair from a mile away.

He had to struggle to keep from grinning. "So whatdya say? You wanna go sit in the shade with me? There's a nice big piss elm hanging over the water there and it's cooler than standing here on the dock in the sun, but not much."

She blinked owlishly at him. "A what elm?"

"Piss elm. Just sorta means a scraggly one. Come on." She looked ready to expire on him, from flustered embarrassment, heat and exasperation. Without waiting for her agreement, he grabbed his cooler, took her arm in a firm grip and led her off the dock, over the rough rock retaining wall and through the grass. One large root of the elm stuck out smoothly from the ground and made a nice seat. Gabe practically shoved her onto it. He was afraid she might faint on him any minute. "Rest there a second while I get you a soda."

She scrambled to smooth her skirt over her legs, covering as much skin as possible, while trying to balance her notepad and adjust her heavy purse. "No, thank you. Really, I just—"

He'd already opened a can. "Here, drink up." He shoved the drink into her hand and then waited until she dutifully sipped. "Feel better?"

"Uh, yes, thank you."

She acted so wary, he couldn't help but be curious about her. She wasn't his type—too pushy, too prim, too...*red*. But that didn't mean he'd let her roast herself in the sun. His mother would hide him if she thought he'd been rude to a lady, any lady. Besides, she was kinda cute with her prissiness. In a red sort of way.

Gabe grabbed another cola for himself, then sat on the cooler. He looked at her while he drank. "So, tell me about these heroes."

She carefully licked her lips then set the can in the grass before facing him. "I'm working on a thesis for college. I've interviewed about a half dozen different men who were recently commended for performing heroic acts. So far, they've all had similar personality types. But you—"

"No fooling? What type of personality do heroes have?"

"Well, before I tell you that, I'd like to ask you a few questions. I don't want your answers to be biased by what the others have said."

Gabe frowned, propping his elbows on his knees and glaring at her. "You think I'd lie?"

She rushed to reassure him. "No! Not consciously. But just to keep my study pure, I'd rather conduct all the interviews the same way."

"But I've already told you, I don't want to be interviewed." He watched her closely, saw her frustration and accurately guessed that wasn't typical behavior of a hero. *What nonsense.*

After a long minute, she said, "Okay, can I ask you something totally different?"

"Depends. Ask, then I'll see if I want to answer."

"Why'd you throw the fish back?"

Gabe looked over his shoulder to where he'd caught the carp, then back. "That fish I just caught?"

"Yes. Why fish if you're not going to keep what you catch."

He chuckled. "You don't get out by the lake much, do you?"

"I'm actually not from around here. I'm just visiting the area—"

"To interview me?" The very idea floored him, and made him feel guilty for giving her such a hard time.

"Yes, actually." She took another drink of the soda, then added, "I rented a place and I'm staying for the month until school starts back up. I wanted to have all my research together before then. I'd thought I was done, and I was due a short vacation, but then I read the papers about you and decided to add one more interview."

"So you're working during your vacation?" He snorted. That was plain nuts. Vacations were for relaxing, and the idea of wasting one to pester him didn't make sense.

"Yes, well, let's just say that, hopefully, I'm combining my vacation with an interview. I couldn't resist. Your situation was unique in that every time you were quoted, you talked about someone else."

"I remember." The people he'd talked about were more interesting than anything he had to say about himself.

"You went on and on about how brave the two little kids were…"

"They were real sweet kids, and—"

"…and you lectured something fierce about drinking and water sports."

"This is a dry lake, which means no alcohol. That damn fool who fell out of his boat could have killed someone."

She gave him a coy look, surprising the hell out of him with the natural sensuality of it. She was so starchy, he hadn't been at all prepared. "But you keep saying the situation wasn't dangerous."

"It wasn't. Not to me." She looked smug, and she wrote something on her paper, making him frown. He decided to explain before she got the wrong idea. "Hell, I've been swimming like a fish since I was still in diapers. I was in this lake before I could walk. My brothers taught me to water-ski when I was barely five years old, and I know boats inside and out. There was no risk to me at all, so there's no way anyone in their right mind can label me a hero."

"So you say. But everyone else seems to disagree."

"Sweetheart, you just don't know Buckhorn. This town is so settled and quiet, any disturbance at all is fodder for front-page news. Why, we had a cow break out of the pasture and wander into the churchyard sometime back. Stopped traffic for miles around so everyone could gawk. The fire department showed up, along with my brother, who's the sheriff, and the *Buckhorn Press* sent all their star reporters to cover the story."

"All their star reporters?"

He grinned. "Yeah. All two of them. That's the way things are run around here. The town council meets to vote on whether or not to change the bulbs in the street lamps and last year when Mrs. Rommen's kitty went missing, a search party was formed and we hunted for three days before finding the old rascal."

She wrote furiously, which annoyed the hell out of Gabe, and then she looked up. "We?"

He tilted his head at her teasing smile, a really nice smile now that he was seeing it. Her lips were full and rosy and... He frowned. "Now, Ms. Parks, you wouldn't expect me to avoid my civic duty, would you? Especially not when the old dear loves that ugly tomcat something fierce."

She grinned at him again, putting dimples in those abundant freckles, making her wide mouth even more appealing, before going back to her writing. Gabe leaned forward to see exactly what she was putting on paper, and she snatched the paper to her chest.

"What are you doing?" She sounded breathless and downright horrified.

Gabe lifted a brow. "Just peeking at what you consider so noteworthy."

"Oh, I'm sorry." She lowered the paper, but the damage

had been done. Dark smears of pencil lead were etched across the front of her damp white blouse.

Gabe nodded appreciatively at her bosom while sipping his cola. "Looks like you'll need to be cleaned up." He said it, then stood. "You should probably head on home to do that."

She quickly stood, too. "But I haven't asked you my questions yet."

"And you won't. I don't want to be interviewed. But just for the hell of it, I turned the fish loose 'cause it's a carp, not that good for eating and a real pain to clean being as they have a mud vein. Bass is more to my tastes. Which doesn't matter any when you're fishing just for the fun of fishing, which is usually how I do it. You should try it sometime." He looked her over slowly. "Cuttin' loose, I mean. It's real relaxing."

He turned to walk away and she trotted to keep up with him. "Gabriel…Mr. Kasper…"

"Gabe will do, unless you're thinking to ask more questions." He said it without looking at her, determined to get away before he noticed anything about her besides her lips, which now that he'd noticed he couldn't stop noticing, or how nicely that starched shirt was beginning to stick to her breasts in the humidity. He still couldn't tell for sure, but he suspected a slight possibility that she was built rather nice beneath all the prim, stiff clothing. And that was the kind of suspicion that could distract a man something awful.

Only she wasn't the kind of woman he wanted to be distracted by. She had an obvious agenda, while he avoided plans and merely enjoyed each day.

"Gabe, really, this isn't a lengthy interview. There's no reason for you to be coy."

He had to laugh at that. Shaking his head, he stepped on the dock and looked at her. He could have sworn he saw another long red tress snap into a curl right before his eyes. Her whole head was beginning to look like corkscrews. Long, lazy, red corkscrews. It was kinda cute in a way... Hell, no. No, it was not cute.

"I've never been called *coy* in my life. I'm just plain not interested in that foolishness." He skimmed off his sunglasses and hat, and placed them on his chair, then tossed a fat inflated black inner tube into the lake. "Now, I'm going to go cool off with a dip. You can either skim out of those clothes and join me before you expire from the heat, or you can go find some other fool to interview. But no more questions." He started to turn away, but belatedly added, "Nice meeting you." Then he dove in.

He was sure his splash got her, but he didn't look to see. At least not at first.

She stood there for the longest time. He was strangely aware of her presence while he hoisted himself into the center of the inner tube and got comfortable. Peeking through one eye, he watched her stew in silence, then glare at him before marching off.

Finally. Let her leave.

Calling him a hero—what nonsense. His brothers were real heroes; even those kids that had kept their cool and not whined could be considered heroic little devils. But not Gabe Kasper. No, sir.

He started to relax, tipping his head into the cool water to drench his hair and lazily drifting his arms. But his neck snapped to attention when he saw Little Red stop beside Rosemary. She pointed at Gabe, then pulled out her damn notepad when Rosemary began chattering. And damn if Ceily and Darlene didn't wander closer, taking part.

Well, hell. She was gossiping about him!

When he'd told her to interview someone else, he meant someone else who wouldn't talk about him. Someone not on the lake. Hell, someone not even in Buckhorn—not even in Kentucky!

Rosemary's mouth was going a mile a minute, and he could only imagine what was being said. He ground his teeth in frustration.

A couple of women in a docked boat started flirting with him, but Gabe barely noticed. He stared at Rosemary, trying to will her to clam up, but not wanting to appear too concerned about the whole thing. What was it with Red, that she'd be so damn pushy? He'd explained he wasn't a hero, that she didn't need him for her little survey or whatever it was she conducted. But could she let that go? Hell, no.

One of the women from the docked boat—a really nice inboard that cost more than some houses—dove in and swam over to him. Gabe sent her a distracted smile.

It was in his nature to flirt; he just couldn't seem to help himself, and he'd never yet met a woman who minded. This particular woman didn't. She took his smile as an invitation.

Yet anytime he'd gotten even remotely close to Red, she'd frozen up like he was a big water snake ready to take a bite. Obviously she wanted into his head, but nowhere else.

Strange woman.

She walked away from Rosemary with a friendly wave, and Gabe started to breathe a sigh of relief—until she stopped a few yards up the incline where Bear, the repairman who worked on boat engines for Rosemary, was hanging around. Gabe helped the man regularly, whenever things got too busy, but did Bear remember that now? Gabe snorted. The old whiskered cuss looked at Red warily, then glanced at Gabe, and a smile as wide as the dam spread across his wrinkled face. Just that fast, Little Red had her pencil racing across the paper again.

"Damn it." Gabe deftly tipped the inner tube and slid over the side into the water. The sudden chill did nothing to cool his simmering temper. Keeping his gaze on the meddling female, he swam—dragging the inner tube—to the dock. But just as he reached it, so did the woman from the boat.

"Ah, now you're not planning to leave just when I got here, are you?"

Gabe turned. He'd actually forgotten the woman, which was incredible. She stood waist deep in the shallow water and from what he could see, she was built like a Barbie doll, all long limbs and long blond hair, and so much cleavage, she fairly overflowed her skimpy bikini bra. She should have held all his attention, but instead, he'd been thoroughly distracted by an uptight, overly freckled, red-headed wonder of a woman who jumped if he even looked at her.

Gabe glanced at Red, and their gazes clashed. He'd thought to go set the little darling straight on how much prying he'd put up with, but he reconsidered.

Oh, she was in a hot temper. Her blue-eyed gaze was glued to him, and her pencil was thankfully still. It was then Gabe realized his female swimming companion had caught hold of his arm—and Red disapproved mightily. She was looking like a schoolmarm again, all rigid, her backbone straight. Well, now. That was more like it.

Gabe turned to the blonde with a huge smile. This might just turn out to be fun.

CHAPTER TWO

ELIZABETH narrowed her eyes as she watched Gabriel Kasper fairly ooze masculine charm over the woman draped at his side. And the woman *was* draped. Elizabeth snorted in disgust. Did all women want to hang on him? Rosemary, Darlene, Ceily and this woman. They seemed to come from all around just to coo at him. No wonder he seemed so...different from the others.

The men she'd interviewed so far had been full of ego over their heroics and more than willing to share their stories with any available ear. They were rightfully proud, considering they'd behaved in a brave, out of the ordinary way that had directly benefited the people around them. Some of them had been shy, some outrageous, but not a one of them had refused her an interview. And not a one of them had so thoroughly ignored her.

No, they'd hung on her every question, anxious to share the excitement, thrilled with her interest, but in a purely self-satisfying way. They certainly hadn't been distracted with her as a woman, eyeing her up and down the way Gabriel Kasper had. She wondered if he thought she was stupid, or just naive, considering the way he'd looked at her, like he thought she wouldn't notice just because he wore sunglasses. Not likely! She'd felt his gaze like a tactile stroke, and it had unnerved her. The average man just didn't look at her that way, and men like Gabe never gave her a thought.

But then Gabe had dismissed her, and that she was more

than used to. Except with the heroes she'd interviewed, the men who wanted their unique stories told.

Damn, Mr. Kasper was an enigma.

"Don't mind that none, miss. Gabe always gets more'n his share of notice from the fillies."

Elizabeth snapped her attention to Bear. His name suited him, she thought, as she looked way, way up into his grizzled face. "I beg your pardon?"

He nodded toward the docks, where Gabe and the woman were chatting cozily. Elizabeth curled her lip. It was disgusting for a woman to put on such an absurd display, especially right out in the open like that. And for Gabe to encourage her so… Good grief, he had a responsibility to the community as a role model after all the attention they'd given him.

"Has he acted any different since becoming a town hero?" During her research, Elizabeth had discovered that people heralded for valor quickly adapted to all the fanfare and added interest thrown their way.

Bear chuckled. "Not Gabe. Truth is, folks in these parts have pretty much always looked up to him and his brothers. I don't think anyone doubted Gabe would do something once he noticed what had happened. Any one of his brothers would have done the same."

"He mentioned his brothers. Can you tell me something about them?"

"Be glad to!" Bear mopped a tattered bandanna around his face, then stuck it in his back pocket. "The oldest brother, Sawyer, is the town doc, and a damn good one to boot. He takes care of everyone from the newborns to the elders. Got hisself married to Honey, a real sweet little woman, about a year back. And that cut his patient load down considerable like. Seems some of the womenfolk coming to see him weren't really sick, just ambitious."

Bear grinned, but Elizabeth shook her head in exasperation.

"Right after Sawyer is Morgan, the sheriff, who generally looks like he just crawled right off a cactus, but he's as nice as they come as long as you stay on his good side." He leaned close to whisper, "And folks in these parts definitely stay on his good side."

"Lovely." Elizabeth tried to picture these two respectable men related to Gabe, who looked like a beach bum, but she couldn't quite manage it.

"Morgan up and married Honey's sister, Misty, just a bit after Sawyer married. He smiles more these days—that is, when she doesn't have him in a temper. She does seem to enjoy riling that boy."

It was a sure sign of Bear's age that he'd call a man older than Gabe a boy.

"Then there's Jordan, the best damn vet Buckhorn County has to offer. He can sing to an animal, and damned if it won't sing back! That man can charm a bird out of a tree or lull an ornery mule asleep. He's still a bachelor."

Good grief. Elizabeth could do no more than blink. Doctor, sheriff, vet. It was certainly an impressive family. "What does Gabe do for a living?"

Bear scratched beneath his chin, thinking, and then he looked away. "Thing is, Gabe's the youngest, and he don't yet know what it is he wants to do. Mostly he's a handyman, sort of a jack-of-all-trades. That boy can do just about anything with his hands. He's—"

"He doesn't have a job?" Elizabeth didn't mean to sound so shocked, but Rosemary had told her Gabe was twenty-seven years old, and to Elizabeth's mind, that was plenty old enough to have figured out your life's ambition.

"Well..."

She shook her head, cutting off whatever lame excuses

Bear was prepared to make. "I got the impression from a few things Rosemary said that he worked here."

A cold, wet hand clamped onto her shoulder, and Elizabeth jumped, then whirled to see Gabe, dripping lake water, standing right behind her. His grin wasn't pleasant, and she wished that she hadn't gotten engrossed in what Bear had to say, that she'd kept at least part of her attention on Gabe.

She looked around him, but his newest female companion was nowhere to be found. Which, she supposed, accounted for his presence. Surely if any other woman was available he'd still be ignoring her.

Gabe nodded to Bear, more or less dismissing him, then pulled Elizabeth around and started walking a few feet away. In a voice that only barely bordered on cordial, he said, "Well, Miss Nosy, I do work here, but I'm not employed here. There's a definite difference. And from now on, I'd appreciate it if you kept your questions to yourself. I don't much like people prying into my personal life, especially when I already told 'em not to."

Elizabeth gulped. No amount of forced pleasantness could mask his irritation. She tried to inch away from his hot, controlling grasp, but he wasn't letting go. So she simply stopped.

Gabe turned to face her. They were once again standing in the bright sun, on a gravel drive that declined down the slight hill, used to launch boats into the lake. The glare off the white gravel was blinding. She had to shield her eyes with one hand while balancing her notepad, pen and purse with the other. Looking directly at him both flustered and annoyed her. He was an incredibly...*potent* male, no denying that. Standing there in nothing more than wet, worn, faded cutoffs—and those hanging entirely too low on his lean hips—he was a devastatingly masculine sight. A sparse covering of light brown hair, damp from his swim, laid over solid muscles in his chest and down his abdomen, then swirled around his navel. He was deeply tanned, his legs long, his big feet bare. He seemed impervious to the sharp gravel and the hot sun. And as she watched, his arms crossed over his chest.

"You be sure and let me know when you're done looking so I can finish telling you what I think of your prying ways."

The heat that washed over her face had nothing to do with the summer sun and everything to do with humiliation.

"I'm sorry. It's just that you don't look like the other men."

He sighed dramatically. "I take it we're talking about the other supposed heroes?"

"Yes."

"And how did they look?"

Elizabeth hesitated, wondering how to explain it. She couldn't just say they had all been fully dressed, because thinking it made her blush more. At the moment, Gabe Kasper looked more naked than not, and even the jean shorts didn't help, considering they were soaked and clinging to his hard thighs, to his... *Don't go there.*

She cleared her throat. "They were all more...serious. They have careers they take great pride in, and they enjoyed telling their stories."

"But I told you, I don't have a story to tell."

"Your friends disagree."

His arms dropped and he scowled at her. Strangely, Elizabeth noticed he was watching her mouth instead of looking into her eyes. It made it easier for her because staring directly at him kept her edgy for some reason. There was so much expression in his eyes, as if he wasn't just looking at her, but really seeing her. It was an unusual experience for her.

But with him looking at her mouth, she felt nervous in

a different way, and without thinking, she licked her lips. His gaze shot to hers, and he stared, eyes narrowed, for two heartbeats while she held her breath and felt faint for some stupid reason. She gulped air and fanned her burning face.

Relaxing slightly, he shook his head, then said, "Look, Lizzy—"

"Don't call me that. My name is Elizabeth."

"And as long you're disregarding my wishes, I think I'll just disregard yours. Besides, Lizzy sorta suits you. It sounds like the proper name for a red-haired girl."

Elizabeth wanted to smack him. But since he'd come right out and all but admitted he wanted to annoy her, she decided to deny him the satisfaction. When she remained silent, he smiled, then continued. "This is all foolishness. Now I'm asking you nicely to let it drop."

"I can't. I've decided you'll make a really good contrast to the other men in my study. See, you're very different, and I can't, in good conscience, leave out such an important factor in my study. In order for the study to be accurate, I need to take data from every angle—"

He raised a hand, looking annoyed enough for his head to explode. "Enough of that already. This is your summer break, right?"

She watched him cautiously. "Yes."

"So why work so damn hard on summer break? Why not just cut loose a little and have some fun before going back to school?" He looked her over again and judging by the tightness of his mouth and the expression in his eyes, obviously found her lacking. "You're so prissed up, you have to be sweltering. No one puts on that many clothes in this heat."

Her shoulders were so stiff they hurt, and her stomach was churning. How dare he attack her on such a personal level? "Obviously someone does. I consider my dress totally appropriate."

"Appropriate to what?"

"To interviewing a hero."

His head dropped forward and he groaned. "You are the most stubbornest damn woman...."

"Me? You're the one who refuses to answer a few simple questions."

Their voices had risen and Gabe, with a heartfelt sigh, took her arm again and started farther up the gravel drive.

"Where are we going?" She had a vague image of him dragging her off and wringing her neck. Even a hero could only be pushed so far, and with the way everyone worshiped him, she didn't think she'd get much help.

"We're drawing attention and it isn't the kind of attention I like."

With a sneer she couldn't quite repress, she asked, "You mean it isn't purely female?"

Glancing her way, he grinned. "That's right."

"Oh, for heaven's sake!"

"Here we go. Have a seat."

Luckily, this time it wasn't a root he wanted to perch her on. The rough wooden picnic table was located beneath a tree—not an elm—and though it was partially covered with dried leaves, acorns and twigs, it was at least shaded.

Elizabeth had barely gotten herself settled before Gabe blurted, "Okay, what is it going to take to get you to back off?"

He wanted to bargain with her? Surprised, but also hopeful because she really did want to add his story to the others—he was proving to be the exception that broke the hero mold she'd mentally formed—Elizabeth carefully considered her answer. Finally, she said, "If you'd just answer five questions..."

"I'll answer one. But it'll cost you."

Her relief died a short death. "How much? I have a job,

but it's barely enough to pay my tuition so I couldn't offer you anything significant—''

He looked so totally and utterly appalled, she knew she'd misunderstood. His expression said so, but in case she hadn't caught on, he leaned close, caging her in with one arm on the picnic table, the other on her shoulder, and said through his teeth, ''You actually think I'd take money from you?''

Elizabeth tried leaning back, but she didn't have much room to maneuver, not without toppling over. ''You...you said you don't have a job.''

''Wrong.'' He looked ready to do that neck wringing she'd worried about. ''I said I'm not employed here. For your information, Red, I more than pay my own way. Not that my financial situation is any business of yours.''

''But...'' It was one of the questions in her survey, though luckily this time she had the good sense to forfeit it. ''Of course not. I didn't mean to suggest—''

''If you want me to answer a question, you'll have to loosen up. And before you start widening those big blue eyes at me again, I'm not suggestin' an illicit affair.''

Her heart almost stopped, but for the life of her she wasn't entirely sure if it was relief or disappointment she felt. No one had ever offered her an illicit affair, and the idea held a certain amount of appeal. Not that she'd ever accept, of course, but still... ''What, exactly, are you suggesting?''

''A swim. In the lake. Me and you.''

The big green murky lake behind her? The lake he'd pulled that enormous fish out of—then thrown it back so it was still in there? The lake where any number of things could be living? Never mind that she didn't even own a bathing suit, the thought of getting into that lake positively terrified her. Hoping against hope, she said, ''I don't understand.''

"It's easy, Lizzy. I want you here tomorrow, same time, wearing a swimsuit instead of all that armor. And I want you to relax with me, to take a nice leisurely swim. Maybe if you loosen up a bit, I won't even mind so much answering a question for you."

To make certain she understood before she agreed to anything, she asked, "And in exchange, you'll answer my questions?"

"No, I'll answer one question. Just one. Any question you like. You can even make notes in that damn little book of yours." He eyed her mouth again, then shook his head. "And who knows, if all goes well, maybe we can work out another deal."

"For another question?"

He shrugged, looking reluctant but strangely resigned.

Elizabeth had the sneaking suspicion he was trying to bluff her, to force her to back out. But she was fascinated. Such unusual behavior for a hero! She could almost imagine the response she'd get from this thesis—if anyone even believed it. But there had to be some redeeming information there, something that would make her research all that more complete, valuable and applicable.

In the end, there was really only one decision she could make. She held out her hand, and after a moment, Gabe took it.

His hand was so large, so tanned. And he felt hot. She gulped, shored up her courage, and with a smile that almost hurt, she said, "Deal."

HE COULDN'T BELIEVE he was running late.

If anything, he'd planned to be on the dock, sunning himself, a man without a care, when she arrived. Truth was, he felt strangely anxious. He grinned at the novelty of it.

"You've been doing a lot of that this morning."

Gabe turned to his brother Sawyer. "What?"

"Smiling like a fool."

"Maybe I have good reason."

"And what would that be?"

"None of your business." Gabe, still grinning, finished running caulk around the windowpane then wiped his hands on a small towel. "That should do you, Sawyer. From now on, don't let kids play baseball in your office, hear?"

Honey hustled up to his side with a tall glass of iced tea. Bless her, he did like all the doting she felt compelled to do. Having a sister-in-law was a right nice thing. "Thanks, Honey."

"What are you so happy about, Gabe?"

Uh oh. He glanced at Sawyer, saw his smirk and concentrated on drinking his tea. Sawyer knew without a doubt that he wouldn't even consider telling Honey to mind her own business. By virtue of being female, she was due all the respect his brothers didn't warrant. He just naturally tempered himself around women—well, all but Red. She seemed to bring out the oddest reactions from him. Damned if he wasn't looking forward to seeing her again.

What would she look like in a bikini?

"There he goes, grinning again."

"Actually," Gabe said, ignoring his brother, "I was just thinking of a woman." That was true enough, and not at all uncommon. In fact, Honey gave him a fond look of indulgence, patted his shoulder, then went to her husband's side. Sawyer sure was a lucky cuss. Honey was a sexy little woman—not that he thought of her that way, her being in the family and all. But he wasn't blind. She was a real looker, and best of all, she loved his brother to distraction.

Sawyer gave a grievous sigh. "He's in lust again. Just look at him."

That drew Gabe up short. Lust? Hell, no, he didn't feel lust for Little Red. Amusement maybe, because she was

unaccountably funny with her freckles and her red corkscrew curls that hung all the way down to her fanny.

And frustration, because she simply had no idea how to
accept no for an answer and she trussed herself up in those
schoolmarm clothes, to the point a guy couldn't even tell
what he was seeing.

Maybe even annoyance, because her stubbornness
rivaled his brother Morgan's, and that was saying a mouth-
ful. But not lust.

He grunted, earning an odd look from Sawyer.

His invitation for a swim was simply his way of keeping
the upper hand. And thinking that, he said to Sawyer, "If
a funny little red-haired woman tries to talk to you about
me, don't tell her a damn thing, okay?"

Sawyer and Honey blinked at him in confusion, but he
didn't bother to explain. He hurried off. Knowing Red, if
he was too late, she'd give up on him and go home. She
wasn't the type of woman who'd wait around, letting a guy
think she'd be happy to see him when he did show up. No,
Red would probably get her back all stiff and go off asking
questions of every available body in the area.

And he really didn't want anyone filling her head with
that nonsense about heroes. Best that he talked to her himself. And that was another reason he'd engineered the date.
No, take that back. Not a date. An appointment. Yeah, that
sounded better. He'd arranged an appointment so that at
least she'd get her stupid story straight.

Hell, he had plenty of reasons for seeing her again, and
none of them were about lust.

He did wonder what she'd look like in a bikini, though.

SHE WAS STILL in full armor.

Gabe frowned as he climbed out of his car and started
down the hill. Judging by the color of that long braid hanging almost to the dock, the woman with her back to him

was one Miss Elizabeth Parks. And she wasn't wearing a bikini. He consoled himself with the fact that at least she was waiting for him. There was a certain amount of masculine satisfaction in that.

The second he stepped on the dock, she turned her head. He noticed then that she was sitting cross-legged instead of dangling her feet in the water. She had her shoes and frilly little white socks on. Socks in this heat? He stopped and frowned at her. "Where's your swimsuit?"

She frowned right back. "I have it on under my dress. Surely you didn't think I'd drive here in it? And you're late."

She turned away and with her elbows on her knees, propped her chin on a fist and stared at the lake.

Gabe surveyed her stiff back and slowly approached. He wasn't quite sure what to expect of her, so he said carefully, "I'm glad you waited."

With a snort, she answered, "You made it a part of the deal. If I want to ask you one measly question, I had to be here." She waved a dismissive hand. "I figured you'd show up sooner or later."

Not exactly the response he'd hoped for. In fact, she'd taken all the fun out of finding her still here. "Well, skin out of those clothes then, so we can get in. It's hot enough to send a lizard running for shade. That water's going to feel good."

She didn't look at all convinced. Peering at him with one eye scrunched against the sunshine and her small pointed nose wrinkled, she said, "The thing is, I'm not at all keen on doing that."

"What?"

"The swimsuit thing. I've never had much reason to swim, and this boat dock is pretty crowded...."

"You want privacy?" Now why did that idea intrigue him? But it was a good idea, not because he'd be alone with her. No, that had nothing to do with it. But that way, if she asked her dumb hero question, no one else would be around to contradict him.

He liked that idea. "We can take a fishing boat back to a cove. No one's there, at least, not close. There might be a few fishermen trolling by, or the occasional skier, but they won't get near enough to shore to look you over too good." He gave her a crooked grin. "Your modesty will be preserved." *Except from me.*

Her face colored. "It's not that I think I'd draw much attention, you understand. It's just not something I'm used to."

With the way she managed to cover herself from shins to throat, he didn't doubt it. "No problem. The cove is real peaceful. I swim there all the time. Come on." He reached down a hand for her, trying not to look as excited as he suddenly felt. "Do you know how to swim?"

She ignored his hand and lumbered to her feet, dusting off her bottom as she did so. "Not really."

Rather than let her get to him, he dropped his hand and pretended it didn't matter. But he couldn't recall ever having such a thing happen in his entire life, and he knew right then and there he didn't like it worth a damn. "Then you'll need a flotation belt. There's some in the boat. You got a towel?"

"My stuff is there." She pointed to the shore where a large colorful beach towel, a floppy brimmed hat and a pair of round, blue-lens sunglasses had been tossed. Next to the pile was her infamous notepad, which made him frown.

Gabe had his towel slung around his neck, his mirrored glasses already in place and his hat on backward. He carried a stocked cooler in his free hand. "Let's go."

He led her to a small metal fishing boat, then despite her efforts to step around him, helped her inside. The boat swayed, and she nearly lost her balance. She would have fallen overboard if he hadn't held on to her.

He managed not to smirk.

He tossed her stuff in to her, then said, "Take a seat up front and put on a belt. If you fall in, it'll keep you from drowning until I can fish you out."

"Like you did the carp?"

Her teasing smile made his stomach tighten. "Naw, I kissed the fish and threw him back in for luck." He glanced at her, then added, "I wouldn't do that to you."

Her owl-eyed expression showed her confusion. Let her wonder if he meant he wouldn't kiss her or he wouldn't throw her back. Maybe keeping her guessing would take some of the edge off her cockiness. He hid his satisfaction as he stepped into the boat and tilted the motor into the water. He braced his feet apart, gave the rip cord a tug, and the small trolling motor hummed to life.

After seating himself comfortably, he said, "We won't break any speed records, but the ride'll be smooth."

"Is this your boat?"

"Naw. Belongs to Rosemary. But she lets me use it whenever I want."

"Because you do work around the dock for her?"

Tendrils of hair escaped her long thick braid and whipped into her face. She held them back with one hand while she watched him. The dress she wore was made like a tent—no shape at all. From what he could see, it pulled on over her head, without a button or zipper or tie anywhere to be found. The neck was rounded and edged with lace, and the sleeves were barely there. But at least it was a softer material, something kind of like a T-shirt, and a pale yellow that complemented her red hair and bright blue eyes.

Gabe pulled himself away from that distraction and reminded himself that lust had nothing to do with his motivation today. He smiled at her. "Is that your question?"

"What?"

"Your one allotted question. You want to know about me working at the boat dock?"

Her frown was fierce. "Just making conversation."

"Uh-huh. You know what I think? I think you figured you'd sneak a whole bunch of questions in on me and I wouldn't notice."

She bit her lips and looked away. Gabe couldn't help but laugh out loud, it was so obvious she'd been caught. Damn, but she was a surprise. She sat there with her little feet pressed primly together—those damn lacy ankle socks somehow looking kind of sexy all of a sudden—while her snowy white sneakers got damp with the water in the bottom of the boat. Her hands were clasped together in her lap, holding onto her big floppy hat, her eyes squinted against the wind and sun. Her freckles were even more noticeable out here on the lake. She wasn't exactly what you'd call a pretty woman, certainly not a bombshell like Sawyer's Honey or Morgan's Misty. But there was definitely something about her....

"Where are we going?"

She sat facing him in the boat, so he pointed behind her to where the land stretched out and the only living things in sight were a few cows grazing along the shoreline. The man-made lake was long and narrow, shaped a lot like a river with vacation cabins squeezed into tight rows along both sides. Several little fingers of water stretched out to form small coves here and there, only a few of which were still owned by farmers and hadn't been taken over by developers. The land Gabe lived on with his brothers had a cove like that, a narrow extension of the main lake, almost entirely cut off from the boating traffic since it was so shallow. But it made for great swimming and fishing, which was what the brothers used it for.

Though they didn't have any cows there, it was peaceful

and natural and they loved it, refusing to sell no matter how many times they were asked and regardless of the offer. They jointly owned a lot of property, and in two spots runoff from the main lake had formed a smaller lake and a pond. Gabe intended to build a house on that site some day.

"We're going *there?*" Lizzy asked, interrupting his thoughts. She sounded horrified.

Gabe bobbed an eyebrow. "It's real private."

"Are the cows friendly?"

"Most bovines are. You just don't want to walk behind them."

"They kick?"

She sounded appalled again, so he had to really struggle to keep from laughing. "Nope. But you have to be real careful where you step."

"Oh."

Slowing the motor, Gabe let the boat glide forward until they'd rounded the cove and nudged as far inside as possible. Someone in years past had installed a floating dock, but it had definitely seen better days. It tended to list to one side, with three corners out of the water and one corner under, covered by moss. But at least it was a good six feet square and didn't sink if you climbed on it.

Gabe threw a rope around a metal cleat on the side of the dock. It was strange, but his heart was already pounding like mad—he had no idea why—and he had to force himself to speak calmly.

He looked at her, saw her shy, averted gaze and felt the wild thrum of excitement. He swallowed hard. "This is as far as we get, so you can skin out of that dress now."

She peeked at him, then away. "Why don't you go ahead and get in, then I'll...inch my way in?"

"Have you ever driven a boat?"

"No."

"Do you know how to start it?"

She glanced dubiously at the pull start for the motor, then shook her head. "I don't think so."

He nodded. "So at least I know you're not plotting on getting me overboard then taking off."

Her eyes widened. "I wouldn't do that." She chewed her lip, looking undecided, then admitted, "It's just that I hadn't figured on how to go about stripping off my clothes out here in the open."

"With me and the cows watching?"

"Right."

He could have offered a few suggestions, but that would be crass. Besides, he was afraid his suggestions would offend her. Likely they would.

Oh, hell, he knew damn good and well they would.

"All right. I'll turn my back. But don't take too long. You can put your folded things on the cooler so they won't get wet." Before he could change his mind, he turned his back, stepped on a seat and dove in. He heard her squeal as the small boat rocked wildly.

The water was shallow, so he made the dive straight out, and seconds later his head broke the water. He could easily stand, so he waded to the dock, keeping his head averted, then rested his folded arms over the edge of the aged wood. He could hear her undressing.

"The water feels great." His voice shook, damn it.

"It's...green."

He cleared his throat. "Because of the moss." She probably had her shoes off already, and those ridiculous, frilly, feminine little socks that looked like they'd come from a fetish catalogue, though he doubted she knew it. He pictured her wearing those socks—and nothing else. The picture was vague because he had no idea what the hell her body looked like, but the thought still excited him. Dumb.

Did she only have on the dress, or was she wearing other

stuff over her suit? He cleared his throat and mustered his control. "Aren't you done yet?"

"Well…yeah."

His head snapped around, and he stared. She stood there, pale slender arms folded over her middle, long legs pressed together, shoulders squared as if in challenge. And her suit wasn't a bikini, not that it mattered one little bit.

"Damn, woman." The words were a choked whisper, hot and touched with awe. It felt like his eyes bugged out of his head.

She shifted nervously, uncrossing and recrossing her arms, taking her weight from one foot to the other, making the supple muscles in her calves and thighs move seductively.

Gabe had no idea if she blushed or not because he couldn't get his gaze off her body and onto her face.

The one-piece suit was simple, a pale lime green, and it covered enough skin to make a grandma happy. But what it left uncovered…

Her plump breasts made his mouth water with the instinct of Pavlov's dog. High, round…he wondered for a single heartbeat if they were real or enhanced. He stared, hard, unaware of her discomfort, her uncertainty. Nothing in the suit suggested it capable of that incredible support. There were no underwires, no lined bra cups. The suit was a sleek, simple design, and it hugged her like her own skin.

The visible outline of soft nipples drew him, making his imagination go wild. He wanted to see them tight and puckered, straining for his mouth.

Breathing deeply, he traced her body with his gaze, to the shaping of her rib cage, the indention of a navel, the rounded slope of her mound.

Heat rolled through him, making his nostrils flare. He could easily picture her naked, and did so, tormenting himself further.

Surely even the cows were agog. She had the most symmetrically perfect feminine body he'd ever seen, and the lake water no longer felt so cool. His groin grew thick and heavy, hot. It was unexpected, this instantaneous reaction he had to her. Women didn't affect him this way. He'd learned control early on and hadn't had an unwanted erection since his teens. He chose when to be involved; he did not get sucked into a vortex of lust!

But there was no denying what he felt at this moment. It annoyed him, with himself, not her. She did nothing to entice him, other than to stand there and let him look his fill.

Just as he'd suspected, her freckles decorated other parts of her body, not just her face. Her shoulders were lightly sprinkled with them—and her thighs. His heartbeat lost its even rhythm. Damn. He hadn't known freckles could be so incredibly sexy.

One thing was certain, he was sure glad he'd brought her here so that every guy on the lake wasn't able to gawk at her.

Hell, he was doing enough gawking for all of them.

Pulling himself together, he cleared his throat again and looked at her face. Her head was down, her long braid hanging over a shoulder, touching a hipbone. He bit his lip, feeling the heavy thumping of his heart, the tautness of his muscles. "Lizzy?"

Her arms tightened around herself. "Hmm?"

Belatedly he understood her anxiety at being on display. He felt like a jerk, and tried for a teasing tone despite the urgency hammering through him. "You comin' in or not?"

"Do I get a choice?"

He didn't hesitate. "No."

Slowly her gaze lifted to his. "You'd better be worth this."

Oh, he'd show her just how worthwhile he could—

No, wait. Wrong thought. He hadn't brought her here for that. He'd brought her here to convince her to forget about her silly ideas of heroism.

He scowled with determination, but his carnal thoughts seemed less and less wrong with every second she stood there, her small body the epitome of sexual temptation. He unglued his tongue and said, "Come on. Quit stalling."

She licked her lips and he groaned, practically feeling the stroke of her small pink tongue.

She glared at him suspiciously, then looked over the side of the boat, looked at him and licked her lips again. "How?"

Without even thinking about it, he found himself wading to the boat, holding up his arms and inviting her into them.

And just like that, she closed her eyes, muttered a quiet prayer and fell in against him.

CHAPTER THREE

GABE FOUND his arms filled with warm, soft woman. It wasn't the first time, of course, but it sure felt different from any other time. Unexpectedly, her scent surrounded him. Lizzy smelled sweet, with a unique hint of musk that pulled at him. Her fingers were tight in his hair, her arms wrapped around his head in a death grip. His mind went almost blank. He could feel her firm, rounded bottom against his right forearm where he'd instinctively hooked her closer, to keep her from falling when she'd jumped in against him. His left arm was around her narrow waist, his large hand splayed wide so that his fingers spanned her back.

More momentous than that, though, was the fact that his face was pressed between her breasts. They certainly felt real enough. Jolted by the sexual press of her body, he froze, not even breathing. She was wrapped around him like a vine, but she didn't seem to notice the intimacy of their position.

Gabe noticed. Damn, but he noticed.

He shifted the tiniest bit so that his hand could cuddle a full, round cheek, and felt the shock of the touch all the way to his throbbing groin. She panted, but not with excitement.

"Lizzy?" His voice was muffled, thanks to having his face buried in lush breasts. His hand on her bottom continued to caress her, almost with a will of its own.

Her arms tightened, her legs shifting to move around his

hips in a jerky, desperate attempt to get closer to him. The movement brought the open, hot juncture of her thighs against his abdomen, and he sucked in a startled, strangled breath. If they were naked, if he slipped her down just a few inches, he could be inside her.

He was losing his grip on propriety real fast.

"Lizzy," he said, speaking low to keep from jarring her, "you're afraid of the water?"

Her growled, "No...*yes,*" almost made him smile. Even now, she tried to hide behind her prickly pride.

"It's okay. There's nothing in here to bother you." Nothing but him, only she didn't need to know that.

"I've never...never swam in a lake before."

Her lips were right above his ear. She sounded breathless, and her voice trembled. "There's nothing to be afraid of," he crooned, and then, because he couldn't help himself, he turned his face slightly and nuzzled his nose against the plump, firm curve of her breast.

She screamed, making his ears ring. In the next instant, she launched herself out of his arms and thrashed her way wildly to the floating dock. The back view of her awkward, hasty climb from the water didn't do a thing to cool his libido. She seemed to be all long legs and woman softness and enticing freckles. The suit, now wet, was even more revealing. Not more revealing than a bikini, but that didn't seem to matter to his heated libido. He watched her huddle on the dock, wrapping her arms around herself, then hurriedly survey the water.

He owed her an apology. That made him disgruntled enough to grouse, "I'll be deaf for an hour. You screech like a wet hen."

Lizzy shook her head, and her teeth chattered. "Something touched me. Something brushed against my leg!"

Gabe stalled. So she hadn't screamed over his forwardness? From the looks of her, he thought, seeing how wild-eyed she appeared, she probably hadn't even noticed that he was turned on, that he'd been attempting to kiss her breast. Making a small sound of exasperation, Gabe said, "It was probably just a fish."

She shuddered in visible horror. "What kind of fish?"

He looked around, peering through the water, which was stirred up from her churning retreat. "There." Pointing, he indicated a small silvery fish pecking at bubbles on the surface of the lake.

Lizzy carefully leaned forward on her hands and knees, making her breasts sway beneath the wet green suit. "Is it a baby?"

He kept his gaze glued to her body. His tongue felt thick and his jaw tight. "No. A bluegill. They don't get much bigger than that."

Her gaze lifted and met his, forcing him to stop staring at her body. "What'd you expect," he asked, "Jaws?"

Her face heated. To Gabe, she looked sexy and enticing and adorable, perched on the edge of the floating dock, her bottom in the air, her eyes wide and her cheeks rosy. Her brows angled. "Are you laughing at me?"

"Nope." He waded over to her then leaned on his forearms. No way could he join her on the dock. His wet cutoffs wouldn't do much to hide his erection. "I didn't realize you were afraid of the water," he told her gently. "You should have said something."

After a deep breath, she sat back. She drew her knees up and wrapped her arms around them. "I was embarrassed," she admitted with a sideways look at him. "I hate being cowardly."

"It's not cowardly to be unsure of things you're not familiar with."

"Will you still answer my question?"

Annoyed that she wouldn't forget her purpose for even a minute, he shrugged. "Get it over with."

Her blue eyes lit with excitement, and she dropped her arms to lean toward him. Her nipples, he couldn't help noticing, were long and pointed.

She smiled. "What were you thinking when you went into the water to save those kids?"

"Thinking?"

"Yes. You saw they were in trouble, and you wanted to help. What did you think about? How you'd get them out, the danger, that your own life wasn't important..."

"Oh, for pity's sake. It wasn't anything like that." Forgetting that he needed to stay in the water, he levered himself up beside her on the dock in one fluid movement. The dock bobbed, making her gasp and flatten her hands on the wood for balance. Water sluiced off his body as he dropped next to her then shook his head like a wet dog. Lizzy made a grab for him to keep from getting knocked in, but she released him just as quickly and frowned at him.

"So what was it like?"

He leaned back on his elbows and surveyed the bright sun, the cloudless sky. "Hell, I don't know. I didn't think anything. I saw the boat, saw the kids—and just reacted." Before she could say anything about that, he added, "Anyone would have done the same."

"No one did do the same. Only you."

He shrugged. "I'd already gone in. There was no reason for anyone else to."

"You were quicker to react."

"Maybe I just noticed the problem first."

When she shifted to face him, Gabe again eyed her breasts. He felt obsessed. Would her nipples be pink or a rosy brown?

She touched his arm. "Were you afraid?"

Annoyed by her persistence, he leaned back on the dock, covering his eyes with a forearm. "That's another question." Gabe wondered if she even realized he was male.

He had a raging hard-on, he'd been staring at her breasts with enough intensity to set her little red head on fire, and she hadn't even noticed. He snorted. Or maybe she just didn't care. Maybe she found him so lacking, so unappealing, he could be naked and it wouldn't affect her.

Her small hand smacked against his shoulder. "Not fair! You didn't even really answer the first question."

He lowered his arm enough to glare at her. "You didn't really swim, so we're even."

Mulish determination set her features, then she turned to the water. Distaste and fear stiffened her shoulders and, amazed, Gabe realized she was going to get in.

"Lizzy…" He reached for her shoulder.

"If a snake eats me, it'll be on your head!" She stuck a toe in the water.

Smiling, Gabe pulled her back. "All right. I'll answer your question."

The tension seemed to melt right out of her. "You will?"

He sighed long and loud to let her know she was a pest. *Yeah, right.* "It beats seeing that look of terror on your face." He flicked her nose as he said it, to let her know he was teasing.

She paid him no mind, speaking to herself in a mumble. "I wish I had my notebook."

Gabe came to his knees, caught the line holding the boat secure and pulled it in. It was a stretch, but he was able to reach her bag and hand it to her. "There you go."

Her smile was beatific. "Thank you."

He gave her a gentlemanly nod. She didn't notice his body, but at least she appreciated his manners. "No problem. Not that I can tell you anything interesting enough to write down."

The look of concentration on her face as she pulled out her notepad told him she disagreed. Gabe thought how cute she was when she went all serious and sincere.

Not that a cute, redheaded virago should have interested him. Beyond making him unaccountably hot, that was.

Nose wrinkled against the glare of the sun, she looked at him and said, "I'm ready."

She looked ready, he thought, unable to keep his mind focused on the fact that he wasn't interested. Posed on the dock as she was, she made a fetching picture. Her long legs were folded to the side in the primmest manner possible, given her body was more bare than not. She tilted her head and pursed her lips in serious cogitation. The bright sunshine glinted off her hair, showing different colored strands of gold and amber and bronze. Midway down, her braid was darker from being wet, and it rested, heavy and thick, along her side. Her skin shone with a fine mist of sweat, intensifying her sweet scent so that with every small breeze he breathed her in.

His skin felt too hot, but not because of the sun.

Gabe wondered what she'd do if he eased her backward and covered her with his body. Would she scream again? He groaned, causing her to lift one brow. She hadn't screamed last time because of him. No, she hadn't even noticed his attention.

"What's wrong?"

Other than the fact he was attracted to a woman who shouldn't have appealed to him and didn't return the favor? He groaned again. "Not a thing." Once again he reclined on the small dock, crossing his arms behind his head. He was too long for the thing, so he let his knees stick over the side and hung his feet in the water. "Let's see. What did I think? Well, I cursed. I know that."

Pencil to paper, she asked, "What did you say?"

"It's not something to be repeated in front of a lady."

"Oh. I understand."

She scribbled quickly across her paper, making Gabe curious. But he already knew she wasn't about to reveal her words to him. "Thing is," he admitted, "I don't really remember thinking anything. I saw the kids and the woman, saw the boat, and I just dove in. I knew they could get hurt, and I knew I could help." He shrugged, not looking at her. "It's no more complicated than that."

"So," she said, her eyes narrowed in thoughtful speculation, "your heroism was instinctive, like a basic part of you?"

"It wasn't heroism, damn it, but yeah, I guess it was instinctive to just dive in and do what I could."

"Did you even think about the danger to yourself?"

Here he was, Gabe thought, lounging in front of her, half naked, and she hadn't even looked at him once. He knew, because he'd been watching her, waiting to see what she'd do when she saw he was aroused. She'd barely noticed him at all except to give him her disapproving looks.

It nettled him that she was on this ridiculous hero kick. He was a man, same as any other, but that obviously didn't interest her at all. He wanted her interest, though he shouldn't have. But looking at her made him forget that she wasn't his type, that he didn't care what she thought, that he was only here today on a lark, as a way to pass the time and have some fun.

He wasn't used to a woman being totally oblivious to his masculinity, and he damn sure didn't like it.

He wouldn't, in fact, tolerate it.

Speaking in a low, deliberately casual tone, he reminded her, "That's another question. I told you I'd answer one."

"But…"

"We could make another deal." He closed his eyes as he said it, as if it didn't matter to him one way or the other. The ensuing silence was palpable. He felt the dock rock the tiniest bit and knew she was shifting. In nervousness? In annoyance? If he looked at her, he'd be able to read the emotions in her big blue eyes. But he didn't want to see if it was only frustration that lit her gaze. He waited, held his breath.

And finally she said, "All right. What deal?"

He opened his eyes and pinned her, his heart pumping hard, his muscles twitching. "I'll answer another question—for a kiss."

She blinked at him, her long, gold-tipped lashes lazily drifting down and up again, as if she couldn't quite believe what he'd said. "A kiss?"

"Mm." He pointed to his mouth. His gaze never left her face, watching her closely. Anticipation, thick and electric, hummed in his veins. "Right here, right now. One question, one kiss."

She shifted again. The lake was still, the only sounds those of a cow occasionally bawling or the soft splash of a frog close to shore. Lizzy nibbled her lips—lush, wet lips. Her gaze, bright and direct, never left his face. She drew a deep breath that made her breasts strain against the clinging material of the suit.

Her blue eyes darkened and her words, soft and uncertain, made him jerk in response.

"What…" she whispered, her breath catching before she cleared her throat and started again. "What if I kiss you twice?"

AT LEAST he was smooth-shaven today, Elizabeth thought as she watched Gabe's face, saw his eyes glitter and grow intent. She felt tense from her toes to her eyebrows, struggling endlessly to keep her gaze on his face and off his lean, muscled body. He was by far the most appealing man she'd ever known—and the most maddening.

When he continued to watch her, his eyes heavier, the blue so hot they looked electric, she made a sound of impatience. "Well?"

In husky tones, he asked, "Two kisses, hm?"

Much more and she'd be racing for the shore. She couldn't take his intensity, the way he stared at her, stroked her with his gaze. Her breasts felt full, her belly sweetly pulled with some indefinable ache. What could he possibly hope to gain with his present attitude? She didn't for a minute think he was actually attracted to her. For one thing, men simply didn't pay that much attention to her. More often than not, she could be invisible for all the notice they took. Secondly, she still remembered his reaction when they'd met. Gabriel Kasper had found her amusing, annoying and, judging by the way he'd looked her over, totally unappealing.

Perhaps, she continued to reason, he only hoped to intimidate her! That would certainly make sense. She swallowed hard and refused to back down. She needed his knowledge. She craved the information that would make her understand what special qualities created a hero. Or a heroine.

His mouth, firm and sensual, wholly masculine, twitched slightly. "Two kisses, two questions."

It was what she'd wanted. And then he added, "Ten kisses, ten questions—but understand, Lizzy, I'm only a man. Kisses are all I can barter and remain a...gentleman." He turned his head slightly toward her, and his voice dropped. "Or does that matter?"

She stiffened. Did he suggest her kisses could make him lose control? Not likely! Mustering her courage, she asked, "Why are you doing this?"

"This...what?"

She waved a hand at his lazy form. "This game. Why trade for kisses? Why trade at all? Is it really so hard to answer a short interview?"

His jaw tightened, and he shut his eyes again. After a moment, still looking more asleep than alert, he said, "You need to loosen up a little, Red. It's a nice afternoon, the sun is warm, the water's cool. We're all alone. Why not play a little?'' He looked at her, his gaze probing. ''Is the idea of kissing me so repulsive?''

She filled her lungs with a deep breath. So she was just a game, a way to pass the time. The arrogant jerk. She'd have to remember to make a note of that, that some heroes were not always perfect in their behavior, some of them enjoyed toying with women.

She straightened her shoulders, refusing to let him intimidate her. ''No, not at all.''

''Then we don't have a problem, do we?''

The only problem, evidently, was her inhibition. But in the face of all she could learn from him, did her reserve really matter? Suddenly determined, she squelched her nervousness and said with firm resolve, ''Okay, a kiss for a question.''

She waited, braced for his sensual assault, but Gabe simply continued to watch her. Not by so much as the flick of an eyelash did he move. Her stomach cramped the tiniest bit and she lifted an eyebrow.

She was both disappointed and relieved when she asked, ''You've changed your mind?''

With one indolent shake of his head, Gabe crooked a finger at her. ''C'mere, Red. You're going to do the kissing, not me.''

In reaction to his potent look, more than her stomach cramped, but the feeling wasn't at all unpleasant.

''Oh.'' She looked at his gorgeous body stretched out in front of her—and started shaking. His shoulders were wide and bunched with muscles, as were his biceps. The undersides of his arms were smooth, slightly lighter than the rest of his skin. She'd never considered a man's armpits sexy before—just the thought was ludicrous—but she'd never seen Gabriel Kasper's. Seeing the hair under his arms was somehow too intimate, like a private showing. She looked away from that part of him.

His chest, tanned and sprinkled with golden brown hair, had the lean hard contours that spoke of a natural athlete. Her pulse fluttered.

His abdomen was flat, sculpted, and if his underarms were too personal, his navel was downright sexual. The way his body hair swirled around it, then became a silky line that disappeared into the very low waistband of his shorts... Her eyes widened.

With his wet cutoffs clinging to his body, there was no way to miss his obvious arousal. Fascinated, she couldn't help but stare for a moment. Never, not in real life, anyway, had she seen an erection. Heat exploded inside her, making her cheeks pulse, her vision blur.

Her gaze flew to his face, desperate, confused, *excited*. His grin, slow and wicked, taunted her. He didn't say a word, and she knew he was waiting for her to back down.

She couldn't. Not now, not with him challenging her. But...

Licking her lips, Elizabeth croaked, "Are you sure we should do this?"

He shrugged one hard shoulder in a show of negligence. "No one will see. Don't be a coward, Lizzy. It's just a kiss."

Just a kiss. She remembered how those women on the dock had hung on him, how every woman who passed in a boat had stared at him with hunger. He was used to kissing, used to so much more. She couldn't recall any other man in all her acquaintance ever demanding such a thing from her. No wonder she was at a loss as to how to proceed. She preferred to arm herself with knowledge, to learn from a book what she didn't understand. But she hadn't known to research this particular theme. She frowned with that thought. Were there books to help you bone up on kissing a sexy-as-sin, half-dressed reclining man?

She eyed him warily. "Why don't you...sit up?" The idea of leaning over him, of being that close to so much masculine flesh, flustered her horribly.

Without hesitation, Gabe shook his head. "Naw, I'm already comfortable. So quit stalling."

He was right; the quicker she got it over with, the better. Like getting a tooth pulled, it meant just a flinch of pain, and then you were done.

Not giving herself time to think about it, she slapped one hand flat on the dock beside his head, bent down and brushed her mouth over his in a flash of movement. She straightened just as quickly and, avoiding his gaze, put her pencil to paper. Her voice shook slightly, but she ignored the tremor as she asked, "Now, when you leaped into the water with the runaway boat, were you afraid?"

"No."

She waited, her pencil ready, but he said no more. Elizabeth rounded on him, her nerves too frazzled for more games. "That's an awfully simplified answer."

He gave her a wry look. "It was an awfully simplified kiss."

Unable to help herself, she looked at his mouth. Her lips still tingled from the brief contact with his. It took all her concentration not to lick her lips, not to chew on them. Her heartbeat was still racing too quickly, her stomach was in knots of anticipation...no! Dread, not anticipation. She had to be philosophical. "You mean, if I made the kiss longer..."

So softly she could barely hear him, he said, "Why don't you give it a try and see?"

She could do this! She was not a fainthearted ninny. Determination stiffened her spine. Sensual awareness sharpened her senses. She gave one quick nod.

Laying the pencil and paper aside, she bent, clasped her palms over his ears to anchor both him and herself, then kissed him for all she was worth.

Never having done much kissing, she had no idea if she was doing it right. But she mashed her mouth tightly to his, turned her head subtly so their lips meshed, and sighed. Or maybe it was more a growl filled with resolution.

His lips felt firm, warm. This close, his scent was stronger, drifting over her, making her insides fill with a new and unexpected need. He was so hot, his skin where they touched almost burning her. Her chin bumped his, their noses rubbed together, and her wrists rested on his silky hot shoulders. She stopped moving her mouth and simply breathed deeply.

Gabe groaned, then promptly laughed, startling her enough that she sat up and stared at him in hurt and confusion.

With a small smile, using only one rough finger, he stroked her bottom lip. His words were as gentle as his touch, and just as devastating. "You haven't done much kissing, have you, Lizzy?"

Indignation would be misplaced; obviously, he could already tell she was inexperienced, so why should she deny it or be embarrassed? He could see what she looked like, had even used the same insulting taunt of Red she'd heard in grade school. He could probably guess at the other names—freckle face and scarecrow. And no doubt he understood the way she'd been ignored in high school, when all the boys were chasing cheerleaders with bubbly personalities and model faces.

None of that hurt her anymore. She had found more important things to do with her time. With an accepting shrug, she agreed. "Pitifully little, actually." And even that was an exaggeration.

Amazingly, his smile turned seductive. He came up on

his right elbow, wrapped the fingers of his left hand around her nape and pulled her close. Against her mouth, he whispered, "Then allow me."

His tongue... Oh gracious. His mouth opened hers with almost no effort. His tongue touched, teased, not really entering her mouth, but making her crazed with small licks and tastes, softly, wetly stroking. She held herself very still so as not to disturb him or interrupt his progress.

Slowly, in infinitesimal degrees, he pulled his mouth away. His hand still held her neck, his fingers caressing, and he stared at her mouth. "You're not kissing me back, Lizzy."

"I..." She hadn't realized he wanted her to. All her senses had been attuned to what he was doing, not what she might do. "Sorry."

With a groan, he took her mouth again, not so gently this time, a hungry greed coming through to curl her toes and make her fingers go numb. Elizabeth leaned into him, tilted her head the tiniest bit to better accept his mouth. She braced her hands against his chest, then jerked at how hot his skin was, the way his chest hair felt on her palms. Her breasts tingled, and below her stomach an insistent tingling demanded her attention.

She panted, and this time when his tongue touched her mouth, she captured it, stroking her tongue against him.

She wasn't sure if it was her heartbeat or his that rocked her. His hand left her head and captured her elbow. She found herself being slowly lowered to the dock, but she didn't care; she just wanted him to go on kissing her like this, creating the overwhelming turmoil inside her. She liked it. She liked him—his taste, his hardness, his scent.

His chest crushed her breasts, but not uncomfortably. It helped to ease the ache there, but then the ache intensified, especially when he moved, abrading her taut nipples. She gasped.

He was braced over her with his elbows on either side of her head. Tentatively, uncertain how far she should go, Elizabeth placed her hands on his back. His tongue stroked deeply and she moaned, arching into him.

Gabe pulled away with a curse. He stared into her eyes, his face so close she could see his individual lashes, and then with another soft curse he sat up and gave her his back.

She struggled for breath, not certain what had happened, if she'd done something wrong. She pressed her palms flat on the rough wooden dock and tried to secure herself. Her head was spinning, her heart beating so wildly she thought it might punch right out of her chest. Her lungs felt constricted, and she couldn't get enough air, which forced her to pant. And there was the most delicious tingling sensation deep inside her.

Gabe ran a hand though his hair, but he kept his back to her. She could see the straight line of his spine, the shift of his muscles as he, too, breathed deeply, quickly. With his attention elsewhere, she devoured him with her eyes. His skin was bronzed, testimony to how much time he spent on the lake, and a striking contrast to his fair hair and burning blue eyes. His damp shorts rode low on trim hips, but all she could see was tanned flesh.

Abruptly he shifted and speared her with a look, as if he'd sensed her regard. Over his shoulder, his eyes razor sharp, he growled, "Ask your damn question."

Still gasping, Elizabeth tried to gather her wits. Question? Her muddled mind came up with one reply. "Are you tanned all over?"

No sooner had the words left her mouth than she realized her mistake. Gabe's eyes widened comically. There was a moment of startled hesitation, then he threw his head back and laughed, the sound bouncing off the placid surface of the lake to return to her again and again, making her brain hurt and her face throb with heat.

Appalled, she started to sit up, but just that quick, Gabe caught her shoulders and pinned her in place.

"Where are you going?" he asked, his voice a husky rumble. His mouth was still slightly curled in amusement.

Elizabeth tried to think. "I...I meant to ask you—"

"I know what you meant," he growled around another smile. "You want me to skin off my shorts so you can get a good look at my backside, just to appease your curiosity?"

Yes. "No, of course not!" He loomed over her, making rational thought impossible. But then, everything about Gabriel Kasper, from their first meeting to now, had been impossible.

"Liar." There was no insult in the accusation. In fact, he said it with amused affection, like an endearment. Then he kissed her again, softly, slowly. Elizabeth felt a constriction in her chest that had nothing to do with the way he held her and everything to do with the realization of all she'd missed in life.

The kiss wasn't consuming, but sweetly sensual. As Gabe lifted his head, he looked at her breasts, gently crushed against the hard planes of his chest. A slight tremble went through him as he swept one fingertip over the upper swell of each breast. "Are these real, sweetheart?"

Her breath strangled at the feel of his hot, rough finger stroking her there, in a place no man had ever touched. Eyes wide, she muttered, "What are you talking about?"

"You have such a sexy body." That taunting fingertip dipped slightly into her cleavage, causing her heart to pick up a quick, almost frantic beat. "And these breasts...so plump when you're so trim everywhere else. So soft when you're mostly firm. I just wondered if Mother Nature had really been so generous, or if you'd had a little help."

She stared at him, her mind blank, unable to think while he was touching her. She was aware of the sun hot against her skin, of the slight breeze that stirred the humid air, of the gentle lapping of the lake on the shore. But all of it was overshadowed by Gabe and the blue flare of his eyes.

Grinning, Gabe murmured, "Maybe I should just find out on my own?" His fingers spread over her chest, just below her collarbone, and jolted her into awareness.

She caught his wrist and stared at him hard. "They're real!" Then, because she was embarrassed over his attention, she muttered, "What a stupid question."

Gabe easily freed his hand from hers and wrapped his fingers around her skull, stroking her hair, smoothing it. "You must have never gone braless in your life."

Heat washed over her face, then down to her breasts. "Of course I haven't."

His thumb rubbed her cheekbone, the corner of her mouth. He shifted, his chest moving over hers, pressing. "Such a little innocent. Such a surprise." He looked at her mouth.

"Gabe?"

"Just one more," he whispered, husky and deep.

She thought to tell him that he'd owe her a lot of conversation for this, that she had plenty of questions he was going to have to answer, but the moment he took the kiss, she forgot all that.

His hand slid down her side to her waist, shaping her, measuring her, it seemed, then drifted to her hip. His touch was sure, his fingers rough, callused. He met bare skin on her upper thigh and made a raw sound of pleasure, causing her to quiver in response.

"So soft," he growled, his mouth against her throat, leaving damp kisses, sucking softly. Overwhelmed, alive, she tipped her head back to make it easier for him. His grip on her thigh tightened, and with little direction from him, she bent her knee and lifted one leg alongside his. The position neatly settled him into the cradle of her hips. She vaguely wondered why she didn't feel crushed, because he was so big, so hard.

He pushed, nestling closer, and his erection rubbed her in the most intimate spot imaginable. She gasped; he groaned.

She'd never felt a man on top of her before. The sensation was...*wonderful.* Scorching, enveloping, gratifying and at the same time stirring new needs.

Gabe dipped the tip of his tongue into her ear. That sensation, too, was astounding. How could such a simple act be so incredibly erotic? She heard his harsh breathing, felt his hot, moist breath and the hammering of his heart. He licked her ear. Stunned for just a moment, she froze, trying to take it all in.

He kissed her again. His mouth ate at hers, his teeth nipping, his tongue stroking. She melted, no longer capable of rational thought, simply reacting to what he did and how he did it.

In the next instant he was gone, sitting up beside her.

Elizabeth blinked in shock, uncertain what had happened or why he had pulled away so abruptly. She lay there, her eyes open but unseeing, trying to assimilate her senses. Gabe never hesitated. He caught her arms just above her elbows and jerked her upright so that she, too, was sitting, although not quite as steadily as he. It took a lot of effort not to flop down. She felt boneless and flushed and limp. Mute, she stared at him.

He gave her a grim, somewhat apologetic look and then she heard the motor. They both turned to stare at the entrance to the lake.

Seconds later a small fishing boat similar to the one they had used rounded the bend into the cove. Two older men, goofy hats hooked with a variety of lures perched on their

heads, concentrated on the long fishing lines they had dragging in the water. Their voices were barely audible over
the steady drone of the trolling motor.

They looked up in surprise when they noticed Gabe. Almost as one, their gazes turned to Elizabeth, and she felt
herself turning pink with embarrassment. Good grief, could
they tell what she and Gabe had been doing? Would they
be able to look at her face and see it all?

Gabe moved, leaning forward to block her from view.
He waved at the men, who waved back and continued to
stare at them until their boat nearly went aground. With a
disgruntled curse, the man in the back redirected their
course and they puttered out of sight.

Gabe turned to her. His eyes were probing and direct.
Unable to look away, Elizabeth thought how unfair it was
that he could completely snare her with just a look. Eyes
so light and clear a blue should have appeared cool, not
fiery and passionate.

His fair hair shimmered beneath the sunshine, mussed
from his swim—and from her fingers. Every muscle in his
tensed body was delineated, drawing her eyes. He watched
her so intently, she almost flinched.

Swallowing hard, Elizabeth tried to think of what to say.
It was nearly impossible to muster a straight, businesslike
face after that…that… She didn't know what to call it. It
was certainly far more than a mere kiss. Admittedly, she
lacked experience, but she was certainly not stupid. She
knew the difference between kissing and what they'd just
done.

It wasn't easy, but she reminded herself of her original
purpose, her continued purpose. All her life she'd struggled
to deal with the idiosyncrasies of heroism, why some had
those qualities and some did not. Having heroism gave you
the ability to change lives, lacking it could leave you forever empty.

She met Gabe's eyes and cleared her throat. "Well, after that, I expect an entire explanation for my thesis."

She hadn't meant to sound so cold and detached; what she really felt was far different from those simple emotions. She'd only meant to stress the point of what they were doing and why.

Gabe's eyes darkened, narrowed, the heat leaving them as if it had never been there. His jaw flexed once, then stilled. He stared at her mouth and said, "You'll get it."

CHAPTER FOUR

HE WANTED to shake her, to... God, he'd never had the inclination to do any more than make love with a woman, laugh with her, tease. But Lizzy had him crazed.

He'd all but taken her on the damn dock, out in the open, on the lake, for crying out loud.

And she'd have let him.

He sensed it in his bones. He knew women, knew how they thought, what they felt, when they were turned on and how to turn them on. Little Red had been wild. She'd bit his bottom lip, sucked on his tongue, lifted her hips into the thrust of his... She'd strained against him, trying to get closer, and her fluttering heartbeat had let him measure each new degree of her excitement. She'd been on the ragged edge. He could have slipped his fingers past the leg band of her suit and stroked her over the edge with very little effort.

But now she watched him as though it had never happened, demanding answers to questions that were beyond stupid.

"I need to cool off." With no more warning than that, Gabe went over the side of the dock. He swam down until he touched the bottom, feeling around for a shell. When he surfaced, Lizzy was hanging over the edge, watching for him anxiously. He pushed wet hair from his face and forced himself not to eye her breasts.

"You scared me!" She stared at him in accusation, looking like a wild woman. Thanks to his hands, long strands of hair had escaped her thick braid in various places, giving her a woolly-headed look, like a damn red thistle. Her smooth cheeks were flushed, making the freckles more pronounced. Her lush mouth, which had felt so hot and hungry under his only moments before, was pressed into a severe line.

Gabe almost laughed. Hell, she wasn't even pretty, not really, and she sure as certain didn't have the right temperament to lure a man. So why had he reacted so strongly?

"Here." He handed her the shell, watched her sit back, bemused, to look it over. "It's just a mussel. The bottom of the lake is littered with them. I dated a girl for a while who used to find live ones and eat them raw."

Lizzy's head jerked up, and she dropped the shell. Her lip curled in a way that made her look ready to vomit. No, she looked far from pretty right now.

Gabe laughed out loud. "Gross, huh? I couldn't quite bring myself to kiss her again after that. I kept thinking of what had been in that mouth. Have you ever seen a live mussel? They're sort of slimy and gray."

She covered her mouth with a hand, swallowed hard, then sat back and glared at him some more. "Are you going to stay in there, or will you get out and answer my question?"

"Answer one for me first, okay?"

Her blue eyes widened, and he had to admit that they, at least, were beautiful. No matter her mood, her eyes were a focal point in her face, vivid and filled with curiosity and intelligence. He liked the color, dark and deep, unlike his faded, washed-out color. With the sun reflecting off the lake, he could see green and black and navy striations in her irises, lending richness to the unique color. As he studied her eyes, her pupils flared, reminding him how quickly she'd gotten aroused with him.

Arousing Little Red was fun, indeed. And from what he

could tell, she could use a little fun in her life. Maybe it'd take some of the starch out of her spine and some of the vinegar out of her speech.

He propped his crossed arms over the edge of the dock, facing her and smiling into her stern face. "Where'd you get that suit?"

Bemused, she looked at herself, then at him. She plucked nervously at the material by her waist. "I...well, I hadn't owned a suit before this. You insisted we needed to swim, so I had to go get one last night. But I couldn't see spending a lot of money on one when this would likely be the only time I wore it. So I grabbed the cheapest one I could find."

"The cheapest one-piece?"

Her lips trembled, fascinating him. "I'm not exactly the type to wear a bikini."

"Why not?" His voice dropped despite his effort to sound dispassionate. "You have an incredible body, Lizzy." He was serious, but he could tell by the way her eyes darkened and she looked away that she didn't believe him.

"Lizzy?" She wouldn't look at him. His heart softened, felt too thick in his chest. Very gently he asked, "When was the last time you looked at yourself naked?"

Her head snapped up, her cheeks hectic with hot color. Her mouth opened twice, but nothing came out. Finally she glared and said with acerbity, "Why do you deliberately try to embarrass me? Is that your idea of fun, to make me feel...feel..."

"Feel what, sugar?" His hand was a scant inch from her small foot, and he caught her ankle, using his thumb to caress her arch. "Shy? You shouldn't. There's not a woman on this lake that looks better in her suit than you. Why don't you know that?"

Her auburn brows snapped down so fiercely, he expected her to get a headache. "I don't know what you're up to,

Gabriel Kasper, but I'm not blind. I'm well aware of how I look, and if it wasn't for you and your ridiculous stipulations, I wouldn't be here now, sitting in this ridiculous suit!"

"You've enjoyed yourself," he felt compelled to remind her, then held on tight when she tried to draw her foot away.

"It was…unexpected." She looked prim and righteous, and he felt his blood heating in masculine reaction to her silent challenge. "As you've already surmised, I haven't done much kissing in my lifetime. I looked at this as sort of a…a learning experience."

Gabe grinned, his thumb still brushing sensually over her foot, making her stiffen. "So I'm sort of a class project, huh? Will you write another thesis? What I did over the summer vacation?"

Like a small volcano erupting, she jerked away and scrambled out of his reach. Her hands flattened on the dock to push herself upright, then she squealed and lifted a finger to her mouth.

Gabe watched her antics with curiosity. "What are you doing?"

"I'm leaving," she grumbled, still looking at her finger. "I realize now that you have no intention of answering my questions, and I can't afford to waste the time with you otherwise."

So he was a waste of time? Like hell! He'd make her eat those words. Gabe levered himself onto the dock, and his weight set it off kilter, causing Lizzy to tilt into him. Her attention was still on her finger.

"I'll answer your damn question, so quit frowning."

She gave him a skeptical, disbelieving look, then went back to frowning.

"What's wrong with you? Did you hurt yourself?" He

leaned over her shoulder to see her hand, and as usual, she pulled it close to her chest as if protecting it from him.

"I have a splinter, thanks to you." As an afterthought, she added, "It hurts."

Gabe wrested her hand away from her body and looked at the injured finger. A jagged piece of wood was imbedded under the pad of her middle finger. "Damn. That sucker is huge."

She tried to pull her hand free. She did that constantly, he realized, always pulling away from him. Well, not constantly. When he'd been kissing her, she'd strained against him.

"I can get it out."

"No!" She tugged again, finally gaining her release. "I can take care of it after I get home. If you're ready to leave?"

Gabe chewed the side of his mouth. "Actually, no, I'm not ready to leave. You have a question for me, and I'll answer it. But first let me take care of this."

"Gabe…"

"Stop being such a sissy. I won't hurt you."

Her chin firmed, her lips pursed, and then she thrust her hand toward him. "Fine. Do your worst."

Without hesitation, Gabe lifted her finger to his mouth. He heard Lizzy gasp, felt her tremble. Probing with his tongue, he located the end of the splinter, then carefully, gently closed his teeth around it. It pulled out easily.

He smiled at her, still with her hand close to his mouth. "There. That wasn't so bad, was it?"

She had that glazed look in her eyes again, like the one she'd had before the fishing boat had interrupted. Unable to help himself with her looking so flustered and shivering, he held her gaze and kissed her fingertip. Her pupils dilated, her lips parting. Damn, but she was quick to react—which made him react, too.

It was if they were connected by their gazes, an intimate hold that he'd never quite experienced before. Gabe touched the tip of his tongue to her finger and heard her inhalation of breath. Her eyes grew heavy, her lashes dipping down. He drew her finger into his mouth and sucked softly. With a moan, she closed her eyes.

Damn, it was erotic. *She* was erotic. Moving her finger along his bottom lip, he said, "Being in the water is second nature to me. It never scares me."

He was shocked by how husky his voice had become, but still, it jarred her enough that her eyes opened. Gabe dipped his tongue between her fingers, licked along the length of one. "I'm as at home in the water as I am on land. Especially this lake. I never once considered there was any danger to me, because there wasn't, so I wasn't afraid."

"Oh."

He moved to her thumb, drawing it into his mouth and tugging gently, just as he might with a breast. The thought inflamed him.

"After the kids and their mother were out of the way, I didn't have time to think or be afraid. I just reacted."

"I...I see."

Her voice was so low and rough he could barely understand her. She watched him through slitted eyes, her body swaying slightly. "I learned to drive boats when I was knee-high to a grasshopper. I started working on boat motors when I was ten, knew more about them than most grown men by the time I was fourteen."

He licked her palm, then the racing pulse in her wrist.

"Because I knew what I was doing, there was no danger, no reason to be afraid."

"I see."

Her eyes were closed, her free hand curled into a fist, her breasts heaving.

"Therefore," Gabe added, as he started to lower her once again, "I'm not what you'd call a hero at all."

Her back no sooner touched the dock than she bolted upright. Her head smacked his chin with the force of a prizefighter's blow. She blinked hard, rubbed her head and scowled at him.

After working his jaw to make certain she hadn't broken anything, Gabe asked, "Are you all right?"

"You've given me a concussion."

He smiled. "I have not." Then: "Why'd you get so jumpy?"

"I need to write everything down before I forget it."

Rolling his eyes, Gabe said, "So you're finally satisfied?" No sooner did the words leave his mouth than he looked at her spectacular breasts, saw her pointed nipples and knew true satisfaction was a long way off. Not that she'd ever admit it.

Her gaze downcast, she said simply, "I'm satisfied—for that question. But I have so many more." Looking at him, a soft plea in her gaze, she asked, "Will it really be so difficult to let me get some answers?"

Damn, he wanted her. He wanted to see that look on her face when she was naked beneath him. It defied reason and went against everything he knew about his preferences and inclinations. She was so far from the type of woman who usually caught his eye that it was almost laughable.

But it didn't change the facts.

Gabe chucked her chin. "I'm willing if you are."

"Meaning?"

There was a note of caution in her tone that made him smile with triumph. "Meaning as long as we stick to our original bargain, I'll answer your questions. One kiss per question."

Lizzy turned her head to stare at the lake. There was a

stillness about her that he hadn't seen before, and it made him uneasy.

"Because this is important to me," she said without inflection, "I'll agree if you insist. But what we've just been doing...that was more than kissing." She turned her big blue eyes on him and added, "Wasn't it?"

Sure felt like more to him! But he'd never admit that to her. He had a feeling that if she knew how she'd turned him on, how close he'd gotten to losing all control, she'd never agree to see him again, much less let him kiss her. "It's not a big deal, Lizzy. You don't have to worry for your reputation or your chastity."

Her lips tightened, giving her a wounded look. Gabe cursed. He'd wanted to reassure her, not make light of their mutual attraction. "I didn't mean..."

"Why?" She turned to face him. "Why is it so important to you to toy with me?"

"I'm not toying with you, damn it."

She obviously didn't believe him. "Do you enjoy seeing me flustered, embarrassed? Do you enjoy knowing this is all very strange to me?"

A direct attack. He hadn't been expecting it, no more than he'd anticipated her vehemence. He watched her, but she once again avoided his gaze. After some thought, Gabe said honestly, "I like you. And it's for certain I like kissing you." She made an exasperated sound, but he continued. "You're different from the women I know around here."

"You mean I'm odd?"

He laughed at the suspicious accusation in her tone and look. "No, that's not what I mean. I've known most of the women in these parts for all of my life. They're entirely comfortable with me and with their own sexuality."

She slanted him a look. "I'm odd."

"No, you are not!" He tucked a long tendril of hair

behind her ear, still smiling. "You're a...contradiction. Sweet and sassy—"

"What a sexist remark!"

"—and pushy but shy. You intrigue me. I guess it's tit for tat. Just as you seem to want to know what makes me tick, I want to know what makes you tick. It's as simple as that."

"It doesn't feel simple."

"That's because you're evidently not used to men paying you attention." She didn't answer his charge, and he frowned. Catching her chin and bringing her face around to his, he asked the question uppermost in his mind. "Why is that, Lizzy?"

She shook her head, her lips scrunched together.

"I figure you must be...what? Twenty-two?"

She looked at the sky. "Almost twenty-three."

"Yet you had no idea how to kiss. What girl gets through high school these days, much less college, without doing some necking?"

She glared at him and growled, "Redheaded, freckled, gangly girls who are shy and bookish, apparently."

Gabe took a telling perusal of her body. "Sweetheart, you're not gangly. Far from it."

She stared at him hard for at least three heartbeats, then asked with endearing caution, "Really?"

Tenderness swelled over him, taking him by surprise. "Didn't your mother ever tell you that you'd filled out real nice?"

She clasped her hands in her lap and shook her head. "My mother died when I was twelve."

Gabe scooted closer to her and put his arm around her sun warmed shoulders. He didn't question his need to hold her, to touch her. "Friends? Sisters?"

Shaking her head, she explained, "I'm an only child. And I didn't really have that many friends in school." As if admitting a grave sin, she added, "I was always very backward until recently."

Gabe squeezed her gently. "You're hardly a robust conqueror now."

"I know. It's not easy for me to do all these interviews, but they're important, so I do them." Her expression turned mocking. "Most of them have been fairly quick and simple."

"Then it's a good thing you ran into me, huh? Because lady, if anyone ever needed shaking up a little, it's you."

"I need to complete my thesis."

"You have the rest of summer break, right?"

She nodded warily, obviously uncertain of his intent.

"So why don't we indulge each other? I'll answer any questions you have, and in return, you'll let me convince you how adorable you are in that bathing suit."

Her chin tucked in close to her chest. "Convince me...how?"

"By what we've already been doing. I won't ever push you further than you want to go, you have my word on that. But I can promise there'll be more kissing." His hand cradled her head. "You won't mind that so much, will you, Lizzy?"

She didn't reply to that, and she didn't look convinced. In a slightly choked voice that gave away her tension, she said, "I need you to be more specific than that."

Gabe chewed it over, trying to think of how to couch his terms so she would be reassured. "Okay, how's this. I'll answer a question and you'll cut loose a little, my choice of how. And before you start arguing, first I want you to go to a drive-in with me. You ever been to the drive-in?"

"With my father when I was young. I didn't even know they still had them."

"You're in for a treat!" And I'm in for a little torture. "We can go over to the next county, to the Dirty Dixie."

He bobbed his eyebrows. "They play fairly raunchy movies—which will probably be another first for you, right?"

Looking dazed, she nodded.

"Perfect. How about this Friday? That's two days away, plenty of time for you to get used to the idea." And plenty of time for him to get a better grip on himself.

She hesitated once again and Gabe held his breath. Then she nodded. "All right. Where should I meet you?"

"Ah, no," he told her gently, knowing she wanted to keep him at a distance and knowing, too, that he wouldn't allow it. "You'll give me your address and phone number. I pick up the women I take on dates, Lizzy, I don't *meet* them."

She seemed to consider that, then shrugged in feigned indifference. Taking up her pencil, she jotted her address and phone number. Gabe accepted the scrap of paper, then slipped off the edge of the dock and waded to the boat to put it in his cooler for safekeeping.

Lizzy, watching him in the water, said, "I'm renting the upstairs from this nice single mother. She has two young children and needed the extra money."

Gabe knew she was prattling out of nervousness. He hated to see an end to the day, but he checked his waterproof watch and saw it was time to go. "We'd better head back. I have some work to do."

"I thought you didn't have a job."

Looking at her from the other side of the boat, he gave her a wide grin. "Angling for another question? All right, I can be generous." He propped his forearms over the metal gunwale and explained, "I don't have a regular job, but I have more work than I can handle. I'm sort of a handyman and this time of year everyone needs something built, repaired or revamped. And that's all I'm telling you, so get that look out of your eyes."

"Spoilsport."

Gabe maneuvered the boat close to the dock. "Since I now know you're afraid of the water—something you should have told me right off—I'll be gallant and hold the boat steady for you to climb in."

"You won't expect me to get in the water again?"

He shook his head at her hopeful expression. "Oh, I imagine we'll get you used to it little by little. After all, what's the use of taking a vacation near a lake if you don't want to get wet? But for today you've had enough."

She couldn't quite hide her relief. "Thanks."

Using exaggerated caution, she scooted off the dock and into the boat. Gabe watched the way her long legs bent, how her breasts filled the snug suit, how her bottom settled neatly on the metal seat, heated by the sun.

Damn, he was in deep. And he couldn't even say why. In the normal course of things, a woman like Ms. Elizabeth Parks shouldn't have appealed to him at all. She was up-tight, pushy, inexperienced…but she was also funny and curious and she had about the sweetest body he'd ever seen.

With a muttered curse against his fickle libido, Gabe hauled himself over the side of the boat, which made her squeal and grab the seat with a death grip. "You can thank me Friday night," he told her, and wondered if he'd be able to keep his hands off her even then. Two days didn't seem like near enough time to get himself together.

But it did seem like an eternity when already he wanted her so bad his hands were shaking.

GABE FELT THE SUN on his shoulders, smelled the newly mown grass and breathed a deep sigh of contentment. Or at least, he'd be content if he could get a redheaded wonder out of his head. He steered the tractor mower toward the last strip of high grass by rote. He and his brothers had so much property, they only kept up the acres surrounding the house. Beyond that, the land was filled with wild shrubs and colorful flowers and mature trees of every variety. It was gorgeous in the fall, when the leaves changed color, but Gabe liked summer best.

His mother used to accuse him of being part lizard, because the heat seldom bothered him, and he was always drawn to the sunshine.

Life had been different since his two oldest brothers had married. Different in a very nice way. He enjoyed having Honey around. She made the house feel homier in some small indefinable ways, like the smell of her scented candles in the bathroom after she'd been indulging in a long soak, or the way she always hugged him when he left the house, cautioning him to be careful—as if he ran around risking his neck whenever he went out the door.

Gabe grinned. He could still recall how Honey had cried when Morgan had moved to his own house. Never mind that it was just up the hill; she liked having all the brothers as near as possible. It was a huge bonus that Morgan had married her sister, Misty. The two women were very close and managed to get together every day, especially since Misty had given birth to an adorable little girl seven months ago. Amber Marie Hudson was about the most precious thing he'd ever seen. And watching his brother fuss over the baby was an endless source of entertainment.

Females flat-out fascinated Gabe, whether they were seven months, twenty-seven or seventy. He didn't think he'd ever tire of learning more about them.

He was pondering what he might learn from a certain redhead when he saw a car pull into their long drive. Gabe stopped the tractor and watched, a feeling of foreboding creeping up his sweaty back. The car, a small purple Escort, looked suspiciously like the one he'd seen Lizzy park at the docks. He'd noticed because the purple clashed so loudly with her hair.

And sure enough, even from this distance, when she

stepped out of the car, there was no mistaking the fiery glint of the sun off her bright head.

Scowling, he put the tractor in gear and headed toward the house. He was aware of a strange pounding in his chest, hoping to intercept her before any of his brothers saw her. Or worse, before Honey or Misty saw her.

But his hopes were vain. Just as he neared the drive the front door opened and there stood Honey, her long blond hair moving gently in the breeze, her killer smile in place.

Oh, hell.

He watched in horror as Lizzy was evidently invited in, as she accepted and as the door closed behind her. The tractor was too damn slow so he stopped it, turned it off and ran the rest of the way.

His chest was heaving and he was dripping sweat by the time he bolted through the front door. No one was in sight. He hurried down the hallway to the family room, finding it empty. He stopped, trying to listen. A feminine laugh caught his attention, and he raced for the kitchen. He had to stop her before she said too much, before she started in with her questions—before anyone found out he'd been kissing her....

He skidded to a halt on the tile floor. The kitchen was crowded, what with Honey and her sister and Amber and Sawyer... Gabe stared at Lizzy, seated at the table with her back to him.

Sawyer was looking her over—not politely, but in minute detail. He leaned over Lizzy with his fingers grazing her cheek, so close to her she could probably feel his breath, for God's sake.

Gabe's brows snapped down to match Sawyer's frown, and he demanded, "What the hell is going on?"

Everyone looked up. Honey was the first to speak, saying, "Gabe. I was just about to come get you."

Misty shook her head at him in a pitying way, as if he'd

gotten himself into trouble somehow, and Amber cooed at the sound of his voice. Gabe ignored them all to stare at his oldest brother.

Of course Lizzy would have to call at lunchtime, he thought darkly, when everyone was bound to be around. Normally Sawyer would have been in his office at the back of the house, treating patients. Luckily, to his mind, Jordan always ate lunch in town. Morgan used to, too, until he married Misty. Now he was likely to show up any minute. Gabe needed to get Lizzy out of the house before she said too much about their association. He could imagine the ribbing he'd take if his brothers knew he was interested in—as in majorly turned on by—a prickly little redheaded witch with freckles!

His face heated at the mere thought.

Then Lizzy turned to look at him, and he knew the heat in his face was nothing compared to hers.

His frown intensified, but for different reasons, as he drifted closer, studying her every feature. "Damn, Lizzy, what happened?"

She was bright pink with sunburn, her nose red, her soft mouth slightly puffy. Without thinking about his rapt audience, he knelt in front of her chair and smoothed a wayward tendril of hair gently behind her ear. God, even the tops of her ears were red!

She licked her lips, looking horribly embarrassed and glancing around at the others. "I'm fine, Gabe," she murmured, trying to get him to stand up while sneaking glances at his family. "There's no reason for this fuss."

He paid no attention at all to her words, too intent on discovering every speck of skin that had been reddened. "I thought you had sunscreen on yesterday."

"I did," she assured him, looking more wretchedly miserable by the minute. "I guess it wasn't strong enough, or maybe it washed off in the water."

Sawyer made an impatient sound, recalling Gabe to the fact that he was on his knees in front of Lizzy, treating her like the most precious woman in the world. He jerked to his feet, but he still couldn't take his concerned gaze off her. "Does it hurt?"

"No." She tried a weak smile, then flinched. "Truly. I'm fine."

Sawyer rudely pushed Gabe aside. "I'm going to give you some topical ointment for the sting. In the meantime, stay out of the sun—" and here he glared at Gabe "—and wear very loose clothes. It doesn't look like you'll blister, but I'd say you're going to be plenty uncomfortable for the next few days."

Honey stepped up with some folded paper towels soaked in cool tea. "This'll help. I'm fair-skinned, too, and it's always worked for me."

Misty leaned close to watch as Honey patted the towels gently in place on Elizabeth's bare shoulders. Gabe realized that Lizzy wore a shapeless white cotton dress, so long it hung to her ankles. He looked closely and could see by the soft fullness beneath the bodice that she wasn't wearing a bra. His heart skipped a beat.

She'd said she never went braless, and her breasts were so firm and round, he believed her. The sunburn must indeed be painful for her to go without one.

To distract himself, he looked around the room and settled on smiling at the baby. At his attention, Amber flailed her pudgy arms from her pumpkin seat on the table, gurgling and blowing spit bubbles. Gabe laughed. "Sorry, kiddo. I'm too sweaty to hold you right now."

Elizabeth watched as he reached out and tweaked the baby's toe, and he knew she was planning on putting that into her little notebook, too. He scowled.

Morgan stepped in through the kitchen door and went immediately to Misty, lifting her into a bear hug that led to a lingering, intimate kiss. The way Misty continued to flush at her husband's touch always tickled Gabe. Morgan had been well and fully tamed.

He turned and hauled Amber out of her chair and against his chest, then nuzzled the baby's downy black hair. Amber squealed as he settled her in the crook of his arm.

Only then did Morgan notice Elizabeth. One dark brow shot up. "Hello."

Misty shook the dreamy look off her face and smiled. "Morgan, this is Elizabeth Parks, a friend of Gabe's."

Morgan's enigmatic gaze transferred to Gabe, and Gabe felt his face heat again. "She looks done to a crisp, Gabe. I suppose you weren't...ah, paying attention to the sun? Had your mind on...other things?"

Gabe stiffened and said, "You know I can't hit you while you're holding the baby. Care to give her to her mother?"

"Nope." He kissed the baby's tiny ear and with a grin turned to Elizabeth. "Nice to meet you, Elizabeth."

She nodded. "And you, Sheriff."

"You're joining us for lunch?"

"Oh. No, please. I just... I'm sorry to impose. Really." Her attention flicked nervously to Gabe as all his interfering relatives assured her she was no imposition at all. "I just had a few questions, if you have the time."

Morgan pulled out a chair. "Questions about what?"

Gabe stepped forward before she could answer. "Lizzy, I'd like to talk to you. In private."

She stalled, staring at him with a guilty expression.

Sawyer nudged him aside. "I've only got fifteen minutes left before I have to see a patient. You can wait that long, can't you, Gabe?"

He wanted to say no, he damn well couldn't wait, but he knew that would only stir up more speculation. So instead he took the cool towels from Honey and began placing them on Lizzy's shoulders. A thought struck him, and he looked at her feet, set together primly beneath the long skirt. She wore thick white socks and slip-on shoes.

He gave her an exasperated look. "Your feet are burned, too, I suppose?"

Not since he'd met her had Lizzy been so withdrawn. She kept her wide eyes trained on him and nodded. In a tiny voice, she admitted, "A little."

Gabe knelt and very carefully pried off her loose loafers, then peeled the socks off her feet. Like a wet hen, Lizzy fussed and complained and tried to shoo him away. He persisted, despite Morgan's choked laugh and Sawyer's hovering attention.

Her feet were small and slender. Looking at how red they were, Gabe had the awful urge to kiss them better, and instead looked at her with a warning in his gaze. "You should be at home, naked, instead of running around all over the place, asking your crazy questions."

Honey gasped. Morgan guffawed, making Amber bounce in delight. Misty smacked Gabe's shoulder.

But Sawyer agreed. "He's right. Wearing clothes right now is just going to aggravate the sunburn. Taking cool baths and using plenty of aloe, and some ibuprofen for the pain, is the best thing you could do for yourself right now." He glared at Gabe. "Of course if baby brother here had remembered that not everyone is a sun worshiper with skin like leather, there wouldn't be a problem."

Gabe gritted his teeth. "I'm well aware of how delicate a woman's skin is. I thought she had sunscreen on. Besides, we weren't really out in the sun that long."

Lizzy stirred uncomfortably. "Gabe's right. This is my fault, not his. I guess I hadn't counted on the sun's reflection off the lake being so strong."

"Water does magnify the sun," Sawyer agreed, then

propped his hands on his hips and asked in his best phy-
sician's voice, "Are you burned anywhere else?"

Lizzy shook her head and at the same time said, "Just
my legs." But as Gabe started to lift her skirt she slapped
his hands away. Her tone was both horrified and embarrassed. "Don't even think it!"

He grinned. She was behaving more like herself, and he
was vastly relieved. He didn't like seeing her so quiet and
apprehensive. "Sorry. Just trying to see how bad it is."

She scowled. "Mostly on my knees, and you can just
take my word on that, Gabriel Kasper."

Morgan leaned back in his seat, both brows lifted. Everyone stared at them, transfixed. Gabe remembered what he
was doing and came to his feet again. How the hell did he
keep ending up on his knees in front of her?

After setting a platter of sandwiches on the table, Honey
said, "Join us for lunch, okay? What would you like to
drink? I have tea and lemonade and—"

"Oh, no. Really, I didn't mean to catch you at a bad
time." Lizzy reached for the towels on her shoulders,
meaning to remove them. "I can just come back another
time if you agree to a short interview."

Gabe let out a gust of relief. "That's a good idea. Come
on, I'll walk you to your car."

But Lizzy hadn't even gotten the first towel removed
before everyone rejected her intentions and insisted she
stay. Hell, they *begged* her to stay, the nosy pests.

Well, they could do as they pleased, Gabe decided, but
that didn't mean he had to stick around and take part in it.
"I'm going to go shower," he announced, and of course,
that was just fine and dandy. No one begged *him* to stick
around! Irritated, he stomped out of the room, but before
he'd even rounded the corner, he heard Morgan start chuckling, and before long, they were all laughing hysterically.

Everyone but Lizzy.

CHAPTER FIVE

ELIZABETH BIT her lip, not sure what was so funny. She hoped they weren't laughing at her, but then Honey gave her a big smile and said, "Gabe is so amusing sometimes."

Elizabeth had no idea how she meant that, and she didn't ask. She cleared her throat and said, "I'm doing a thesis on heroes for my college major. I've been working on it for some time, and I'd just about finished, then I heard about the boating incident here last summer and decided to add Gabriel to my notes."

Morgan tilted his head. "What boating incident?"

That set her back. His own brother wasn't aware of what had happened? But Misty waved a hand and explained to her husband, "I'm sure she's talking about Gabe saving that woman and her children, right?"

Elizabeth nodded.

"That was right after our wedding. Morgan wasn't paying much attention to what happened around him back then."

Morgan gave his wife a smoldering look. "You're to blame for that, Malone, not me. Can I help it if you're distracting?"

Honey laughed. "Stop it, you two, or you'll embarrass our guest." She sat herself on her husband's lap, and Sawyer wrapped his arms around her. "Gabe is a real sweetheart, Elizabeth. We just enjoy teasing him a little."

Elizabeth could attest to the sweetheart bit. From what she'd found out so far, there didn't live a finer example of the term *lady's man.* She cleared her throat. "So you *do* remember the event?"

"Sure." Honey settled comfortably against her husband's wide chest. To Elizabeth's amazement, Sawyer Hudson managed to eat that way, as if having his wife on his lap was a common occurrence. He quickly devoured three sandwiches, which was one less than Morgan ate. Misty and Honey each nibbled on a half. Since they were insistent, Elizabeth took a bite of one herself. She hadn't realized she was hungry until then.

The sunburn had made her so miserable she'd only wanted to find something to do, to keep her mind off it. Her skin felt too tight, itchy and burning. Clothes were a misery—Sawyer Hudson was right about that. But she simply wasn't used to parading around naked and had decided to take her mind off it by finding out more about Gabe before their trip to the movies.

"Can you tell me about it?" Elizabeth asked after a large drink of icy lemonade. With the cool towels on her shoulders and the uncomfortable shoes off her feet, she felt much better.

"Sure." Honey looked thoughtful for a moment, then turned to Morgan. "You ended up arresting the driver of that boat, right?"

Morgan growled, his tone so threatening that Elizabeth jumped. "The fool was drunk and could have damn well killed somebody. If it had been up to me, he'd have lost not only his boating license, but his driver's license, as well. As it turned out, though, he was banned from the lake, got a large fine and spent a week in jail. Hell, that poor woman was so shook up, Sawyer had to give her a sedative."

Sawyer nodded and his tone, in comparison to Morgan's was solemn. "She thought one or both of her kids would be hurt. She was almost in shock." Then he smiled. "When

I got there, I found Gabe with a kid in his arms, one wrapped around his leg, and the woman gushing all over him. The look of relief on Gabe's face when he spotted me was priceless.''

Elizabeth reached for her bag on the floor by her chair and extracted her notebook and pencil. ''Can you describe it for me?''

''What?''

''The look on his face.''

Sawyer appeared startled by her request, then shrugged. ''Sure.''

IT WAS ONLY fifteen minutes before Gabe rejoined them, his shaggy blond hair still wet and hanging in small ringlets on the back of his neck, his requisite cutoffs clean and dry. Elizabeth had already taken page after page of notes, supplied by all the family members, and she was ecstatic to finally have someone agree with her that Gabriel Kasper's actions had, in fact, been heroic.

When Gabe saw her notebook out, he glared and stomped over to snag the last sandwich on the platter.

Elizabeth drew in a deep breath as he leaned past her, but all she could smell was soap. When Gabe had entered earlier, the earthy scent of damp male flesh warm from the sunshine had clung to him—an enticing aphrodisiac. That wonderfully potent scent, combined with the sight of him, had made her nearly too breathless to talk. She hadn't thought she'd see him today. When she'd called the number Bear gave her, Honey had told her Gabe would be working all day. Elizabeth hadn't realized she meant working around his own home.

She also hadn't realized they'd all make such a fuss about her sunburn. She felt like an idiot for getting burned in the first place. She, better than anyone, knew how easily the sun affected her. She'd even brought along the sunscreen to apply often, keeping it in her bag. But she'd been sidetracked by Gabe and kissing and the erotic feelings he'd engendered. She hadn't thought once about overexposure.

Honey stood to make more sandwiches since Morgan had started prowling around for a cookie and Gabe had only gotten one sandwich. Once his lap was vacated, Sawyer excused himself, saying he'd go fetch the aloe cream he wanted Lizzy to use.

Gabe downed a tall glass of iced tea, and Elizabeth watched his throat work, saw the play of muscles in his arms and shoulders as he tipped his head back. He lowered the glass, caught her scrutiny and frowned at her. He opened his mouth to say something, but at that moment, Morgan thrust the baby into Gabe's arms and he got distracted by a tiny fist grabbing his chest hair.

The contrast between Gabe, so big, so strong, golden blond and tanned, and the tiny dark-haired baby held securely in his arms made Elizabeth's chest feel too tight. She'd have thought a man like him, a Lothario with only hedonistic pleasures on his mind, wouldn't have been so confident while holding an infant. But Gabe not only held the baby without hesitation, he blew raspberries on her soft belly and nibbled on her tiny toes.

Elizabeth decided it was time to make a strategic retreat. She knew, despite his gentle touch with the baby, that he was angry with her. She supposed that negated her deal with him; there'd be no movies at the drive-in. But at least, she told herself, trying to be upbeat instead of despondent, she'd gotten what she wanted. She had an entire notebook full of details, and hadn't that been her single goal all along?

Sawyer reappeared with a large tube of ointment and handed it to Elizabeth. "Put that on every hour or so, or whenever your skin feels uncomfortable. It's mostly aloe. You can keep it in the refrigerator if you like. Drink as much water as you can—rehydrating your skin will help it feel more comfortable. Oh, and take cool baths, not showers. Showers are too stressful to the damaged skin. If it doesn't feel better by tomorrow evening, give me a call, okay?''

Feeling horribly conspicuous, Elizabeth nodded. "How much do I owe you for the cream?"

"Not a thing. I'll take it out of Gabe's hide later."

Since Gabe smirked at that, Elizabeth assumed it was a joke. "Thank you." She glanced at Gabe, then away. "For everything."

Sawyer kissed his wife, his niece and his sister-in-law, then went off to work again. They were a demonstrative lot, always hugging and patting and kissing. It disconcerted her.

Misty and Honey and Gabe all walked her to the door. Gabe was deathly quiet, which she felt didn't bode well since he was usually joking and teasing. As she stepped onto the porch, Honey said, "Misty and I are having lunch in town tomorrow. Would you like to join us? The restaurant where Misty works part-time has fabulous beef stew on Friday afternoons. And afterward, we can all go to the library. I know they must have kept records of the local paper there on file. You could see the firsthand reports of Gabe's—" she glanced at her brother-in-law with a wicked smile "—daring feat."

Gabe gave Honey a look that promised retribution, but she just laughed and hugged him.

Misty added, "It'll be fun."

Aware of Gabe spearing her with his hot gaze, knowing he expected her to turn the women down, Elizabeth nonetheless nodded. "All right. Thank you."

She could have sworn she heard Gabe snarling.

Misty took the baby from Gabe's arms. "Great. If you

know where the diner is, we could meet you there at eleven."

"That'll be fine."

"Perfect. We'll see you then!"

Misty and Honey retreated together, and suddenly Elizabeth wished they were still there. Gabe looked ready for murder.

It was his own fault, she decided, refusing to cower. She raised her chin, gave him a haughty look and turned toward her car. Gabe stalked along beside her.

"What are you doing here, Red?"

Uh-oh. He really was angry. "In each of my studies, I've included the accountings of family members whenever possible."

"But you and I had a deal."

Had. She was right, the deal was no longer valid. Disappointment swamped her, but she fought it off. It had been foolish to look forward to her time with Gabe. He was the epitome of a town playboy. He'd amuse himself with her while she was in town, and when she left he'd never think of her.

But she knew already she'd never be able to forget him. Pathetic, she decided, and deliberately tamped down her regret. She opened the car door and tossed in her bag. She hadn't been able to carry it with the strap over her shoulder because of the burn. She was anxious to follow Sawyer's advice and get naked. Her clothes felt like sandpaper against her sensitive skin.

Gabe watched her closely and she managed a shrug. "You never told me I couldn't talk with your family."

"Bull." He leaned closer, crowding her by putting one hand on the roof of her car, the other at the top of the door frame. "You knew damn good and well I didn't want you snooping around. That's why I agreed to answer your questions myself."

With him so close, her heart thundered. Memories washed over her and her belly tingled in response. She couldn't seem to stop staring at his mouth and swallowed hard. "I understand. If…if you want to cancel the rest of it, I won't argue with you."

Gabe stiffened. "Cancel the rest of what?"

The hair on his chest was still slightly damp, as if he'd dried in a hurry. She'd never in her life known a man who paraded around in such a state of undress almost continually. She didn't think he was deliberately flaunting himself for her benefit so much as he was totally at ease with his own body, aware he had no reason for shame or reserve. She curled her hands into fists to keep from touching him.

"The…the drive-in, the…having fun and loosening up." Pride made her add, "I thought it was a dumb plan all along."

He tipped up her chin with an extremely gentle touch. "Oh, no, you don't," he growled. "You're not backing out on me, Lizzy."

"But…" She faltered, caught by the intensity in his gaze. "You're angry."

"Damn right. And we'll discuss my anger tomorrow. At the movies. If you think I'm going to let you breach our deal now, especially after all your damn snooping, you've got another thing coming."

"Oh." Elizabeth couldn't think of anything else to say. Relief was a heavy throbbing in her breasts. "Okay."

Once again she stared at his mouth and felt her lips trembling in remembrance of how he'd kissed her, how he'd tasted, how hot his mouth had been.

Breathless again, she whispered, "Gabe?" and even she could hear the longing in the single word.

Gabe's nostrils flared and suddenly he cursed. He leaned forward and took her mouth with careful hunger, that single rough finger beneath her chin holding her captive. The kiss was long and deep and Elizabeth grabbed his shoulders, though he didn't return the embrace. His tongue thrust in, hot and wet, and she accepted it, stroking it with her own, moaning softly.

When Gabe lifted his head a scant inch, she said, "Oh, my."

He smiled. "Yeah." There was a husky catch in his voice.

She realized she was practically hanging on him and jerked back. "I didn't mean—"

Again Gabe touched her chin, making her meet his eyes. "You can believe I'd have had you close, Lizzy, if I wasn't afraid of hurting you." His voice dropped and he asked, "Are your thighs burned?"

She couldn't seem to get enough oxygen into her lungs. "A little."

"Your arms?"

"Some."

His mouth barely touched hers. "Your breasts?"

She drew a shuddering breath. "Just..." She sounded like a bullfrog and cleared her throat. "Just the very tops, where the suit didn't cover."

"Want some help with that cream?"

New heat washed over her, making her light-headed. "No! I can manage just fine on my own."

His mouth twitched with a grin. "Spoilsport."

"I should go." She should go before she begged him to help her with the cream, before she attacked his mostly naked body. Before she made a total fool of herself. She had to remember that to Gabe, this was just a game, a way to pass the time while indulging her curiosity. He wasn't serious about any of it. As far as she could tell, he wasn't overly serious about anything.

"All right." Gabe straightened, then gave her another frown. "Don't think I'm not mad over you showing up here. But we'll talk about it when I pick you up for the drive-in, when I'll be assured of a little privacy.''

No sooner did he say it than he looked struck by that thought and twisted to look behind him. Elizabeth peered over his shoulder just in time to see a curtain drop and several heads duck out of sight. Gabe cursed.

Unable to believe what she'd seen, Elizabeth asked, ''They were spying on you?''

Gabe looked livid but accepting. ''Don't sound so incredulous. I'd have done the same.''

''You would have?''

''Sure.'' Then he laughed and scrubbed both hands over his face. ''Oh, hell, the cat's out of the bag now. I'm never going to hear the end of it.''

''The end of what?'' Surely he wasn't embarrassed because he'd been a hero. That didn't make any sense at all.

''Never mind.'' He turned to her, shaking his head. ''Maybe I should just do like Morgan and build my own place. 'Course, Honey'd probably have a fit.''

Elizabeth had a hard time keeping up with his switches in topic.

Gabe pointed toward a spot on a hill overlooking the main house. ''See that house up there? That's Morgan's. He and Misty moved in there last year. Until then, we all lived in the house together. Morgan lived in the main part of the house with Sawyer and his son, Casey. Have you met Case yet? No? Well, you're in for a treat. Hell of a kid.''

She reached for her notebook to jot down the name, but Gabe caught her wrist with a sigh. ''Forget I said that. Leave Casey alone.''

''But you said...''

''You've done enough meddling, Red.''

There was definite menace in his tone. Elizabeth committed the name to memory, determined to write it down as soon as she was away from Gabe. To distract him, she said, "Tell me about these living arrangements."

He gave her a narrow look, then shook his head. "Why not? There's no secret there. I live in the basement. I have my own entrance and it's nicer than most apartments. Jordan lives in the rooms over the garage."

Elizabeth frowned. "Four grown men all live together?"

"Yeah." Gabe squinted against the sun, then his eyes widened and he cursed. "Damn it, here I am, keeping you out in the sun again! Woman, don't you have any sense at all? Get on home."

"But—"

"No buts. I'll give you a family history on Friday. *After* I explain how disgruntled I am with you for trespassing with my family."

Elizabeth huffed. "I didn't trespass. Honey invited me over."

"Yeah, I just bet she did."

Elizabeth sat carefully in the car, trying not to scrape her tender flesh on the seats. Gabe closed her door for her, then leaned in to give her another quick kiss. "Drive careful. And when you get home, get naked."

"Gabe," she admonished, embarrassed by his frank suggestion. She wondered if she'd ever get used to him.

She started the engine and put the car in reverse. Gabe leaned in the window once more. "And Elizabeth?"

She paused. Gabe stared at her unconfined breasts in the loose dress, then whispered, "When you're naked, think of me, okay?" He touched the end of her nose and sauntered away.

Elizabeth stared after him, goggle-eyed and flushed, her heart pounding so hard she could hear it—and dead certain that she'd do exactly as he had asked her to.

GABE CURSED HIMSELF the entire way there, but he couldn't make himself not go. He tried to talk himself out of it. He'd even made other plans—then had to cancel them.

He was worried about her, and damned if that wasn't a first. He'd never had a woman consume his thoughts so completely.

But the sunburn was his fault and he felt responsible. Plus he'd yelled at her and she was so sensitive, so inexperienced, she probably felt bad because of it. Besides, he wanted to know what his damn meddling brothers had told her, because they hadn't given him so much as a clue. Even Misty and Honey were staying mum, refusing to reveal a single word.

Gabe squeezed the steering wheel tight and called himself three kinds of a fool, because the bare-bones truth of it was that he wanted to see her. There. He'd admitted it. He liked her and he wanted her.

He pulled into the driveway on the quiet suburban street just outside of Buckhorn County and turned off the ignition. The house was an older redbrick two-story with mature trees and a meticulously trimmed lawn. As he got out of the car, Gabe wondered if Elizabeth had done as ordered and stripped down. Was she naked right now? Maybe lounging in a soothing tub of cool water?

He shoved his hands into his pockets and climbed the outside stairwell to the upper floor at the side of the building. Miniblinds were pulled shut over the only full-size window. That was good, he thought, just in case she was naked.

Gabe rocked on his heels, took a deep breath and knocked. There was no answer. Briefly he considered turning away in case she was asleep. But it was still early, not quite nine o'clock, so he knocked again, harder.

A muffled sound reached him from the other side of the door, and then he heard Lizzy call, "Who is it?"

She didn't sound as if she'd just awakened, but she did

sound wary. Probably she didn't get that many callers, especially not at night.

He felt a curious satisfaction at that deduction. "It's me, Red. Open up."

There were more muffled sounds, and finally the door opened the tiniest bit. One big blue eye peeked at him through the crack in the door. "Gabe. What in the world are you doing here?"

Rather than answer that, because he had no answer, he said, "Did I wake you?"

"Oh. No, I was just... Is anything wrong?"

"Yeah." He pushed against the door, and she hastily stepped out of the way. "I wanted to check...on...you." Gabe stared. His gut clenched and his toes curled. Lizzy had her hair all piled up on top of her head, and she wore only a sheet wrapped around her breasts. Loosely. Very loosely. In fact, if it wasn't for one small, tightly clenched fist, the sheet would have fallen. And good riddance, Gabe thought.

He shoved her front door shut with his heel. He knew he should say something, but he just kept staring.

Lizzy cleared her throat. "I was getting ready to put on some more of that ointment your brother gave me. It helps a lot, but it doesn't last all that long."

Gabe looked past her to the open kitchen nook. On the table sat a bowl of water and the tube of ointment Sawyer had given her. "I'll help you."

Her eyes flared wide. She shook her head, making that huge pile of hair threaten to topple. Her shoulders were bright pink, but just on the top, thank goodness. Most of her back, from what he could tell, was fine. But her breasts... Gabe swallowed. The sheet was white and damp in places around her chest; she must have been putting on cool compresses, he decided.

He was a man. He'd act like a man. Gabe put his arm

around her sheet-covered waist and steered her toward the tiny kitchen. Her living room was minuscule, holding only a sofa, a single chair and some shelves. A thirteen-inch television was centered on the shelves and around that were some plants. The only other things in the spartan rented room were a few books and two photos. He'd check out the photos later, but for now he wanted to help ease her discomfort.

Her feet were bare and looked adorable peeking out from beneath the sheet. Pink, but adorable. Gabe looked at her breasts again, surreptitiously, so she wouldn't notice. The tops of her breasts, from just beneath her collarbone to somewhere beneath that white sheet, were sunburned.

"Here, sit down."

She remained standing. "Gabe, I'm perfectly capable of taking care of this myself."

"But why should you when I can help? I know it can't be easy to reach your shoulders."

Her mouth twisted, her eyes downcast. Her long auburn lashes left shadows on her cheeks from the fluorescent light overhead. He wanted to kiss her.

"I'll get dressed."

"Don't."

She stared at him, unblinking.

"Please, Lizzy?" He kept his tone cajoling, soothing. "Sit down and let me help, okay? It'll make *me* feel better, I promise."

Still she hesitated, and finally she heaved a sigh. "Oh, all right." She lowered herself carefully into the straight-back chair. "But if you hurt me," she warned, "I'm going to be really angry."

His hands shook as he stared at her shoulders. "I'll be as gentle as I can."

He lifted the tube of cream and realized it was cool. Lizzy must have been keeping it in the refrigerator, just as

Sawyer had suggested. He squeezed a large dollop onto his fingertips, then very carefully began smoothing it over her skin. Her head dropped forward and she shivered.

"Cold?"

"It's supposed to be."

"I'm not hurting you?" Her skin was so delicate, even without the sunburn.

"No."

There was a tiny quaking to her voice that made everything masculine in him sit up and take notice. Velvety soft curls on the back of her neck got in his way, and he used one hand to lift them while spreading the cream with the other. Her neck was long and graceful, her hair somewhat lighter here, more like a golden strawberry blond. "Feel better?"

"Mm. Yes."

Gabe looked at her arms, saw they were pink and stepped to her side. He lifted her arm and said, "Brace your hand on my abdomen."

She jerked her hand as if he'd suggested she cut it off. She held it protectively to her chest so he couldn't take it again.

Gabe smiled. "C'mon, Lizzy. Don't be shy. I just want to put the cream on you, and I'm even wearing a shirt. There's no reason to act so timid."

Her spine stiffened. "I am not acting timid! I'm just not used to how you...how you constantly..."

He could imagine what she'd eventually come up with, so he decided to help her. "How informal and comfortable and at ease I am? Yeah, that's true. Touching someone isn't a sin, sweetheart." He pried her arm loose, being careful not to hurt her, then pressed her hand to his abdomen. His muscles were clenched rock hard, not on purpose, but in startling reaction to the feel of her small hand there. "See. That's not so bad, is it?"

A tiny squeak.

Gabe lifted a brow, still covering her hand with his so she couldn't retreat. "What was that?"

Lizzy glared at him and said, "No. It's not…awful."

Laughing, Gabe released her and reached for the cream. "Now just hold still."

He could feel her trembling as he spread the sticky aloe cream up and down her slender arm. She felt so soft, so female, which he supposed made sense. It even made sense that his overcharged male brain immediately began to imagine how soft she was in other, more feminine places, like her inner thighs, her belly and lower.

He felt himself hardening and wanted to curse. Like a doomed man, he continued with his ministrations, torturing himself, but enjoying it all the same.

With only one hand to hold it, her sheet started to slip. Gabe froze as she made a frantic grab for it, his breath held, but she managed to maintain her modesty.

Sighing, he went to her other side, determined to behave himself. He was not a boy ready to take his first woman. He was experienced, mature… There was absolutely no reason for all the anticipation, all the keen tension.

His voice gruff, he said, "You know the drill."

She looked away from him even as she thrust out her arm. Nervously, she said, "I have to admit I'm a little surprised to see you so fully dressed. I was beginning to think you didn't own any shirts or slacks."

He looked at his white T-shirt and faded jeans. The jeans were so old, so worn, they fit like a second skin—which meant that if she bothered to look at all, she'd see he had an erection. Again.

But of course she didn't look. Gabe studied her averted face and smiled. "Are you disappointed that I came fully clothed, Lizzy?"

In prim tones, she replied, "Not at all."

He didn't quite believe her. Sure, he felt the tension, but then, so did she. She was practically vibrating with it. Yet she'd deny any attraction. Most women came on to him with force; this tactic was totally unusual…and intriguing.

She turned her face even more, until her chin almost hit the chair back. Gabe bit his lip to keep from laughing. Elizabeth Parks was about the most entertaining woman he'd ever met. It was probably a good thing she wouldn't be here long or he'd get addicted to her prickly ways.

But until she left, he told himself, he might as well put them both out of their misery.

CHAPTER SIX

ELIZABETH DIDN'T quite know what to think when Gabe moved in front of her, insinuating his body into the small space between the Formica table and the chair where she sat. Every one of her nerve endings felt sensitized from the way he'd so gently stroked her. And now his lap was on a level with her gaze.

Her eyes widened. *He was turned on!* It wasn't just *her* feeling so sexually charged. But unlike Gabe, she was the only one uncertain how to continue, or if she even should.

Gabe leaned very close and gripped the seat of the chair in his large hands. Elizabeth yelped when he lifted it and moved it far enough for him to kneel in front of her. Her heart beat so hard she felt slightly sick, her vision almost blurring.

He smelled of aftershave mingled with his own unique scent. Never in her life had she noticed a man's smell before. She wished she could bottle Gabe's particular aroma—she'd make a fortune. There couldn't be a woman alive who wouldn't love his enticing scent.

His lips grazed her ears and he said softly, "I'm going to finish putting the cream on you, then we're going to do a little experimenting, all right?"

The soft, damp press of his mouth on her temple served as a period to his statement. He phrased his comment as a question, but given the heat suffusing her, it had to be rhetorical.

Her hands opened and closed fitfully on the sheet. "What exactly do you mean?"

Leaning back on his haunches, Gabe stared at her and caught the hem of the sheet. "Your legs are burned, too." His rough palms slid up the back of her calves all the way to her knees, baring them as the sheet parted.

Elizabeth pressed herself back in the chair, her legs tightly clenched together, her toes curled. Good Lord, surely he didn't mean...

The sheet fell open over her thighs, barely leaving her modesty intact. She tried to hold it closed at her breasts and still push his hands away, but Gabe wasn't having it.

"Shhh. Shh, Lizzy, it's all right." He held perfectly still, not moving, not rushing her, waiting for her to calm down and either acquiesce or reject him.

"You're looking at me!" she said, not really wanting him to stop but unable to contain her embarrassment.

"Just your legs, sweetheart. And I've already seen them, right?"

She sucked in a quick, semicalming breath. He was right, in a way. "It just...it feels different."

"Because you're naked beneath the sheet?" His fingers continued to stroke up and down her calves, pausing occasionally to gently explore the back of her knees with a touch so gentle, so hot.

She'd had no idea the back of a knee could be an erogenous zone!

Gabe watched her, waiting for an answer. She forced the words past the constriction in her throat. "Yes, because I'm naked beneath the sheet."

"Am I hurting you, Lizzy?"

She shook her head, heated by the tone of his voice, the careful way he was treating her.

"Do you like this?" He began stroking her again, avoiding her sunburned areas while finding places that were ultrasensitive but nonthreatening.

His hands were so large, so dark against her paler complexion. Working hands, she thought stupidly, rough and callused. She gulped. Words were beyond her, but she managed a nod. She did like it. A lot.

Gabe met her gaze with a smoldering look, his eyes blazing, his tone low and soothing and seductive. "Relax for me, sweetheart. I'm not going to do anything you don't want me to do."

Relaxing was the absolute last thing she could accomplish. Her thoughts swirled as he reached for the cream and squeezed a large dollop into his palm. She had no real idea what he intended, but the look on his face told her it would be sensual and that she'd probably enjoy it a great deal.

Should she allow this? How could she not allow it? Never in her entire life had a man pursued her. Certainly not a man like Gabe Kasper. She could do her thesis and indulge in an episode that might well prove to be the high light of her entire life. Who was she kidding, she thought. It was already the highlight of her life!

She squeezed her eyes shut and held her breath, trying to order her thoughts, and suddenly felt his fingertips stroke up the inside of her thigh.

She moaned long and low, unable to quiet the sound. It came as much from expectation as from his touch.

"Look at me, Lizzy."

He was asking a lot, considered how tumultuous her emotions were at the moment. It took several seconds and the stillness of his hand on her leg for her to finally comply.

Gabe was breathing roughly. His mouth quirked the tiniest bit. "I don't know what it is about you, Red, but you make me feel like I'm going to explode." His fingers moved in a tantalizing little caress that made her breath catch. "Have you ever played baseball?"

She blinked, trying to comprehend the absurd question. "I...no."

Gabe nodded. "I'll teach you baseball. But probably not the kind of sport you think I mean." Still holding her gaze, he bent his golden blond head and pressed a soft, damp kiss onto her burned knee. "Much as I'd like to do otherwise, I think we'll just try first base tonight. If you don't like it, say stop and that'll be it. If you do like it, then tomorrow at the drive-in, we'll go to second base. Do you understand?"

He continued to place soft, warm kisses on her skin. Seeing his head there, against her legs, when no man had ever even gotten within touching distance before, was a fascinating discovery. She couldn't have conjured up something so hot, so erotic, in her wildest dreams.

"I think so." Her throat felt raw, but then she had an absolutely gorgeous hunk of a man kneeling at her feet, staring at her with lust, his hot fingers stroking her leg. "Is what you're doing now considered first base?"

Very slowly, Gabe shook his head. "No, this is just torture for me." He gave her a rascal's grin, and his blue eyes darkened. "For right now, I'm going to just finish putting on the cream. I want you as comfortable as possible. But to keep us both distracted, I'd like to learn a little more about you, okay?"

She probably would have agreed to anything in that moment. She was equally mesmerized and frantic and curious. "All right."

On his knees, Gabe opened his legs so that they enclosed her; his chest was even with her lap. He scooped more of the cream from his palm and began applying it in smooth, even strokes that felt like live fire. Not painfully, but with incredible promise.

"Tell me why you chose heroism for your thesis."

Oh, no. She couldn't explain that, not right now, not to

him. She cleared her throat, trying to disassociate her mind from his touch so she could form coherent words. "I'm majoring in psychology. Most of the topics have been done to death. This seemed...unique."

Gabe tilted his head. "Is that right? What gave you the idea for heroism?"

She bit her lip, trying to sort out what she could tell him and what she couldn't. "I've always been fascinated by the stories of people who managed to muster incredible courage or strength at the time of need."

"Like the adrenaline rush? A woman who lifts a car to free her trapped child, a man who ignores burns to rescue his wife from a house fire. Those types of things?"

"Yes." The adrenaline rush that made saving someone important possible. Her throat tightened with the remembrance of how she'd failed, how she'd not been able to react at all, except as a coward.

"Hey?" Gabe finished her legs and carefully replaced the sheet, surprising her...disappointing her. "Are you all right, babe?"

His perceptiveness was frightening, especially when it involved a part of herself she fully intended to keep forever hidden. She went on the defensive without even stopping to think what she was doing or how he might view her response. Meeting his gaze, she said, "I'm not sure I like all these endearments you keep using. And especially not 'babe.' It sounds like you're talking to an infant."

Rather than hardening at her acerbic tone, his expression softened. "There's something you're not telling me, Lizzy."

Panic struck; she absolutely could not bear for him to nose into her private business. He was everything she wasn't, and she accepted that. But she didn't want her face rubbed in it. "I thought you were going to teach me about baseball!"

One side of his mouth kicked up, though his eyes continued to look shadowed with concern. "All right." He touched her chin with a fingertip. "Baseball is something we play in high school, but somehow I think you missed out on that."

His searching gaze forced her to acknowledge that with a nod. "I was very shy in high school."

"There was just you and your father, right?"

"Yes. But we were very close."

Gabe looked at her chest and she felt her breasts tighten in response. "That's good. But it can't make up for all the shenanigans and experiments and playfulness that teenagers indulge in with each other."

"My father," she admitted, willing to give him some truths, "tried to encourage me to go out more often. He was more than willing to supply me with the popular clothes and music and such. On my sixteenth birthday he even bought me a wonderful little car. But I wasn't really interested."

Talking was becoming more difficult by the moment. She knew Gabe was listening, but he was also caressing her with his eyes, and she knew what he saw. Her nipples were peaked, pressing against the white sheet almost painfully. But she liked the way he looked at her and didn't want him to stop.

With a bluntness that stunned her, Gabe suddenly said, "I'm going to touch your breasts. That's first base. All right?"

He didn't wait for her permission, but got more of the cooling cream and prepared to apply it her chest. Elizabeth held her breath, frozen, not daring to move for fear he'd stop—and for fear he wouldn't. She was excited, but also cautious. Whenever she'd imagined getting intimate with a man, she hadn't envisioned all this idle chitchat. She'd always assumed things would just…happen. She'd pictured getting carried away with passion, not having a man tease and explain and ask permission.

With the cream in one palm, Gabe closed his free hand around her wrist and gently pried her fingers from the sheet.

"Breathe, Lizzy."

She did, in a long choked gasp. The sheet slipped, but not far enough to bare her completely. Gabe's nostrils flared and his cheekbones flushed. He carried her shaking hand to his mouth and pressed a kiss into her palm, then placed her hand on her lap.

She tried to prepare herself but when she felt the cream on her skin she jumped. Again, Gabe whispered, "Shh…" in a way that sounded positively carnal. She was oblivious to the sting of her burned skin as his fingers dipped lower and lower. The edge of his thumb brushed her nipple.

His gaze leaped to hers, so intense she felt it clear to her bones. He leaned forward to blow on her skin. "I should be shot," he whispered, "for letting your sweet hide get burned like this."

His breath continued to drift over her, making gooseflesh rise, making her shiver in anticipation. His lips lightly touched the upper swell of her right breast. But that wasn't the only touch she was aware of. His hair, cool and so very soft, brushed against her and his hard muscled thighs caged her calves. Against one shin, she felt his throbbing erection.

She moaned.

Gabe nuzzled closer to her nipple, very close, but not quite touching her there. "I like that, Lizzy, the way you make that soft, hungry little sound deep in your throat. It tells me so much."

His lips moved against her skin, adding to her sensitivity. She wasn't used to playing games, and she sure as certain wasn't used to wanting something so badly that her entire body trembled with the need. It wasn't a conscious decision

on her part, but her hands lifted, sank into his hair and
directed his mouth where she wanted it most.

Gabe gave his own earthy, raw groan just before his
mouth clamped down on her throbbing nipple, suckling her
through the sheet. Her body tensed, her back arching, her
fingers clenching, her head falling back as her eyes closed.
It was by far the most exquisite thing she had ever experienced. With her eyes closed, her senses were attuned to
every rough flick of his tongue, the heat inside his mouth,
the sharp edge of his teeth. She wanted to savor every sensation, store them all away to remember forever. Breathless,
she whispered, ''It's...it's not like I thought it'd be.''

Gabe stroked with his tongue, soaking the sheet and ply-
ing her stiff nipple. ''No?'' His voice was a rough rasp and
he sat back to view his handiwork, eyeing her shimmering
breasts with satisfaction.

She didn't care. He could look all he wanted as long as
he kissed her like that again. Shaking her head, Elizabeth
ignored the way some of her hair tumbled free. ''No,'' she
admitted. ''I used to daydream about a man doing that some
day.'' She stroked his head, luxuriating in the cool silk of
his thick hair. ''But never a man like you, and it never felt
quite that...deep.''

His hands settled on either side of her hips, his long
fingers curving to her buttocks. Heavy-lidded, he watched
her. ''What do you mean by deep?''

Elizabeth placed her hand low on her belly. ''I feel it
here. Every small lick or suck...I feel it inside me.''

Gabe groaned again, then feasted on her other nipple.
Elizabeth let her hands drift down his strong shoulders, then
farther to his upper arms. She felt half insensate with the
pleasure, half driven by curiosity to explore his pronounced
biceps. His arms were rigid, braced hard on the chair and
her behind.

He leaned back again, his breath heavy, his mouth wet.

Still he looked at her body, not her face. "What did you mean, a man like me?"

Elizabeth had to gather her wits, had to force her eyes open. Gabe lifted one hand and, with the edge of his thumb, teased a wet nipple. The sheet offered no barrier at all, and when she looked down, Elizabeth could see that the sheet was all but transparent.

She wanted his mouth on her again.

"I always thought…" She swallowed hard, trying to form the correct words. "I'd hoped that some day I'd get intimate with a man, but I assumed he'd be more like me."

Slowly, Gabe's gaze lifted until he was studying her intently. But his hand was still on her breast, still driving her to distraction. "Like you, how?"

She shook her head. "Boring. Introverted. Something of a wallflower. Homely."

She gasped as Gabe lurched to his feet and glared at her. Her mouth open in a small O, her eyes wide, she watched him, uncertain what had caused that sudden, heated reaction.

Gabe propped his hands on his lean hips, and his chest rose and fell with his labored efforts to gain control. His eyes were burning, his brows down, his mouth a hard line.

He shook his head and made a disgusted sound. "Damn it, Red, now you've gone and made me mad."

GABE WATCHED HER struggle to follow his words. She looked like sin and temptation and sweetness all wrapped together. Her heavy dark red hair was half up, half down, giving her a totally wanton look. Her skin was flushed beyond the sunburn, her eyes heavy lidded with sensuality but somewhat dazed by his annoyance.

It made him unreasonably angry for her to put herself down, though what she'd said had mirrored his earlier thoughts. Looking at her, he doubted any man could think her unattractive. He sure as hell didn't.

Reminded of that, he stalked a foot closer and grabbed her wrist, carrying her hand to his groin. Her mouth fell open as he forced her palm against his erection. "You know what that means, Red?"

She nodded dumbly, so still she wasn't even breathing.

"What? Tell me what it means?"

Her eyes left his face to stare at her hand, then to his face again. "That you're excited."

"Right. Do you think I'd get excited over a homely woman?"

She didn't answer.

He moved her hand, forcing her to stroke him, driving himself crazy. "The answer is no," he said with a rasp. "Now here's another question." The words were forced out through his teeth because Lizzy was no longer passive. Her hand had relaxed, opened, and her fingers curved around him. In a moment of wonder, Gabe realized he was the first guy she'd ever touched.

It was a heady thought.

He wasn't having an easy time controlling himself, but two deep breaths later, he finally managed to say, "Do you think, Red, that this happens to me often?"

"Yes."

That one breathy whispered word nearly made his knees buckle. He released her wrist and stepped back, but she leaned forward at the same time, maintaining the contact. "Well, you're wrong." He nearly strangled when she licked her lips in innocent, unthinking suggestion, her gaze still glued to his crotch. Gabe growled and said, "If you stroke me one more time you're going to see the consequences."

He clenched his fists, tightened his thighs, and luckily she let him go. When he could focus again, Gabe looked at her. Blinking rapidly, Lizzy continued to study his body. Suddenly aware of his renewed attention, she looked him in the eyes and asked, "Can I feel you some more?"

Yes. "No, not right now."

"When?"

He nearly choked on a laugh. "You persistent, curious little witch," he accused.

"You...you don't want me to?"

"I want you to too much."

Her tongue came out to stroke her lips again, making his blood thicken. "Then..."

"Tomorrow," he said quickly, before she could push him over the edge with her wanton questions. Knowing she wanted him, knowing he'd be the first man she'd ever explored, that she'd learn from him, was possibly the strongest aphrodisiac known to man. "At the drive-in. We'll go to second base, remember?"

Her eyes were dreamy. "You promise?"

Gabe gave one sharp nod while stifling a reflexive groan. He'd never survive. Was she wet right now? He'd be willing to bet she was, wet and hot, and he knew in every fiber of his being that she'd be so tight she'd kill him with pleasure. "I should go."

She came to her feet so fast she nearly stumbled over the sheet. Gabe caught her by the upper arms, heard her sharp intake of breath as his hands closed tightly on her burned skin, and he cursed himself. He released her, but she didn't step away; she stepped closer.

He felt like a total cad. "I can't believe I'm here seducing you when you're in pain." He'd aroused her, but there wasn't much chance of satisfying her without also causing her a lot of discomfort. She was so sunburned that just about any position would be impossible.

Her big eyes stared at him with wonder. "You were seducing me?"

Gabe stared at the ceiling, looking for inspiration but finding none. "What the hell did you think I was doing, Lizzy?"

She said simply, "Playing with me."

"Oh, yeah." A fresh surge of blood rushed to his groin, making him break out in a sweat. He felt every pulse beat in his erection, and ground his teeth with the need to finish what he'd started.

He was so hard he hurt and he knew damn well he'd have a hell of a time sleeping tonight. "I'll play with you, all right. Playing with a woman's body is about the most pleasure a man can expect. And when a woman has a body like yours...I'm not sure I can live through it."

She stared at him while she chewed on her lips, and he could almost see the wheels turning. Gently, he touched a finger to her swollen mouth. "No, sweetheart, we can't tonight. You're in no shape to tussle with a man, and I'm too damn horny to be as careful as I'd need to be."

Her eyes flared over his blunt language, but he was too far gone to attempt romantic clichés. She touched his chest tentatively. "Would...would you like to just stay and talk for awhile?"

So you can work on seducing me? He knew he should say no, should remove himself from temptation, but he couldn't. She looked so hopeful, so sweet and aroused, he nodded. "Sure. Why don't you go get a dry sheet and I'll pour us some drinks. Sawyer did say you should have lots of fluids."

Her smile was beatific. "Okay."

Gabe watched the sassy sway of a perfect heart-shaped bottom and groaned anew. Damn, she was hot, and her being unaware of it only made her more so.

He found two tall glasses in the cabinet and opened the tiny apartment-size fridge. There was orange juice, milk and one cola. He poured two glasses of orange juice and carried them into the living room. When he set them down, he again noticed the pictures on the shelves and walked closer to examine them.

One was of a much younger Lizzy. Her red hair gave her away, although in the photo she wore long skinny braids and had braces on her teeth. Gabe grinned, thinking she looked oddly cute. An older woman with hair of a similar color, cut short and stylish, smiled into the camera while hugging Lizzy close. Her mother, Gabe decided, and felt a sadness for Lizzy's loss. No child should ever lose a mother at such a young age.

The other picture was of her father, sitting in a straight-backed chair, with Lizzy behind him. She had one pale hand on his shoulder; neither of them were smiling. Her father looked tired but kind, and Lizzy had an endearing expression of forbearance, as if she'd hated having the picture taken. She was older in this one, probably around seventeen. She was just starting to grow into her looks, he decided. Her freckles were more pronounced, her eyes too large, her chin too stubborn. Added years had softened her features and made them more feminine.

As Gabe went to replace the framed photograph on the shelf, he caught sight of an album. Curious, thinking to find more pictures of her and her life, Gabe picked it up and settled into the sofa. A folded transcript of her grades fell out. As he'd suspected, Lizzy was an overachiever, with near perfect marks in every subject. She'd already received recognition from the dean for being at the head of her class. He shook his head, wondering how anyone could take life so seriously. Then he opened the album.

What he found shocked him speechless.

There were numerous clipped articles, all of them focusing on her mother's death. They appeared to be from small hometown papers, and Gabe could relate because of all the fanfare he'd gotten in the local papers when he'd stopped the runaway boat.

Only these articles didn't appear to be very complimentary. Keeping one ear open for signs of Lizzy's return, Gabe began to read.

Girl fails to react: Eleanor Parks died in her car Saturday night after being forced off the road by a semi. The overturned car wasn't visible from the road, and while Elizabeth Parks escaped with nonfatal injuries, shock kept her from seeking help. Medical authorities speculate that, with timely intervention, Mrs. Parks may well have survived.

Appalled, Gabe read headline after headline, and with each word, a horrible ache expanded in his heart, making his chest too tight, his eyes damp. God, he could only imagine her torment.

Daughter Slow to React: Mother Dies
Unnecessary Death—The Trauma of Shock
Daughter Stricken with Grief—Must Be Hospitalized
Father Defends Daughter in Time of Grief

What could it have felt like for a twelve-year-old child to accept the guilt of her mother's death? Not only had she lost the one person she was likely closest to, but she'd been blamed by insensitive reporters and medical specialists.

Feeling a cross between numbness and unbearable pain, Gabe carefully replaced the album beneath the photos. He thrust his fisted hands into his pockets and paced. So this was what had her in such an all-fire tizzy to interview heroes. He grunted to himself, fair sick of the damn word and its connotations. How could an intelligent, independent woman compare her reactions as a twelve-year-old child to those of a grown man? It was ludicrous, and he wanted to both shake her and cuddle her close, swearing that nothing would ever hurt her again.

He swallowed hard against the tumultuous, conflicting emotions that left him feeling adrift, uncertain of himself and his purpose. When he heard her bedroom door open, he stepped away from the shelves and crossed the carpeted floor to stare at her with volatile feelings that simmered close to erupting. They weren't exactly joyous feelings, but feelings of acute awareness of her as a woman, him as a man, of the differences in their lives and how shallow he'd been in his assumptions.

Lizzy, wrapped in a very soft, pale blue terry-cloth robe, widened her eyes at him and asked carefully, "Gabe? What's wrong?"

It felt like his damn heart was lodged in his throat, making it hard to swallow, doubly hard to speak. He hated it, hated himself and his cavalier attitude. Gently he cupped her face in his palms and bent to kiss her soft mouth, which still trembled slightly with the urges he'd deliberately created. He'd thought to say something soothing to her, something reassuring, but as her mouth opened and her hands sought his shoulders, Gabe decided on a different approach.

He'd get Lizzy over her ridiculous notions of guilt. He'd make her see herself as he saw her—a sexy, adorable woman filled with mysteries and depth. And he'd make damn sure she enjoyed herself in the bargain.

CHAPTER SEVEN

ELIZABETH FELT like she was floating, her feet never quite touching the ground. She said hello to the people she passed on the main street while heading to the diner to meet Misty and Honey Hudson. She hadn't had much sleep the night before, having been too tightly strung from wanting Gabe and from the slight lingering discomfort of her sunburn.

Today it was a toss-up as to which bothered her more. Gabe had stayed an additional hour, but he hadn't resumed the heated seduction. Instead, he'd been so painstakingly gentle, so filled with concern and comfort, it had been all she could do not to curl up on his lap and cuddle. He'd have let her. Heck, he'd tried several times to instigate just such a thing.

By the time he'd left and she'd prepared for bed, she'd been tingling all over, ultrasensitized by the brush of his mouth, the stroke of his fingertips, his low husky voice and constant string of compliments.

He thought her freckles were sexy. He thought her red hair was sexy. Oh, the things he'd said about her hair. She blushed again, remembering the way he'd looked at her while speculating on the contrast of her almost-brown brows and the vivid red of her hair, wondering about the curls on the rest of her body.

He was big and muscular and outrageous and all male. She'd already decided that if he was willing to begin an involvement, she'd be an utter fool to rebuff him. The things he made her feel were too wonderful to ignore.

When she entered the small diner, several male heads turned her way. They didn't look at her as Gabe did, but rather with idle curiosity because she was a new face. She located the women, talking to a waitress at the back of the diner in a semiprivate booth. They all had their backs to her as she approached.

She was only a few feet away when she heard Misty say, "I think he's dumbstruck by his own interest. She's not at all the type of woman he usually goes after and he doesn't know what to make of that."

Honey laughed. "That's an understatement. Sawyer told me Gabe started chasing the ladies when he was just a kid, and he usually caught them. By the time he was fifteen, they were chasing *him*."

The waitress shook her head. Elizabeth recognized her as one of the women who'd been at the docks the day she'd first tracked down Gabe.

"That's nothing but the truth," the woman said. "Gabe can sit on the dock and the boats will pull in or idle by just to look at him. He always accepts it as his due, because it's what he's used to. I remember how he reacted when Elizabeth first showed up there. He didn't like her at all, but then she didn't seem to like him much, either, and I sorta think that's the draw. He's not used to women not gushing all over him."

"I just hope he doesn't hurt her. Gabe is a long way from being ready to settle down for more than a little recreation. But every woman he gets together with falls in love with him."

Misty agreed with her sister. "He's a hedonistic reprobate, but an adorable one."

Elizabeth was frozen to the spot. She wasn't an eavesdropper by nature, but she hadn't quite been able to an-

nounce herself. *In love with Gabe?* Yes, she supposed she
was halfway there. How stupid of her, how naive to think
he'd be truly interested in her for more than a quick tumble.
As the women had implied, he evidently found her odd and
was challenged by her.

The differences between her and Gabe had never felt
more pronounced than at that precise moment. Because she
was so inexperienced, not just sexually but when it came
to relationships of any kind, she knew she'd be vulnerable
to a man's attention. And Gabe wasn't just any man. His
interest in her, no matter how short-term, was like the quin-
tessential Cinderella story. Gabe was more than used to
taking what he wanted from women, not in a selfish de-
mand, but in shared pleasure. He'd assumed Elizabeth understood that, and that the enjoyment of playtime would be
mutual. And it would be. She'd see to it.

A short, humorless laugh nearly choked her...and drew
the three women's attention. Elizabeth mentally shook her
head as she stepped forward with a feigned smile. None of
it mattered; she still wanted him, wanted to experience everything he could show her, teach her. She wanted to really
truly *feel* once again. Since her mother's death and the ap-
pearance of the harsh, dragging guilt, it seemed as if she
hadn't really been living, that anything heartfelt or lasting
had been blunted by the need to make amends, to understand her weakness.

Her heart hurt, but pride would keep her from showing
it. She'd accept Gabriel Kasper on any terms, and he'd
never know that she dreamed of more. She'd enjoy herself,
without regrets, without demands.

Despite her past, she deserved that much.

The waitress, looking cautious, indicated a chair. "Hey,
there, Elizabeth. Remember me?"

Again, Elizabeth smiled. "Ceily, from the boat docks,
right? Yes, I remember. I hadn't realized you worked

here." She carefully lowered herself into her seat and nodded at both sisters. Honey and Misty looked guilty, and Elizabeth tried to reassure them by pretending she hadn't heard a thing. "I hope I'm not too late?"

"Not at all," Misty said quickly. Her baby was sitting beside her in the booth on a pumpkin seat. "I hope you don't mind that I brought Amber along."

Elizabeth leaned over slightly to peer at the baby. "How could anyone ever object to that darling little angel?"

When she'd been a young girl, still fanciful and filled with daydreams, Elizabeth used to imagine someday having a baby, coddling it as her mother had coddled her, but she'd set those fantasies aside when she'd accepted her shortcomings.

Misty beamed at the compliment. "Strangely enough, she looks just like Morgan."

Ceily snorted at that outrageous comment. "Come on, Misty. I've never seen that little doll manage anything near the nasty scowl Morgan can dredge up without even trying."

Honey laughed. "That's true enough. But if Misty is even two minutes late to feed her, she has to contend with scowls and grumblings from both father and daughter. And I have to admit, they do resemble each other then. It sometimes seems to be a competition to see who can complain the loudest."

Misty slid a gentle finger over her sleeping daughter's cheek. "Morgan can't stand it if she even whimpers, much less gives a good howl. I swear, he shakes like a skinny Chihuahua if Amber gets the least upset."

Ceily made a sound of amused disgust. "I never thought I'd see the day when the brothers started settling down into blissful wedlock."

Honey nudged Elizabeth, then quipped in a stage whisper, "Not that Ceily's complaining. I think she's the only female in Buckhorn County who isn't pining for our men."

Being included in that "our men" category made Elizabeth blush, but no one noticed as Ceily broke loose with a raucous laugh. "I know the brothers far too well. We've been friends forever and that's not something I'd ever want to screw up by getting…romantic."

"A wise woman," Honey said, between sips of iced tea. "I think they all consider you something of a little sister."

Ceily bit her lip and mumbled under her breath, "I wouldn't exactly say that." But Elizabeth appeared to be the only one who'd heard her.

Ceily took their orders and sauntered off. Elizabeth watched her surreptitiously, wondering just how involved the woman had been with the brothers. She was beautiful, in a very natural way, not bothering much with makeup or a fancy hairdo. She looked…earthy, with her light tan and sandy-brown hair. And Elizabeth remembered from seeing her in her bathing suit at the boat dock that Ceily was built very well, with the type of lush curves that would definitely attract the males.

She was frowning when Honey asked, "How's the sunburn?"

"Oh." Elizabeth drew herself together and shrugged. "Much better today. Your husband's cream worked wonders. Would you thank him again for me?"

Honey waved away her gratitude. "No problem. Sawyer is glad to do it, I'm sure."

Misty looked at her closely. "You don't look nearly as pink today. I guess it's fading fast."

Forcing a laugh, Elizabeth admitted, "I can even wear my bra today without cringing."

"Ouch." Misty looked appalled by that idea. "Are you sure you should? This blasted heat is oppressive."

It was only then that Elizabeth realized she was trussed

up far more than Misty and Honey were. While they both wore comfortably loose T-shirts and cotton shorts with flip-flop sandals, Elizabeth had put a blouse under her long pullover dress and ankle socks with her shoes.

Deciding to be daring, she asked, "Does everyone dress so casually here? I mean, do you think anyone would notice if I wore something like that?" She indicated their clothes with a nod.

Honey laughed out loud. "Heck, yes. Gabe would notice! But then I get the feeling he'd notice you no matter what you wore. Watching him blunder around yesterday like a fish out of water was about the best entertainment we've had for awhile."

Misty bit her bottom lip, trying to stifle a laugh. "Gabe teased both Sawyer and Morgan something terrible when they got involved with us. Now he's just getting his due."

"But we're not involved." Even as she said it, Elizabeth felt her face heating. She hoped the sisters would attribute it to her sunburn and not embarrassment.

"Maybe not yet, but Gabe's working on it. I've gotten to know him pretty good since Sawyer and I married. He dates all the time, but he never mentions any particular woman. You he's mentioned several times."

Elizabeth didn't dare ask what he'd said. She could just imagine. "I think I'll buy myself some shorts today."

"Good idea. This is a vacation lake. Very few people bother to put on anything except casual clothes."

Ceily sidled up with Elizabeth's drink and everyone's food. Misty was having a huge hamburger with fries, but Honey and Elizabeth had settled on salads.

Misty made a face at them. "It's the breast-feeding, I swear. I never ate like a hog before, but now I stay hungry all the time. Sawyer says I'm burning off calories."

Honey pursed her lips, as if trying to keep something

unsaid, then she appeared to burst. "I wonder if it'll affect me that way."

Misty froze with her mouth clamped around the fat burger. Like a sleepwalker she lowered the food and swallowed hard. "Are you...?"

Honey, practically shivering with excitement, nodded. Elizabeth almost jumped out of her seat when the two women squealed loudly and jumped up to hug across the table.

"When?" Misty demanded.

"In about six months. Late February." Honey leaned forward. "But keep it down. I don't want anyone else to know until I tell Sawyer."

"You haven't told him yet?"

"I just found out for sure this morning." She turned to Elizabeth. "We hadn't exactly been trying not to get pregnant, if you know what I mean, so it won't be a shock. But I still think he's going to make a big deal of it."

Wide-eyed, Elizabeth had no idea what to say to that. She was...stunned that the sisters had included her in such a personal, familial announcement. She'd never in her life had close female friends. She'd always been too odd, too alone, to mix in any of the small groups in school.

But as it turned out, Elizabeth didn't need to reply. Honey and Misty went back to chattering while they ate, and Elizabeth was loath to interrupt.

Finally, they wore down and simply settled back in their seats, smiling. The silence wasn't an uncomfortable one, and Elizabeth found herself wondering about several things.

Trying to shake off her shyness, she asked, "Do you hope it's a boy or a girl?"

Honey touched her stomach with a mother's love. "It doesn't really matter to me. Amber is so precious—a girl would be nice. But then, Casey is such an outstanding young man that I think a son would be perfect, too."

Using that statement to lead into another question, Elizabeth pulled out her paper and pencil. "Do the brothers have any sisters?"

"Not a one. They only have male sperm, to hear them tell it." Misty had a soft, almost secret smile on her face. "Morgan calls Amber his little miracle."

Honey sighed. "Sawyer even warned me before we were married that I should resign myself to baby boys. The way they dote on Amber, as if none of them had ever seen a baby girl before, is hysterical. I keep telling them she's no different from Cascy when he was an infant, but they just look at me like I'm nuts."

Elizabeth grinned at that image. "In a nice sort of way," she ventured cautiously, so she wouldn't offend, "they seem a bit sexist."

"Oh, they're sexist all right! And very old-fashioned, but as you said, in a nice way. They insist on helping a woman whenever they can, but they'd refuse to admit it if *they* needed help."

"Not that they ever do," Honey added. "They're the most self-reliant men I've ever seen. Their mother made sure they could cook and clean and fend for themselves."

Misty leaned forward to speak in a whisper. "Morgan says all he needs me for is to keep him happy." Her eyebrows bobbed. "You know what I mean." Then she settled back with a blissful sigh. "But then he'll show me it's so much more than that. We talk about everything and share everything. He unloads his worries at night over dinner and he says he misses me all day when he's working."

"Do you still work here in the diner?"

"Part-time, just for the fun of it. It keeps Morgan on his toes. He has this absurd notion that every guy in town comes here to eat just to ogle his wife." She laughed. "In truth, there's not a guy around who would look for more than two seconds for fear of incurring Morgan's wrath."

"He has a temper?"

"No, not really."

Honey choked, accidentally spraying iced tea across the table. Alarmed, Elizabeth quickly handed her a napkin. Biting back a laugh, Honey mumbled, "Sorry."

But Misty wasn't offended. "You should talk," she said primly. "Morgan is still bragging about that fight Sawyer had over you."

"What about Gabe?" Elizabeth asked. "Is he a hell-raiser?"

"Gabe? Heck, no, Gabe's a lover, not a fighter. Not that I doubt he could handle himself in any situation."

Elizabeth tried to sound only mildly curious as she pursued that topic. "He has himself something of a reputation, doesn't he?"

Misty shrugged. "I suppose, but it's not a bad one. Folks around here just love him, that's all."

"You know," Elizabeth said thoughtfully as she set aside her pencil and propped her elbows on the table, "I think it's amazing that he did something so heroic and yet he shrugs it off as nothing."

Honey waved her fork dismissively. "They're all like that. They're strong and capable and well-respected and they don't really think a thing of it. To them, it's just how things are—they're nothing special. But I know not a one of them would sit on the sidelines if someone needed help. That's just the way they are."

For over an hour, the women talked, and Elizabeth took page after page of background notes on the brothers, Gabe specifically. If some of her questions had nothing to do with her thesis...well, that was no one's concern but her own.

When the lunch ended and she was ready to go, Elizabeth thanked both women. Misty had her wide-awake daughter cradled in her arms, cooing to her, so it was

Honey who touched Elizabeth's arm and said, "I hope we've been some help."

Elizabeth could read the look in Honey's eyes and understood her meaning. She smiled in acknowledgment. "You don't have to worry. I know Gabe is still sowing his wild oats, so while I'm enjoying interviewing him, I'm not going to expect undying love. I'm a little more grounded in reality than that."

Honey bit her lip then shared a look with her sister. Misty sighed. "He really is a doll, isn't he?"

"Yes, he is. But he's a rascal too, and I'm well aware of just how serious he is, which isn't very. Besides, I'm only here for the summer. I have another semester of college to go and then job hunting before I can ever think of getting attached to anyone. Gabe is fun and exciting, but I know that's where it ends."

Misty slid out of the booth to stand before Elizabeth, her brow drawn into a thoughtful frown. "Now, I'm not sure you should rule everything out."

Honey agreed. "He is acting darned strange about all this."

"It doesn't matter." Elizabeth knew they wanted to be kind, to spare her. "I'm not letting anything or anyone get in the way of my goals."

"What are your goals? I know you said you're doing your thesis on the mystique of heroes, but why?"

"I'm hoping to go into counseling. Too often the ordinary person tries to compare herself to the true heroes of the world and only comes up lacking, which is damaging to self-esteem. I'd like to be able to prove that there are real, tangible differences to account for the heroes."

Before either sister could remark on that, Elizabeth asked for directions to Jordan's veterinary office. He was the only brother she hadn't spoken to yet. From what she'd heard, this particular brother was vastly different in many ways, but still enough to melt a woman's heart.

She looked forward to grilling him.

GABE WRAPPED HIS ARM around Ceily from behind, then gave her a loud smooch on her nape. "Hey, doll," he growled in a mock-hungry voice.

Jumping, Ceily almost dropped the tray of dirty dishes loading her down, and would have if Gabe hadn't caught it in time.

Rounding on him, Ceily yelled, "Don't do that, damn it! You about gave me a heart attack."

"Shh." Gabe grinned at her. "I don't want anyone to know I'm here."

Ceily seemed to think that was very funny, judging by her crooked grin. "If you're looking for your newest girl-friend, she already left."

Disappointment struck him, and he muttered a low curse that made Ceily's grin widen. "Do you know where she went?"

She took the tray from him and set it in the sink. "Maybe."

"Ceily…"

With a calculating look, she said over her shoulder, "I need a leaking faucet fixed. I can talk while you repair."

Gabe didn't want to waste that much time, but he reluctantly agreed. Ceily was one of his best friends, and she made one hell of a spy. Though she didn't gossip, she always seemed to know anything and everything that was said in her diner. "All right. Show me the sink."

Five minutes later Gabe was on his back, shirtless to keep from getting too dirty, trying to tighten a valve. The job was simple, but Ceily needed new plumbing in a bad way. "I can fix it for now, hon, but we're going to need to make major repairs soon. When's good for you?"

Ceily was at his side on a stool, taking a quick break while business was slow. "You just give me the word and I'll make the time."

Seconds later, Gabe shoved himself out from under the sink and sat up. "All done. So start talking."

Ceily checked the sink first, saw it was dry and nodded. "She went to see your brother Jordan, but she said she's also going to do some shopping." Ceily gave an impish smile. "She wants to dress more casual, like Misty and Honey."

Gabe groaned. Misty and Honey had chic comfort down to a fine art. The women could wear cutoffs and T-shirts and look like sex personified. "I'll never live through it."

Ceily thought that was about the funniest thing she'd ever heard. Gabe used her knee for unnecessary leverage and came to his feet. "You care to share the joke?"

"You don't think it's amusing that the mighty Gabe Kasper, womanizer and renowned playboy, is being struck down by a prim little red-haired wallflower?"

Anger tightened his gut for an instant before Gabe hid it. He didn't like anyone making fun of Lizzy, but he knew Ceily hadn't meant to be nasty. She, like him, was merely surprised at his interest in a woman who was so different from his usual girlfriends.

But then, that was precisely why he felt so drawn to her.

He began lathering his hands in the sink while he gathered his thoughts. Ceily tilted her head at his silence, then let out a whistle.

"Well, I'll be. You really are smitten, aren't you?"

"Smitten is a stupid word, Ceily," he groused. "Let's just call it intrigued, okay?"

"Intrigued, smitten…doesn't matter what you call it, Gabe, you've still got it bad." She crossed her arms and leaned against the wall. "Care to tell me why?"

Gabe lifted one shoulder in a shrug as he dried his hands on a frayed dish towel. "Lizzy is different."

"You're telling me!"

Gabe snapped her with the towel. "You *are* feeling sassy today, aren't you?"

She yelped, then rubbed her well-rounded hip. There was a time when Gabe would have helped her with that, but he had no real interest in touching any woman, even playfully, except Lizzy. She had invaded his brain, and it was taking a lot of getting used to.

Ceily was still frowning when she said, "It's not every day I get to witness the fall of the mighty Gabe."

Lifting one brow, Gabe announced, "I didn't fall, I jumped."

"So it's like that, huh?"

Gabe propped one hip on the side of the sink and watched Ceily. She was his friend and he'd always been able to talk with her. He loved his brothers dearly, but he could just imagine how they'd react if he started confessing to them. He'd never hear the end of it.

"It's damn strange," he admitted, "if you want the truth. One minute I didn't like her at all, then I was noticing all these little things about her, then I was lusting after her...."

"Uh, I hate to point this out, Gabe, but you tend to lust over every available, of-age woman you meet."

"Not like this." He shook his head and considered all the differences. "You know as well as I do that most of the women have come pretty easy for me."

Her look was ironic. "I have firsthand knowledge of that fact."

Gabe looked up, startled. A slow flush crept up his neck. "I wasn't talking about you, doll." He reached out and flicked a long finger over her soft cheek. "We were both too young then to even know what we were doing."

Ceily's smile was slow and taunting. Despite the fact

they'd once experimented a little with each other, their friendship had grown. Gabe was eternally grateful for that.

"As I recall," she purred, teasing him, "you knew exactly what you were doing. And it was nice for my first time to be with someone I trusted and liked."

Gabe felt as though he was choking. Ceily hadn't mentioned that little episode in many years. And never would he point out to her exactly how inept he'd been back then. When she found the right guy, she'd realize it on her own. Curious, since she *had* brought it up, he asked, "Did you ever tell anyone?"

"Nope. And I know for a fact you haven't, so don't get all flustered. Besides, I'm not carrying a torch for you, Gabe. It was fun, but I want more."

Gabe slid off the sink to give her a bear hug. Ceily was a very special person. "I know. And you'll find it. You deserve the very best."

She returned his hug and said with a hoity-toity accent, "I tend to think so." Then she shoved him back a bit. "But I know what you mean. All the women for miles around come running when you crook your little finger."

"Not all." Gabe almost chuckled at the image she described, but felt forced to admit the truth. "I have been turned down a time or two, you know."

Ceily scoffed. "Never with anyone who mattered."

Gabe stared at her, and her eyes widened. "Oh, wait! Are you telling me Elizabeth Parks turned you down?"

Scowling, Gabe shoved his hands in his pockets. "I'm not telling you anything about Elizabeth. My point was just that most women want me because of my reputation, because they think I'm good-looking or sexy—"

Ceily bent double laughing.

Gabe glared. "Oh, to hell with it. There's no talking to you today."

He started to skirt around her, but she caught him from

behind and held on to his belt loops, getting dragged two feet before he finally stopped. Still chuckling, she gasped, "No, wait! I want to hear what it is that she wants from you."

Gabe heaved a deep sigh, then without turning to look at her, he admitted, "She thinks I'm some kind of damn hero and she wants to learn more about me, about my character and my family. She looks at me with this strange kind of excitement and...almost awe. Not for what *we* might do, or for what I might do to her, but for who she thinks I am. Damn, Ceily, no woman has ever done that before. And she hasn't pursued me at all for anything else. If I'd be willing to go on answering her damn questions, she'd be happy as a lark to leave it at that."

Last night, Gabe reminded himself, she'd been more than willing to do other things. But she hadn't come to him, he'd gone to her. He'd set about seducing her when he hadn't found it necessary to seduce a woman in ages.

And even then, he had the feeling that if he'd stuck her damn pencil in her hand, she'd have stopped cold in the middle of his sensual ministrations to start taking notes on his character. Now that he knew why it was so important to her, he not only felt turned on by her physically, he felt touched by her emotionally.

Seduction was a damn arousing business.

Ceily let go of his belt loops and smoothed her hand over the breadth of his back. "Poor Gabe. You really are adrift, huh?"

"I'm gonna turn you over my knee, Ceily."

She laughed at such a ridiculous threat. "No, you won't. Because I can give you some valuable advice."

Very slowly Gabe turned to face her. "Is that right?"

"Yep. You see, I heard Elizabeth tell your sisters-in-law that she has no intention of hanging around here once school starts. She's an academic sort and she has big plans for her life. If you hope to be part of those plans, you'd better get cracking, because I got the feeling that once she's gone, she won't be coming back.''

CHAPTER EIGHT

WHEN GABE let himself in through the back entrance of Jordan's veterinary clinic, he found Elizabeth and Jordan leaning over an examination table. Their backs were to him, but he could see that Lizzy was cuddled close to Jordan's side, Jordan's arm was around her shoulders, and they were in intimate conversation.

Gabe saw red.

"Am I interrupting?" He had meant to ask that question with cold indifference, but even to his ears it had sounded like a raw challenge.

Jordan looked at him over his shoulder; he was smiling. "Come here, Gabe. Take a look." Then he added, "But be very quiet."

His brother's voice had that peculiar soothing quality he used when treating frightened or injured animals. It was hypnotic and, according to all the women, sexy as hell.

Gabe barely stifled a growl. If Jordan was using that voice on Lizzy, he'd—

A very fat, bedraggled feline lay on the exam table, licking a new batch of tiny mewling kittens. Gabe glanced up at the look on Lizzy's face and promptly melted.

Big tears glistened in her vivid blue eyes and spiked her lashes. As Gabe watched, she gave a watery smile and sniffed, then gently rubbed the battered cat behind what was left of an ear.

Softly, Jordan explained, "She got into a tussle with a neighboring dog and lost. No sooner did she get dropped off than she started birthing. Eight kittens." Jordan shook his head. "She's a trooper, aren't you, old girl?" Jordan stroked his hand down the cat's back, earning a throaty purr.

Lizzy sniffed again. "She's a stray. Jordan says she's undernourished, so we didn't know if the kittens would be all right or not." She peered at Gabe with a worried expression. "They are awfully small, aren't they?"

Gabe smiled. "Most kittens are that tiny."

"And how...yucky they look?"

Jordan chuckled. "She'll have them all cleaned up and cozy in no time. The problem now is getting her into a pen. I hate to move her after she's just given birth, but I can hardly leave her and the babies here on the table."

Lizzy seemed to be considering that. "Do the pens open from the top or the front?"

"Both."

"Then... Well, maybe we could just take the table cover and all, and put her in the pen. I mean, if you hold the two top corners, and Gabe holds the two bottom corners, and I sort of guide it in and make sure no babies tumble out... Would that work do you think?"

To Gabe's annoyance, Jordan smiled and kissed Lizzy's cheek. "I think that's a brilliant idea. Gabe, keep an eye on this batch while I go find a big-enough pen. I'll be right back."

Gabe stepped next to Lizzy. "You've been crying." Just being close to her made him feel funny—adrift, as Ceily had said. He didn't know himself when he was this close to her, and he sure as hell didn't recognize all the things she made him feel.

Lizzy bit her lip, which looked extremely provocative to Gabe. "I've never seen babies born before. It's amazing."

Gabe slipped his arm around her and nuzzled her ear.

Keeping his hands, or his mouth, to himself was out of the question. "Did you help Jordan?"

She laughed softly. "Mostly I just tried to stay out of his way."

Jordan said from behind them, "I couldn't have done it without her. She has the touch, Gabe. No sooner did she stroke that old cat than she settled down and relaxed some. I was afraid I was going to have to sedate her, but Elizabeth's touch was better than any shot I could give."

Gabe made a noncommittal sound. He knew firsthand just how special Lizzy's touch was.

Within minutes they had the mother and all her babies cozied up in the pen and set in a warm corner where there was plenty of sunshine and quiet. The mother cat, exhausted after her ordeal, dozed off.

"Will she be all right?" Gabe asked.

Elizabeth answered him. "Jordan said none of her injuries from the dog are significant. He cleaned up some scrapes and scratches, one not too horrible bite, and then she started birthing." Laughing at herself, Lizzy admitted, "When she let out that first screeching roar, I thought she was dying. Jordan explained to me that she was just a mama in labor."

Jordan, trying to slip clean dry bedding in around the mewling kittens, said, "Gabe, why don't you show Elizabeth around the rest of the clinic?"

Lizzy's eyes widened. "Could you? I'd love to see it."

Since Gabe would love to get her alone, he agreed.

Everything about Elizabeth Parks fascinated him—her softness, her freckles, her temper, her awe at the sight of a yapping puppy or a sleeping bird. She was complex in many ways, crystal clear in others. By the time they were done looking around, Jordan had finished with the kittens and he showed no hesitation in embracing Lizzy again.

Gabe wanted to flatten him.

"Come back any time, Elizabeth." He glanced at Gabe. "We can talk more."

"I'd like that. Thank you."

Gabe knew his ears were turning red, but damn it, he didn't want her hanging around Jordan. He didn't want her hanging around any man except himself.

And he still wasn't too keen on her discussing him with everyone. God only knew what she might hear!

She finally stepped away from Jordan and faced both men. "I have to run off now. I have more errands to get through."

She backed to the door as she said it, keeping a close watch on Gabe.

"What errands?" he asked suspiciously.

"Oh, the usual." She reached for the doorknob and opened the door. "The library, the grocery store...a visit with Casey."

The last was muttered and it took a second for it to sink in. Gabe scowled and started toward her. "Now wait just a damn minute—"

"Sorry! Gotta go." She hesitated, then called, "I'll see you tonight, Gabe!"

She was out the door before he could catch her. He would have given pursuit if Jordan hadn't started laughing. At that moment, Gabe's frustration level tipped the scales and he decided Jordan would make a fine target. Slowly he turned, his nostrils flared. "You have something to say?"

Jordan was his quietest brother, but also the deepest. He kept his thoughts to himself for the most part, and tended to view the world differently than the rest of them. He was more serious, more sensitive. Women loved him for those qualities.

What had Elizabeth thought of him?

Gabe waited and finally Jordan managed to wipe the grin off his face. "I'd say Elizabeth Parks is pretty special."

Gabe's muscles tightened until they almost cramped. He hadn't thought her special at first, but now that he did, he didn't want anyone else—anyone male—to think it. "Me, too," he snarled.

Jordan was supremely unaffected by his anger. "Going to do anything about it?"

"It?"

Jordan shook his head as if he pitied Gabe. "You remind me of a junkyard dog who's just sniffed a female in heat. You're trying to guard the junkyard and still lay claim to the female."

"I'm not at all sure I like that analogy."

Jordan shrugged. "It fits. And if I was you, I'd get my head clear real quick."

Because he wasn't sure how to do that, Gabe didn't comment. Instead, he asked, "What did you think of her?"

"Sexy."

That single word hit him like a solid punch in the ribs. He wheezed. "Damn it, Jordan…"

"What? You think you're the only one to notice?" Again, Jordan shook his head. "I've got a waiting room full of clients, so I'll make this quick. No, Elizabeth's sex appeal isn't up-front and in your face. But it only takes about two minutes of talking with her, of watching her move and hearing her voice and looking into those incredible blue eyes to know she's hotter than hell on the inside."

It was so unlike Jordan to speak that way that Gabe was rendered mute.

"If you could have seen how gentle her hands were when she touched that frightened cat, well… You can imagine where a man's mind wanders when seeing that. And the look of discovery on her face when the first kitten appeared, and her husky voice when she's getting emotional…" Jordan shrugged. "It doesn't take a rocket scientist to know those same qualities would carry over into the rest of her life. She's sensitive and tenderhearted and something about her is a little wounded, making her sympathetic to boot."

Gabe rubbed both hands over his face, those elusive emotions rising to choke him.

Jordan slapped him on the back. "Add to that an incredible body... Well, there you have it."

"I'm sorry I asked," Gabe moaned.

Jordan turned his brother around and steered him toward the door. They were of a similar height and build, but Gabe was numb, so moving him was no problem. "Go. I have work to do."

Gabe was just over the threshold when Jordan said his name again. Turning, Gabe raised one brow.

"I talked you up real nice, told her what a sterling character you have, but somehow I got the impression she's given up on you already." Jordan shrugged. "Not that she isn't interested, because I could tell she is. I'm not sure what you've been doing with her, and it's certainly none of my business, but every time she said your name, she blushed real cute."

Eyes narrowed, Gabe muttered, "That's sunburn."

"No, that was arousal. Credit me with enough sense to know the difference."

Gabe started back in and Jordan flattened a hand on his sternum, holding him off. "The thing is," Jordan said with quiet emphasis, "her thoughts are as clear as the written word, and from what I could tell, she's determined that what she feels is only sexual. So if that's not what you want, I'd say you have a problem. One that you better start working on real quick."

It was the second time in one day that Gabe had been given that advice. Without another word he stomped off, his mind churning with confusion. Yes, he wanted more, but how much more? Hell, he barely knew the woman. And she did have an education to finish, one that was obviously important to her.

All he could do, Gabe decided, was take it day by day. He'd get inside her brick wall, get her to talk to him, and maybe, with any luck, he'd find out that Elizabeth wanted him for more than a sexual fling or a college thesis.

But for how much more was anyone's guess.

ELIZABETH FELT like a puddle of nerves on the drive to the movies that night. In quite a daring move, she'd changed from her earlier clothes into another dress, this one a tad shorter, landing just below her knees, and with a bodice that unbuttoned. She felt downright wanton. Not because the clothing was in any way revealing, but because of why she'd chosen it in the first place.

Thinking of Gabe's hands stealing under her skirt in search of second base or opening her buttons to linger on first base had her in a frenzy of anticipation.

Nervously, she glanced at his profile. He was quiet, his jaw set as he concentrated on driving. His strange, introspective mood seemed to permeate the car. She cleared her throat and said boldly, "Do you realize how many firsts I've had since meeting you?"

He jerked, his gaze swinging toward her for a brief instant. "What's that supposed to mean?"

She had to make him understand, Elizabeth thought. The last thing she wanted to happen, now that she was getting into the novelty of this unique courtship, was for Gabe to feel pressured and back off. His sisters-in-law had been clearly concerned that she might get hurt. Perhaps Gabe would worry about the same thing. But if she reassured him that they wanted the same thing, a pleasant way to pass the time during her visit, with no strings attached, then he'd feel free to continue his wonderful attentions.

And they were wonderful. Gabe made her feel sexy,

when all her life she'd felt plain to the point of being invisible. He made her feel feminine when she'd never paid much attention to her softness before, except that it made her weaker, less competent in a crisis. And he made her feel sexually hungry when she hadn't even known such a hunger existed.

"I like your brother."

Gabe shot her a dark look. "Which one?"

"Well, all of them, but I was talking about Jordan. He's different from the rest of you."

Gabe's hands squeezed the wheel tightly. "Yeah? How so?"

"Quieter. More…intense. He's so gentle with the animals. I felt totally at ease with him, and that was certainly a first."

Gabe's jaw locked so hard she wondered that he didn't get a headache. "You're not at ease with me?"

Around Gabe she was tense and so hot she thought she might catch fire. But she wouldn't tell him that. "It was just different with Jordan. And he let me help with that cat. I've never seen babies born before." Her voice softened, but she couldn't help it. Seeing the tiny little wet creatures emerging was a true miracle. "Have you? Seen babies born, I mean?"

"Sure." Gabe glanced at her, then at the road. "Jordan keeps all kinds of pets around the house. We all like animals, Lizzy. He's not different in that."

"But Jordan's… I don't know. More discreet than the rest of you. Softer."

"Ha!" Gabe shifted in his seat, looking disgruntled. "Don't let Jordan fool you! He's quieter, I'll give you that. But he's a man, same as I am."

"Gabe, I didn't mean to draw a comparison." She couldn't understand his reaction. It was almost as if…no.

There was no way Gabriel Kasper could be jealous of his brother. She decided to change the subject.

"I had lunch with Honey and Misty today."

Gabe's brows pulled down the tiniest bit. "Did you enjoy yourself?"

"Yes." Elizabeth pleated the edge of her skirt with her fingertips. "I've never really hung out with other women before. It was fun. The things they talk about…"

There was a strange darkness to his eyes as he asked, "What things?"

She shrugged. "Women things." She had no intention of telling him Honey was pregnant. Now that she'd been initiated into the wonders of doing lunch with the ladies, she'd didn't want to do anything to ruin it. When Honey told her husband the news, then Gabe would find out. "Shopping, Amber, men. Things like that."

In a reflexive movement, Gabe's hands tightened on the steering wheel. "What about men?"

"Nothing in particular. Just fun stuff. It was a first for me. I hadn't realized how enjoyable that could be, chatting and laughing with other women. I've never quite fit in like that before, but they're so nice and accepting. I like your sisters-in-law."

Gabe stopped for a red light and turned to face her. "I like them, too. A lot." He tilted his head, studying her, and there was something in his eyes, some vague shadow of consideration. "C'mere, Lizzy."

Oh, the way he said that. It was so much more than an invitation to close the space between them. The heat in his eyes made it more. The low growl of his voice made it more. She looked at the seat where Gabe's large hand rested. Warming inside, she scooted over as much as her seat belt would allow. It was close enough to feel his heat, his energy, to breathe in his wonderfully musky male scent.

Last night she had imagined burying her nose against his

neck, drinking him in and tasting his hot skin with her tongue…. She gulped a large breath of air and tried to get control of herself. She was turning into a nymphomaniac!

Immediately, Gabe's rough palm settled on her thigh in a possessive hold that thrilled her.

"How's your sunburn today?" he murmured, gently caressing her.

Staring at his dark hand on her leg, she shrugged. "Much better. It was a little tender this morning, but now I hardly notice it at all."

He slipped his fingers beneath the skirt of her dress and began tracing slow, easy circles on her flesh. Her breathing deepened. "And this? Does this hurt you, Lizzy?"

She shook her head, too startled, too excited to speak.

The light turned green and Gabe pulled away. He used one hand to steer while his gentle fingers continued to pet her bare skin. "Tell me what other firsts we're talking about."

His warm touch was hypnotic and she found her legs parting just a bit so his searching fingers could drift lazily up the sensitive inside of her knee. "Swimming in a lake."

"Oh, yeah." He flashed her a grin. "Think you might want to be daring and try it again sometime?"

This must be old hat to him, Elizabeth thought, as he easily maneuvered the car one-handed while deliberately arousing her with the other. He was such a rogue.

"Yes." She'd try anything Gabe wanted her to. She trusted him.

"Any other firsts?"

"Well, there's…this." She indicated his hand beneath her skirt, slowly inching higher. She sucked in air and concentrated on speaking coherently. "The kissing and touching and the way you…talk to me."

He glanced at her and she said, "I love the way you talk

to me, Gabe. No man has ever spoken so intimately with me, much less said the kinds of things you say."

"You've known a lot of fools, sweetheart."

Her smile trembled. "There, you see? And all this business with first base and drive-in movies. I feel like I'm just starting to really see the world."

Gabe squeezed his eyes closed for a heartbeat, and she added, "You're also by far the most unique hero I've interviewed, so I suppose that's a first, as well."

How in the world she'd managed to string so many words together, she had no idea. Her thoughts felt jumbled, her nerve endings raw. Leaning slightly toward him, she touched his shoulder. "Gabe, can I ask you something?"

Twilight was settling in on the small town, making it almost dark enough to hide what they did with each other. Elizabeth smoothed her hand over his shoulder, then down to squeeze his biceps. She soaked in the feel of the soft cotton T-shirt over solid muscle. Gabe felt so good.

He worked his jaw. "You can ask me anything, babe."

Hesitantly, she explained, "It's sort of a request."

His hand left her as he pulled into a gravel lot behind several other cars, waiting to pay at the drive-in entrance. Elizabeth looked around in wonder. People milled about everywhere, some walking to a concrete-block building that she assumed housed the cameras and perhaps a concession stand. Others leaned in car windows talking to neighbors. Some were sitting outside their cars or trucks or vans, watching the sky darken and the stars appear. The screen was huge, situated in front of row after row of metal poles holding speakers. It fascinated her.

"Ask away."

"Oh." Turning to Gabe, she bit her bottom lip, then because she was unable to look at him and ask her question, she gave her attention to the surrounding lot. "Would it be okay if I touched you, too? I mean, like with first base and second base? Touching you last night...that was another first. I had no idea a man felt so...contradictory."

His Adam's apple bobbed when he swallowed hard. He adjusted his jeans, slouched behind the wheel a bit more and closed his eyes. "Contradictory, how?"

Elizabeth knew her face was flaming. Actually, her whole body was flaming. In a rough, strangled whisper, she said, "Soft in some places, so hard in others. Sleek and alive. I'd...I'd like to feel your chest, under your shirt, and I'd like to feel you...*there*, inside your jeans."

Gabe groaned, then laughed. He rested his forehead against the steering wheel for one second, then swiveled to snare her with his gaze. "Are you absolutely sure you want to see a movie?"

Not quite understanding, Elizabeth glanced at the billboard announcing which titles would be playing tonight. The first movie was *Tonya's Revenge*. Probably an action movie, she decided—not her favorite. But while it didn't sound exactly scintillating, she was very curious. "I'd like to see at least a bit of it, since this is another first for me. Why?"

Gabe hesitated to answer as he pulled up to the small cashier's window and handed over a couple of bills. The attendant, evidently someone Gabe knew based on his greeting and his curiosity as he speared a flashlight into the car to check out Elizabeth, winked and handed Gabe his change. "Enjoy the movie," he said with a wide grin. Gabe answered with a muttered oath.

Elizabeth looked around as Gabe parked the car toward the back of the lot. Already people had set up lawn chairs and blankets or turned their trucks around to relax in the truck beds. Gabe moved as far away from the others as he could.

"You don't want to stay, do you?" Elizabeth didn't want to force him into something he was reluctant to do.

Gabe's frown became more pronounced. "I'm having second thoughts, that's all."

Her stomach pitched in very real dread. "Second thoughts? You mean you don't want to—"

In a sudden move, Gabe grabbed her by the back of the neck and hauled her close, then treated her to a hot, deep, tongue-licking kiss that left her shaken. With his mouth still touching hers, he said, "I want," he assured her in a low growl. "But I'd rather be back at your apartment where I could get you naked and feast on you in private."

Elizabeth could barely get her heavy eyelids to open. Her heart felt ready to burst, her skin too tight, her breasts and belly too sensitive. Breathless, she asked, "And you'd let me touch you, too?"

"Hell, yeah." He kissed her again, short and sweet. "But I don't want you to miss any firsts here, sugar. And every American woman should experience the drive-in at least once. Better late than never, I suppose."

Elizabeth nuzzled his warm throat, just as she'd imagined doing. She luxuriated in his exotic, enticing scent. What would it be like to have that scent surrounding her all night long? Trying to follow the conversation, she asked, "Because the movies are good?"

Gabe grinned, but it was a carnal grin, filled with determination and sultry heat. "No, baby." He held her a little closer, his hand splayed on the small of her back. "It's because getting groped at the drive-in is practically a tradition. You can't really be at the movies without doing at least a little petting. The lights are dim, the movie's boring and all that body heat builds up. It's just natural to get a little frisky."

Elizabeth considered that, then slowly slid both hands up Gabe's chest to his shoulders, then around his neck. "How about if I want to do a lot of petting?"

"Then I'll maybe last through half a movie. *Maybe.*"
He cradled her head between his hands and rubbed her
cheekbones with his thumbs. "But I'm not making any
promises, sweetheart, so don't say I didn't warn you."

CHAPTER NINE

She was driving him crazy. Lizzy's sweet, hot mouth opened on his throat and she made a nearly incoherent sound of discovery and excitement. "You taste so good, Gabe. Do you taste the same all over?"

Feeling her soft lips move against his skin, he tightened painfully from toes to scalp. He wanted to let her explore, to take her time and experience everything, but he wasn't sure he'd live through it. "You can find out later," he murmured, and just saying the words almost sent him off the deep end while images of her mouth on his abdomen, his thighs, in between, fired him. He groaned.

She leaned back slightly and looked at the movie. "What?"

There was a breathless excitement to her tone as she anticipated another love scene on the big screen. He'd had no idea Lizzy would be so receptive to the somewhat cheesy, low-grade erotic film that was playing. Watching her while she watched the movie, he wedged his palm beneath her breast and felt the frantic racing of her heartbeat.

She amused him. And fascinated him. Grinning, he teased, "Lizzy. I'm surprised you can even see the movie the way we've steamed up the windows."

Her smile was pleased and filled with feminine power. "I'd read about fogging windows in books before, but I thought it was an exaggeration."

Forget amusement. Her naïveté made him rock hard with lust and soft as butter with affection. Bringing her mouth to his, he said against her lips, "Just looking at you is enough to steam the place up," then proceeded to thoroughly feast on her mouth. He'd never tire of her taste, her warmth. The small, sexy sounds she made when he gave her his tongue, or when he coaxed her tongue into his mouth.

She grew quickly impatient with kissing and started tugging on his T-shirt, untucking it from his jeans.

Gabe, always willing to oblige, set her a bit away from him and pulled it over his head. Within a heartbeat she was back, her eyes luminous in the dark interior of the car, her small hands eagerly sliding over his hot skin. Whether on purpose or not, he didn't know, her thumbs brushed over his nipples and he jerked. She stared, wide-eyed, at his reaction, made a sound of discovery and deliberately delved her hands into the hair on his chest again.

"Sweet mercy..." Gabe groaned, knotting his hands against the seat and dredging up thoughts of work, of the lake, anything to try to regain some measure of control.

Then her mouth touched his right nipple and he felt her gentle, moist breath, the tentative flick of her small pink tongue...and he was gone.

"Sorry," he rasped. "I can't take it." He saw the disappointment in her gaze and choked on a strangled breath. Holding her slim shoulders to keep her at bay, he said, "Not here, sweetheart. It's just too much. You're too much. I don't understand it, but..."

She didn't look convinced, so he caught her hand and carried it to his erection, then hissed a painful breath as the contact made his entire body clench.

"You see what you're doing to me?" he asked. He knew his voice was harsh, guttural, knew he'd started to sweat and that his hands were shaking. "It's insane. I've made out in this drive-in hundreds of times, but I've never been this close to losing all reason."

"Really?"

He blinked at her look of wonder, minutely regaining his wits. She honestly had no idea of her appeal or her effect on the male species. "Yeah. I'm sorry, babe, but it's the truth." For the first time in his life, his salacious past embarrassed him a bit. Lizzy was so innocent, so pure, that he felt like a total scoundrel. "My mother should have locked me up or something," he muttered, his long fingers still encircling her wrist, holding her hand immobile against him. "Sawyer told her to often enough. Morgan even tried it a few times. But I was always more wild than not and I was determined to get my fill and..."

He trailed off as he realized how fascinated she was, soaking up his every absurd word. Good God, he hoped she didn't put any of that in her damn thesis!

Shaking her gently, he added, "Lizzy, listen to me. There's something about you...."

She tilted her head at him in a measure of pity. "What? My freckles? Come on, Gabe. I've never heard of freckles inspiring lust. Or red hair that's too curly. Or..."

Gabe curved his hand around one lush breast. He could feel the warmth and softness of her, the incredible firmness of virgin flesh. "How about a body made for a man?" he growled. "Or a smile that's so sweet I feel it inside my pants."

She gasped.

"Or skin so soft it makes me crazy wanting to feel it all over my body. Or the way you talk, the things you talk about, your innocence and your daring and your—"

She pressed her fingers over his mouth, her eyes squeezed shut. He parted his lips and ran the tip of his tongue down the seam of her middle and ring finger, probing lightly. She snatched her hand away and panted.

"I want you, Lizzy."

Her eyes opened slowly and they glowed. "I want you,

too.'' She gulped in air, then added, "Just for the summer, for this one time in my life, I want to experience everything I've never felt before. When I go back to school and my old life-style and my plans, when I start my formal training, I want it to be with new knowledge. I don't want to be inexperienced anymore. I want to loosen up, as you suggested.''

Gabe took her words like an iron punch on the chin. *Just for the summer, just for the summer...*

Damn her, no! He wouldn't give up that easy. But he also didn't want to scare her off. He'd give her everything she asked for and more. He'd drown her in pleasure so intense she'd get addicted. She wouldn't be able to do without him. He'd tie her so closely to him she wouldn't even be able to think about walking away from him.

He had no idea what the murky future held, but for the first time in his life he was anxious about it. A year from now? Who the hell knew? Lasting romantic relationships weren't his forté, but he'd seen his two oldest brothers work it out, and that was nothing short of a miracle. One thing he was certain about: a month from now he'd still be wanting her, today, tomorrow...maybe indefinitely. He wanted, he *needed*, a chance to see what was happening between them.

Gabe reached to the floor of the car and picked up the box of popcorn they'd bought earlier. He put it in her lap. "Hold onto that."

"Gabe?"

He didn't look at her again as he stuck the speaker out the window and hooked it into place on its stand. A lot of people would recognize his car, and they'd know he was leaving early. They'd probably even deduce why. For Lizzy's sake, he hated that, but couldn't think of an alternative. It would be worse if he ended up doing things with her here that he knew damn good and well should be done in private. And his control was too strained. Already he wanted her so bad he felt sweat forming on his naked back and at his temples, though the night had cooled off and was comfortable.

Even without the speaker in the car, he heard the on-screen moaning and looked up. *Tanya's Revenge* wasn't much in the way of evil intent. Gabe figured she planned to physically, sexually wear out her adversary, then gain her revenge—whatever it might be. Lizzy was spellbound. She'd watched every sex scene with single-minded intent.

His heart pounded in his chest as he considered doing all those things to her, and how she would react. "Put your seat belt back on."

Without tearing her gaze from the screen, she obeyed. His car started with a low purr and then they were maneuvering out of the lot. Once the screen was no longer in view, Lizzy turned toward him. He could feel her curiosity, could almost hear her mind working, thinking about what she'd watched and wondering if they'd do things like that together.

"Damn right we will," Gabe said, answering her silent question. Lizzy fanned herself, but otherwise held quiet. They reached her place in record time. In one minute flat they were inside with the door locked and Gabe had her pressed to the wall, giving his hands and his mouth free rein.

ELIZABETH held her breath as Gabe's right hand stroked down her side, over her waist, her hip, then to the back of her knee. He pulled her leg upward so that she was practically circling his hips—then he thrust gently.

A moan escaped her. She could feel the fullness and hard length of his erection through his jeans as he deliberately rocked against her in a parody of sex. His mouth, open and damp, moved over her cheek to her arched throat. "I want to be inside you right now, babe. I *need* to be inside you."

"My…my bedroom," she muttered, nearly incoherent, more than ready to accommodate him. But Gabe shook his head.

"You have to do some catching up. I want you to be as hot as I am."

She tried to tell him that she already was, but then his mouth covered hers and his tongue licked past her lips and she could barely think, much less speak.

His hand, rough and incredibly hot, smoothed over her bare thigh to her panties. Elizabeth couldn't stop her instinctive reaction to his hand on her bottom, exploring, first palming one round cheek then gliding inward to touch her in the most intimate spot imaginable.

"Easy," he whispered against her mouth. "Damn, you're wet. You do want me, don't you, sweetheart?"

"Yes…" She felt like she was falling, though her back was flat against the wall with Gabe's hard torso pinning her in place.

"Let's get these out of the way." He released her leg and hooked both hands into the waistband of her panties beneath her skirt. It felt naughty and exciting and achingly sexual the way he went to one knee in front of her to strip off her underclothes. "Step out of them," he instructed.

Like a sleepwalker, Elizabeth lifted first one foot and then the other. Her sandals were still in place, but Gabe had no problem tugging her panties off around them. She waited for him to stand, but he didn't, and she looked down.

His face was flushed, his eyes burning hot as he kneaded the backs of her thighs. He looked at her and didn't smile. Instead he leaned forward and kissed her through her cotton dress, making her suck in a startled, choking breath. Her

hands automatically sought his head and her fingers
threaded into his cool blond hair.

"Gabe?"

"You smell good," he said, nuzzling into her. Her knees
threatened to give out, but his palms moved to cuddle her
naked backside, keeping her upright. "So good."

"I...I can't do this." Even as she said it, her hands
clenched in his hair, directing his attentions to a spot that
pulsed with need. His mouth opened and his breath was
incredibly hot, almost unbearable. She felt the damp press
of his tongue through her clothes and she cried out.

Gabe shot to his feet in front of her and took her mouth
in a voracious kiss meant to consume her. She couldn't
breathe, couldn't react, couldn't think. She felt wild, this
time lifting her leg to wrap around him without instruction.
Both his hands covered her breasts, squeezing a bit roughly,
but she loved it, loved him and the way he made her feel.

He started on the buttons of her dress and had them all
free within seconds. The bodice opened just wide enough
for him to tug it down her shoulders and beneath her
breasts. The dress framed her, caught at her elbows and
pinning her arms to her sides. "Gabe?" She struggled,
wanting to touch him, too.

The dress pulled taut and forced her straining breasts
higher. Her nipples were stiff, pointed, and with a low
growl Gabe bent and sucked one deep into the heat of his
mouth, his rough tongue rasping over her, his teeth holding
her captive for the assault.

She screamed. Her body arched hard against his. Gabe
switched to the other nipple and his hands went under her
skirt, one lifting her thigh, the other cupping over her belly
then delving into her moist curls. She knew she was wet,
could feel the pulsing of her body. His fingers were both a
relief and a torture as he moved them over her hot flesh,
stroking, then parting slick, swollen folds.

She pressed her head against the wall, feeling a strange tension begin to invade her body.

"We'll go easy," he promised, but the words were so low, so rough, she could barely understand them. "Right here, sweetheart," he murmured, and she felt a lightning stroke of sensation as one fingertip deliberately plied her swollen clitoris. Gasping, she tried to pull away because the sensation was too acute, but there was no place for her to go.

"Don't fight me," he whispered around her wet nipple, licking lazily. "Trust me, Lizzy."

She couldn't. The feelings were coming too fast, too strong. Her muscles ached and tightened, then tightened some more. Her vision blurred as heat washed over her in waves. She tried to tell him it was too much, but her words didn't make any sense and he ignored them anyway, listening more to her body than what she had to say. His fingertip felt both rough and gentle as he continued to pet her, concentrating patiently on that one ultrasensitive spot, driving her insane.

Her climax took her by surprise, stealing her breath, making it impossible to do more than moan in low gasping pants, going on and on.... Her body bowed, but Gabe held her securely, not stopping his touch, pushing her and pushing her. He moaned, too, the sound a small vibration around her nipple as he sucked strongly at her. His left forearm slipped beneath her buttocks, keeping her on her feet as her knees weakened, forcing her to feel everything he wanted her to feel.

When finally she slumped against him, spent and exhausted, his hold gentled, loosened. She was no longer crushed against his body, but remained in his embrace, gently rocking. His palm cupped her, holding in the heat, and he said, "I can still feel you pulsing."

Embarrassment tried to ebb into her consciousness, but

Gabe didn't give it a chance to take hold. He kissed each breast, her throat, her chin. Putting his forehead to hers, their noses touching, he whispered, "That was incredible, Lizzy."

If she'd had the strength she would have laughed. Gabe was a master of understatement. Slowly she opened her eyes and was seared by the heat in his. While she watched, he removed his palm from her and raised his hand to her face. His gaze dropped to her mouth and with one wet fingertip, he traced her lips.

She sucked in a startled breath, but couldn't think of a thing to say. Still watching her, Gabe slowly licked her upper lip, then pulled her bottom lip through his teeth to suck gently. "You taste as sweet as I knew you would."

She couldn't move. Her eyes opened owlishly. Good grief, she'd never been in this situation before, never even imagined such a thing! He hadn't shared intercourse with her, but she supposed this was one form of lovemaking. Only…against her front door? With her panties off and his clothes still on and his magical fingers…

"Cat got your tongue?" he asked while smoothing her hair from her face.

"I…" She swallowed hard. "I don't know what to say."

"How about, 'Gabe I want you.'" His gaze moved over her face in loving detail, his fingers gentle on her temple. She noticed his hands shook.

"Gabe, I want you."

The smile she'd already fallen in love with lighted his face. "Thank the lord. I haven't come in my pants since I was a teenager, but it was a close thing, babe. A very close thing."

"Oh." The things he said, and how he said them, never ceased to stupefy her. She was still considering the image he'd evoked with his words when Gabe scooped her up in his arms and started across the floor. She held on tight, charmed by the gallantry. This was another thing, like fogged windows, that she thought only happened in books.

"Sunburn okay?" he asked. He wasn't even straining to hold her weight.

She sighed, totally enamored of his strength. "What sunburn?"

Gabe laughed, a sound filled with masculine satisfaction and triumph—wholly male, hotly sexual. Rather than put her on the bed, he stood her beside it, and with no fanfare at all, caught the hem of her dress and whisked it over her head. Her arms caught in the sleeves for just a moment, making her feel awkward, but Gabe wasn't deterred. He freed her easily, then stepped back to look at her.

She still wore her sandals, was her first thought. Second was that the way he looked at her was almost tactile, like a stroke across her belly, penetrating deep to where the need rekindled and came alive once again.

Without a word Gabe kicked off his shoes as he surveyed her body. He unbuttoned his jeans, slid down the zipper and shucked both his jeans and his shorts. Lizzy was given time to look all she pleased—which was a lot. Gabe stood still for her, except to reach out with his right arm and stroke her nipples with a knuckle.

He swallowed at her continued scrutiny. "Put me out of my misery, Red. Please."

His hips were narrow in contrast to his wide chest. His abdomen was hard and flat, his navel a shallow dent surrounded by golden brown hair that felt soft to the touch. His shoulders were straight, his legs long and strong and covered in hair. His groin... She gulped, then reached out to encircle him with her hand and squeezed. So hard and so strong, his erection flexed and he made a small strangled sound. His hands fisted; his knees locked. One glistening drop of fluid appeared on the tip, fascinating her. She spread it around with her thumb, and heard his hissing breath.

"You're playing with fire, babe."

"You're so beautiful," she breathed, then started slightly when he growled and reached for her.

"Come here, Elizabeth. Let me hold you."

But as she stepped up to him he stepped forward and carried her down to the bed. Balanced on one elbow above her, he began exploring her body again.

"I love all these sexy little freckles." He traced around her breasts, skimming just below her puckered nipples, then trailed down her abdomen to her belly button. He dipped his baby fingertip there before moving over her hipbones and her upper thighs. His hand cupped her between her thighs and she groaned, knowing exactly how he could make her feel. "And this fiery red hair," he said. "I've never seen anything like it."

Elizabeth squirmed as he parted her, as one long finger pushed deeply into her.

His gaze met hers. "Does that hurt?" he asked huskily.

She shook her head. "No, please, Gabe." She spread both hands over his chest, reveling in the heat of his skin, the way his heart galloped. She loved touching his nipples and hearing his breath hitch.

"Open your legs more, Lizzy. That's it. Another finger, okay? I want to make sure you're ready, that I won't hurt you."

His words didn't make much sense to her, though she tried to listen closely. She was attuned to his scent, his touch, the warmth of his big body. She turned her face toward him to watch as her hands glided over him.

"I can't wait anymore," he growled.

Good, she thought, already so tense she ached. If she hadn't been so unused to the intimacy, she'd have demanded he get on with it, but she wasn't quite that daring yet. All she could do was try to urge him to haste with her touch.

Gabe reached for his discarded jeans and removed a condom. Curious, Lizzy stroked his body as he slipped it on, letting her palm cup him beneath his erection, where he was heavy and warm and soft. His eyes nearly closed as he groaned, and then he was over her, his entire big body shaking as he forced her legs wide and opened her with gentle fingers.

"Lizzy, look at me."

She did, snared by his beauty, by the savage hunger in his hot blue eyes. He took her in one long slow thrust and she cried out, not in pain but in incredible pleasure. Her hips lifted of their own accord, trying to make the contact as complete as possible.

Gabe slid both hands beneath her bottom and lifted her, pushing deep, retreating, pushing in again, causing the most incredible friction. "Put your legs around me, sweetheart."

She did, crossing her ankles at the small of his back, squeezing him tight. His hairy chest crushed her breasts, and she tried to rub them against him, tried to feel as much of him as she could. The sensation of him being inside her, her tender flesh stretched tight around him, was almost unbearable. The explosive feelings began building again and she struggled toward them, her head tipped back, her eyes squeezed closed.

But then Gabe cursed and paused for one throbbing heartbeat. With another muttered oath he lowered himself to her completely, opened his mouth on her throat and began thrusting hard and fast, his groan building, his body rock hard and vibrating, and Lizzy held him, enthralled as he came. She forgot her own needs, satisfied to smooth her hands over his damp back, through his silky soft hair and straining shoulders.

Gabe relaxed against her, breathing deep, his arms keeping her close, her legs still around him. After several minutes he muttered against her throat, "Sorry."

Lizzy kissed his shoulder. "For what?"

"For leaving you." He leaned up and looked at her and there was a deeply sated expression to his eyes, a tenderness that went bone deep. "I'll make it up to you in just a little bit."

Elizabeth smiled and touched his face. "I'm fine."

"I want you better than fine," he said, and he kissed her, a long, slow, leisurely kiss. He didn't seem in any hurry to stop kissing her. After a while he sat up to remove the condom—another first for her! Without much talking he carried her into the bathroom where they both soaked in a cool tub. Gabe made her wild with the way he bathed her, stroked her, teased her. After that, he seemed insatiable.

She could barely keep her eyes open after two more climaxes and a lot of new firsts, but when he settled into the bed with her, she found the foresight to ask, "Are you staying all night?"

"Yes." He pulled her to his side and pressed her head to his shoulder.

His assumption that he was welcome amused her, but then, she wanted him to stay. "Shouldn't you tell someone where you are so they won't worry?"

"I'm twenty-seven years old, sweetheart. I don't have to account for myself to my brothers."

"What about Honey? Will she worry?"

He went still, then cursed softly. "Don't move." He padded naked from the bed into the kitchen where her only phone hung on the wall. After a few seconds she heard him say, "I won't be home tonight."

There was a pause. "Yeah, well, I thought Honey might—" He laughed. "That's what I figured. See ya tomorrow."

He came back to bed and settled himself. "You were

right. Sawyer said she would have worried.'' He kissed her forehead and within seconds he was breathing deeply.

Elizabeth stroked his chest, wondering how often he spent the night with women, if this meant anything to him at all, if she had the right to hope he'd stay with her whenever possible.

It was a long time before she, too, dozed off. But thinking of Gabe and how strong and independent and capable he was only served to slant her dreams with miserable comparisons of all the things he was, and all the things she wasn't.

And sometime in the middle of the night, the nightmares returned.

CHAPTER TEN

GABE WAS generally a sound sleeper, but then, contrary to popular belief, he seldom had a very sexy, very warm woman cuddled up to his side when he slept. Because he lived with his brothers, and because his nephew, Casey, was there, he hadn't made a habit of flaunting his social life. Having Lizzy at his side was a unique and pleasant experience.

And while he'd had no problem sleeping, he was never at any moment unaware of her curled against him.

When her skin grew warmer and her breathing deeper, he stirred. She mumbled something in her sleep and he turned his head to look at her, making a soft, soothing sound. Her hand suddenly fisted against his chest, and her head twisted from side to side.

Frowning, Gabe came up on one elbow. *"Lizzy?"* She didn't answer him. He touched her cheek and felt it wet with tears. His heart pounded. "Hey, come on, sweetheart. Talk to me."

In the dim moonlight filtering through the curtains, he could barely make out her features. He saw her mouth move, crying soundlessly, then heard a small whimper, and another, each gaining in volume.

"Lizzy?" Gabe held her closer and stroked her hair. "You're dreaming, sweetheart. Wake up." He made his voice deliberately commanding, unable to bear her unconscious distress.

Suddenly her body went rigid as if she'd just suffered a

crushing physical pain. She screamed, harsh, tearing sounds that echoed around the silent bedroom. Her arms flailed wildly and she hit him in the chest, fighting against him, against herself. Gabe pinned her arms down and rolled her beneath him.

"Wake up, Lizzy!"

Sobbing softly, she opened her eyes and stared at him. For one instant she looked lost and confused, her eyes shadowed, then she crumbled. Gabe turned to his side and held her face to his throat. "It's all right. It's all right, sweetheart."

She clutched him, and his heart broke at her racking cries. Gabe felt his eyes get misty and crushed her even closer, wanting to absorb her pain, to somehow be a part of her so he could carry some of her emotional burden.

Long minutes passed before she finally quieted, only suffering the occasional hiccup or sniff. Gabe kissed her temple, then eased her away from him. He kept the lights off and said, "Don't move, baby. I'm going to go get you a cool cloth."

He was in and out of her bathroom in fifteen seconds. When he walked in, Lizzy was propped up in the bed blowing her nose. She had her knees drawn up to her chest, the sheet wrapped around her. The first thing she said was, "I'm sorry."

"Don't make me turn you over my knee when you're already upset." Gabe scooted into bed beside her and manfully ignored the way she tried to inch away from him. He caught her chin and turned her face, then gently stroked her with the damp washcloth. "You have no reason to be sorry, Lizzy. Everyone has bad dreams every now and again."

A long silence threatened to break him and then she muttered, "It wasn't a dream."

Gabe propped his back against the headboard and handed

the washcloth to Lizzy. She pressed it over her swollen eyes. Utilizing every ounce of patience he possessed, Gabe waited.

Finally she said, "I'm a little embarrassed."

"Please don't be." He kept his voice soft but firm. "I'm so glad I was here with you." His arm slipped around her shoulders and she didn't fight him as he pulled her close. "I care about you, Lizzy. Will you believe that?"

She nodded, but said, "I don't know."

Rubbing his hand up and down her bare arm, he asked, "Is it so strange for someone to care about you, sweetheart?"

"Someone like you, yes."

"What about someone not like me?"

She went still. "There's...things about me you don't know."

Gabe tightened his hold, anticipating her reaction. "You mean the awful way your mother died?"

As he'd predicted, she jerked and almost got away from him. "What do you know about that?"

"I read the articles you saved."

"How dare you!" She struggled against him, but Gabe held her tight.

"Quit fighting me, honey. I'm not letting you go." Probably not ever. It was several seconds before she went rigid against him. Gabe could feel her hurt, her anger. But he wanted to get past it, and the only way he saw to do that was to force his way. He spread his fingers across the back of her head and kept her pressed to his shoulder. "That's why you're so all-fired determined to understand this nonsense about heroism, right?"

She shuddered, and another choking sob escaped her before she caught herself. "You...you can't understand. You aren't like me. You saw a way to help and you instinctively acted. I...I let my mother die." Her hands curled into his shoulders, her nails biting, but Gabe would have gladly accepted any pain to help her. "Oh, God. I let her die."

Unable to bear it, Gabe pressed his face into her neck and rocked her while she continued talking.

"We were in a car wreck. I...I was changing the radio station trying to find a song Mom and I could sing to. We did that all the time, playing around, just having fun. It was raining and dark. Mom told me to turn the radio down, and I started to, but then a semi came around the corner and Mom had to swerve..."

Her voice had an eerie, faraway quality to it. Gabe wondered how many times, and to how many people, she'd given this guilty admission. The thought of her as a twelve-year-old child, awkward and shy, suffering what no child should ever suffer, made him desperate with the need to fix things that were years too distant to repair.

"The car went off the road and hit a tree. Mom's door was smashed shut, the windshield broken. She was... bleeding. I thought she was dead and I just screamed and got out of the car and crouched down on the gravel and the mud, waiting and numb. Too stupid to do what I should have done."

"Oh, Lizzy." Gabe kissed her temple, her ear. He murmured inanities, but she didn't seem to hear him.

"The nearest telephone was only two miles away. If...if I'd gone for help...she'd have lived if only I hadn't frozen, if I hadn't become a useless lump crying and waiting to be helped when I was barely hurt." Her hand fisted and thumped once, hard, against his shoulder. "She was pinned in that damn car unconscious and bleeding to death and I just let her die." Sobbing again, her tears soaking his neck, she whispered, "By the time another car came by and found us...it was too late."

Keeping her in the iron grip of his embrace, Gabe reached for the lamp and turned the switch. Lizzy flinched

away from the harshness of it, but Gabe was so suffused
with pity, with pain and mostly with anger, he refused to
let her hide. Her ravaged face was a fist around his heart,
but he never wavered in his determination. Forcing her to
meet his gaze, he said, "You were twelve goddamned years
old! You were a child. How in the hell can you compare
what a child does to a grown man?"

She looked stunned by his outrage. "I was useless."

"You were in shock!"

"If I'd reacted…"

"No, Lizzy. There is no going back, no starting over.
All any of us can do is make the most of each day. You're
such an intelligent woman, so giving and sincere, why can't
you see that you were an innocent that day?"

"You…you said you read the articles."

"And I also know how the damn media can slant things
deliberately to get the best story. One more human death
means little enough to them when people pass away every
day, some in more horrific circumstances than others. But
a human-interest story on a young traumatized girl, well,
now, that's newsworthy. You were a pawn, sweetheart, a
sacrifice to a headliner. That's all there is to it."

"I let her die," she said, but she sounded vaguely uncertain, almost desperate to believe him.

"No." Gabe pulled her close and kissed her hard. "You
don't know that. It was dark, it was raining. Even if,
through the trauma of seeing your mother badly injured,
you'd been able to run to the nearest phone, there's no
guarantee that you'd have gotten there safely, that you'd
have found help and they'd have made it to her in time."

She searched his face, then reached for another tissue.
After mopping her eyes and blowing her nose, she admitted
in a raw whisper, "My dad has said that. But I'd hear him
crying at night, and I'd see how wounded he looked without my mother."

Gabe cupped her tear-streaked cheeks, fighting his own emotions. "He still had you." He wobbled her head, trying to get through to her, trying to reach her. "I know he had to be grateful for that."

Her smile trembled and she gave an inelegant sniff. "Yes. He said he was. My father is wonderful."

Relief filled him that at least her father hadn't blamed her. The man had obviously been overwrought with grief. Gabe couldn't begin to imagine how he'd react if something happened to Lizzy. If he ever lost her, he'd—

Gabe froze, struck by the enormity of his thoughts. He loved Lizzy! It didn't require rhyme or reason. It didn't require a long courtship or special circumstances. He knew her, and she was so special, how could he not love her?

He touched the corner of her mouth with his thumb, already feeling his body tense with arousal and new awareness. "You're a wonderful person, sweetheart, so you deserve a wonderful dad."

Her eyes were red-rimmed, matching her nose, and her lips were puffy, her skin blotchy. Gabe thought she was possibly the most beautiful person he'd ever seen. The sheet slipped a bit, and he looked at her lush breasts, the faint sprinkling of freckles and the tantalizing peak of one soft nipple.

He tamped down his hunger and struggled to direct all his attention to her distress. "Will you believe me that you weren't to blame, Lizzy?"

She bit her lip, then sighed. "I'll believe you don't blame me. But facts are facts. Some people possess heroic tendencies, and some people are ineffectual. I'm afraid I fall into the latter category."

Gabe caught her hips and pulled her down so she lay flat in the bed. He whisked the sheet away. "Few people," he said, while eyeing her luscious body, "are ever given the opportunity to really know if they're heroic or not." He placed his palm gently on her soft white belly. "Personally, I don't think you can judge yourself by what a frightened, shy, injured twelve-year-old did."

She stared at his mouth, firing his lust. "That's…that's why I'm studying this so hard. I want to help other adolescents to understand their own limitations, to know that they can't be completely blamed for qualities they don't possess. We're all individuals."

"And you don't want any other child to hurt as you've hurt?"

Her beautiful eyes filled with tears again. "Yes."

"I love you, Lizzy."

Her eyes widened and she stared. Stock-still, she did no more than watch him with wary disbelief. Gabe had to laugh at himself. He hadn't quite meant to blurt that out, and he felt a tad foolish.

Elizabeth was everything he wasn't. Serious, studious, caring and concerned. She had a purpose for her life, while he'd always been content to idle away his time, shirking responsibilities, refusing to settle down, priding himself on his freedom. She was at the top of her class, while he'd gone from one minor to another, never quite deciding on any one thing he wanted to do in his life. His time in college had been more a lark than anything else; he'd gone because it was expected. He'd gotten good grades because his pride demanded nothing less, but it had been easy and had never meant anything to him.

Lizzy would never consider letting someone like him interrupt her plans. She was goal-oriented, while he was out for fun. She'd told him that she wanted the summer with him, but she'd never even hinted that she might want more than that.

Trying to make light of his declaration—though he refused to take it back—he said, "Don't worry. I won't start writing you poetry or begging you to elope."

She blinked and her face colored, which added to her already blotchy cheeks and red nose, giving her a comical look. Gabe forced a grin and kissed her forehead. Damn, but he loved her. He felt ready to burst with it.

"Have I rendered you speechless, sweetheart?"

She swallowed hard. "Yes." Then: "Gabe, did you mean it?"

"Absolutely." He cupped her breast and idly flicked her soft nipple with his thumb until it stiffened. "How could I not love you, Lizzy? I've never known anyone like you. You make me laugh and you make me hot and you confuse my brain and my heart."

She scrunched up her mouth, trying not to laugh. "How...romantic."

Gabe shifted, settling himself between her long slender thighs. "I'm horny as hell," he admitted in a growl, letting her feel the hardness of his body. "How romantic did you expect me to be?"

She looped both arms around his neck and smiled. "Thank you, Gabe."

"For what?"

"For making me feel so much better." Her fingers caressed his nape, and she wound her legs around him, holding him, welcoming him. "For being here with me now, for saying you love me."

He started to reassure her that he hadn't said the words lightly, that he meant them and felt them down to his very soul. But he held back. Similar words hadn't crossed her lips, and he needed time to get himself together, to sort out this new revelation. So all he said was, "My pleasure," and then he kissed her, trying to show her without words that they were meant for each other whether she knew it yet or not.

He felt as if his life hung in the balance. He needed her, but he didn't know if he could make her need him in return.

SAWYER STOOD behind him, leaving a long shadow across the planks of wood that extended over the lake. Gabe didn't bother to turn when he asked, "You want something, Sawyer?"

"Yeah. I want to know why you're mangling all those nails."

Gabe looked at the third nail he'd bent trying to hammer it into the new dock extension he was building for his brother Morgan. Normally he did this kind of work without thought, his movements fluid, one nail, one blow. Over the years he'd built so many docks, for his family and for area residents, that he should have been able to do it blindfolded. But he'd hit his damn thumb twice already and he was rapidly make a mess of things.

In a fit of frustration he flung the hammer onto the shore and stomped out of the water, sloshing the mud at his feet and sending minnows swimming away. Sawyer handed him a glass of iced tea when he got close enough.

"From Honey?"

"Yeah." Sawyer stretched with lazy contentment. "She was all set to bring it to you herself, but I figured you might not welcome her mothering right now, since you've been a damn bear all week."

Gabe grunted in response, then chugged the entire glassful, feeling some of it trickle down the side of his mouth and onto his heated chest. "Thanks."

Sawyer lowered himself to the dry grass and picked at a dandelion. He wore jeans and nothing else, and Gabe thought it was a miracle Honey had let him out of her sight. Ever since she'd announced her pregnancy three weeks ago, Sawyer had been like a buck in rutting season. When Honey was within reach, he was reaching for her, and there was a special new glow to their love. Honey wallowed in her husband's attentions with total abandon. It was amusing—and damn annoying, because while their marriage grew visibly stronger every day, Gabe watched the time slip by, knowing Lizzy would be heading back to school soon. Three and a half weeks had passed, and he was no closer to tying her to him than he had been when he'd met her. Not once had she told him how she felt about him, yet their intimacy had grown until Gabe couldn't keep her out of his mind. He had one week left. One lousy week.

It put him in a killing mood.

Cursing, he looked at the clouds, then decided he might as well make use of Sawyer's visit, since it was obvious that's what Sawyer intended by seeking him out. He looked at his oldest brother and said grimly, "I'm in love."

Sawyer's smile was slow and satisfied. "I figured as much. Elizabeth Parks?"

"Yeah." Gabe rubbed the back of his neck, then sent a disgruntled glance at the half completed dock. "I might as well give up on this today. My head isn't into it."

"Morgan'll understand. He's not in a big hurry for the dock, and we've got plenty of room to keep the boat at the house. Besides, he suffered his own black moods before Misty put him out of his misery."

"But that's just it." Gabe dropped down beside Sawyer and stretched out in the sun. The grass was warm and prickly against his back, and near his right ear, a bee buzzed. "I don't see an end in sight for my particular brand of misery. Lizzy is going back to school. I've only got a few more days with her."

"Have you told her you love her?"

"Yep. She was flattered." Gabe made a wry face and laid one forearm over his eyes. "Can you believe that crap?"

A startled silence proved that wasn't exactly what Sawyer had been expecting to hear. Compared to the way he and Morgan had fought the notion of falling in love, it was no wonder Sawyer was taken off guard.

"You've only known her a few weeks, Gabe."

"I knew I loved her almost from the first." He lowered his arm to stare at his brother. "It was the damnedest thing, but she introduced herself, then proceeded to crawl right in under my skin. And I like it. It's making me nuts thinking about her going off to college again, this time with the knowledge that she's sexy and exciting and that plenty of men will want her. She hadn't known that before, you know. She thought she was too plain, and it's for certain she was too quiet, too intense. But now..."

"Now you've corrupted her?"

Gabe couldn't hold back his grin. "Yeah, she's wonderfully corrupt. It's one of the things I love most about her."

Lizzy was the absolute best sex partner he'd ever had. Open, wild, giving and accepting. When she'd said she wanted to experience it all, she hadn't been kidding. Gabe shivered with the memory, then suffered through Sawyer's curious attention. No way would he share details with his brother, but then, there was no way Sawyer would expect him to.

And just as special to Gabe were the quiet times when they talked afterward. He'd shared stories about his mother with her, and in turn Lizzy had told him about her childhood before the accident. Their mothers were exact opposites, but both loving, both totally devoted to their children.

She'd cried several times while talking about her mom, but they were bittersweet tears of remembrance, not tears of regret or guilt. Gabe sincerely hoped she'd gotten over her ridiculous notion that she'd somehow held responsibility for her mother's death. He couldn't bear to think of her carrying that guilt on her slender shoulders.

"How much longer will she be in school?" Sawyer asked.

"Depends." Gabe sat up and crossed his forearms over his knees, staring sightlessly at the crystal surface of the lake. The lot Morgan had chosen to build on was ideal, quiet and peaceful and scenic. But Gabe preferred the bustle of the bait shops, the boat rentals, the comings and goings of vacationers. He'd always loved summer best because it was the season filled with excitement and fun on the lake. He'd invariably hated to see it coming to an end, but never more so than now, when the end meant Lizzy would leave him.

"Depends on what?" Sawyer pressed.

"On what she decides to do. She could easily graduate this semester and be done, but knowing Lizzy she may well want to further her education. She's so damn intelligent and so determined to learn as much as she can."

"We have colleges closer that she could transfer to."

"She's never mentioned doing that." It took him a moment to form the words, and then Gabe admitted, "I don't want to get in her way. I don't want to lure her into changing her plans for me, when I don't even have any plans. I've spent my whole life goofing off, while Lizzy is the epitome of seriousness." He met his oldest brother's gaze and asked, "What right do I have to screw with her life when my own is up in the air?"

Sawyer was silent a moment, and just as Gabe started to expect a dose of sympathy, Sawyer made an obnoxious sound and shook his head. "That is the biggest bunch of melodramatic bull I've ever heard uttered. You don't want to get in her way? Hell, Gabe, how can loving a woman get in her way?"

"She has plans."

"And you don't? Oh, that's right. You said you've screwed around all your life. So then, that wasn't you who helped Ceily rebuild after the fire at her restaurant? And it wasn't you who worked his butt off for Rosemary when her daddy was sick and she needed help at the boat docks?

I doubt there's a body in town who you haven't built, repaired or renovated something for.''

Gabe shrugged. "That's just idle stuff. You know I like working with my hands, and I don't mind helping out. But it's not like having a real job. I can still remember how appalled Lizzy was when she first came here and found out I wasn't employed. And rightfully so.''

"I see. So since you don't have an office in town and a sign hanging off your door, you're not really employed?''

Gabe frowned, not at all sure what Sawyer was getting at. "You know I'm not.''

Sawyer nodded slowly. "You know, when I first started practicing medicine, a lot of the hospital staff in the neighboring towns claimed I wasn't legitimate. I worked out of the house so I could be near Casey, and there's plenty of times when I don't charge someone, or else I get paid with an apple pie and an invitation to visit. It used to steam me like you wouldn't believe, that others would discount what I did just because I didn't take on all the trappings.''

Gabe scowled. "It's not at all the same thing. You're about the best doctor around.'' Then anger hit him and he asked, "Who the hell said you weren't legitimate?''

"It doesn't matter now.''

"The hell it doesn't. Who was it, Sawyer?''

Laughing, Sawyer clapped him on the shoulder. "Forget it. It was a long time ago and what they thought never mattered a hill of beans to me. And now I have their respect, so I guess I proved myself in the end. But the point is—''

"The point is that someone insulted you. Who was it?''

"Gabe. You're avoiding the subject here, which is *you*.'' Sawyer used his stern, big-brother voice, which Gabe waved away without concern. He was too old to be intimated by his oldest overachiever brother. Sawyer didn't mind now that he had Gabe's attention again. "The point is, you damn near make as much money as I do, just by doing the odd job and always being available and being incredibly good at what you do. If it bothers you, well, then, rent a space in town and run a few ads and—'' Sawyer snapped his fingers ''—you're legitimate. An honest-to-goodness self-employed craftsman. But don't do it for the wrong reasons. Don't make the assumption that it matters to Elizabeth, because she didn't strike me as the type to be so shallow.''

''She's not shallow!''

Just as Gabe had ignored Sawyer's annoyance, Sawyer ignored Gabe's. ''I have a question for you.''

''You're getting on my nerves, Sawyer.''

''Have you let Elizabeth know that you'd like things to continue past the summer? Or is she maybe buying into that awesome reputation of yours and thinking you want this just to be a summer fling?''

The rustling of big doggy feet bounding excitedly through the grass alerted Sawyer and Gabe that they were being joined, and judging by the heavy footsteps following in the wake of the dog, they knew it was Morgan and his massive but good-natured pet, Godzilla. Gabe twisted to see his second-oldest brother just as Morgan snarled, ''Let me guess. Sawyer is giving you advice on your love life now, too?''

''Too?'' Gabe lifted a brow, then had to struggle to keep Godzilla from knocking him over. The dog hadn't yet realized that he was far too big for anyone's lap. Gabe shoved fur out of his face, dodged a wet tongue and asked, ''Sawyer gave you advice?''

''Hell, yes.'' Then: ''Godzilla, get off my brother before you smother him.'' Morgan threw a stick into the lake and Godzilla, always up for a game, scrambled the length of the half-built dock and did a perfect doggy dive off the

end. All three men watched, then groaned, knowing they'd
get sprayed when Godzilla shook himself dry.

"That damn dog has no fear," Morgan grumbled.

Gabe made a face. "He must get that from you."

Morgan returned his attention to Gabe. "Sawyer fancies
himself an expert on women just because Honey walks
around with a vacuous smile on her face all the time."

Sawyer's grin was pure satisfaction. "Just because Misty
prefers to give you hell instead—"

"She gives me hell because she loves getting me riled."
Morgan chuckled. "She claims I'm a wild man when I'm
riled."

Gabe muttered, "You're always a wild man," then had
to jump out of the way when Godzilla ran to Morgan and
dropped the stick at his feet. Morgan was wearing his uni-
form, but the shirt was unbuttoned and his hat was gone.
He quickly threw the stick again, this time up the hill toward the house and dry land.

"So what's the answer here, Gabe? Does your little redheaded wonder know you're in this for the long haul?"

Sawyer leaned around Gabe to see Morgan. "He told her
he loved her."

Morgan raised a brow. "Is that so?"

Gabe wanted to punch them both, but instead he muttered a simple truth. "She's never returned the sentiment."

"Hm." Morgan and Sawyer seemed to be putting their
collective brains together on that one until Morgan's cell
phone beeped. He took it off his belt and flipped it open.
"Sheriff Hudson." He grinned, and his voice changed from
official to intimate. "Hi, babe. No, I'm just trying to
straighten out Gabe's love life. Seems he's not going to
finish my dock until I do." Morgan waited, then said,
"Okay, I'll tell him."

To Gabe's disgust and Sawyer's amusement, Morgan

made a kissing sound into the phone, then closed it and clipped it on his belt. "That was Misty."

Sawyer laughed outright. "I never would have guessed."

"Gabe, it seems your little woman is headed over to see Jordan, only Jordan told Misty he had to make a house call for an injured heifer and would be away from the office for a bit. Jordan wants you to go over and make his apologies for him."

Sawyer looked at Gabe. "Why is Elizabeth hanging around with Jordan?"

With obvious disgruntlement in every line of his body, Gabe shoved himself to his feet. "Lizzy has some harebrained notion that Jordan is different, somehow nicer than the rest of us."

Morgan and Sawyer looked at each other, then burst out laughing. Gabe ignored them and snatched up his dirt- and sweat-stained T-shirt before Godzilla could step on it. Sitting on a large rock, he shoved his feet into his unlaced sneakers. His brothers were still laughing. "It's not that funny," he told them, then grinned when Godzilla threw himself into Morgan's lap, his tongue hanging in doggy bliss. Morgan made a face, resigned, and rubbed the dog's shaggy ears.

Sawyer wiped his eyes, damp from his mirth. "Elizabeth doesn't know Jordan very well, does she?"

"If you mean, has she ever seen his temper," Gabe asked, "the answer is no. I got the feeling she doesn't think Jordan *has* a temper."

Morgan choked, but there was admiration and pride in his voice when he said, "Jordan is so damn sly. He hides it well. Most women don't realize that he's only civilized on the outside."

"As long as you don't mess with his animals, or anyone he cares about, he keeps it together. But get him on one of his crusades..." Sawyer shook his head in wonder at the way his middle brother could handle himself when provoked.

Even Gabe grinned at that. Jordan gave the impression of a quiet peacemaker—and to some extent, he was. But when quiet tactics didn't work, he was more than capable of resorting to what would. "He does seem to like championing the underdog, doesn't he?"

Morgan stroked Godzilla's wet back. "Literally."

After yanking on his shirt, Gabe faced his brothers. He had his hands on his hips and a nervous chip on his shoulder. "I'm going to ask Elizabeth to give us a chance. I'm going to tell her how things'll be." He pointed an accusing finger at both of them. "But if this backfires on me, I'm coming back and kicking both your asses."

As Gabe strode away, Sawyer yelled, "Good luck."

Morgan muttered loud enough for Gabe to hear, "Never thought I'd see the day when Gabe would have women troubles."

Gabe sincerely hoped today wasn't the day, either, because he just didn't know what he'd do without Ms. Elizabeth Parks in his life.

GABE FOUND LIZZY pacing outside the front of Jordan's clinic. Her hands were clasped together, her expression frightened. Not knowing what had happened, Gabe left his car in a hurry and trotted toward her. Lizzy looked up, saw him and relief flooded her entire being.

She ran to him. "Gabe, something's wrong!"

Gabe reached for her shoulders, but she pulled away and sprinted toward the clinic door. "Listen to the animals. They're never that noisy. They're all making a racket."

Gabe could hear the whine of dogs, the screech of cats. He frowned. "Jordan always keeps them calm, but Jordan isn't here."

Lizzy put her hands to her mouth. "Something's wrong. I just know it."

Gabe considered her worry for only two seconds, then said, "Okay, just hang on, hon. I'm going in."

"How?"

For an answer, Gabe picked up a rock and tapped the glass out of a window. The howling and crying became louder with the window open—and then they smelled the smoke.

"Oh, God." Gabe jerked off his shirt, wrapped it around his hand and safely removed the broken glass. "Quickly, Lizzy. I'll go in and unlock the door. Use the cell phone in my car to call Morgan. He'll send people here. Hurry."

Lizzy ran off and Gabe carefully levered himself over the windowsill. The smoke wasn't very thick yet, but he could smell the acrid stench of burning plastic and paper. Gabe ran to the door and unlocked it, then pushed it wide open. He wasn't really given a chance to see what was burning or why, not with so many animals calling for attention. He hefted the first big cage he came to and hauled it outside.

Lizzy was back. "Morgan's on his way. What can I do?"

"Just pull these cages away from the house as I bring them out."

"But there's too many of them!"

"Just do it, Red. We don't have time to talk about it." Gabe didn't know how sick the animals were, if it was safe to open the cages... He raced inside and hauled two more out. He almost tripped over Lizzy. She had a big empty cage that she was dragging over the threshold. She had to pry open the double doors before it would fit through. Gabe frowned at her. "What the hell are you doing?"

Without answering, she ran in. She opened three pens filled with cats and began carrying the cats—without the bulky cages—outside. She got several scratches for her efforts, but the empty cage she'd taken outside was quickly filled. As Gabe worked he watched her make trip after trip, occasionally repeating the process of setting up an empty cage. The animals, penned together, might hurt each other in the excitement, but they wouldn't die.

The smoke was thicker, filling the air while frantic animal growls and cries echoed off every wall. Gabe hadn't seen any signs of an actual fire, but then the smoke tended to mask things. He had enough trouble just breathing. As Gabe struggled to release an older German shepherd, he tripped over a pile of feed and went down. His head hit the edge of a metal cage, and he saw stars.

"Gabe!"

As if from a distance he heard Lizzy calling him, and panic engulfed him. Was she hurt? He tried to raise himself, but everything spun around him. And then she was there, her arm supporting his head. She coughed several times before she was able to say, "Gabe, you have to stand."

Gabe could tell she was crying, and it cut him deeply. "Lizzy?"

"Please, Gabe. Please." She tugged on him and finally he managed to get his rubbery legs to work, leaning heavily against her. Something warm ran into his right eye, and he wondered vaguely what it was before Lizzy's insistence that he move forced him to concentrate on her demands. It was slow going, the smoke so thick he couldn't see at all.

Then blessedly clean air filled his lungs and he dropped to the ground. Lizzy knelt over him, her soft hands touching his face. "Oh, my God. You're bleeding."

Gabe said, "The animals…"

Elizabeth swabbed at his face with the hem of her dress, giving him a peek at her panties as she did so. "You've got a nasty cut."

"I'll be fine," he muttered.

She ran off but she was back within seconds. "Here, hold this against your head. Can you do that, Gabe?"

She handed him a soft pad, and he realized it was from the clinic. He pressed it hard to his head to stem the flow of blood.

"Don't you dare move, Gabriel Kasper." Her voice shook, thick with smoke and, he thought, perhaps emotion. "And don't you be seriously hurt, either." He saw her wipe tears from her face with a soot-covered hand, and he tried to smile at her, but his head was pounding painfully. "I'll never forgive you if you're seriously hurt."

Before he could reassure her she was gone and a new panic settled in. Dear God, she'd gone into the clinic! Gabe summoned all his strength to stand, to fetch her and keep her safe, and then he heard the sound of approaching sirens and knew Morgan was almost there. He'd take care of things. But Gabe was needed still; he had to help her....

Morgan's big hands settled on Gabe's shoulders. "Don't move, Gabe."

"It's just a knock on the head. Stupid cage got in my way."

Morgan pressed him down. "Damn it, I said don't move, you stubborn fool!" Speaking to someone else, Morgan said, "Go ahead. I'll take care of my brother. Get the animals out."

"Lizzy?" Already Gabe's head was starting to clear, even as a throbbing pain settled in. The sirens were blasting, not helping one bit, keeping the animals frenzied and his head pulsing. He glared at Morgan. "Get Lizzy."

"She's inside?" Morgan jerked to his feet, but at that moment Lizzy stumbled through the doorway, aided by two firemen. She had a box of mewling kittens in her arms, and she was a dirty mess. "Here she comes now."

Morgan went to her and took the box of kittens. "Sawyer was right behind me. He'll fix Gabe up good as new."

Gabe watched her lean against Morgan for just an instant, then she straightened and hurried to Gabe.

"Shh. It's all right, babe. I'm okay. I just got knocked silly." He pulled her to his side as he carefully sat up. "Morgan! Shut the damn sirens off."

Morgan barked a few orders, and one fireman rushed to do as he was told. When silence settled in, Gabe touched Lizzy's blackened face. "Are you all right?"

She wasn't listening to him. She'd spotted Sawyer and she ran to him, then practically dragged him to Gabe. He had Jordan with him, and Jordan looked frozen with shock.

"What the hell happened?" As Sawyer spoke he opened his bag and began swabbing off Gabe's face. To Lizzy he said, "Head wounds bleed like the very devil. If he's not hurt anywhere else then he should be fine."

Gabe took pity on Jordan. "I'm fine, Jordan. Go check your animals."

Jordan looked at Sawyer and got his nod of confirmation. "Looks like he'll need a few stitches, but that's all."

"Thank God." Jordan, still looking somewhat sick and so furious he could chew nails, headed for the clinic door.

An hour and a half later, everything had quieted down. There was a lot of smoke damage to the clinic, but very little had burned. It hadn't taken a large investigation to discover that a pet owner who'd come in earlier had evidently thrown a cigarette into the trash can in the bathroom. The can was metal, so other than the walls and floor in that room being singed, the damage was mostly smoke-related. It would take quite a bit of work, and a professional crew, to get everything clean again and to rid the clinic of the smell. Jordan had a strict no-smoking policy. Gabe couldn't remember ever seeing his brother look so ravaged, or so livid.

Gabe was propped up against a tree, his head bandaged, watching the proceedings with frustration since Sawyer had flatly refused to let him help out. Lizzy had continued to work with Jordan until they had every animal accounted for and loaded into covered truck beds. Luckily, not a single animal had suffered a serious injury from the small fire, but they were frightened and skittish and Jordan was using his mesmerizing voice to calm them all. He looked like hell warmed over, but his tone didn't in any way match his expression. It was lulling and easy and sank into the bones, reassuring even the most fractious animal.

Lizzy returned to Gabe's side again and again, and each time he told her he was fine. Then she'd flit off to do more work. She had to be exhausted, but she kept on. He was so damn proud of her, he could barely contain himself.

As if she'd heard his thoughts, she glanced at him, then hurried to his side. "Do you need something to drink?"

On her knees beside him, she smoothed his hair and touched his cheek. Gabe caught her hand and carried it to his mouth. "Mm. You taste like charcoal."

She grinned. "I imagine I smell like it, too." She glanced at Jordan. "Sawyer recommended he move the animals into your garage until the clinic can be cleaned. It'll take a few days. Poor Jordan. He looks devastated."

"I know how he feels." She faced him, her brow puckered in confusion, and he said, "You scared the hell out of me, Lizzy, when you ran back in there without me. For all I knew, the place was burning to the ground. I kept thinking about you getting hurt...."

"I was careful."

"But what if you'd stumbled like I did? How the hell would I have gotten you out of there?" Her expression softened, and she leaned forward to gently kiss his mouth.

"I didn't mean to worry you."

"I love you." He hadn't said it again since she'd had her nightmare, and now he couldn't keep the words contained. Her eyes widened. "What?" he asked, sounding a little sarcastic. "You thought I made it up the first time? Not a chance."

"Oh, Gabe." Tears welled in her eyes, and Gabe held his breath, waiting to see what she would say.

Then Jordan appeared, and he hauled Lizzy to her feet. "I've been so busy trying to see to things, I haven't even thanked you yet."

Jealousy speared through Gabe as he watched Jordan lift Lizzy onto her tiptoes and kiss her soundly. She blushed, but she didn't pull away.

"This is going to be inconvenient as hell for a few days," Jordan said, hugging her tight, "but at least all the animals are safe."

Lizzy finally pulled back. She smiled and started to say, "Gabe's the real..." but then her words tapered off and she put a hand over her mouth.

Jordan raised a brow. "Real what? Hero? I'd say you both are. Not only did you get all twenty-three animals outside, you even managed to get my baby brother out with only a knock to his hard head. That took a lot of guts, sweetheart, and I want you to know how much I appreciate it."

After Jordan walked away, Gabe took pity on Lizzy and tugged her down beside him. She was mute, her dirty face blank. Gabe kissed her ear. "How's it feel to be a heroine? Will you add your own experiences to your thesis?"

She blinked owlishly at him. "But I didn't..."

"Didn't what?" He smoothed a long red sooty curl behind her ear. "Didn't risk your life for those animals? Didn't face injury without a thought? Didn't do what had to be done almost by instinct?"

"But..." She sucked in a deep breath. "I was so scared."

"For yourself?"

She stared into his eyes, bemused. "No, not at first. I

was afraid for you, and for the poor animals. But now I'm shaking with nerves." She held out her hand to show him, and Gabe cradled it in his large hand.

"Only a fool wouldn't react after going through something like this. You think after that boating incident I wasn't something of a wreck?"

"You said you weren't afraid."

"I was mad as hell at that fool for falling out of his boat. I wanted to tear something apart, and since I couldn't get hold of him, I punched a hole in my wall, then had to repair it." He gave her a sheepish grin. "It's all just reaction. Anger, fear... I've even seen people start laughing and not be able to stop. You're trembling. I got violent. We're the same, sweetheart, but we're also different. And what you did today is no less significant than what I did a year ago."

She seemed to consider that for a long time, and Gabe was content to hold her. Finally, without quite looking at him, she said, "I don't want to be a coward, Gabe."

"You're not."

She bit her bottom lip. "Have you enjoyed spending your time with me these last few weeks?"

His heart started pounding. His palms got damp. Gabe didn't give away his reaction when he answered, keeping his tone mild. "I told you I love you. So of course I love spending time with you."

She nodded slowly, then curled tighter to his side, keeping her face tucked under his chin. "How many women have you loved?"

Wrapping a red curl around his finger, he said, "Hm. Let's see. There's my mother. And now Honey and Misty."

She punched his ribs. "No, I mean romantically."

"Just you, sweetheart."

"You've never told another woman that you loved her?"

"No. Though plenty of women have told *me* that."

She was so surprised, she leaned back to glare at him. "Really?"

Gabe flicked the end of her nose. "Really. Just not the one woman I wish would tell me."

She swallowed hard. Her blue eyes were round and filled with feminine daring. Gabe held his breath.

"What would you think," she asked slowly, "of me finishing school and coming back here to stay?"

Afraid to move, Gabe said, "Are you considering doing that?"

"I think, since you love me, and since I love you, it'd make sense."

He let his breath out in whoosh. "You little witch!" He laughed and squeezed her, then winced as his head pounded. "Why haven't you told me before now?"

"I wasn't sure if I'd dreamed it or if you'd want me around forever. I wasn't sure if I was making too much of things. I'm not very good at figuring out this whole romantic business. But I do love you. I can't think of much besides you."

Going for broke, Gabe said, "You know you'll have to marry me." He frowned at her just to let her know he was serious. "You can't tell a man you love him and then not marry him."

Her face lit up and her smile was radiant, despite the black soot on her cheeks and the end of her nose. "I have to finish out my semester first. But that won't be too long."

"I can wait. I don't want you to give up anything for me." Then he shook his head. "I take that back. I want you to give up your guilt. And your free weekends because I'll be coming to see you whenever you're off school. And I most definitely want you to give up any thoughts of other men, or—"

She touched his face. "Okay."

Gabe grinned so hard his head hurt. "I just love an agreeable woman."

EPILOGUE

"QUIT LOOKING so disgruntled."

Gabe frowned at Jordan, his face red, his fists clenched. "I can't believe you stole her right out from under my nose."

"She came to me willingly, Gabe. And besides, I need her."

"So do I!"

Jordan shrugged indifferently. "You can get anyone to answer your damn phones, but Elizabeth has the touch. The animals love her. More than they love me, sometimes, and that's a truth that hurts."

Gabe looked at his wife, all decked out in snowy white, her beautiful red hair hanging in long curls down her back. He wanted to get the damn reception over with so he could get her alone.

"Uh, Gabe, your lust is showing."

Gabe considered flattening his brother, but then he saw Lizzy smile and she looked so happy, he knew he had to give in gracefully. "All right, so she can be your assistant. I guess I can hire someone else." He had taken Sawyer's advice and opened a shop in town. He had more business than he could handle, but he enjoyed it so he wasn't complaining. He'd thought Lizzy would work with him, but she'd opted to sign on with Jordan, and he had to admit she had a way with animals.

She was so special she made his heart swell just looking at her.

"So magnanimous," Jordan uttered dryly. "I had no idea you had these caveman tendencies."

"I didn't, either, until I met Lizzy."

"She got a fantastic grade on her thesis. Did she tell you she's been approached about adding it to a text?"

Gabe scowled. "She's my wife. Of course she told me."

Jordan laughed, then quickly held up both hands. "All right, all right. Quit breathing fire on me. I'm sorry I mentioned it."

Thank God she'd kept his name anonymous, Gabe thought, disgruntled by the instant popularity of her *Mystique of Heroes.* He snorted. What a stupid subject. But evidently not everyone thought so; Lizzy had received several calls from men wanting her to interview them. Gabe would have liked to hide her away somewhere, but watching her bloom was a distinct pleasure, so he put up with all the other men ogling her and tamped down his jealousy.

After all, she'd married him.

Jordan nudged him with his shoulder. "She's getting ready to throw the bouquet. This always cracks me up the way the women fight over it."

Ready to get back a little of his own, Gabe said, "I noticed all those women lining up are eyeing you like a side of beef. You'll be next, you know."

Jordan shook his head, then downed the rest of his drink. "You can forget that right now. I'm rather partial to my bachelor ways."

"You just haven't met the right woman yet. When you do, I bet you get knocked on your ass so quick you won't know what hit you."

Jordan was ready to refute that when suddenly the women all started shouting. He and Gabe looked up to see that Lizzy had thrown the bouquet, but her aim was off. It came sailing across the room in a dramatic arch. Right toward Jordan.

He almost dropped his drink he was so surprised, but when the flowers hit him in the chest, he managed to juggle everything, and was left standing there holding the flowers.

Gabe laughed out loud, Lizzy covered her mouth with a hand to stifle her giggles and Jordan, seeing a gaggle of women rushing toward him, muttered, "Oh, hell."

Gabe looked at his wife and winked, then whispered to Jordan, "You better make a run for it."

And he did.

Gabe smiled as Lizzy headed toward him, looking impish and beautiful and so sexy he decided the reception was well and truly over. He kissed her as soon as she reached him, then whispered against her lips, "That was a dirty trick to play on my brother."

She grinned. "I was tired of all the women here looking at you with broken hearts. It's time for Jordan to be the sacrificial lamb."

Gabe shook his head with mock sympathy. "Damn, I feel sorry for him."

Startled, Elizabeth leaned into his side and asked, "Why?"

Taking her by surprise, Gabe hoisted her up in his arms, which left her delicate white gown loose around her legs, giving everyone a sexy peek. Over the sound of the raucous applause from all the attending guests, Gabe whispered, "Because the prettiest, sexiest, smartest female is already taken—and I have her."

Elizabeth laughed. "You are a charmer, Gabe."

He started out of the room, holding her close to his heart. Right before he disappeared through the doorway, he looked up and saw Jordan backed against a wall, women surrounding him. Gabe shook his head.

He wished his only single brother all the same love that he'd just found.

The women looked determined enough to see that he got it.

JORDAN

CHAPTER ONE

THE SWINE.

Jordan Sommerville stared at the hand-painted sign positioned crookedly over the ramshackle building. Visible from the roadway, the sign boasted some of the worst penmanship he'd ever seen. The bright red letters seemed to leap right out at him.

He cursed as another icy trickle of rain slid down the back of his neck. He could hear the others behind him, murmuring in subdued awe as they took in the sights and sounds of the bar. It was late, it was dark, and for September, it was unseasonably cool. Surely there didn't exist a more idiotic way to spend a Friday night.

The idea of trying to convince a bar owner to institute a drink limit, especially a bar owner who had thus far allowed quite a few men to overimbibe, seemed futile. Jordan started forward, anxious to get it over with.

Somehow he'd become the designated leader of the five-man troop, a dubious honor he'd regretfully accepted. The men had been organized by Zenny, a retired farmer who was best described as cantankerous on his good days. Then there was Walt and Newton, who claimed to be semi-retired from their small-town shops, though they still spent every day there. And Howard and Jesse, the town gossips who volunteered for every project, just to make sure they got to stick their noses into anything that was going on.

Jordan stopped at the neon-lighted doorway to the seedy saloon and turned to face the men. A strobing beer sign in the front window illuminated their rapt faces. Jordan had to shout to be heard over the loud music and laughter blaring from inside the establishment.

"Now remember," he said, and though he used his customary calm tone, he infused enough command to hold all their attention, "we're going to *talk.* That's all. There'll be no accusations, no threats and absolutely, under no circumstances, will there be any violence. Understood?"

Five heads bobbed in agreement even as they looked anxiously beyond Jordan to the rambunctious partying inside. Jordan sighed.

Buckhorn County was dry, which meant anyone who drank had the good sense to stay indoors and keep it private. There'd been too many accidents on the lake, mostly from vacationers who thought water sports and alcohol went hand in hand, for the citizens to want it any other way.

But this new bar, a renovated old barn, had opened just over the county line, so the same restriction didn't apply. Lately, some of its customers had tried joyriding through Buckhorn in the dead of the night, hitting fences, tearing up cornfields, terrorizing the farm animals, and generally making minor mayhem. No one had been seriously injured, yet, but in the face of such moronic amusements, it was only a matter of time.

So the good citizens of Buckhorn had rallied together and, at the suggestion of the Town Advisory Board, decided to try talking to the owner of the bar. They hoped he would be reasonable and agree to restrict drinks to the rowdier customers, or perhaps institute a drink limit for those that leaned toward nefarious tendencies and overindulgence.

Jordan already knew what a waste of time that would be. He had his own very personal reasons for loathing drunks. He would have gently refused to take part in the futile endeavor tonight, except that he and his brothers were considered leading citizens of Buckhorn, and right now, due to a nasty flu that had swept through the town, Jordan was the only brother available to lead.

With a sigh, he walked through the scarred wooden doors and stepped inside. The smoke immediately made his lungs hurt. Mixed with the smells of sweat and the sickening sweet odor of liquor, it was enough to cause the strongest stomach to lurch.

The dank, dark night worked as a seal, enclosing the bar in a sultry cocoon. The walls were covered with dull gray paint. Long fluorescent lights hung down from the exposed ceiling beams, adding a dim illumination to an otherwise gloomy scene.

Men piled up behind Jordan, looking over his shoulder, breathing on his neck, tsking at what they saw as salacious activity. Which didn't, of course, stop them from ogling the scene in deep fascination. Jordan could almost feel their anticipation and knew the evening was not destined to end well.

Hoping to locate someone in charge, Jordan looked around. A heavy, sloping counter seated several men, all of them hanging over their beers while a painfully skinny, balding man refilled drinks with the quickness of long practice. At the end of the bar stood a massive, menacing bouncer, the look on his face deliberately intimidating. Jordan snorted, seeing the ploy for what it was; a way to keep the peace in a place that cultivated disagreements by virtue of what it was and the purpose it served.

There were booths lining the walls and a few round tables cluttering up the middle of the floor. Overall, the place seemed crowded and loud, but not lively. An atmosphere of depression hung in the air despite the bawdy laughter.

Then suddenly the noise of conversation, clinking glasses and rowdy music died away. In its place a heavy, expectant hush filled the air. Jordan felt the hair on his arms tingle with a subtle awareness. Everyone stared at a low stage to the left of the front door, almost in the center of the bar. It couldn't have been more than eight feet wide and ten feet long. A faded, threadbare curtain at the back of the stage rustled but didn't open.

Jordan stared, feeling as mesmerized as everyone else, though he had no idea why. Behind him, old man Zenny coughed. Walt eased closer. Newton bumped into his left side.

Slowly, so slowly Jordan hardly noticed it at first, music from a hidden stereo began to filter into the quiet. It crackled a bit, as if the speakers had been subjected to excessive volume. It started out low and easy and gradually built to a rousing tempo that made him think of the *Lone Ranger* series. All the men who'd previously been loud were now subdued and waiting.

The curtain parted just as the music grabbed a bouncing beat and took off like a horse given his lead. Jordan caught his breath.

A woman, slight in build except for her truly exceptional breasts, burst onto the stage in what appeared to be an aerobic display except that she moved with the music...and looked seductive as hell.

He'd seen his three sisters-in-law do similar steps while exercising, but then, his sisters-in-law didn't have breasts like this woman, and they were always dressed in sweats when they worked out.

And they sure as certain didn't perform for drunks.

Nearly spellbound, Jordan couldn't pull his gaze away. His mouth opened on a deep breath, his hands curled into fists and his body tightened. The reaction surprised him and kept him off guard.

As he stared he realized the woman wasn't exactly doing a seductive dance. But the way she moved, fluid and graceful and fast, each turn or twist or high kick keeping time to the throbbing beat, had every man in the bar—including Jordan—holding his breath, balanced on a keen edge of anticipation.

She wore a revealing costume of black lace, strategically placed fringe, and little else. The fringe glittered with jet beads that moved as she moved, drawing attention to her bouncing breasts and rotating hips. Her legs were slender, sleekly muscled. She turned her back to the bar, and the fringe on her behind did a little *flip—flip—flip.* Jordan's right hand twitched, just imagining what that bottom would feel like.

He cursed under his breath. The costume covered her, and yet it didn't. He'd seen women at the lake wearing bikinis that were much more revealing, but none that were sexier. She kept perfect time with the heavy pulsing of the music and within two minutes her shoulders and upper chest gleamed with a fine mist of sweat, making her glow. Her full breasts, revealed almost to her nipples, somehow managed to stay inside her skimpy costume, but the thought that they might not kept Jordan rigid and enrapt.

Next to him, Newton whispered, "Lord have mercy," and the same awe Jordan felt was revealed in the older man's voice. Jordan scowled, wishing he could send the men back outside, wishing he could somehow cover the woman up.

He didn't want others looking at her. But he could have looked at her all night long.

His possessive urges toward a complete stranger were absurd, so he buried them away behind a dose of contempt while ignoring the punching beat of his heart.

The audience cheered, screamed, banged their thick beer mugs on the counter and on the tabletops. Yet the woman's expression never changed. She didn't smile, though her overly lush, wide mouth trembled slightly with her exertions. She had a mouth made for kissing, for devouring.

Her lips looked soft and Jordan knew with a man's intuition exactly how sweet they'd feel against his own mouth, his skin. Every now and then she turned in such a way that the lighting reflected in her pale gray eyes, which stared straight ahead, never once focusing on any one man.

In fact, her complete and utter disregard for her all-male audience was somehow arousing. She looked to be the epitome of sexual temptation, but didn't care. She might have been dancing alone, in the privacy of her bedroom, for all the attention she gave to the shouting, leering spectators.

Feigning nonchalance, Jordan crossed his arms over his chest and decided to wait until her show ended before finding the proprietor. Not because she interested him. Of course not. But because right now it would be useless to start his search, being that everyone was caught up in the show.

Despite his attempt at indifference, Jordan's gaze never left her, and every so often it seemed his heartbeat mirrored her rhythm. Beneath his skin, a strange warmth expanded, pulsed. Something about her, something elusive yet intrinsically female, called to him. He ignored the call. He was not a man drawn in by flagrant sexuality. No, when a woman caught his attention, it was because of her gentleness, her intelligence, her morals. Unlike his brothers—who were the finest men he knew—he'd never been a slave to his libido. They'd often teased him about his staid personality, his lack of fire, because he'd made a point of keeping his composure in all things. *At least most of the time.*

His eyes narrowed.

Short, golden brown curls framed her face and were beginning to darken with sweat, clinging to her temples and her throat. It was an earthy look, dredging up basic primal appetites. Jordan wondered what those damp curls would feel like in his fingers, what her heated skin would taste like to his tongue. How her warmed body would feel under his, moving as smoothly to his sexual demands as it moved to the music.

As the rhythmic beat began to fade, she dropped smoothly to her knees, then her stomach. Palms flat on the floor, arms extended, she arched her body in a parody of a woman in the throes of pleasure. The move was blatantly sexual, deliberately seducing, causing the crowd to almost riot and making Jordan catch his breath.

Her face was exquisite at that moment, eyes closed, mouth slightly parted, nostrils flaring. Jordan locked his jaw against the mental images filling his brain—images of him holding her hips while she rode him in just that way, taking him deep inside her body.

He wanted to banish the thoughts, but they wouldn't budge. Anger at himself and at the woman conflicted with his growing tension.

He knew every damn man in the place was imagining the same thing and it enraged him.

In that instant her eyes slowly opened and her glittering gray gaze locked on his. Jordan sucked in a breath, feeling as though she'd just touched him in all the right places. They were connected as surely as any lovers, despite the space between them, the surroundings and the lack of prior knowledge. Her eyes turned hot and a bit frightened as they filled with awareness.

Then she caught herself and with a lift of her chin, she swung her legs around and came effortlessly to her feet.

Scowling at the unexpected effect of her, Jordan tried, without success, to pull his gaze away. There was nothing about a mostly naked vamp dancing in a sleazy bar for the delectation of drunks that should appeal to him.

So why was he so aroused?

He hadn't had such a staggering reaction to a female since his teens when puberty had made him more interested in sex than just about anything else. But he'd grown up since then. He was a mature, responsible man now. He was...

The music died away to utter silence. The hush in the room was rich and hungry.

She wasn't beautiful, Jordan insisted to himself, attempting to argue away his racing heartbeat, his clenched muscles and his swelling sex. In fact, she was barely pretty. But she was as sexy as the original temptation, her appeal basic and erotic.

Over the silence, Jordan detected the sound of her heavy breathing with the force of a thunderclap. A roar of approval started the massive applause, and within seconds the room rocked with the sounds of masculine appreciation and entreaties for more. Jordan continued to watch her, not smiling, not about to encourage her. He waited for her to meet his gaze again, but she didn't. She looked straight ahead, deliberately ignoring him.

Anger simmered inside him, warring with lust.

Slowly, still struggling for breath, she took a bow. He hadn't noticed until that moment that she wore high heels. Amazing, he thought, remembering how she'd moved, the gracefulness of her every step. Her legs looked especially long in the spiked heels.

She tottered slightly as if in exhaustion, appearing young and vulnerable for the space of a heartbeat. Money was thrown onstage, some of it hitting the open urn positioned at the edge, most of it landing around her feet. She didn't bend to pick it up or acknowledge the money in any way. She merely stood there, as proud and imperious as a queen while the men payed homage, begging her for more, emptying their pockets.

If Jordan hadn't been watching her so closely, he wouldn't have seen her hands curl into fists, or the way her soft mouth tightened. With one last nod of her head, she turned to leave the stage. That's when the trouble started.

Two men reached for her, one catching her wrist, the other stroking her knee and thigh.

A wave of rage hit Jordan with such force, it nearly took him to his knees.

He couldn't dispute his own reaction, and started toward her. At almost the same time, the bouncer pushed himself away from the back wall, but Jordan barely noticed him. He kept his gaze on the woman's face as she tried to pull her hand free, but the drunken men had other plans. One of them attempted to press money into her hand while he suggested several lecherous possibilities, egged on by his buddy.

Others seconded the drunks' suggestions, throwing more money, making catcalls and urging her to another dance... and more.

She firmly refused, and again tried to step away. Her gaze sought out the bouncer, but he'd been detained by a table full of younger men who were insisting the woman should continue.

Jordan reached the edge of the stage just as she said, "Go on home to your wife, Larry. The show's over."

Her deep throaty voice was filled with loathing and exhaustion. It affected Jordan almost as strongly as the sight of the drunk's rough hand wrapped around her slender wrist. He barely restrained himself from attacking the man, and that alone was an aberration. Jordan had never considered himself a violent or overly aggressive person.

"Let the lady go."

Reacting to the command in Jordan's tone, the man released her automatically, only to turn on Jordan with a growl.

"Who the hell are you?" As he asked it, Larry took a threatening step forward.

Jordan gave him a stark look of contempt. In as reasonable a voice as he could muster, considering his mood and the obstreperous noise of the bar, he said, "You're drunk and I'm not. I'm bigger in every way. And right now, I'd like to tear you in two." Jordan watched him, his gaze unwavering. "Does it really matter who I am?"

Larry reeked of alcohol, as if he'd been at the bar all day. Perhaps that accounted for his loss of good sense. But for whatever reason, he disregarded Jordan's warning and attempted a clumsy punch. Jordan leaned back two inches so that Larry's limp fist whipped right past his jaw, then he stuck his foot out, gave the smaller man a shove, and sent him sprawling. Larry screeched like a wet hen, but when he hit the dusty barn floor he landed hard, and he didn't look sober enough to get back up.

"Oh, for heaven's sake…" The dancer's words were muttered low, but Jordan heard her. He glanced up. The other man stepped back quickly at the look of menace in Jordan's eyes. Unfortunately, he still had his hand hooked around the woman's knee and his sudden retreat pulled her off balance. With a loud gasp, she stumbled right off the edge of the low stage and would have landed next to Larry if Jordan hadn't caught her.

The impact of her small, lush body caused Jordan to stumble, too, but he easily regained his balance and, acting on pure male instinct, wrapped his arms tightly around her bottom. Her belly landed flush against his lower chest, her ripe breasts pressed to his face. Jordan stood, for a single instant, stunned.

Her small hands felt cool on his burning skin, the contrast maddening. Braced against his shoulders, she pushed back and Jordan was able to see her angry face.

"Are you *insane?*" she demanded.

"At this moment?" Jordan asked, unable to concentrate on anything of import, not with those incredible breasts a mere breath away. "I believe so."

He held very still, feeling trapped by her nearness, by

the deep timbre of her voice, her warm, gentle weight, her seductive movements. Her body was lithe and supple, soft, despite her determination to push away from him. Acutely aware of one firm breast pressing into his jaw, he could see far too much cleavage to allow for divided attention.

Her black lace bodysuit dipped low in front, displaying the paleness and lush roundness of her breasts; the material was so sheer he could plainly make out the outline of her puckered nipples, thrusting noticeably against the material. His mouth went dry. He was so hard he hurt.

He wanted to taste her.

Contrary to all reason, to the situation, to the crowd around them, *to his own basic nature,* he wanted to draw her into the heat of his mouth, lick her, taste her, hear her husky moans. He'd only need to turn his head a scant two inches and…

His breath came faster, his stomach cramped.

Her naked thighs were sleek and smooth and warm against his forearms, which he had crossed beneath her bottom. Up close, her overdone makeup was even more apparent—but then, so was her allure. Jordan met her gaze and they each stalled.

Her pale skin was tinged pink from exertion and embarrassment. Her nose was narrow, tilted up on the end like an innocent pixie's, her mouth so full and soft he could almost feel the effect of it against his skin, making his body throb. Her face was a perfect oval, her cheeks a little too round, her chin a little too stubborn. But those arctic gray eyes…

He'd never seen any like them.

Her breath caught sharply as he studied her mouth. With a burst of near panic, she began her struggles anew. Her efforts to free herself from his hold set them off-kilter and Jordan fell back a step.

A rickety table overturned as he bumped into it, spilling

several drinks. Jordan, feeling a little drunk himself as he breathed in the smell of her musky, heated skin, especially strong between her soft breasts, attempted to regain his balance and apologize at the same time.

He wasn't given a chance. This time the man swinging his meaty fist had better aim. Jordan quickly tried to set the dancer on her feet even as he ducked. He wasn't fast enough to do either.

His head snapped back from a solid clip in the jaw. Pain exploded, but Jordan didn't lose his hold on the woman. In fact, his arms felt locked, unable to open even when he wanted them to.

Ears ringing from the blow, Jordan allowed his anger to erupt. Because of how he held her, that fist had come entirely too close to touching a woman.

His head now clearer, Jordan gently released his feminine bundle and moved her behind his back, keeping her there when she attempted to stall the fight. He eyed the man who'd struck him, and with a sharp, lightning-fast reflex that was more automatic than not, Jordan used the backward sweep of his bent arm to slam his elbow into the man's jaw. His blow was far more powerful than the one he'd received, and the man sank like a brick in water. Other than his arm, Jordan hadn't moved—and his mood was deadly.

All hell broke loose.

The bouncer who'd just witnessed Jordan's retaliation came charging forward. Jordan sighed. He wasn't a regular, which he supposed meant he was automatically tagged as the troublemaker.

Looking quickly around for the older men who'd come with him, Jordan found them safely ensconced in the far corner near the front door where they could watch while staying unharmed. He didn't have time to breathe a sigh of relief.

The bouncer grabbed Jordan's arm and jerked him forward. Normally Jordan would have attempted to talk his way out of the confrontation. He wasn't, in the usual course of things, a combative man. But the bar had opened up to a free-for-all. Chairs flew around him, bottles and glasses were thrown. Men were shouting and punching and cursing.

Jordan locked his jaw. He needed to get the woman out of harm's way, and he needed to take his cohorts back to Buckhorn. Before he had time to really think about what he would do, he ducked under the bouncer's meaty arm and came up behind him. The guy was huge, easily four inches taller than Jordan's six foot one, with a neck the size of a tree trunk. Jordan gripped the man's fingers and applied just enough negative pressure for the big guy to issue a moan of pain. Jordan wrapped his free arm around the bouncer's throat and squeezed.

"Just hold still," Jordan said in disgust, wondering what the hell he should do now. He ducked a body that came staggering past, inadvertently hurting the bouncer further. Damn, things had gotten out of hand.

Jordan wasn't a fighter, but he had grown up with two older brothers and one younger. Being the pacifist in a family full of physical aggressors, he'd been taught to give as well as take. Not that he and his brothers had ever had any serious fistfights. But his brothers played as hard as they fought, so Jordan had learned how to hold his own.

Morgan, his second oldest brother, was built like a solid brick wall and Jordan had practiced up on him most of his life. There were few things that Morgan enjoyed more than a good skirmish. And though he was beyond fair, Morgan always finished as the victor.

Jordan knew how to handle the big ones. Morgan had generously seen to that.

Sirens sounded outside, adding to the confusion. In strangled tones, the bouncer demanded to be released, but Jordan ignored him, maintaining his awkward hold and refusing to lose the upper hand. Using the large man as a shield, Jordan turned to the woman and shouted, ''Get away from here.''

She hesitated for only a moment, sending a regretful look at the money scattered across the stage. Then her gray eyes met his and she nodded her agreement. But before she could go, her eyes widened and she looked beyond Jordan. He twisted just in time to avoid getting hit from behind. The bouncer ended up taking the brunt of the blow, which left him cursing and very disgruntled, but still very alert. Jordan raised his brows. It was a good thing he'd immobilized the big bruiser, because he wasn't at all certain he could have bested him face-to-face.

He turned back in time to see the woman scrambling up onto the stage. In her retreat, she gave Jordan a delectable view of her bottom in the skimpy costume. Despite his precarious position—having his arms filled with an outraged bouncer—Jordan felt his heartbeat accelerate at the luscious sight of her. She was almost to the curtain when several policemen charged through the doors.

With a feeling of dread, Jordan saw the officers draw their guns as they issued the clichéd order of *"everybody freeze."*

Zenny, Walt, Newton and the others were nowhere in sight, having evidently made a run for it when they heard the sirens. At least they'd managed to avoid this situation, Jordan thought. In fact, he'd be willing to bet they were already halfway back to Buckhorn, anxious to begin spreading tales of his night of debauchery. This was likely more excitement than any of the older citizens had experienced in many years, and the only thing that might compare would be the joy of telling others about it.

Jordan's thoughts were interrupted when a young officer climbed onto the stage and approached the dancer. She looked like she wanted to run, but instead she faced him with a defiant pose and began arguing. Dressed as she was, her attitude was more ludicrous than not. A mostly naked woman could hardly be taken seriously.

Jordan started toward her, bustling the bouncer along with him, meaning to intervene. But before he'd taken two steps another officer stepped in front of him. All around them, men were shouting curses and arguing, which did them no good at all. Having no choice, Jordan released the bouncer, who began shaking his hand and cursing and promising dire consequences. He was quickly handcuffed and urged into the crowd of men being corralled outside. The officer turned to Jordan with a frown.

Knowing there was no hope for it, Jordan merely held out his hands and suffered the unique experience of being handcuffed. Beside him, men attempted to argue their circumstances, and were shoved roughly out the door for their efforts. Jordan shook his head at the demeaning display while still keeping one eye on the woman. Someone, he thought, should at least offer to let her get dressed.

"You're not from around here, are you?" the officer asked Jordan.

"No, I'm from Buckhorn." He gave the admission grudgingly, but he already knew there was no way to keep this stupid contretemps from his brothers. They'd rib him about this for the rest of eternity.

The officer lifted a brow and grinned with a good deal of satisfaction. "That's a break. You can just wait in my car while I notify the sheriff of Buckhorn. He can deal with you himself and save me the trouble."

When the officer started to pull him away, Jordan asked, "The woman...?"

"I'd worry about my own hide if I was you," he said, then added, "That Buckhorn sheriff is one mean son of a bitch."

Since the sheriff was none other than his brother Morgan,

Jordan was already well aware of that fact. He lost sight of the woman as he was escorted outside through the rain and into the back seat of a cruiser where he cursed his fate, his libido and his damned temper, which had chosen a hell of a bad time to display itself. The car he'd arrived in was long gone, proving his supposition that the others had headed home.

The car door opened again and an officer helped the woman inside. She faltered when she saw Jordan sitting there, staring at her in blank surprise. "Oh, Lord," she whispered with heartfelt distress. She dropped back into the seat and covered her face with her hands. "Just when I think the night can't get any worse...."

Jordan breathed in the scent of her rain-damp skin and hair, acutely aware of her frustration, her exhaustion. He settled into his seat and realized that despite how she felt, the night had just taken a dramatic turn for the better as far as he was concerned.

CHAPTER TWO

"You LIVE IN Buckhorn?" he asked, which was the only conclusion he could come up with for why she was now in the car with him.

When she didn't answer, the officer gave him a man-to-man look and said, "According to her license, she does."

Jordan leaned forward to see her face, but with her hands still covering it, that wasn't possible. He gently caught her wrists and tugged them down. Their handcuffs clinked together.

Softly, attempting to put her at ease, he asked, "Whereabouts? I've never seen you before." And he sure as certain would have remembered if he ever had. Even if she'd been fully clothed and doing something as mundane as shopping for groceries, he felt certain he'd have paid special attention to her. There was something about her that hit him on a gut level.

Just being this close to her now had his muscles cramping in a decidedly erotic way. Like the effects of prolonged foreplay, the sensation was pleasurable yet somewhat painful at the same time, because of the imposed restraint.

Their gazes met, his curious, hers wary and antagonistic. She looked away. "Where I live," she said under her breath, "is no concern of yours."

The officer answered again, disregarding her wishes for privacy. "You know that old farmhouse, out by the water tower? She moved in there."

The woman glared at the officer, who did manage to look

a bit sheepish over his quick tongue. He leaned farther into the car to remove her handcuffs and place her purse in her lap. Jordan stared at her narrow wrists while she rubbed them, feeling his temper prick at the thought that she might have been hurt.

She wore no jewelry—no wedding band.

The officer spared him a glance. "If I remove your handcuffs, too, do you think you can behave yourself?"

It rankled, being treated like an unruly child, but Jordan was too busy staring at the woman to take too much offense. He silently held up his hands and waited to have them unlocked. The woman stared out her window past the officer, ignoring Jordan completely.

"What are we waiting for?" Jordan asked, before the officer could walk away.

"The chief agrees that Sheriff Hudson can deal with the both of you. Our jail is overcrowded as it is, and it's going to be a late night getting everyone's phone calls out of the way. Just sit tight. Hudson's already been called."

Jordan groaned softly. Morgan had his hands full taking care of Misty tonight. She was laid low with the nastiest case of flu Jordan had ever seen, and with their baby daughter to contend with, Morgan wouldn't appreciate being called out. Of course, his brother Gabe or one of his sisters-in-law, Honey or Elizabeth, would gladly give a helping hand. But that meant they then ran the risk of getting the flu, too.

Jordan forced his gaze away from the woman and dropped his head back against the seat. "I'm never going to hear the end of this."

She shifted slightly away from him, though she was already pressed up against the door. Jordan swiveled his head just a bit to see her. The night was dark with no stars visible, no moonlight. Shadows played over her features and exaggerated her guarded frown. She looked quietly, disturbingly miserable. And she was shivering.

No wonder, he thought, calling himself three kinds of fool. The outfit she wore offered no protection at all from the rainy night air. Though it was September, a cool wet spell had rolled into Kentucky forcing everyone into slightly warmer clothes. Jordan studied her bare shoulders and slim naked limbs as he removed his jacket. It was damp around the collar, but still dry on the inside, and warm from his own body heat.

Aware of her efforts to ignore him, he held it out to her, his gaze intent. "Put this on," he told her, using his most cajoling tone. "You're shivering."

Very slowly, she turned her head and looked at him with the most distant, skeptical expression he'd ever seen on a female face. "Why are you talking like that?"

Jordan started in surprise. "Like what?" he asked, not quite so softly or cajoling.

Her frown was filled with distrust…and accusation. "Like you're trying to seduce me. Like a man talks to a woman when they're alone together in bed."

Jordan couldn't have been more floored by her direct attack if she'd clobbered him. Totally bemused, he opened his mouth, but nothing came out.

She made a sound of disgust. "You can stop wasting your time. I'm not interested. And no, I don't want your jacket."

Taken off guard, Jordan frowned. All his life, women had told him he had the most compelling voice. He could lull a wounded bear to sleep or talk grown men out of a fistfight. At the ripe old age of thirty-three, he'd garnered a half dozen wedding proposals from women who said they loved to just listen to him talk, especially in bed.

But right then, at this particular moment, he didn't even

think about trying to be persuasive. He even forgot that he *could* be persuasive.

"Don't be a fool," he growled. "You'll end up catching your death running around near naked like that."

Her arms crossed over her middle and her neck stiffened at his exasperated tone. A heavy beat of silence passed before she rounded on him. Her eyes weren't cool now. They were bright and hot with anger.

"I can't believe you got me into this fix," she nearly shouted, "then have the nerve to try to seduce me and—"

"I wasn't trying to seduce you, damn it!"

"—and to criticize me!"

Distracted by the way her crossed arms hefted her breasts a little higher, Jordan was slow to respond. He managed to drag his gaze up to her very angry face again, and he scowled. "*I* got you into this fix? Honey, I'm the one who was trying to help you out!"

She thrust her jaw toward him in clear challenge. She was so close, her sweet hot breath pelted his face. "I'm not your damn *honey,* mister, and I didn't need your help. I deal with Larry in one way or another nearly every night. He's a regular at the bar—a regular drunk and a regular pain in the butt. But I know how to handle him." Her lip curled, and she added with contempt, "Obviously, you don't."

Jordan let his hand holding the jacket drop to the seat between them. Never in his life had he been at such a loss for words. He rubbed his chin, scrutinizing her until she squirmed. Good. Her discomfort, in the face of her hostility, gave him a heady dose of satisfaction.

"Ah." He cocked one brow. "I think I understand now."

"I seriously doubt that."

He shrugged. "I suppose any woman with enough guts to display herself as you did tonight must know how to handle the pathetic drunks who want to grope her. I'm sorry I interfered. Would Larry have given you a bigger tip?''

She choked on an outraged breath. ''You hypocrite! I had you pegged from the start. You sit there and condemn me, yet you were at the bar, weren't you? You'll gladly watch, even as you look down your nose at the entertainment.''

Jordan leaned closer, too, drawn to her like a magnet, wishing he could lift her into his lap and hold her close and feel all that angry passion flush against his body. She practically vibrated with her fury, and for some fool reason it turned him on like the most potent aphrodisiac.

''I was there,'' Jordan said, ''to protest the place, not to support your little display.''

Her eyes widened and her chest heaved; Jordan couldn't help it, he stared at her breasts. They were more than a handful, shimmering with her frustration, creamy pale and looking so soft. His palms itched with the need to scoop those luscious breasts out of her bodice and weigh them in his hands, to flick her nipples with his thumbs until they stiffened, until she moaned.

He swallowed hard and met her gaze, knowing his look was covetous, knowing that she knew it, too.

''So,'' she said, and to his interest, she sounded a bit breathless despite her efforts at acerbity, ''you're a vigilante? One of those crazy people who protests all the sinners, people who drink or dance or have fun of any kind?''

''Not at all.'' They were both so close now, a mere inch separated them. She wasn't backing off any more than he was, and her bravado served as another source of excitement. He'd never met a woman like her.

Jordan felt the clash of wills and the draw of sensual interest. ''My only concern,'' he murmured, distracted by her warmth, her scent, ''is the inebriated men who leave the bar and enter my county. *Your* county. They've caused

a few problems which I'd like to see taken care of before
someone ends up hurt or even killed.''

Her gaze dropped to his mouth. Jordan drew a deep
breath, trying to remember what it was he had to say. ''I
had intended to talk to the owner, nothing more. But then,
I didn't realize you liked being felt up by Larry.''

Her gaze jerked back to his. Her bottom lip quivered
before she stilled it, making Jordan wonder if it was caused
by upset at his nasty words—*why* was he being nasty, damn
it?—or from the distinct chill of the night. He felt the first
nigglings of shame for baiting her. In the normal course of
things, he never intentionally insulted women. He was gentle and understanding. But this wasn't a normal night, she
wasn't the average woman, and his reactions to her were
as far from the expected as he could get.

''He touched my leg,'' she said succinctly, ''and before
he would have touched anything else, Gus would have
stopped him.''

''Gus?'' A tiny flare of jealousy took him by surprise.

''The bouncer. The one you…''

''Ah.'' Jordan saw a hint of color sweep over her face
and touched her cheek with his fingertips, gently smoothing
a damp curl aside. ''The big bruiser I stopped from knocking me out. Why the hell was he attacking me, anyway?''

She didn't protest his touch. They were both breathing
too hard, too fast. She lifted one delicate shoulder in a way
that made her breasts shift, teasing him with the possibility
of gaining a peek at her taut nipples. He was disappointed
to see she stayed securely inside the bodice. Jordan shook
his head and tried to force himself to concentrate on their
conversation, impossible as that seemed.

''He doesn't know you,'' she said. ''And you looked—''
She peeked up at him, a slight frown marring her brown.
''Well, you looked furious.''

''I was furious.'' His voice dropped to a whisper, making

her eyes, shadowed and cautious, widen on his face. "I thought someone was going to hurt you."

Her lips parted.

Outside the car, one man struggling against being arrested fetched up against the door closest to the woman. She jumped, letting out a startled gasp. Without even thinking about it, Jordan clasped her shoulder, offering comfort and reassurance. Her soft skin tempted him and it was all he could do to keep the touch impersonal, to keep from caressing her. But she also felt cool against the warmth of his hand, making him frown.

A lot of activity was going on around them, though he hadn't been aware of it moments before. Above the din of complaints and drunken shouts, Jordan heard the sheriff arguing that he'd been called one time too many to the bar, and now he was forced to actually do something, just so he could get some peace.

Apparently that *something* was a series of arrests, and it didn't matter that Jordan hadn't been drinking, that he hadn't started the fight, and that he'd had nothing to do with the other numerous times the disgruntled sheriff had been summoned.

"Nice place you work at." Jordan continued to smooth his fingers over her skin, unable to force himself to move away from her.

"It pays the bills," was her straightforward reply, then she suddenly seemed to realize his touch and turned to glare at him.

Jordan again held up the coat. "Do you really want my brother to see you looking like that?"

"Your brother?"

"The Buckhorn sheriff. If I know Morgan, he's liable to be here any minute. I'm sure I'll get the brunt of his anger, but believe me, there'll be a heady dose for you, too, since he'd had his evening all planned and it didn't include a jaunt out into the rainy night. Wouldn't you rather be wearing a little more armor than lace and fringe?''

Her hands knotted together in her lap. ''Do you think he'll keep us for the night?''

She looked so fragile and delicate, so damn young, Jordan had a hard time reconciling the confident, aloof vamp she'd been on the stage with the concerned, shivering woman she was now. She simply didn't strike him as a person hardened to life, a woman brazen enough to be comfortable with her earlier display.

It was Jordan's turn to shrug. ''Who knows? He has no tolerance for ignorance, regardless of the fact we're related. But then again, he's very fair and you and I weren't to blame for what happened in there.''

Her glare said differently. Jordan smiled. ''Okay, so you think I was to blame. Is that any reason to sit there freezing?'' He traced the line of her throat with one fingertip. ''Your skin is like ice.''

A slight shudder ran through her and her eyes closed. Jordan stared, feeling what she felt, the connection, the instantaneous sexual charge. Like a touch of lightning, it sizzled along his every nerve ending, making him so acutely aware of her he hurt. He'd never known anything like it and he had no idea how to deal with it. He wanted, quite frankly, to pull her down into the seat and strip off her costume and cover her with his body. He wanted to warm her with his heat. He wanted to take her, right now, right here, to brand her with his touch.

There were no gentle words of admiration in his mind, no thoughts of cautious seduction. He felt savage, and it shook him.

After a shuddering breath, she moved away from his caressing fingers and accepted his coat. He helped her to slip it on, watching her contortions in the limited space of the back seat, seeing the thrust of her breasts as she slipped first one arm though, then the other. She lifted slightly to settle it behind her, and Jordan petted the material down her narrow back, all the way to the base of her spine. She felt supple and firm and he relished the sound of her quickened breath.

He smiled at how the sleeves completely hid her hands, curiously satisfied at seeing her in his coat and feeling somewhat barbaric because of it. She trembled so badly she couldn't quite manage the buttons. Jordan brushed her small, chilled hands away and did them up for her. In a voice affected by being so close to her, he whispered, "Better?"

"Yes, thank you."

Her voice, too, sounded huskier than usual, proving to Jordan that he wasn't sinking alone. No. Whatever strange affliction he felt, she felt it, too.

The urge to touch her again was strong, and he gave into it, tucking a damp curl behind her ear. Her hair was as soft as her skin, baby fine, intriguing. It was cut into various-length curls that moved and bounced when she turned her head. Along her nape, the hair had pulled into adorable little ringlets. He lifted those small curls out of the collar of his coat. "I'm Jordan Sommerville," he said, and heard the increasing rush of her breath.

Staring down at her hands, she replied, "Georgia Barnes."

"Georgia? As in a Georgia peach?"

"Don't start." Then she blinked and looked up at him. "Sommerville? I thought you said Sheriff Hudson was your brother?"

"Half brother," Jordan explained. He felt the old bitterness rise up, nearly choking him.

Her head tilted in a curious way. "The sheriff is your younger brother?"

"No. Morgan is the second oldest, right behind Saw-

yer.'' Jordan didn't feel like explaining. If he was in Buckhorn, he wouldn't have to, because everyone there knew
everyone else's business. In fact, he decided she must either
be very new to the area or very isolated, not to have already
heard the stories herself.

There was no disapproval in her tone when she asked,
''Your mother has been married twice?''

Jordan sighed, seeing no hope for it. At least Georgia—
what a name, probably just used as a stage name—was
talking to him. ''My mother's first husband died in the
service after giving her two sons, Sawyer and Morgan. She
married my father, but not for long because he became a
miserable drunk shortly after the wedding.''

He saw her eyes glittering in surprise, saw her soft mouth
open. Jordan cupped her chin and touched her bottom lip
with his thumb, hungry for the taste of her, as unlikely as
that seemed. He barely knew her, and for the most part he
didn't like what he did know, but he felt as though he'd
wanted her forever.

Without meaning to, without even wanting to reveal so
much, he added, ''By all accounts, my father was the type
of man who would have loved this bar—as well as that
little show of yours.'' Slowly, he looked her over in his too
large coat, her honey-brown hair wispy and curled with
perspiration and rain, her flamboyant makeup smudged.

Her slender bare thigh rested only a few inches beside
his, taunting him with its nearness. His hand was large
enough that he could cover the entire front of her thigh
with his splayed fingers. He could caress her skin, parting
her legs as he inched higher and higher until he cupped her,
felt her heat, her softness. The material of her bodysuit
would offer no obstruction at all. He could…

He muttered a low curse. With the drizzling rain outside
sealing them in, her musky scent seemed to permeate his
brain. It filled him with lust so strong he felt it in his heart-

beat, tasted it on his tongue. He'd never been thrown so off balance in his entire life.

''My father,'' Jordan said in a raw voice, ''would have been right up there with the others, sweetheart, throwing money on the stage, urging you on, and doing his damndest to buy your favors. But seeing you tonight...'' He hesitated and his hand opened on the back of her head as he thrust his fingers through her silky hair, urging her closer, watching her pupils expand wildly. ''...I can almost forgive him for that.''

Jordan's words trailed off into a whisper as her eyes slowly closed, her lips parting on a hungry breath. Her invitation was clear, and he leaned toward her, already growing hard in anticipation of taking her mouth. He couldn't believe this was happening, and he couldn't stop it.

She gave a soft moan as he kissed the very corner of her lips, and another when he tilted his head and brushed his mouth over hers. Her lips parted on the third moan and Jordan took her, his tongue immediately sinking deep, his mind shutting down on everything except the hot taste of her, the wild, savage way she made him feel.

A loud rapping on the window jarred him out of his lust-fogged stupor.

Georgia jumped back, gasping, one hand at her throat as her face drained of color. It didn't take a rocket scientist to know she was mortified, that she'd been as carried away as Jordan. He leaned past her to see his largest brother scowling through the window.

Morgan's hair was plastered to his skull, his face was unshaven and he wore a plain T-shirt and jeans, testimony to the fact that he'd been at home, not on call. He must have driven at top speed, Jordan realized, to have gotten to the bar so quickly.

Morgan's requisite badass look was firmly in place, the one that had kept Buckhorn citizens in line for some time now—the same look that made them all respect him as a man fully capable of handling any situation.

Not in the least daunted by that black expression, Jordan shoved his door open and stepped out of the car, addressing Morgan over the roof. "You've got about the lousiest damn timing of any man I've ever known!"

Morgan, red-eyed and looking mean, made a sound reminiscent of a snarl. "I'm leaving that distinction to you, Jordan. And you better have one helluva good excuse for this, otherwise I'm liable to kick your ass all the way home—where my sick wife and fussing baby girl are waiting."

Jordan prepared to blast him with his own ire, made hotter out of unreasoning sexual frustration. But he'd barely gotten two sputtering words out before Georgia shoved her door open, making Morgan back up a pace. She climbed out of the police car, faced him with a serene expression fit for a queen, and said, "You can handle this little family squabble later. I, for one, would like to get this over with so I can get home."

IT WAS ALL Georgia could do to keep herself from trembling. The man staring down at her had the most ferocious demeanor she'd ever witnessed on man or rabid dog. Besides being enormous, he was dark and so layered in thick muscle she felt dwarfed beside him.

And here she'd thought Jordan was huge.

Actually, the two men were of a similar height, but where Jordan appeared athletic, lean and toned, this man looked like he could eat gravel for breakfast.

Despite her resolve, she began quaking like a wet Chihuahua. And then suddenly Jordan was at her side.

"Knock it off, Morgan. You're scaring her."

When Jordan's hands settled on her shoulders, she didn't move away. She should have, being that Jordan had the power to turn her knees to jelly and her insides to fire. *She'd let him kiss her.* The reality of that wasn't to be borne.

The man had the most sinfully seductive voice she'd ever heard, even when insulting and baiting her. She'd done the unthinkable, all because his voice had softened her, melting away her will and her resolve. She scowled at herself, feeling the shame claw at her. She didn't like men—not at all. Not for friends, certainly not for lovers.

Most definitely not for a one-night stand, which from what she could deduce, was what Jordan Sommerville was after. He'd made no pretense of liking her or approving of her in any way. The arrogant jerk.

She forced herself to meet the sheriff's gaze. "Actually, you're not. Scaring me, that is." The lie sounded credible even to her own ears, though neither man seemed to believe her. "So if it's all the same to you I'd just as soon get out of this rain and get going."

Morgan snorted, eyeing her with a mix of clear annoyance, and perhaps a touch of approval. "So anxious to spend a night in jail, are you?"

She nearly staggered. "Jail? But…" Her stomach suddenly felt queasy, her knees weak. She couldn't, absolutely couldn't stay away all night. Swallowing hard, and hating what she had to say even before the words left her mouth, she forced herself to meet the sheriff's gaze. "I have to go home. Tonight."

Morgan's eyes narrowed. "Got a husband waiting for you?"

She shook her head and felt a raindrop slither down her nose. "Two children."

Jordan's hands bit reflexively into her shoulders. "*What?*"

Georgia felt hemmed in by testosterone. The sheriff looked too grim by half, and she could feel the tension radiating off Jordan. She shifted her shoulders slightly at the pressure of his fingers and he loosened his hold, then turned her around to face him.

"You have kids?" His eyes were like green fire.

She lifted her chin. "Yes."

The shock on his face was replaced with disgust. "Where the hell is your husband?"

She owed him nothing, certainly no explanations. "Ex-husband. And I have no idea." Jordan's brows smoothed out, and she added, "But wherever he is, I hope he stays there. Now, are you done with your interrogation?"

The sheriff snorted. "Maybe you should ask me that."

Jordan, no longer looking like a thundercloud, pulled her behind his back. Georgia couldn't see around him, but she heard him plain enough as he addressed his brother.

"You're not going to arrest her, Morgan, and you know it, so quit taking your bad temper out on her."

The sheriff seemed to be spoiling for a fight. "Or what?"

"Or I'll tell Misty."

Georgia had no idea who Misty was or why her name would make the sheriff relent, but that's exactly what happened. Sheriff Hudson still sounded annoyed, but no longer so angry. "It's a lousy night for you to do this to me, Jordan."

"Yeah, well, it wasn't my idea for you to be called, you know."

"No? What was your idea? To start an all out brawl? I thought you came along to see that there was no trouble, not to insure that there was."

"I didn't cause the trouble. I was only…"

His words trailed off as Georgia stepped around him and headed for the bar. If the fool men wanted to stand around in the rain and discuss the situation to death, that was fine with her. But now that she felt certain she wouldn't be locked up, she had a better way to spend her time.

Before she'd gone five feet, Jordan's hand closed around her elbow. "Where do you think you're going?"

With a sigh, she drew up short and turned to face him. She shook back one of the long sleeves of his jacket to free a hand, and then shoved her hair out of her face. Her makeup, she knew, was a disaster.

Not that she cared.

Jordan's hold on her arm was gentle. His light brown hair hung over his brow, now more wet than otherwise, and his eyes reflected the bar lights, appearing almost...hungry. She looked quickly away. "I've got money on the stage. If I don't get it now, Bill will abscond with it and I'll have wasted the night for nothing. Since you two don't seem in a big hurry to rush off, and the other sheriff is apparently done inside—"

"Bill?"

He did seem to get hung up on every male name she mentioned. "The owner of the bar. The man you came to see before you got...sidetracked." She tried to pull away but Jordan wasn't letting go.

He turned to Morgan. "Can you give us just a moment?"

"Just." Morgan didn't look happy over the concession, but then, she doubted that this one ever looked happy. "Malone will only stay in bed when I'm there to force her to it. Otherwise, you know how she is. She'll be up and running around, making herself feverish again...."

"We'll be quick. Why don't you go warm up the car?"

With a shrug, the sheriff turned away. Georgia watched him go with relief. "Who's Malone?"

"His wife, Misty."

So it was his wife that Jordan had threatened him with? That seemed curious to Georgia.

"Why does he call her Malone...never mind." Disgusted with herself, Georgia turned away. She didn't care about these men or their strange ways. She walked briskly into the bar, doing her best to ignore the warm touch of Jordan's hand on her arm as he kept pace with her. Even through his coat sleeve, she could feel his strength, his heat. And for some absurd reason, she reacted to it. He had her thinking things she hadn't thought in years, contemplating pleasures she was certain didn't even exist.

Bill was just scooping up the money off the stage when they walked in. Jordan released her and she marched forward, saying sweetly, "Why thank you, Bill. I so appreciate you looking after my money for me."

Bill had the kind of slick good looks that he assumed would get him anything he wanted from women. To Georgia, his perfectly styled blond hair, dark blue eyes, and capped teeth only emphasized what a fraud he was. She didn't trust him one iota and never would.

Bill flashed her a surprised look. "Georgia! I thought you were gone."

"Almost." She stuck out her hand expectantly and Bill tucked the money closer to his chest. "I'm waiting," she said, well used to having to deal with Bill and his miserly ways. Like most men, he had a self-serving streak a mile wide, a selfish attitude whenever it came to money and he didn't hesitate to screw someone when he thought he could get away with it.

"What about the damages to my bar?" he blustered, and cast a nasty look at Jordan Sommerville.

Georgia glanced at Jordan, too, and saw that he had an expression almost as fierce as his brother's. It was the same look he'd worn earlier, when Larry had held on to her wrist. He'd said he was furious...because he thought she might be hurt.

She turned away. "That wasn't my doing, Bill, and you know it. Take up your grievances with the boys locked away. But give me my money." When Bill still dithered, looking undecided as to whether or not he had to obey, she narrowed her eyes and said, "You know I can dance any-where, Bill. Don't push me. I need the money."

With a foul curse that would have embarrassed her as little as a month ago, Bill thrust the wad of bills into her hands. Most of them were ones, but altogether, it should amount up to a hundred dollars or more, money she needed to make repairs to the house she'd recently bought. With a sugary sweet, utterly false smile, she muttered, "Thank you."

She turned to Jordan, saw his look of contempt, and sniffed. Sanctimonious jerk. "I'm ready if you are."

Jordan held the saloon door open for her and kept stride with her on the way to the large black sport utility vehicle his brother drove. Some official car, she thought, eyeing the shiny black four-wheel-drive Bronco.

The two sheriffs had been talking, but as she and Jordan neared the vehicle, they parted ways. Sheriff Hudson got behind the wheel.

The rain had almost let up, but a chill had settled in that seemed to seep into her bones. Her bare legs were freezing and she'd somehow managed to step into a puddle, getting both feet soaked. She would have changed clothes, but the sheriff was in an obvious hurry to get going and she didn't want to push her luck. The quicker she got this over with, the quicker she could get home. She was so weary she ached all the way down to her toes and more than anything she needed a good night's sleep.

But once she got home, there would be chores to do. If she didn't get some of the laundry taken care of, they'd all be running around naked. She had no doubt the sink was full of dishes, and there were bills that had to be paid before she lost her utilities.

She was so drawn into her thoughts, she nearly tripped over Jordan when he held the front door of the Bronco open for her. Belatedly, she realized he expected her to ride to the sheriff's station sandwiched between two overwhelmingly male bodies.

"I'll sit in back," she offered, hoping she sounded merely casual, not concerned.

Jordan narrowed his gaze on her. "You'll ride up front. I want to talk to you."

He appeared determined and unrelenting, so she looked past him to see the sheriff. "Excuse me," she said, and Morgan Hudson turned his head to look at her, then lifted one black brow. "I'd prefer to ride in the back like any other criminal being arrested."

Morgan opened his mouth to say something, but snapped it shut when she yelped. Jordan's hands were secure on her waist as he literally tossed her into the front seat and climbed in beside her too quickly for her to do anything about it. He looked at his brother and said, "Drive," and with a slight, barely suppressed chuckle, the good sheriff did just that.

CHAPTER THREE

GEORGIA STEAMED, she was so angry. At herself as much as at the two outrageous, oversized men. They'd driven a few minutes in silence when she finally couldn't hold it in any longer and growled, "I don't like you."

Jordan started, evidently surprised that she'd spoken after being quiet for so long. And Morgan grinned. She'd already decided that the sheriff was either frowning or grinning—there wasn't much middle ground.

"Which of us are you talking to?" Morgan asked.

She was just disgruntled enough to bark, "Both." Unfortunately, Jordan seemed unfazed by her pique and Morgan was amused.

She was still pondering what to do and how to get everything done tonight when Jordan gave Morgan directions to her home, telling her without words that he was indeed familiar with the old farmhouse she'd bought.

But more important than that, she realized they were taking her straight home, rather than to the station.

"Excuse me," she said, giving her attention to the sheriff while doing her best to ignore Jordan pressed up against her side, "but if you're only going to take me home, why did I just leave my car at the bar? Do you realize what a nuisance this will be now for me to get it?"

Morgan shrugged. "Don't worry about your car. We'll take care of it in the morning. Isn't that right, Jordan?"

Jordan made a noncommittal sound that she wasn't interested in deciphering. "I don't *want* you to take care of it!"

Jordan stared out his window. Morgan glanced at her, then back to the road. "Not much choice, now. There was a lot going on. I figured it'd be easier this way, rather than hassling with the arresting sheriff. He wanted you two taken off, so I took you off. And as to that, I suppose I should give you a ticket or something." She watched the sheriff rub his thick neck, as if pondering a difficult predicament. "You see, the thing is, Jordan said you weren't to blame and I've never known him to tell me a pickle. But I gotta say, I am curious as hell as to why you were picked up, why you were there in the first place, and why you're dressed that way."

He leaned around to see Jordan, and added, "And what the hell you've got to do with it."

Though she knew the sheriff was only trying to distract her, Georgia stiffened. "He has nothing to do with me! But he did attempt to intervene…well, sort of…"

Jordan made another exasperated sound and interrupted. "I don't need you to explain for me, Georgia."

She shrugged, stung by his biting tone. "Fine." Crossing her arms, she leaned back in the seat, silent again.

Morgan began to whistle. After a moment, he said thoughtfully, "I think I have it figured out."

"Morgan," Jordan said by way of warning.

"You're a dancer at the bar, right?" At her stiff nod, he continued. "And Jordan here got a little too enthused over your…skill. Understandable. Although Jordan is a little slow on the uptake sometimes, at least where women are concerned—"

"Oh, for God's sake."

Georgia listened, fascinated despite herself.

"You see," Morgan said in something of a whisper, leaning toward Georgia, "in the last few years my brothers and I have all tied the knot. All except Jordan, and that leaves him sort of vulnerable to all the hungry single ladies looking to get hitched. He's so busy trying to fend them off, he's forgotten just how pleasant a nice, warm woman can be.''

Georgia blinked. "I really don't think—"

"It's obvious to me that old Jordan here has lost his finesse. I'd be willing to bet he tried to defend your honor or something like that, is that right?''

Jordan growled, but Georgia paid him and his nasty temper no mind. This night had been endless and she'd had just about enough. "You think, perhaps, that I don't have any honor to defend just because I work for a living?''

Morgan surprised her by shaking his head. "Not at all. I don't make those type of assumptions about ladies. Malone'd have my head if I did, seeing as I once made a horrid assumption about her.''

Before she could ponder that particular scenario too long, Jordan slapped one hand down on the dash and twisted in his seat to face them both. "You want the nitty-gritty details, Morgan? Is that it?''

"Of course.''

Jordan glared at his brother, and Georgia could feel his hot breath as he leaned around her. Being stuck between these two big oafs was not her idea of fun. She pressed farther back in her seat.

"All right, fine." The words were ground out from between clenched teeth. "She finished dancing and some bozo started groping her leg. He wouldn't quit when she asked him to and I stepped in. Unnecessarily, it would seem, at least according to Ms. Barnes.''

Slowly, Georgia turned toward him. She heard his brother mutter, *"uh-oh"* under his breath, yet all her attention was now on Jordan.

"For your information," she said in a slow, precise tone,

"I work all week in the bar as a waitress. I deal with those bozos day in and day out. I know them, and I know just how to get them to back off. *Without* throwing any punches or starting any riots."

"Uh…" Morgan said, attempting to intervene, "Jordan actually punched someone?"

"Several someones!"

"Only two."

Morgan cleared his throat. "You dress like that to serve drinks? You must make some hellacious tips."

Contrary to what she'd just said, Georgia felt like throwing her own punch. "I dress like this to dance on the weekends because it pays a lot better than serving drinks through the week, and unlike some people—" she fried Jordan a look "—I have obligations, and have to do whatever I can to make ends meet."

The car slowed as Morgan pulled into her driveway. Even as angry as she was, a curious peace settled over her at being home. She'd loved the big old house on sight and dreamed of renovating it into a home her kids could finally be proud of, a home that would last them forever.

It needed work, no denying that. But the yard was spacious, giving the kids plenty of room to play. And the air out here in the country was clean, fresh, putting new color in her mother's cheeks. The house represented everything Georgia had ever wanted or needed for her family.

Her fist curled around the strap of her purse, now filled with the money that had been thrown onstage. With a little luck, a lot of determination, and enough fortitude, she *could* make everything right. She had to. Her options were sorely limited.

Morgan turned the car off and Georgia, pulled from her thoughts, realized Jordan was staring at her mouth. Again. Heat rushed through her like a tidal wave, stealing her breath until she nearly choked.

How did he keep doing this to her? He'd made it clear he didn't approve of her, yet he wanted her. And if she was honest with herself, she was far too aware of him as a man. *Absurd.* She'd sworn off men!

"It looks to me," Morgan said softly, "as if a couple of small obligations have been waiting for you."

"What?" Georgia twisted around at the considering tone of the sheriff's voice, only to see her son and daughter standing anxiously in the open doorway of the house, their noses practically pressed to the storm door. She knew in an instant that something was very wrong. They should have been long in bed. Her mother never let them to the door without her.

In a single heartbeat her distraction with Jordan disappeared, as did her exhaustion. All that remained was mind-numbing fear.

"Oh, God." Georgia practically climbed over Jordan, who did his best to get the door open for her and to get out of her way. He didn't even complain when her elbow clipped him in the nose and she stepped on his foot.

"Georgia, wait!"

She heard his alarmed tone as he followed her from the car, heard Morgan talking low, his words concerned. And then her daughter Lisa, only six years old, threw the front door open and dashed across the yard in her long nightgown. Georgia forgot all about the men.

"MOMMY!"

Jordan nearly slipped on the wet grass. Knowing she was a mother and seeing a little girl address her as such were two entirely different things. His heart punched hard against his ribs when Georgia dropped to her knees, unconcerned with the soggy ground, and caught her daughter up to her.

"Lisa, what is it, honey? What's wrong?"

The little girl was crying too hard to make sense. A queer

feeling of resentment—she'd left the child to dance in a bar, for God's sake—and tenderness, seeing her now, holding the child so closely, made Jordan almost breathless. He stepped closer and with a hiccup, the little girl looked up at him. She had huge brown eyes with spiked wet lashes and was about the cutest thing he'd ever seen.

Keeping a wary gaze on him, the little girl mumbled, "Grandma is sick. She won't wake up."

"Oh, my God!"

Just that quick, Georgia was back on her feet. She'd picked up the little girl and was running hell-bent across the lawn. Her high heels sank into the ground, hindering her a bit, but in no way holding her back.

Jordan rushed after her, aware of Morgan right behind him. He followed her down a short hall as she called out, "Mom!" in a heart-wrenching panicked voice.

Lisa clung to Georgia's shoulders and said in a wavering voice, "She's in her room."

They passed a family room with a television playing and every light on, toys all over the floor, then a dining room that held only one rickety table—still covered with dishes.

At the end of the hall, to the right, was a kitchen, and to the left, Georgia threw open a door then halted. Jordan could see her heaving, see the rigidity of her shoulders. Slowly, she set the girl on her feet and moved forward. "Mom?"

Jordan watched the little girl move to a corner, trying to make herself invisible. Beyond Georgia, lying in a rumpled bed, a slender woman of about sixty rested on her back, her eyes closed, her chest barely moving—until she started coughing.

Lisa cried. Jordan didn't know what the hell to do. Then Morgan was there and he went down on one knee in front of Lisa. "Hi, there. I'm the sheriff and a friend of your mom's. Are you okay?"

Lisa covered her face with her hands, hiding, and then she nodded. Seeing that Morgan had things under control there, at least as much as was possible, Jordan stepped close to Georgia and knelt by the bed. She was busy checking her mother over, her movements efficient and quick.

She glanced at Jordan. "We have to get her to the hospital. She has weak lungs and it looks like she's gotten a bad cold or something."

Jordan frowned in concern. "A cold can do this to her?"

"Yes." Georgia's voice was clipped as she moved to a portable oxygen tank and dragged it to her mother's bedside. As she sat beside her mother and pulled her into a sitting position, the older woman's eyes opened. Again, she started coughing.

"It's all right now, Mom. I'm going to take you to the hospital.

"I'm sorry, honey—"

"Hey, none of that! I love you, remember?" She glanced at Jordan. "You're going to have to take us since you left my car behind." Then, as if just realizing it, her eyes widened in alarm and she said, "Lisa, where's Adam?"

A small towheaded child peeked around the doorframe.

"They're not used to men in the house," Georgia explained, then gave her son a small smile. "Come here, sweetie. It's okay. Grandma's going to be fine."

With the oxygen over her face, the older woman did seem to be breathing easier. She kept dozing off, which alarmed Jordan, but Georgia was holding it all together. The little boy inched his way in the door. He looked to be around four and clung to his mother's knee, hiding his face in her lap.

Jordan felt thunderstruck, and at that moment, he almost hated himself.

With renewed purpose, he stood. "I can carry her out to the Bronco. Morgan—"

"I'll call it in," Morgan said before Jordan could finish. He smiled at the little girl and smoothed a large hand over her head. "Can you find some shoes and a jacket for you and your brother?"

She peeked between her fingers, then nodded.

"Good girl."

Georgia smiled an absent thanks at Morgan. "Hang on, Mom. We'll have you there in no time."

Jordan knelt beside her and added his own arm to support her mother. "Why don't you get her coat and shoes for her? I'll do this."

Georgia hesitated, her eyes on her mother's face. "Her lungs are weak from emphysema. Sometimes, if she overdoes it, she needs the oxygen so we always keep it handy. She knows—" Her voice broke and frustrated tears filled her eyes. Angrily, she swiped them away. "She knows that any kind of illness for her is serious. But…she never complains."

Jordan watched her struggle to pull herself together. He covered her hand on the oxygen mask and asked, "Are you all right?"

Lips tightly pressed together, she nodded, then pushed to her feet. She found her mother's slippers beneath the bed. When she started looking around the room, Jordan changed his mind on the coat.

"Let's just wrap her in a blanket. It'll be easier for her, and the hospital will put her in a gown when she gets there anyway." Jordan didn't say it out loud, but judging by the difficulty her mother had breathing, he thought she might have pneumonia. With his own brother being a doctor, he'd seen enough cases of it. Plus her skin was pale and dry and too warm, indicating a high fever.

Georgia took a deep breath and wrapped her mother in a pretty quilt. Jordan saw the tears glisten in her eyes again and knew he'd made a horrible mistake.

IT HADN'T taken long for them to be on their way. With the combined efforts of Morgan and Jordan, things had just fallen into place. They were obviously men accustomed to taking charge. Georgia didn't know how she felt about that, but she did know she was glad not to be alone.

Lisa and Adam were buckled into the front seat with Morgan, thoroughly distracted from any worries as Morgan let them play with his radio and turn on his lights. It amazed her that a man so large, so commanding, could summon up such a gentle tone for children. Right now, as he smiled at Adam, he looked like a big pushover, when her first impression of him would never have allowed for such a possibility.

He'd already spoken with the hospital and they were ready and waiting for them to arrive. The flashing lights, which amused her kids, were necessary; Morgan drove well past the speed limit. But at this time of night, the streets were almost clear of traffic.

"It's usually about an hour's drive to the hospital." Jordan watched her closely as he spoke, but then, he'd hardly taken his gaze off her since she'd first noticed him at the bar. "At least from our house. But I'd say you're fifteen minutes closer, and with Morgan driving and no cars on the road, it shouldn't take much longer."

Georgia realized he was trying to put her at ease. She appreciated his efforts. Morgan's, too. The kids, after their initial bout of shyness and upset, had taken to him with hardly any reserve. He had an easy way about him that would naturally draw kids.

She had a feeling Jordan would be the same when he wasn't busy tending to her mother's care. She'd seen how he'd looked at her children, the softness in his eyes. He was a man of contradictions—harsh one minute, soft the next. Always strong and confident.

At the moment, with her knees shaking and her heart

beating too fast, she resented his strength even as she relied on it. *She* had to be strong. And she never wanted to depend on another man for anything.

They sat in the back, her mother propped between them on the carpeted floor of the storage area. Georgia supported her mother with an arm around her waist, offering her shoulder to lean on.

Streetlamps glowed, their lights flashing into the moving car with a strobe effect. They cast dark, shifting shadows over Jordan's profile, but in no way detracted from his look of genuine concern. He was an incredibly handsome man, Georgia decided, and obviously very caring.

"Almost there," he said with a reassuring smile. "Just hang on." His mesmerizing voice soothed her as nothing else could. Even her mother, dozing and waking every few minutes, wasn't immune to it. Georgia held her close, but it was Jordan's hand she gripped like a lifeline, his voice that occasionally coerced her eyes open.

Georgia leaned close and kissed her mother's cheek. Everything would be all right. She had to believe that.

JORDAN KEPT HOLD of the woman's limp hand while watching her closely for any signs of distress. Her breathing was still ragged, occasionally racked by harsh coughing, but the oxygen had helped. That, and the fact that she knew she was almost at the hospital.

Georgia looked like hell. Though she tried to hide it, her own distress far outweighed her mother's. At that moment, Jordan wanted so badly to hold her close, to protect her. There seemed to be so much he hadn't understood. Her house was a shambles, inside and out. It had potential, but it would take a lot of sweat and money to make it what it could be.

Her children, adorable little moppets who had taken a cautious liking to Morgan, had her look about them. Lisa had the same golden-brown hair, though long enough to be in a braid, and Adam's hair was pale blond. They both had brown eyes, not Georgia's gray-blue, but the intensity in their gazes was the same as hers.

How the hell did she keep it all together? Between being a single parent of two young children, and her mother's health, not to mention the work needed on her house, she had her hands full.

He couldn't keep his gaze off her and glanced at her again just as she rubbed one tear-filled eye with a fist. She'd done that several times, refusing to let the tears fall, never mind that she had good reason, that most women would have bowed under the stress of the night. Her makeup was an absolute mess, leaving dark smudges on her cheeks and all around her eyes. Jordan reached into his pocket and retrieved a hanky.

"Hey," he said softly, and Georgia pulled her gaze away from her mother long enough to send him a questioning look.

He reached over and used the edge of the cotton hanky to wipe her eyes. "You look like a Halloween cat," he teased, and she gave him the first sincere smile he'd seen. It about stopped his heart. In that moment, with smeared makeup, rain-frazzled hair and a red nose, she was the most beautiful woman he'd ever seen.

Taking the hanky from him, she scrubbed at her face, removing the worst of the smudges. "I hate this stupid makeup, but Bill insists." She grinned at her mother and added, "She gives me heck about it all the time. According to Mom, I look like a call girl. But then, I suppose that's Bill's intent."

Jordan glanced at the front seat. Luckily, her kids were oblivious to the conversation. "What do you tell them?"

Almost immediately her expression turned carefully blank. She adjusted the quilt over her mother's shoulder, refusing to meet his gaze. "That I have to work. That I'm a dancer. They've seen *Muppets On Ice* and think it's something like that."

She shrugged and Jordan suddenly realized she was still wearing only his coat over a very revealing, enticing costume. He wanted to curse his own stupidity. Why the hell hadn't he thought to grab her some decent clothes before they'd left the house? Everyone in the hospital would be staring at her.

As if she'd read his thoughts, she said, "It doesn't matter." She leaned over her mother, saw that her eyes were open and alert and smiled. "Does it, Mom?"

The older woman tried for her own smile beneath the oxygen mask, and gave one slight, negative shake of her head.

Georgia sighed. "What am I going to do with you, Mom? You're just too darn good to me."

Her mother gave her a ferocious frown, and Georgia's eyes filled with new tears. She laughed to cover them up. "No, don't yell at me. Just save your breath."

Jordan couldn't bear to see her pain. "It'll be all right, Georgia."

"Yes, of course it will." She looked up at him. "I just thought of something. You two haven't been introduced. Mom, this is Jordan Sommerville, White Knight extraordinaire. And that hulk driving—don't know if you got a good look at him, but he *is* a hulk—he's Morgan Hudson, Jordan's half brother and the sheriff of Buckhorn. Jordan, this is Ruth Samson."

Jordan nodded his head formally. "Glad to make your acquaintance, Ms. Samson." He didn't bother to tell Georgia that she needn't have explained his relationship to Morgan quite so precisely. They'd all been raised together, and were as close as any full-blooded brothers could be.

"Speaking of brothers," Morgan said from the front seat

as he handed a cell phone over his shoulder to Jordan, "call Gabe and tell him to go sit on Malone. I don't want her up running around."

Jordan took the phone, and then noticed the look of guilt on Georgia's face. Their eyes met and she winced.

"I'm sorry you got pulled away from your wife, sheriff."

Morgan blared his sirens for a second as he rolled through a red light, alerting any traffic and making the kids squeal. He said to Georgia, "Don't worry about it. Gabe can handle things. And Malone will understand. She's stubborn, but she has an enormous heart."

"He's madly in love," Jordan said dryly, explaining away his brother's description of his wife. He dialed the phone and Gabe immediately answered. Jordan skipped the niceties and asked, "Who's with Misty?"

"Lizzy's looking after her," Gabe said, then: "We've been waiting to hear from you."

Jordan covered the phone and said to Morgan, "Elizabeth's with her."

"Not good enough. Malone can bulldoze her. Tell Gabe to go."

Jordan rolled his eyes. "Morgan wants you to go sit on Misty and make certain she stays in bed."

"I will. But do you need anything? Misty said you were brawling at a bar or something."

There was an undertone of laughter in his youngest brother's voice. "No, I was not brawling."

He'd thought Georgia was distracted, but at his words, one slim brow went up. Jordan shook his head and explained as briefly as possible what they were doing. "We'll be at the hospital in just a few minutes."

Gabe whistled low. "Damn. You want me to send Casey over there? He just got home from a date. His car is still warm."

Jordan thought about it for two seconds. "Yeah, that might not be a bad idea." He eyed Georgia's mostly naked legs and exposed cleavage. Turning slightly away from her, he muttered, "Have Casey bring a change of clothes, okay? From one of the women." Then he rethought that and added, "Make it a big shirt, maybe one of yours or Sawyer's."

"Chesty, is she?"

"Yeah."

Through an undertone of laughter, Gabe said, "I'll see what I can do."

"Thanks. I imagine we'll be at the hospital for a spell, and I know Morgan would like to head home."

Morgan heard him and said, "Hey, I'm in no rush." But Jordan knew that he was, that he wanted to be with Misty and Amber. A more doting father and husband had never been created.

"Will do," Gabe said. "Tell Morgan not to worry—and if you need me just give a buzz."

"Thanks, Gabe." He closed the phone and turned to Georgia as Morgan pulled into the hospital lot.

She tilted her head. "Another brother?"

"The youngest, and most recently married. With only one anniversary to his credit, Gabe still considers himself a newlywed. He's sending my nephew, Casey, here. I hope you don't mind, but I thought he could bring you—"

"Clothes. I heard."

She hadn't quite looked at him and it frustrated him. "Look, Georgia, I don't mean to criticize exactly—"

She interrupted his awkward explanation. "Believe me, I'll be grateful to get into something different." She glanced down at her own breasts and made a sound of disgust. "I don't wear this stuff by choice."

Jordan nodded, uncertain what he could say to that. She

looked hot enough to tempt a saint, and he supposed that was the main reason for wearing the outfit on stage.

To his surprise, she said, "Thanks for thinking of it."

"No problem." With her sitting so close to him, and having so much skin exposed, it was a wonder he'd been able to think of anything else. "Unfortunately, it'll take Case a little while to get here."

Morgan pulled right up to the emergency entrance, and what with his flashing lights and the earlier call, it only took about fifteen seconds before a stretcher was rolled out to the Bronco and Ruth was being taken inside.

Georgia looked overwhelmed by the speed at which things were happening. She rushed to get her kids out of the car, trying to reassure them and keep sight of her mother as she was being whisked away.

Jordan touched her arm as she started to lift Adam from the front seat. "Go on, Georgia." She glanced up at him, clearly distracted. "Get your mother settled and appease the hospital officials with all the paperwork they'll need. The kids and I will meet you in the waiting room when you're done."

She looked at him as though he was insane, cuddling her children closer in a protective gesture and attempting to walk around him. Jordan moved to her side and kept pace with her hurried stride. Both kids stumbled along while staring up at him.

Just as the automatic entry doors opened with a swoosh, he heard Morgan call out that he'd park and be right in. Jordan waved him off.

"Georgia…"

Her high heels clicked on the tiled floor. "Come on, kids. We have to hurry."

There was a note of brittle urgency in her voice that tortured him. No woman should ever be put in such a position. Jordan again took her arm, this time pulling her to a stop. The children seemed fascinated. "Georgia, listen to me."

Utter exasperation, exhaustion, and near panic filled her face. *"What?"*

Well aware of the kids' engrossed attention, and at how close Georgia was to losing it, Jordan spoke softly, giving her a very direct look. "You can trust me, sweetheart. I swear it."

She shook her head, her face pale.

"We'll be in the waiting room," he added, ignoring her refusal, "just around the corner, drinking hot chocolate and watching television and talking." He reached out for Lisa's hand, praying she wouldn't shy away from him, and let out a breath when she released her mother and moved to his side. Her shy smile showed one missing front tooth.

Jordan enclosed her tiny hand in his own. To Georgia, he said, "Did I tell you my oldest brother is a doctor? Well he is. Everyone at the hospital knows Sawyer, though he's always chosen to work from home, treating the people of Buckhorn. He has an office at the back of the house. His son, Casey, is the one who's bringing you some clothes."

She looked around and bit her lip when she saw her mother being wheeled beyond a thick white door. A nurse stood there, papers in hand, waiting for Georgia.

Jordan felt something against his side and looked down. Adam, chewing on the edge of his coat collar and staring up with big brown eyes, leaned trustingly against Jordan's thigh. His heart swelled with an indefinable affection. He put his hand on the boy's downy head and said again, "You can trust me, Georgia."

She wavered, probably aware she had few choices, then dropped to her knees. Pulling the coat collar from Adam's mouth, she said, "If you have to use the bathroom, or get hungry, tell Mr. Sommerville, okay?"

Adam nodded, then gave her a huge hug. Lisa was next. "We'll drink hot chocolate," she said, mimicking Jordan.

Georgia's smile was misty. "Okay, sweetie, but not too much. It'll keep you awake."

Adam tilted his head. "But we can't sleep here, huh?"

"Sure you can." Georgia grinned, kissed him again, then stood. "There's probably a nice soft couch for you to get comfy on. If you get tired, just close your eyes and pretend you're at home. And before you know it, I'll be right back."

Jordan watched her stride quickly to the desk, her legs looking absurdly long in the high heels. Her shoulders were stiff beneath his jacket, her hands fisted on the strap of her purse. Every line of her body bespoke tension and exhaustion and fear.

A nurse, repeatedly looking Georgia over in her sexy costume, waited for her behind the desk. After Georgia had seated herself and began digging through her purse, no doubt hunting up an insurance card for her mother, Jordan looked down at the kids. Adam raised his arms and, without thinking about it, Jordan lifted the boy. He was stocky, more compact than his sister who looked almost fey she was so slight. Small arms wrapped around his neck.

"Hot chocolate," Adam said, trying for an adolescent dose of subtlety, "sure sounds good." Jordan bit back a smile. It didn't make any sense and he knew he must be losing his mind, but despite all the chaos, despite the horrid situation and his worry for Georgia and his disapproval of where she worked, he felt good, from the inside out.

Probably better than he had in months.

Oh, hell.

CHAPTER FOUR

CASEY PULLED IN the hospital parking lot and turned off the engine. He'd driven his father's car, a spacious sedan, rather than the truck he usually favored. As he understood it, Jordan was with a woman and her two children—too many people to fit into the truck. He was anxious to hear what story his uncle Jordan told to explain all this.

But for the moment he was more concerned with how to handle Emma Clark.

The truck, being a stick shift, would have guaranteed some space between them. But the car had bench seats, and Emma scooted much too close. She smelled nice, damp from the outdoors and sweet like a female. He was far from immune. She reached for his knee before he could open his door.

"Just a second, Case." Her voice was low, throaty. "Why're you in such a hurry?"

Very calmly, Casey took her wrist and lifted her hand away. She was the most brazen girl he knew, and the most insecure. It was something in her big brown eyes, something she tried real hard to hide.

Twining his fingers with hers, he couldn't help but notice how small boned she was, how her hand felt tiny in his own. "It's almost one in the morning, Emma." The parking lot was well lit, sending slashes of light across her features, making her eyes look even bigger than usual. "What were you doing out on the road alone?"

She rolled one shoulder beneath the shirt he'd insisted

she put on. He'd been left in nothing more than an under-shirt, but that was better than seeing her traipse around half-naked. He still couldn't believe she'd been moseying down the damn highway so late, wearing her short white shorts, sandals, and a hot-pink halter top that left more bare than it covered. He'd recognized her world-class behind the moment his headlights had hit her. Of course he'd offered her a ride.

Of course she'd accepted. Emma had been after him for months.

"A shrug is not an answer, Em."

She shrugged again, smiling at him and flipping her bleached-blond hair behind her. Casey assumed her natural hair color was a dark brown, judging by her brows and thick lashes. Although that could be makeup, too. She wore a lot of it. She looked...brassy. Almost cheap. And though he had no intention of telling her so, she made him sweat.

"I got mad at my date," she said in her low drawl, "so I took off." Her mouth, shiny with lip gloss that a few of the guys had told him tasted like cherries, tilted up at the corners. "Why d'you care?"

Casey snorted at that lame explanation and defensive response, deciding not to question her further. At seventeen, Emma's idea of a date was to be picked up long enough to add to her already questionable reputation, then get dropped off again. He'd never understand her, but he couldn't help feeling sorry for her.

Just as he couldn't help wanting her.

"C'mon. I need to get inside." When he got out of the car, she scrambled out, too, and rushed around to him.

"You're not mad at me, are you?"

He pulled the bag of clothes from the back seat, sparing her a quick glance. "It's really none of my business, Emma."

She looked hurt for a moment, then the shirt slid off her

shoulder and his gaze dropped to her scantily covered chest.
He turned abruptly away.

She ran to keep up with him as he headed inside. Thankfully it had stopped raining, but the air felt too cool and
still too damp. Water dripped from every tree, shrub and
building. He felt a bit chilled. Or at least he had moments
ago, before he'd noticed that the night air had caused her
nipples to tighten.

He wouldn't look at her there again.

Once inside, he made his way to the waiting room, where
he assumed he'd find his uncles. His stride was long, a little
too fast, but a small smile curled his mouth as he remembered Gabe relaying the evening's events. His uncle Jordan
in a fight? It sounded absurd, although he'd grown up hearing stories of the few occasions when Jordan had lost it,
giving into his fierce temper. It wasn't something Casey
had ever seen, but he'd believed it was possible.

Jordan was just so…intense. Especially about things he
really believed in.

Or people he cared about.

Casey rounded the corner to the open waiting area and
stopped short at the sight of Jordan with a little boy sound
asleep in his lap. There was a chocolate mustache on the
kid, and he was snoring softly. Casey grinned. Jordan had
a poleaxed expression on his face, as if deep in thought.

Morgan sat on the floor opposite a tiny girl with a glass-
topped coffee table between them, playing Go Fish. Casey
had stopped so abruptly, Emma bumped into his back. His
breath caught as he felt her soft, young body flush against
his. Her hands settled low on his hips and she went on
tiptoe, her warm lips touching his ear as she whispered,
"Sorry."

Casey ignored her.

"Have I missed anything important?"

Jordan glanced up, then raised one finger to his mouth,

cautioning Casey to be quiet. Carefully, his movements very slow, Jordan removed the bundle from his lap and put the boy on the couch. He covered him with his coat. With a wide yawn and a little squirreling around, the kid resettled himself into a rolled-up lump and dozed off again.

Morgan laid his cards down and pushed to his feet. "'Bout time you got here." He nodded to the little girl. "Lisa here is a card shark."

Lisa—long brown hair in disheveled braids—grinned at what she obviously considered a compliment. Morgan tugged on one of those braids with affection. "Maybe she'll be gentler with you, Casey."

Casey leaned in the wide door frame. "I dunno. She's got that ruthless look about her."

Lisa looked up at him, blinked, and kept on looking. Like a natural-born flirt, she batted her long eyelashes at Casey and gave him a wide, adoring grin. She even sighed.

Morgan turned to Jordan. "Would you look at that? She's only six and even she's smitten by him."

Jordan grunted. "He's worse than Gabe."

"Or better."

Casey laughed out loud, well used to their razzing. "Kids just like me."

Morgan looked at him from under his brows. "Females just like you, you mean."

Casey shrugged. It was true, as far as it went. The females did seem to like him. Since he'd first become a teenager, they'd been after him. Not that he had any intentions of getting permanently caught.

Morgan glanced around the waiting room. It looked like chaos with empty foam cups and candy wrappers and kids shoes on the floor. "You okay here now," he asked Jordan, "or do you want me to stick around?"

Jordan stretched tiredly. "We're fine. Go on home. You're starting to get worry lines."

Case walked the rest of the way into the room, keeping
his voice as low as his uncles'. "And here I thought those
were laugh lines caused by his sunny disposition." Morgan
swatted at Casey, making him duck. "Gabe told me to tell
you that Misty is sound asleep, konked out from the medicine Sawyer gave her, so you don't have to keep fretting."

Morgan's shoulders—wide as an ax handle—softened
with relief. "And Amber?"

Thoughts of his little cousin, now nearing the terrible
twos, which on her weren't so terrible, made Casey
chuckle. "She wore herself out chasing Gabe in a pillow
fight. Last I saw her, she was as zonked as the little guy
there." He indicated the boy on the couch.

Jordan rubbed his chin, appearing somewhat exhausted
and ultimately pleased at the same time. It was a strange
expression for him. "That's Adam, Georgia's son."

"Georgia?"

Morgan leaned forward and said in a whisper, "The bar
dancer who Jordan fought over."

"I did *not* fight over her."

"Shh!" Morgan gave him a severe frown for his raised
voice.

Jordan glanced at Lisa, who was oblivious as she attempted to shuffle the cards, which sent them all flying to
the floor. "It was a misunderstanding," he growled in a
lowered voice.

Casey noticed his uncle's color was a bit high and
choked back a grin. "Hey, whatever you say, Jordan."

Morgan shook his head, then looked beyond Casey with
a questioning frown. Casey turned and saw that Emma had
backed up until she was against the wall beside a plastic
floor plant. It almost seemed she was trying to be invisible,
which of course was impossible for a girl who looked like
Emma.

He frowned. So brazen one minute—especially when they were alone—and so timid the next.

He held out his hand. "Emma, have you met my uncles?"

Her big brown eyes widened at the attention given to her, and she swallowed hard. For the first time that Casey could ever remember, her face turned bright red. "I've... um, that is, I know who they are of course, but we've never actually been introduced or anything."

Since Casey still stood there with his hand out, she finally stepped forward and took it, the embarrassed heat positively pulsing in her cheeks.

He rubbed her knuckles with his thumb, trying to reassure her. Damned if he knew why. "Emma, my uncle Jordan and my uncle Morgan."

Strangely enough, she did an awkward curtsy of sorts, then looked appalled at herself. "Uh,...hi."

Morgan grinned, which always made him look menacing. "You two out on a late date?"

"No." Casey turned her loose so fast, both his uncles scowled at him. He hadn't meant to hold her hand anyway. "I just picked her up."

Jordan raised both brows at that.

Emma pulled the shirt tight around her and folded her arms beneath her breasts. "Casey is just...giving me a ride. Home, I mean."

"But you live in Buckhorn," Morgan pointed out. "Isn't that right?"

"Yeah." Even her neck turned red. "I was...um, headed that way, but Casey said he needed to come here first, then he'd drop me off later."

Morgan glanced at Casey, then back at Emma. "If you're in a hurry to get home, I can drop you off on my way. I'm heading out now."

Jordan made a disgusted sound and stepped in front of

Morgan. Casey knew he was trying to shield Emma, since Morgan tended to always look a bit like a marauder. "You and Casey can both head out. I think they'll probably get Georgia's mother settled in her own room soon."

Emma glanced at Casey. He took his time thinking about it, not wanting to embarrass her, but not wanting to give her the wrong impression either. "You want to call your folks first, so they won't be worrying?"

"No."

She said that far too quickly and Jordan and Morgan shared a look. It didn't surprise Casey; he'd already figured out Emma's home life wasn't exactly ideal. If it had been, no way would she have been walking home alone at this time of night. Or done half the other things her reputation suggested. He turned back to his uncles.

"You're sure you don't want me to stick around, Jordan?"

Jordan gave Casey a searching look before he shook his head. "We'll be fine."

As Casey handed him the keys to the car, Morgan took Jordan's arm. "I want to talk to Jordan for just a minute, Case. Can you keep an eye on the kids?"

Lisa looked up and sighed at him again. Casey smiled. "No problem."

"Thanks. I'll bring the Bronco around and wait out front for you both."

THEY WERE barely around the corner when Morgan asked, "What the hell is Casey doing out so late with that girl?"

Jordan shrugged. "Hell if I know. But I don't think there's anything going on between them."

"Why not?"

"She doesn't look like his usual type."

Morgan snorted. "Like Georgia is your usual type?"

Jordan almost faltered. He did frown. "Who says I'm even interested?"

Morgan came to a complete stop and turned to give Jordan an incredulous look. "Well, let's see. You can't look at her without tensing up. And that hard-on you had while arguing with her might be a good clue."

Jordan flushed. And it made him madder than hell, because not a single one of his other damned brothers would have. They'd have grinned, hell, they might've even bragged. They would not, however, have turned red. But Jordan wasn't at all pleased that all he had to do was breathe in Georgia's scent and he wanted her. Bad.

Morgan shook his head. "It's a full moon tonight, did you know that? Maybe that accounts for a few things. Like Casey showing up with a girl that I know damn good and well has a reputation that far exceeds the one Gabe had at her age. And that's saying something."

"Are you sure about that?" Jordan frowned, concern for his nephew overshadowing his embarrassment. And talking about Casey was definitely preferable to talking about himself. Or Georgia. Or him and Georgia.

"Yeah. It's a long sad story and I'm too damn tired to go into it tonight. Besides, I reckon Casey has a handle on things. Though she's not eighteen yet, so if you get the chance, warn him to be careful, okay?"

Jordan nodded. While Casey was only eighteen himself, he gave the impression of being much, much older.

"At least it's stopped raining." The doors slid open as Morgan approached them. He looked outside, giving Jordan his back as he surveyed the starless sky. With a nonchalance that didn't fool Jordan for a minute, Morgan asked, "Should we expect you back at the house tonight?"

Jordan hadn't really thought about it, but now that he did... He dropped his head forward, brooding. His muscles felt tight and he rolled his shoulders, trying to relieve some of the tension.

But there was no hope for it. "She doesn't have a car," he said, stating an obvious fact. "Hers is still at the bar."

Morgan nodded. "I know."

"It doesn't seem right to leave her and two kids at a house alone, with no transportation. What if something happened? What if she no sooner got home and her mother needed her?"

"And odds are," Morgan interjected, going right along with him, "even if her mother rests easy tonight, Georgia'll still want to check on her first thing in the morning, so she'll probably need a ride. Assuming you all get to go home tonight at all." Morgan faced him again. "I can't see you leaving her here alone."

"No, I wouldn't do that." Jordan gestured at the mostly quiet hospital. "With the kids and everything...."

"Yeah." Morgan tilted his head, his expression thoughtful. "So I guess we'll see ya sometime in the morning." He stepped into the open doorway. "Let me know tomorrow if there's something I can do to help."

"Thanks."

"Oh, and Jordan?"

Wishing his damn brother would just go away, Jordan raised a brow. "What?"

Morgan grinned. "It's going to get worse before it gets better. I just thought I should let you know that."

Jordan stiffened. "You don't know what the hell you're talking about."

"On the contrary, I married Malone, didn't I? I know exactly what I'm talking about. And my advice would be not to fight it."

"It?"

"The whole chemistry thing."

"Oh, for the love of—"

Morgan shrugged. "You should just give up right now, and save yourself a pound of heartache. Tell her what it is you want. Be up front with her."

Tell her that he wanted to strip her naked? That he wanted to bury himself inside her and spend all night finding ways to make her climax—and the fact that she was a mother, that she danced for drunks, that she didn't appear to particularly like him, hadn't blunted his need one bit? "She has two children, Morgan."

"So? She's still sexy as hell. Any man who's seen her in that getup she's wearing tonight can damn sure vouch for that. Besides, the more you fight it, the worse it is. You're caught. You might as well accept it."

Morgan walked away before Jordan could correct him, before he could assure him that he wasn't *caught* at all! He was turned on, to where he couldn't seem to stop shaking, to stop wanting.

But that was all it was.

Hell, Morgan had taken one look at Misty Malone and started acting the fool. He'd fallen head over ass for her in a single heartbeat.

But he wasn't Morgan. Just as he wasn't Sawyer or Gabe. He wasn't looking for a wife, had no desire for home and hearth, and even if he was, Georgia wouldn't qualify as wifely material. Not for him.

Still, maybe Morgan was right. What did he have to lose if he told her flat out that he wanted her? She had reacted to him, he wasn't imagining that. Maybe that chemistry mumbo jumbo had some truth to it. Maybe she wouldn't mind an uninvolved sexual relationship.

Jordan swallowed hard at the mere thought, imagining her saying yes, imagining her peeling off that skimpy costume for him....

Oh, hell. *Her outfit.* If she came back to the waiting room before Jordan could head her off and give her the change of clothes, who knew how Casey might react. There was no doubt he'd be surprised, because who would expect a woman to be running around a hospital dressed as she was?

He didn't want Casey to accidentally hurt her feelings with his shock. And he didn't want his nephew ogling her either.

Unfortunately, Jordan reached the waiting room just in time to see Georgia stumble over her own feet. She stared toward Casey, who'd stood when she entered the room.

"Who," Georgia asked, eyeing the way her daughter clung to Casey's hand, "are you?"

"He's Casey," Lisa said.

Casey smoothed his dark blond hair out of his eyes, then held out his free hand. "I gather you're Lisa's mother?"

Georgia looked mesmerized, then gave him her hand. She tipped her head back to see Casey's face, before looking him over with awe. "Why, I wonder, did I think you'd look like an average kid?"

Casey grinned, showing off his killer smile and shaking her hand gently. "I don't know, ma'am."

"Is the whole family like you?"

Emma, who had been sitting quietly on the couch by Adam's feet, spoke up. "Yes, they are."

"Incredible."

Jordan stepped up behind her. "Casey brought you a change of clothes."

"Oh, yeah." Casey reached for the bag and offered it to her. "Honey, my stepmother, wasn't sure what size you might be, so she told me to apologize and explain that she sent things that would adjust." To Jordan, he said, "She refused to send her a man's shirt."

Georgia looked into the bag and pulled out white, elastic waist cotton slacks, a soft pink cotton T-shirt, and a long sleeved matching cardigan. There was even a pair of slip-on casual canvas shoes.

She glanced back up at Casey with a grateful smile. "Please be sure to tell her how much I appreciate this. And I promise to return the clothes right away."

Casey skipped a look toward Jordan before smiling. "You can tell her yourself. She said to invite you and your family over to the big cookout at the end of the month. Honey likes to show all our neighbors how much she appreciates them by having this huge get-together. It worked out real well last year, so she wants to make it a traditional gathering."

Jordan choked and considered stuffing Casey into the damn bag. Georgia, he noticed, looked panicked.

"But…" She sputtered, her gray eyes wide, "We're not neighbors!"

"You live in Buckhorn?"

Georgia nodded.

"Close enough." He ignored Jordan when he added, "You don't have to wait till then to visit though. Our house is pretty far off the main road without any other houses close by. Honey said to tell you she'd love the company anytime you feel up to visiting."

Lisa clapped her hands together, staring with naked adoration toward Casey. "Can we, Mommy, please, please, please?"

"But…"

Casey ruffled Lisa's hair, then turned to the couch, caught Emma's hand and pulled her to her feet. She tried to hang onto his hand, but Casey made that impossible. "We've got to go before Morgan leaves without us."

Georgia hustled after him. "Wait! Please, tell your stepmother—"

"Honey."

"Yes, well, tell Honey that I appreciate the offer, but I can't possibly come."

"Jordan'll bring you." Casey stared at Jordan, knowing

exactly what he was doing. His brown eyes warmed to glittering amber as he said, "He wouldn't want to disappoint Honey."

Keeping a relationship purely sexual, Jordan thought, would be pretty damn tough if the whole family got to know her. But then he looked at Lisa, and he gave up with a sound somewhere between a growl and a sigh. "No, I don't want to disappoint Honey."

Georgia held the clothes clutched to her spectacular chest, her pale gray eyes flared with dismay, her golden brown hair practically standing on end.

And perversely, Jordan said, "I insist. It'll be fun."

"But…"

He turned away and bid Casey and Emma good-night, noticing that Casey was staying just out of Emma's reach. He shook his head.

"What?"

Georgia stood beside him. He could smell her, warm and sweet, and he wanted to press his nose into her neck, taste her skin. "My nephew," he said in a rough voice, filled with lust, though she didn't seem to know it, "didn't even notice what you're wearing."

He hadn't quite realized it until he said it. But not once did Casey look her over. He'd kept his gaze respectfully on her face, his manner as polite and friendly as ever.

Georgia looked down at herself. "I know you think I should be embarrassed." She met his gaze, her eyes now somber, sad. "But I'm just too worried."

Jordan touched her cheek. That didn't seem like enough so he put his arm around her shoulders and led her to the chair Casey had just vacated. Luckily, there was no one else in this particular waiting room. Earlier a man had come in with a badly cut finger, and a woman had shown up with a twisted ankle. But they had each been attended to and no one had shown up since.

Once Georgia was seated, her hands twisting in the clothing Honey had sent, Jordan asked, "What did they say about your mother? How is she?"

He knelt in front of her, unable to stop touching her. This time his hands rested on her knees. Her skin was so incredibly warm, so silky, he wanted to part her thighs, wanted to tip up her face and kiss her deeply as he moved between her legs. Her thighs were strong, he'd seen that as she danced, and he could only imagine how tightly she'd hold him.

She didn't seem to notice his touch or his preoccupation, or else she didn't care.

Jordan shook himself. Adam snored nearby on the couch and Lisa was starting to get bored with the cards. She'd taken to deliberately scattering them, and the last time they'd flown everywhere, she hadn't bothered to pick them back up.

He had to get hold of himself. Lusting after a woman in front of her children wasn't something he ever would have done. He wouldn't do it now. Out of all the brothers, he was the one most circumspect, most discerning.

"Will she be all right, Georgia?"

Georgia nodded. "Mom has emphysema. My father was a big cigar smoker and they say it was his secondhand smoke that…" She looked furious for a moment, then started over. "She's never been a smoker herself. In fact she hates the things."

"Me, too." He took one of her hands, and she didn't pull away.

"They think she has bronchitis. With her lung disease, that's a big problem. They're going to keep her a few days, put her on IV antibiotics, do a breathing treatment every four hours or so. As soon as they get her settled in her room and I make sure she's got everything she needs, I'll be able to head home. I just don't want to go until I know—"

"Of course not. There's no rush."

She gave him a distracted, grateful nod.

"When was the last time you ate?"

She looked at him as if he were crazy. "I'm not hungry. But the kids…" She glanced over at the couch. Jordan looked, too. Lisa was still sitting on the floor, but she'd slumped sideways, sound asleep, her head mere inches from her brother's big toe.

Jordan grinned. "I fed them. It wasn't the most nutritional meal going. Just sub sandwiches from the vending machine with chips and hot chocolate."

She rubbed her forehead with a shaking hand. "I should have thought of it. Thank you. It didn't even occur to me…"

"Hey." Jordan leaned lower to see her averted face. Very gently he touched her chin. "You had your hands full."

"I'll pay you back. How much was it?"

Her polite query set his teeth on edge. "I don't want your money, Georgia."

To his surprise, she came to her feet, making him quickly stand so he wouldn't be stampeded. "It's not your job to take care of my children."

Jordan crossed his arms over his chest and stared down at her, studying her set expression. "I don't mind helping out."

Her soft lips flattened into a hard line. The way she squeezed Honey's clothes, they'd be all wrinkled by the time she got them on. Not that he was in any hurry for her to change now that they were virtually alone. The kids were asleep, Casey and Morgan had left, the hospital was quiet.

She looked incredible, sexy and tousled and earthy. His

breath came a little faster. "You're going to need more help, you know."

She rounded on him, nearly dropping the clothes. Her eyes, circled with smeared mascara and exhaustion, turned stormy gray. She kept her voice low, but it sounded like a growl. "We'll manage just fine."

"Georgia…"

Her chin lifted. "You can leave now. I'm sorry I kept you so long. I lost track of the time, but now that I know my mother will be all right, I can—"

Very gently, he interrupted her. "You know I'm not going to leave."

"Don't be ridiculous. It's…" She looked around for a clock.

"It's very late." Jordan kept his tone soft and easy, soothing her. He had no idea why she'd suddenly turned defensive, except that she probably hadn't eaten for a while, her mother was sick, and she'd nearly been arrested.

And he couldn't stop thinking about getting her naked and under him. Or over him. Or…

He felt like a complete bastard. "Listen to me, Georgia." He waited until her eyes lifted to his. "I'm going to drive you home after everything is taken care of here."

"Why?" She stared at him, her face flushed. "You don't even know me. And what you do know about me, you disapprove of. You certainly don't owe me anything."

"Georgia." He said her name like a caress. He didn't mean to, but he did. "No man would leave you here alone like this."

She laughed at that, a mean, bitter laugh. "You are so wrong."

It took a lot of effort not to get riled, not to react to his sudden suspicions. But she was too upset right now, too overwhelmed, for him to start interrogating her. There'd be plenty of time for him to learn more about her past later. He'd see to that. "How else would you get home?"

"We can take a cab." She drew a shuddering breath. "Since I got my money from Bill, I can easily afford—"

Jordan took her shoulders and pulled her closer to him, leaning down so that he could whisper. The very last thing he wanted to do was wake the children.

Her eyelashes fluttered at his nearness, but she didn't look into his eyes. She stared at his mouth instead.

"I'm taking you home, Georgia. Accept it. We'll get your car tomorrow and then you can check on your mother and, after all that, we'll talk about the cookout my family has planned."

She covered her ears with her hands and pulled away. "I have to change now. Will you…" She made a disgusted sound. "Will you stay here with Lisa and Adam?"

"Of course." Why was she covering her ears? It wasn't like he'd been being abusive. He'd offered her help. He'd been gentle, calm. He hadn't told her that he wanted her, that just touching her damn shoulders and bringing her close had nearly driven him to his knees and made him semierect.

He watched her walk away, and decided that he *would* tell her. Tonight.

He wasn't at all sure he could last another day this way.

CHAPTER FIVE

THE CAR RIDE home was mostly silent. There wasn't a single other vehicle on the road, the kids were sound asleep and the clouds had finally cleared enough to let the moonlight dance over the wet streets. Overall, it was a sleepy, relaxing, lulling ride.

But she was far from relaxed. "Jordan...I'm sorry I lost my temper with you."

Jordan glanced at her as if surprised that she'd spoken. Aside from getting her arrested, he'd been wonderful, and she'd been a raving bitch. All because he scared her.

And when she was around him, she scared herself. The man didn't need to say anything important, not even anything seductive, and she wanted him. An intolerable situation, and she was far too tired to deal with it.

She could hear the smile in his mellow, mesmeric voice when he spoke. "No problem. You've had a rough day."

Georgia made a sound of agreement, leaned her head back and closed her eyes. Maybe if she didn't look at him, if she didn't see his wide, hard shoulders, the thickness of his muscled forearms, the way his light brown hair caught the moonlight and how deep, how seductive his green eyes were when he turned them toward her—well, maybe it would help. But she doubted it. He was a sinfully gorgeous male, tall and strong and hard, but she'd seen strong attractive men before, dealt with them every night at the bar. No, it was much more than Jordan's looks, much more than his physical attributes.

All the man had to do was mutter two syllables and she wanted to melt. Something about his voice affected her deep down inside, stripping away her defenses. It made her imagine awful, wonderful things.

She shook her head, more at herself than anything he did or said. "I appreciate the ride home. And how you carried the kids out. I could have managed, but—"

"But you've had enough to deal with." He reached across the seat and his large hand squeezed her shoulder. Even through the borrowed T-shirt, his touch was electric. She caught her breath, not wanting him to know how he affected her, how amazingly turned on she was even at this moment.

She'd had very little sleep over the past two days. She'd worked a double shift and dealt with the threat of being arrested, then the gut-wrenching fear over her mother's health. She had no idea how she was going to manage to work and take care of her mother at the hospital, with no baby-sitter. Things looked very grim.

But still she wanted him when she never wanted any guy. She'd long since considered herself immune to the normal urges most women felt. So what if Jordan was an uncommonly patient and wonderful man? She shouldn't care that he was gorgeous and as finely built as a Greek statue, or that he had a voice warm enough to melt butter.

She knew he disapproved of her, and that should have taken care of the rest. But somehow, maybe because her children seemed so taken by him, his disapproval didn't matter.

"You deserve to take a break, Georgia. And I like your kids. Adam reminds me a little of Casey when he was that age. Constant motion right up until he runs out of steam."

A distracting topic if ever there was one. She gladly accepted it. "Your nephew certainly took me by surprise."

Jordan's smile was gentle and filled with pride. "He's

an amazing kid. Only eighteen, but I swear he has more common sense, more backbone and maturity than a lot of men twice his age. We pretty much raised him ourselves, you know.''

She didn't know. Since she'd moved to Buckhorn, she'd kept to herself except for her work. And she certainly hadn't tried to form any friendships at the bar. She didn't have time to gossip with neighbors, or go out of her way to get to know anyone. ''We, meaning you and your brothers?''

''That's right. Casey's mother couldn't deal with a newborn infant, and she took off. Sawyer, my oldest brother, the one who's a doctor? He was still in medical school when Case was born, but he brought him home from the hospital and that was that. I was…let's see, fifteen at the time. And I remember being absolutely fascinated. I looked up to Sawyer and Morgan a lot, and I'd always seen them in a one dimensional way, you know?''

''Yes.'' She saw most men in a one dimensional way— *selfish*. Her father, her ex, her boss, the men who threw money at her while she was on stage…. She squeezed her eyes shut at that thought, praying that none of the men were spending grocery or bill money. Some of them, she was sure, couldn't afford what they tossed at her while downing drink after drink, night after night. And if she thought about that too much, she felt miserably guilty.

But the brothers, even the nephew, had thrown her for a loop. They were unlike any men she'd ever known. Their very posture spoke of confidence and honor and respectability. She found herself intrigued.

Because she knew it had been true for her father, and true for her ex, she asked, ''Things changed a lot with a baby in the picture?''

She waited for Jordan's complaints on the hardships of

keeping up with an infant. Once again, he took her by surprise.

"I wouldn't say they changed, just adjusted a bit. In a good way. Sawyer was always so straight-faced, so serious. And then there he was, cuddling this little squirt and grinning all the time and looking so happy to change a diaper or give a bath."

Georgia stared at him. When she'd had Lisa, she'd always felt the same way. Everything her baby did she'd thought was magical and amazing. But she'd never considered that a man might have that outlook. "You're serious?"

Nodding, Jordan said, "I used to think nothing could pull Sawyer from his books, not even a beautiful woman. But if Casey made a noise, he was there, checking on him, smiling at him."

Jordan grinned with the memories, then shook his head. "Morgan was always the rowdiest. He fought for the fun of fighting. Everyone still jokes about him bordering on the side of savage."

"I can see that."

Jordan glanced at her quickly before returning his attention to the road. "He makes a hell of an impression, doesn't he? He's kept our town peaceful, usually with little more than a look. But whenever he touched Casey, he was so gentle. It boggled my mind. Now, with his own daughter, Amber, who's heading on two, he's the same. I swear he could wrestle buffalo with one arm and hold her close with the other, making sure not a one of her little curls got ruffled. He makes a hell of a sheriff, and an even better dad."

"You have an impressive family." Beyond impressive really. Having only met Jordan and Morgan, she should have been prepared for Casey. How could he have been anything less than spectacular, surrounded by such incredible uncles?

Jordan gave one nod. "Yeah, I think they're pretty great. Gabe, the youngest, started his own business not too long ago and already he's got more work than he can handle. He can build or repair anything, and after his marriage he decided he needed to get things a little more on track."

"On track how?"

"Before he met Elizabeth, he just worked when the mood struck him—or if someone needed something. He was always willing to help out. But Gabe preferred to spend his time in other pursuits. I doubt there was ever a day when he was without female company. Women flocked to him. It was almost uncanny. From the time he learned the difference between males and females, every girl in the area was after him, and he took advantage of it. They spoiled him rotten."

Jordan said that with a fond smile, making Georgia shake her head.

"The worse his reputation got, the more they seemed to come after him. It used to drive my mother nuts until she and Brett retired to Florida."

His poor wife, Georgia thought. A man like that never settled down, never really gave up his old ways....

Jordan touched her cheek. "Why are you frowning?"

She'd been so absorbed in her thoughts, she hadn't realized she frowned. "No reason."

"Come on, Georgia." He turned down the old road leading to her house. It was bumpy and filled with muddy puddles thanks to the rain. "I could almost see the evil thoughts going through your brain."

"Not evil. Just...realistic."

"Like?"

She didn't appreciate being pushed. She didn't appreciate having him affect her this way, either. Perhaps it would be best to tell him up front exactly how she felt so he'd leave tonight and not come back. That would be the most intelligent course to take.

So then why did the possibility make her feel so desperate?

Georgia cleared her throat, peeked at her kids to make certain they were still sleeping soundly. "Very well. If you're sure you want to hear this?"

"I do."

"I imagine," she said slowly, measuring her words, "that any man who's used to running from one woman to the next, to indulging every sexual whim, is not likely to settle down with only one woman, just because he says a few vows. If it's in his nature to be a...sexual hedonist—"

Jordan laughed. "Gabe is that."

"—then he'll always be a hedonist."

"True. I won't argue with you there. All of my brothers are very sexual." He glanced at her and shrugged. "There's nothing wrong with that, by the way."

Georgia didn't bother to argue with him on it. She did, however, wonder if he included himself in the "very sexual" category.

No! She did not wonder. She didn't care. Refusing to look at him, she stared out her door window and watched the passing shrubbery on the side of the road. Even in the darkness, everything looked wilted by the rain.

Without her encouragement, Jordan continued. "Gabe is still a man, still very interested in sex, and I can't see that ever changing. But now he does all his overindulging with his wife."

Lord, how had she gotten onto this subject? She felt so hot, her window was beginning to steam. "If you say so," she mumbled, hoping he'd let it go.

But of course he didn't.

"You don't believe me?" When she didn't answer, he whistled. "Must have been a hell of a marriage you had."

Georgia denied that with a shake of her head. "The marriage was fine. It was the end of the marriage that was hell."

So softly she could barely hear him, Jordan asked, "Because you still loved him?"

"No." By the time the divorce was finalized, she knew she'd been living a fairy tale, created and maintained all in the fancy of her mind. She'd seen what she'd wanted to see, not what had really been there. "No, I didn't still love him. And it didn't matter that he had never really loved me. But he never loved his kids, either. And that I can't understand."

"I'm sorry."

"Why?" His voice had that low, hypnotic sound to it again, making her insides tingle, making her breasts feel too full. It pulled at her until she wanted to lean toward him, wanted to press her face into his throat and breathe in his scent, feel the warmth of his hard body. "What difference does it make to you?"

Jordan turned into her driveway and cut the engine. "Maybe I can explain it once we get inside." His gaze, glittering bright, held her. "Go unlock your front door and I'll carry the kids in."

She quickly shook her head, dispelling the trance he'd put her in with that melodic voice. "No. Thank you. You've done enough and I insist on repaying you for your—"

"I'm walking you in, Georgia." His tone was now firm and commanding. His large hand cupped her cheek, tipping up her chin. "We have a few things to say to each other."

"We have nothing to discuss!"

"Mommy?" Lisa sat up, rubbing her eyes and looking around in confusion.

With one last glare at Jordan—where she couldn't help but notice that he appeared understanding and sympathetic still—Georgia got out of the front seat, then opened her daughter's car door. "Sweetheart, we're home." She unfastened Lisa's seat belt and smoothed her tangled bangs out of her face. "Wait right here while I go unlock the door, then I'll get Adam and we'll all go in, okay?"

She'd forgotten to turn on a porch light before they left, and the path to the front door, broken and overgrown with weeds, would have been impossible if Jordan hadn't flipped the headlights back on. Her hand shook as she struggled to get the key into the lock and open the front door. But when she turned around, she almost fell over her daughter.

Jordan stood there, Adam snuggled blissfully unaware in his arms while Lisa held on to one of his belt loops. He gave her a gentle smile and said, "Move."

Like a zombie, Georgia stepped out of the way. What choice did she have? None. As a matter of fact, Jordan, with his quiet, calm ways, had been taking away her choices from the moment she first saw him.

She closed the door and started after him, hearing Lisa direct him to Adam's room at the top of the stairs. Lisa followed him, then veered off to her own bedroom. Georgia went to her first, helping her to get her nightgown on and tucking her into bed.

"I didn't brush my teeth."

Georgia smiled and pressed a kiss to Lisa's forehead. "You'll brush them twice tomorrow morning, okay?"

"Okay. I love you, Mommy."

Tears blurred her eyes for a moment. She was just so tired. And she had so very much to be thankful for. "Oh baby, I love you, too." She scooped her daughter up for a giant bear hug. "So, so much."

"Will you tell Jordan g'night for me?"

"Of course I—"

"I'm right here." Jordan stepped out of the shadows and sat on the edge of Lisa's bed, practically forcing Georgia to scamper out of his way. He was an enormously large man and took up entirely too much space. "Thanks for helping me out so much today, Lisa. I appreciate it."

Her teeth flashed in a quick smile. "It was fun. Except for grandma gettin' sick."

Jordan stroked her hair. "You were asleep, but your mother assures me that your grandma will be fine. The doctors are going to take very good care of her, and before long, she'll be back home."

Lisa nodded, then looked back at her mother. "Who's going to baby-sit us when you go to work?"

Georgia had been standing there in something of a stupor, amazed and a little appalled at how at ease Jordan seemed to be with her daughter, and how at ease her daughter was with him. There hadn't been many men in their lives, certainly not one who would smooth a blanket and stroke back a wayward curl.

Her father had never been close to her, much less his grandchildren. He'd died without ever knowing how truly wonderful Lisa and Adam were. Her ex-husband had walked away from them without a backward glance. But Jordan Sommerville had not only cared for them, he'd done so willingly, and even claimed to have enjoyed himself.

Seeing him now, she could believe him.

The lump in her throat nearly strangled her. She did not want to like him, not at all. But it was getting harder to stick to that resolve.

Forestalling her daughter from saying too much, Georgia said, "It's all taken care of, sweetie. I'll tell you about it in the morning. But for now, you need to get to sleep. The sun will be up before you know it."

Just like that, Lisa rolled to her side, snuggled her head into her pillow, and faded back to sleep.

Jordan smiled as he stood. In a low whisper that made every nerve in her body stand on end, he said, "Children are the most amazing creatures. Awake one minute, zonked out the next.''

Georgia turned off the bedside lamp, throwing the room into concealing darkness. Only the dim light from the hallway intruded. She headed for the door. ''My children are very sound sleepers. Once they're out, not much can wake them.''

She turned to pull the door shut and found herself not two inches from Jordan. He looked down at her, his gaze lazy and relaxed. Her heartbeat jumped into double-time. She stared at his mouth—and he moved out of her way.

Georgia decided not to look at him again, but it turned out not to be a worry. He didn't follow her to Adam's room. Instead he headed back downstairs.

She found Adam still in his jeans and T-shirt, but his shoes had been pulled off and the blankets pulled over him. Her heart swelled at the sight of his teddy bear clutched in his arms. How had Jordan known to give it to him? It was a certainty her son hadn't awakened enough to ask for it. But he might have missed it in the middle of night.

She sighed, kissed him gently—which prompted a snuffled snore—and smiled. She left his room with her thoughts in a jumble, pausing in the hallway for a good three minutes while she tried to figure out how to get rid of Jordan, how to remove him without looking totally ungrateful for all he'd done.

Honesty, she decided, might be her best course. She'd simply tell him outright that she neither wanted nor needed his help—not anymore. She'd thank him for all he'd done that day, regardless of the fact that part of the trouble had been his doing.

Then she'd tell him good-night, and that would be that.

She headed into the kitchen, her back stiff with resolve, and found him making coffee. Before she could speak he

turned to her and his expression was so intense, so...
sensual, she caught her breath.

"We have to talk," he said, and just those simple words,
muttered low and rough, made her heart pound too sharply,
her body too warm. She literally trembled with need, and
it made her angry and scared and frustrated. How could he
affect her this way? He stepped toward her and touched her
cheek. "But first, why don't you go get showered and get
all this makeup off? The coffee—I found decaf so it won't
keep you up—should be done by then."

With her breath coming fast and low, her stomach in
knots, Georgia nodded. He was making her coffee, one of
her favorite things on this earth. And it sounded heavenly.
He sounded heavenly. Lord, what a combination.

She hadn't stood a chance.

JORDAN HAD himself well in check. He would stop reacting
like a teenager with raging hormones, where the sight of a
girl's panties could put him into a frenzy of carnal greed.
Hell, he could see a woman *without* her damn panties and
still control himself. He would be calm. He would explain
to Georgia that he wanted her, that he thought they should
take advantage of the incredible chemistry...no, not incredible. Just good old chemistry. Nothing special, but there
was no reason why they couldn't get together and, as mature, reasonable adults, have a brief affair.

It only made sense. There was no reason for them *not* to
indulge their mutual desire. She was a divorced woman
working in a bar. It wasn't like she was a prim and proper
virgin.

But even as Jordan listed in his mind all the reasons that
they should and could get together to take the edge off the
urgent, burning hunger threatening to consume him, he
worried that she'd refuse.

Damn, even looking at her sink full of dirty dishes made

him want her. The whole house was a wreck, and rather than make him disdainful, it drove home to him how over-whelmed she was. He looked around again and wondered which issue he should resolve first: his lust, or the fact that he was going to give her a helping hand whether she wanted him to or not.

The old house was silent except for the creaking of the pipes as she showered. His hands shook and his vision blurred as he imagined her naked, wet and soapy and slick and…

He groaned aloud. The shower shut off and he pictured her drying her lush breasts, her flat belly, her thighs….

To distract himself, he started on the dishes. She needed a dishwasher, but there was really no place in the ancient kitchen to put one. The cabinets were a tad warped, some of them mismatched, and they'd been painted many times. They weren't very deep, but there was certainly an abun-dance of them. Too many, in fact.

The linoleum on the floor, besides being of a singularly ugly design, was cracked and starting to peel. The ceiling, which he guessed to be just beneath the shower judging by the noise, had water stains, indicating that at least a few of those squeaky pipes were leaking.

He was done with the dishes, all of them stacked on a dishtowel to air dry, when the coffee finished dripping. She'd be getting dressed now… Jordan forced himself to keep busy.

Right off the kitchen was a glass-enclosed patio that opened to the backyard. Vents in the floor-to-ceiling win-dows were opened about an inch, letting in the cool, damp night air. Jordan, who needed a little cooling off, carried his coffee into that room and looked out at the backyard. Beautiful, he thought, even with the rough grounds. There was an enormous oak tree that probably provided an abundance of shade to the room during the hottest part of the day.

A padded glider, two chairs, a few rattan tables that had seen better days, and various toys scattered about filled the room to overflowing.

Light from the kitchen slanted across the floor, mixing with the softer, gentler moonlight. The wind stroked the trees, making the shadows dance. The house, while in need of repair, was perfect. It would take only a few pets—and a man—to make it a complete home.

Jordan held his coffee cup with a barely restrained grip. What was she doing now? How would she dress? He imagined she'd look vastly different in regular clothes, with her hair freshly shampooed and all her overdone makeup gone.

And then finally he heard her.

"Jordan?"

"Right here." The words, whispered low, barely made it past the restriction in his throat. He didn't turn to face her, attempting to get himself back under control first. But damn, it was impossible. It was insane.

He could smell her, he thought with an edge of urgency, sweet and warm and so damn female. Even fresh from her shower, he detected her scent. He felt like a bull in full rut.

He cleared his throat. "There's a cup of coffee waiting for you on the counter."

Her footsteps were nearly silent as she padded to the kitchen and back. He knew she was coming out to him.

"Thank you." She, too, had lowered her voice, and there was an edge of wariness in her tone. He heard her sip, then heard the creak of the glider as she sat down. "I should have known you'd make great coffee."

It sounded like an accusation. Slowly Jordan turned to face her. Moonlight touched her in selective places—over the crown of her hair, making it glow a soft gold, across her shoulders now covered in a baggy white cotton pullover, and her knees, bare from the sloppy gray sweatshorts she wore. There were thick white ankle socks on her feet.

Not a seductive outfit, at least not deliberately. But then, nothing that she'd done to him had been deliberate. Most of her face was hidden, but he saw enough.

"My God, you're beautiful." Without the makeup, she looked young and innocent and...distressed. Because of him?

Her quiet laugh was incredulous. "Hardly that. Only my mother, who loves me dearly, would ever call me beautiful."

Jordan heard the words, but he couldn't quite comprehend them. Not with her sitting there making him shake with the most profound emotions he'd ever experienced.

She laughed again, nervously this time as he continued to stare. "But I suppose anything is an improvement after the war paint, especially since it had all been smudged. I nearly scared myself when I looked in the mirror."

She took another drink of the coffee, then set the mug beside her on the floor. With a loose-limbed dexterity that amazed him, she twisted one leg up across her lap and began massaging her foot. "Now, about our talk."

Jordan looked at her foot, so small and feminine, less than half the size of his own. He breathed hard and felt like an idiot. How the hell could her feet raise his fevered urgency to the breaking point? He searched his beleaguered brain for an ounce of logic.

"You're going to need some help for the next few days." Damn, he hadn't meant to blurt that out.

She paused, looking up at him with a blank sort of disbelief. She forced a smile. "We'll be fine."

In for a penny, in for a pound.... "Who will watch your children," he asked, "while you visit your mother at the hospital? I assume you'll want to visit her?"

That got her frowning. "Of course I will! I'm not going to just leave her there...."

"I didn't think so." The love she felt for her mother, the closeness, was as obvious to him as her feelings for her children. It had pained him to witness her worry, her fear. All his life, he'd had his family around him, his mother, his brothers, ready to share any burdens, ready to support him in any way they could. But the one person Georgia had was now ailing, and it turned him inside out trying to imagine how the hell she could cope with that reality.

His own mother was the epitome of female strength, her love and loyalty unshakeable, unquestionable. She was fierce in her independence, and God help anyone who tried to come between her and her family.

He knew if it was his mother in the hospital right now, he'd move heaven and earth for her. But Georgia didn't have his financial or familial resources.

Georgia needed him, and his mother would be the first to have his head if he didn't insist on helping. As much as it pained him, he was going to have to put lust aside, at least for the time being.

"What will you do when you have to work?" Jordan asked. "Do you have any baby-sitters? Other than your mother, I mean."

Her head snapped up and she dropped her foot back to the floor. Jordan had a feeling she was ready to pounce on him. He quickly set his own coffee cup on the rickety rattan table and stepped close enough so that she couldn't come completely to her feet without touching him.

He waited, hoping, his breath held. But with no more than a wary look, she retreated.

He settled both hands on her shoulders and gave her his patented stern look. "Is it true, Georgia? Or do you have someone you can call to help out until your mother gets well?"

They were still speaking in hushed tones, and her voice sounded gruff with emotion when she answered. "Of course I have people I can call."

Jordan knelt down in front of her. His long legs encased hers; he surrounded her, wanting her to know he'd protect her, that she could trust him. "Who?"

Silence filled the room. Jordan loved the way her gray eyes darkened, making her thoughts easy for him to read. Others would consider her eyes mysterious, but he understood her. He *knew* her.

Finally, after long seconds, she shook her head.

His heart swelled painfully. "There's no one, is there?" She turned away and he whispered, "Georgia?"

"No."

Without conscious decision, he began caressing her shoulders, feeling the smoothness of her, the softness. In a tone so low he could barely hear himself, he said, "Don't ever lie to me again, Georgia. It's not necessary. Whatever men you've known—"

She laughed at that, a sound without much humor.

"—I'm not like them. You can trust me."

She stared at his mouth. "Oh, I know you're different, Jordan. No doubt about it. But don't you see? That's part of the problem."

"You want to explain that?"

"Why not?" Her hand trembled when she touched his jaw, and her voice was husky with wonder. "I've found it very easy to ignore most men, even the men yelling crude suggestions from the audience when I dance. But I can't ignore you. You make me feel different. You…affect me." Then with a frown: "I don't like it."

For the first time in his life, Jordan's knees felt weak. He sucked in air, trying to fill his lungs enough, trying to dredge up just a little more calm. This was important and he wanted it resolved.

He cupped her face, pulled her forward to the edge of her seat until her breasts were soft and full against his chest, until he could feel her thundering heartbeat, meshing with his own. "You affect me, too."

And then he kissed her.

Her lush mouth softened, warmed, under his. She made a small sound of confusion and her hands settled on his shoulders, her fingers biting deep into his muscles.

He tasted her deeply, his tongue pushing gently into her mouth, making them both groan. Jordan was a hairsbreadth away from taking her completely when he forced himself to lift his mouth away. They both struggled for breath. "This is insane," he whispered.

She nodded, staring into his eyes with a mix of wonder and fear.

"Here's what we're going to do." He used the tone that made women agree with him no matter what. He considered it successful, given that she rested her head on his shoulder and her hands still held him tightly.

"I'll see to the children," he insisted, "after I've taken care of all my appointments. With a little rearranging, I think I can be done by three each day, which means you'll have plenty of time to visit with your mother, and then get into work, right?"

With an obvious effort, she pulled herself away from him. She looked dazed, but said, "Sometimes I waitress in the afternoons, too."

Jordan barely resisted the urge to kiss her again. "You work alternate shifts?"

"No. Sometimes I work both. We…that is, I need the money. This house has a lot of repairs that have to be done and…"

It seemed the words came from her unwillingly. "Shh. I understand. When I can't make it, Casey or one of my other relatives will help out. You'll love them. They're all terrific with kids.''

She didn't reply to that, either to deny or accept his offer. Jordan looked at the weariness etched into every line of her body. It was no wonder she looked so tired, so utterly defeated. "You were finishing up a double shift today, weren't you?"

"Yes."

He lifted one hand to her cheek and used his thumb to stroke her cheekbone. "How many hours do you usually work in a day?"

"However many I need to."

Her matter-of-fact answer hit him like a slap. He looked up at the ceiling, wanting to roar with frustration. Since meeting her, he'd been indulging visions of wild lechery while she was barely able to stay on her feet. He felt like a complete and total bastard, an unfeeling—

"What is it you do, Jordan? You said you have appointments?

It wasn't easy to tamp down his anger at the thought of her working herself into the ground, especially at that sorry place. But her exhaustion was a palpable force, wearing her down, *wearing him down,* and he couldn't bring himself to add to it. He reminded himself that she needed his strength, not his temper. Not his lust.

"I'm a vet." He moved to sit beside her on the glider and as she turned toward him, he took her hand. The unusual day had brought them a closeness that might normally have taken a week or more to achieve. He'd seen her vulnerability, and her strength. But they'd had little time to actually get to know one another. He'd rectify as much of that as he could right now.

"I've always loved animals and they've always loved me. I feel gifted, because they respond to me."

"It's your voice," she said, and she smiled.

Jordan shrugged. All his life he'd heard about his mystical voice, but so far, Georgia had seemed quite capable of resisting him. "Why don't you have any pets? The yard is plenty big enough and the kids would love it."

"So would I. But pets cost money. They need food and shots and...not only would it cost too much, but I don't have much spare time left. The kids are too young to be solely responsible for a pet, and my mother does enough as it is."

Jordan decided to think on that. As isolated as she was in the big house, a dog would be ideal. He said, "I have a clinic not that far from here. That's why it'll be easy for me to help you out with the children. They like me, Georgia, so that shouldn't be a problem. And if you still have any doubts about my character, well, ask around town tomorrow. Anyone can tell you that I'm good baby-sitting material."

She looked down at their clasped hands, then tugged gently until he freed her. Scooting over a little to put some space between them, she again pulled her foot into her lap and began rubbing. In a ridiculously prim voice considering they were sitting alone in the darkness and he'd had his tongue in her mouth only moments before, she said, "I don't want to impose on you."

"I'm offering, and besides—" he tipped her face toward him "—what other options do you have?"

Her eyes closed and she sighed. "Options? I don't have many, do I? I've often wondered what my life would be like with more options."

Jordan growled out a sigh. She was the most exasperating woman he'd ever met. "I'm trying to give you some options, sweetheart."

"Don't call me that."

Jordan ignored her order. "I want you to be able to visit

your mother and work without having to worry about Lisa or Adam.''

Her eyes slanted his way, heavy with fatigue. ''You don't approve of me.''

Fighting the urge to shake her, Jordan frowned. ''Wrong. I don't approve of where you work. They're two entirely different things.''

She laughed at that, and focused on flexing the arch of her left foot with intense concentration.

Jordan caught her wrists. ''What are you doing?''

''My feet hurt.'' Her tone was abrupt, as if that particular question had annoyed her more than anything else. ''Try staying on your feet all damn day—in high heels no less— and your feet'll hurt, too.''

He flexed his jaw. He told himself to just leave. He even cursed himself privately in the silence of his own mind. But it didn't make one whit of difference. He was already so far off track, he had no idea where he was going, but was just as intent on getting there.

''Lay down.''

She reared back as if he'd struck her. *''What?''*

Jordan caught her hips and pulled her toward him so that she landed flat on her back on the flowered cushions. She was stunned for a moment, not moving, and before she could gather her wits he deftly flipped her onto her stomach. He had her feet in his lap and his gaze glued to the sight of her rounded ass in the loose shorts, by the time she started to struggle. He must have masochistic tendencies, he decided, tightening his grip on her ankles, holding her secure.

Georgia levered up on stiffened arms, gasping in outrage—until his fingers moved deeply over the arch of her left foot, then up and over her toes. She gave a long, husky, vibrating groan.

The sound of her unrestrained pleasure made Jordan

break out in a sweat. Her shoulders went limp and her head dropped forward as if her neck had no strength to hold it up. "This isn't fair."

"What?"

"A voice that seduces, perfect coffee, and now a foot massage." She groaned again. "Ohmigod, that feels good."

Jordan closed his eyes and applied himself to giving her the best damn foot rub she'd ever had in her life. "Relax," he ordered, though he was so rigid a mere touch would have shattered him.

She obeyed. She dropped flat to the glider and rested her head on her folded arms. Every few seconds she moaned in bliss, stretching her toes like a cat being petted.

Jordan was so hard he hurt. He desperately wanted to slide his hands up the backs of her firm thighs, to slip his fingers beneath the loose hem of the shorts she wore. Probably, he reasoned, she'd thought the shorts to be unappealing because they were old and gray and faded. But the material hugged her curves and they were loose enough in the legs that he could now see all the way to the tops of her thighs.

He slid his hands up her warm, resilient calves. She had excellent muscle tone, and even as he stroked her, kneading her flesh, feeling her muscles relax, he admitted he was beyond pathetic when a woman's muscle tone brought him to the edge.

Feeling like a damn lecher, he lifted one of her legs and was even able to see the edge of her panties, which—contrary to all he'd been telling himself—nearly made him erupt with carnal greed.

In a rasp totally unlike his normal seductive tone, he said, "Agree to my help, damn it."

She sighed, adjusted her head more comfortably and murmured in a barely there voice, "It wouldn't be right."

Affronted, Jordan realized she was on the verge of sleep. Conflicting emotions bombarded him. Lust was there, tearing at his resolve, making his guts cramp, but there was also a throbbing explosion of tenderness, enough to expand his heart and tighten his lungs.

"I want to help you, Georgia."

She sighed, and in the next instant started to snore softly. A reluctant smile curved his mouth. Never in his benighted life had a woman fallen asleep on him. It was a novelty he could have lived without, but then it occurred to him that perhaps this was exactly what he needed to gain the upper hand.

"Georgia?" He continued working the tendons in her feet, something he knew from experience that all women seemed to enjoy. Personally, if a female was going to rub him, he could think of better places than his feet.

She didn't reply and after he gently placed her foot in his lap, he reached up and shook her shoulder.

She never stirred.

Jordan sat back with a grin. She'd said her children were very sound sleepers and now he knew that it was an inherited trait.

Beyond his feelings of triumph—because he really did have her now—it dawned on him that she was as vulnerable as a woman could be with a man, so she must trust him to some degree. And he wasn't above taking advantage of it.

He stroked her hair, silky soft and warm. He indulged his need to touch her, to learn the textures and curves of her face, her neck, her shoulder. Her spine was graceful, leading down to that superior rump that looked so damn tantalizing there before him, like an offering.

He was an honorable man, so he kept his hands on safe ground, but he looked at every inch of her, then whispered, "I've got you now, sweetheart."

And still she didn't move.

It took a lot of willpower to walk away from her, to find a blanket to cover her with and then to walk out of the room. But he managed it; he had a lot of fortitude when something really mattered.

And this mattered. Much as he hated to admit it, it mattered too damn much.

CHAPTER SIX

GEORGIA WOKE with the sunlight bright in her face. She didn't move, at first making an attempt to orient herself. Something wasn't right. She squinted; why was there so much light?

As her eyes adjusted, she saw the huge oak in her backyard through dirty windows, stately and still, not a single leaf stirring. There must be no wind, she thought, now that the dreadful rain had obviously ended.

And then it dawned on her that she wasn't in her own bed where she should be, or she certainly wouldn't be looking at the backyard. She was, as incredible as it seemed, in the enclosed patio curled up on the glider under a quilt.

She was still putting those thoughts together in the cobwebs of her mind when she heard a faint, muffled laugh. Lisa, then Adam. They sounded happy and for just a moment she thought everything was as it was supposed to be, as it had been the day before. Her mother, an early riser, was probably making coffee and the kids liked to hang next to her, waiting for cereal, chattering nonstop. Georgia always got up when she heard the kids, even though she was still exhausted and even though she knew her mother would complain and tell her to sleep more—and then she heard another deeper, more masculine laugh.

Jordan!

She jerked upright so fast the glider rolled, nearly spilling her onto the floor. Her heart racing, she remembered everything, her near arrest, her mother's illness—that orgasmic foot rub Jordan had been giving her late last night.

She twisted to face the kitchen behind her, and sure enough, that was Jordan's rough-velvet voice whispering, "Shhh. We don't want your mother to wake up yet. She had a long night."

Adam, sounding a bit blurry as if he hadn't been awake long himself, said, "Mommy always gets up with us, even when grandma grouches at her 'bout it."

Lisa bragged, "She won't hear anything, but she always hears us. Even when we're quiet. Grandma says that's a mommy's sixth sense."

"You've got an excellent mommy." Jordan said that with conviction, and Georgia wondered if he meant it. More likely he was merely trying to appease the kids. "But today we'll try to let her catch up on sleep."

Lisa asked, "Can I have the next pancake?"

Pancake?

"Absolutely. I can't believe you've eaten two already. Are you sure they're in your belly? You didn't hide one behind your ear?"

Lisa laughed again and Adam joined her.

Georgia nearly choked. She'd been sleeping so soundly one minute, and jarred awake the next, that she felt nearly drunk as she staggered to her feet in righteous indignation and groped her way toward the kitchen. Jordan was feeding her children? He had invaded her kitchen? What in the world was he doing here so early? The kids knew better than to go anywhere near the doors without her or their grandmother. She'd reminded them again and again that they were never ever to open the door to anyone.

Georgia stopped in the entryway, her thoughts scattering at the sight of Jordan. He looked...*gorgeous.* Sinfully gorgeous. His light brown hair was mussed, his jaw rough with beard stubble, his sleeves rolled back over his thick fore-arms. And he wore an apron around his waist.

For the first time she understood the appeal of "barefoot and pregnant in the kitchen". Jordan's bare feet looked very sexy, and though he wasn't in the family way, he was being domestic—which she assumed was the point. He smiled at Lisa and it made her heart expand painfully against her rib cage. Georgia rubbed a hand under her breast, trying to ease the constriction, but it didn't help.

God, the man looked good standing at her stove. He looked good with her children, too. And he looked far, far too good in her life.

Both kids wore aprons as well, tied up under their arm-pits and with the hems dragging near the floor. They were huddled around the stove while Jordan used a turkey baster to put pancake batter on the griddle with complex precision.

"I'm an artist," he proclaimed, and both kids quickly agreed.

Curiosity swamped her, and when she finally got her hungry gaze off Jordan and onto the griddle she saw that he was making the most odd-shaped pancakes she'd ever seen. They were…well, they looked like faces. And fish. And…

"Mommy!"

Adam rushed to her, nearly knocking her off her feet as he barreled into her legs. Jordan looked up with a frown. Lisa ran to her and took her hand.

It was traditional for them to share kisses and hugs first thing in the morning, and this morning was no different.

It wasn't traditional, however, for a very large, very sexy man to be looking on. A man with noticeable chest hair showing through the open collar of his shirt. A man with very warm, appreciative eyes.

Maybe the kids hadn't let him in. Maybe—she gulped—he'd spent the night! She couldn't seem to remember anything after he'd started working on her feet. Nothing except how incredibly good it had felt.

Heat rushed into her face and Jordan smiled as if he knew exactly why she blushed. Georgia ignored him, holding both children close, relishing the feel of their small arms tight around her neck, their sweet, familiar smells. She could never truly regret the mistakes in her life, because it was those mistakes that had given her Lisa and Adam.

But that didn't mean she wanted to make those mistakes again. Having a male stranger invade her life so easily not only showed her irresponsibility, but her stupidity. She couldn't let it happen. She *wouldn't* let it happen.

She'd barely straightened when both kids began extolling Jordan's virtues, how funny he was, his culinary expertise, his artistic talent. He'd already promised to show them new kittens at his office, and to take them along the next time he had to treat a horse or cow.

Like a damn new puppy, they wanted to keep him. Forever.

Georgia ground her teeth together and concentrated on getting her sluggish brain in gear. Adam demanded her attention with the typical enthusiasm of a four-year-old boy.

It was an effort, but Georgia hefted his sturdy little body into her arms. He clasped her face and said, "We been cookin'!"

"So I see." Her words ended on a jaw-splitting yawn and since her hands were full holding up her tank of a son, she couldn't quite cover her mouth.

Jordan ushered Lisa away from the stove with a gentle touch. "Not too close, hon. I want to get your mother some coffee before she topples over, and you never know when a pancake might explode. So don't go near the griddle without me, okay?"

Lisa held her sides as she laughed, but she did as he asked, settling into her chair at the table.

Without her permission, Jordan relieved her of Adam's weight, holding her son as if he had the right, as if he'd known how unsteady she still felt, and to her further annoyance, Adam clung to him.

Cooking, coffee, foot massage, and now coddling her kids; the man knew his way into a woman's heart.

Jordan handed her the coffee cup as a replacement for Adam. "Here. You look like you could use this."

Fragrant steam rose from the cup, making the coffee impossible to resist. She took one long hot sip and felt her head begin to clear. "Nothing on earth," she said with relish, "tastes better than that first sip of coffee in the morning."

His eyes took on a warm glow. "Oh, I don't know about that." He looked at her mouth, and heat shot down her spine, doing more than the coffee had to revive her.

Jordan smiled at her as he deftly seated Adam at the table and put a square pancake on his plate. "Why don't you sit down, Georgia, and I'll tell you what the hospital had to say this morning."

Her brain threatened to burst. Georgia glanced at the clock and saw it was only eight. "You've called them already?"

"Yes. I thought you'd probably want to know something as soon as you woke."

He was right, of course. Not only did he excite her, he read her mind.

"They said your mother rested peacefully through the night and that she's doing much better this morning. The doctor will be in to see her sometime between eleven and one, so I thought you'd like to be there." He looked her over, taking in the rumpled clothes she'd slept in. "I'd planned to wake you in an hour or so to give you time to get ready."

Wake her? She was both relieved and slightly disappointed to have missed that happening. She couldn't remember the last time she'd been awakened by a man. Before the divorce, she was always the one up first. To have Jordan wake her…it would have been a novel experience.

Dazed, Georgia looked around the kitchen. For the first time she could remember since moving in, it was spotless. Not a dish out of place, other than the ones now loaded with the odd pancake shapes. The counters were all spotless, the floor clean, the sink polished. Even the toys that were forever under foot had all been put away. The dozens of colored pictures by Adam and Lisa were neatly organized on the front of the refrigerator.

She frowned and cast a suspicious glare at Jordan. Had he been cleaning all night to accomplish so much? And why would he do such a thing anyway? Her father and her ex-husband had considered that women's work.

"Would you like a pancake?"

Her eyes narrowed at his continued good humor and solicitousness. "No."

"I can make it in the conventional shape if the fun stuff scares you."

He knew damn good and well that it was he who scared her, not his ridiculous pancakes. She considered strangling him.

"They're the best pancakes I've ever tasted!" Lisa said with her mouth full, her lips sticky with syrup. Georgia saw the box of pancake mix—the same that they always used—sitting on the cabinet, and raised her brows at Jordan.

"It's all in the preparation," he explained. "Any chef can tell you that."

She drank the rest of her coffee, in desperate need of the caffeine if she was expected to spar with him after just rising. Last night had been the best sleep she'd had in ages, when she'd thought she'd be awake fretting all night.

With that superior gentleness that made her want to

smack him, Jordan took her arm and led her to a chair. "Yes, there's more coffee," he said, saving her from having to ask.

He refilled her cup and she scowled. "Cooking, cleaning, serving. What are you? My fairy godmother?"

Leaning close to her ear, he whispered, "I'm just a man who wants you, sweetheart. And we did make that wonderful agreement last night."

She straightened so abruptly she bumped his chin with the back of her head. To his credit, he didn't curse, but he did give her a long look as he rubbed away the ache. Luckily the kids were digging into their food and not paying attention.

"What agreement?" she growled as he moved away, a man without a care in the world.

"We can go over all the details, as per your request," he said easily, "right after you get cleaned up and dressed."

"I don't remember any request!"

"Oh. Well, you were very groggy. Which was why you said it'd be better to finalize our plans—you do remember the plans?—in the morning." He turned to the stove and put three round pancakes on a plate, buttered them, and set them before her.

She had no recollection of the conversation at all. Certainly not about any plans. But those pancakes...the smells were incredible, making her stomach rumble loudly. Everyone looked at her. Lisa pointed and laughed.

Jordan pulled his own chair up close to hers. "When did you eat last?"

His gaze was too perceptive, too intrusive, demanding an honest reply. The problem was, she couldn't remember. The days tended to blur together when she worked double shifts.

He shook his head. "If you're going to burn the candle at both ends, you really need to refuel, you know."

"That's mixing your metaphors just a bit, isn't it?"

"Maybe. But the point is still valid, I swear." He watched her as she took her first bite, and smiled when she closed her eyes in bliss. "Good?"

"Very." She gave him a reluctant look, and added, "Thank you."

He touched her, stroking one long finger over her cheekbone and jaw, the side of her throat. "That wasn't so painful, now was it?"

Georgia froze for a heartbeat, mesmerized by that seductive tone and achingly tender touch. Then she shook herself and looked pointedly at her children, who were watching the byplay with an absorbed fascination. She supposed having a man at the breakfast table was even more unique for them. She doubted they remembered their father much, and what they would have remembered had nothing to do with peaceful family breakfasts together.

Jordan never missed a beat. "If you little beggars are done, why don't you go get your teeth brushed and pull on some clothes while your mother and I talk?"

"Talk about what?" Lisa wanted to know.

"Why, about you both visiting Casey again today, this time at our home. I live right near a long skinny lake. Casey can take you fishing while your mother and I visit the hospital and fetch your car back home from where she works."

Lisa and Adam immediately started jumping up and down, squealing and begging.

"That's enough," Georgia said. The kids quieted just a bit, but their eyes were still bright and wide with hope.

She stared at Jordan, her face so frozen it hurt, and murmured, "That's low, even for you."

He looked guilty for a flash of an instant, then resolve

darkened his eyes. "I'm a desperate man. And we did make that bargain—"

"Kids," she interrupted, "go ahead and get dressed. And Lisa, remember you wanted to brush your teeth twice, okay?"

"Are we going to see Casey?"

Not if she could help it. "I'll have to think about it, sweetie. There's a lot I have to get done today."

The kids trailed out, dragging their feet, their expressions despondent. Damn Jordan for putting her in this position. Her children had so few outings these days, what with her working all the time. She knew how much they'd love a visit to a lake. But the more time she spent with Jordan, the weaker her stand on independence seemed to feel. She had to make it on her own. She *had* to.

When Georgia heard their footsteps at the top of the creaky stairs, she rounded on Jordan, blasting him with all her fury. "How dare you!"

After one long, silent look, Jordan began carrying dishes to the sink. "You're just being stubborn, Georgia. Why should the kids be cooped up at the hospital while you're visiting your mother? They'll enjoy being in the fresh air, and I already spoke with Casey this morning and he agreed—"

"I didn't agree." She left her chair and faced him with her hands on her hips. "They're *my* children and I know what's best for them."

"True." Jordan leaned back on the sink and silently studied her. "I'm not questioning your parenting skills, honey. It only took me about two seconds of seeing you with them to know how much you love them, and that they're crazy about you. But you did agree." When she stared at him blankly, he added, "Last night? Don't tell me you don't remember any of it?"

Her heart lurched at his continued insistence. Last night?

So much of it, once he'd touched her feet, was a blur. She'd been so tired, so stressed....

"You told me," Jordan said calmly, "that taking the kids to Casey would be fine. Sawyer is going to meet me at the hospital, and while you're visiting, he and I will fetch your car. Afterwards we'll pick up the kids and I'll take you all to dinner."

Georgia felt like a deflated balloon. Surely she hadn't discussed all that with him? But he looked so positive, so sure of himself. And she *had* been beyond weary, ready to simply cave in under the exhaustion and worry. It was conceivable that she might have said things she now couldn't remember.

She just didn't know.

Her head hurt and she rubbed her fingers through her badly tangled hair. She felt Jordan's large firm hands settle on her shoulders and pull her close. She tried to resist him and the comfort, the security that he offered. She really did. But he brought her up flush against his strong, solid body and began rubbing her back. The man's voice wasn't the only thing magical about him. His fingers were pretty amazing, too.

It had been so, so long since anyone stronger, bigger than she had held her. Her muscles turned liquid at the wondrous feel of it.

Jordan's whiskery jaw brushed her temple as he spoke. "Just stop being so defensive and think about this logically, okay? We're not bad people, sweetheart. Casey will enjoy keeping your rugrats entertained for a few hours. He adores children. We all do. And Lisa already adores Casey. He's responsible. He won't let anything happen to them."

"But—"

He tipped up her chin. "But you're still worried? Please don't be. Not now. When things get straightened out and your mother is back home, then you can give me hell, okay?''

She couldn't help but laugh. "I don't want to give you hell. It's just that…I don't understand you."

"And that worries you?"

With complete honesty, she said, "Yes."

"Well, I don't quite understand myself right now, either, so I'm afraid I can't offer any explanations. I just know I want to help out. Is that so bad?"

She searched his face, looking for answers while confusion swamped her. "We barely know each other, Jordan."

"But it doesn't seem to matter, does it?" His gaze warmed and his touch changed. Just like that, he went from comforting to being all male. All interested male. He looked at her mouth and then kept on looking. "I can't believe how you make me feel."

"Jordan?" Her lips trembled. Her entire body trembled. Nothing should feel like this, so good and so scary and so…right.

He bent toward her. His breath teased her lips as he whispered, "What you do to me should be illegal."

Oh, the way he said that! He'd turned the full power of his bewitching voice on her and, combined with the memory of that sensuous foot rub of the night before, she was a goner. "Oh, my…"

He stole her breathy exclamation with his mouth as he kissed her. Knowing that she should resist, and being able to resist, were two entirely different things. His mouth was hot, incredibly hungry, and damp. She kissed him back, unable not to. His taste was indescribable. Hot and feverish. His hands were gentle on her face, a stark contrast to the consuming carnality of the kiss, eating at her, nipping with his teeth, sucking at her tongue as he groaned low in his throat and kissed her again and again.

Her hands curved around his shoulders and the feel of him, of solid muscle, bone and sinew flexing against her palms made her insides curl with raw desire. He arched her into his body and gave her his own tongue, tasting her deeply, pressing the hard planes of his body into her softness. Her breasts throbbed and ached, their galloping heartbeats mingled, and between her thighs....

Somehow she found herself backed up to the cabinets. With no effort at all, Jordan lifted her and the second she was balanced on the edge of the counter, he stepped between her thighs. She could feel the long, hard ridge of his erection, throbbing against her. His hand curved up her side and then over her breast, and it was so wonderful she cried out.

Jordan cursed as he kissed his way to her throat, to the sensitive skin beneath her ear. "I want you."

She wanted him, too. She held on to him, unable to think beyond the need. He was between her legs, leaving her open and vulnerable and she liked it. She liked the way he moved against her, stroking her with a tantalizing touch that brought her so close to completion even though they were both completely dressed and for the most part standing. She'd never realized that such a thing was possible, but she felt her muscles tightening, felt the spiral of delicious heat curling in her belly and below.

His fingertips brushed over her aching nipple, then pinched lightly and she almost lost it, almost came right there in her kitchen with a man who was hardly more than a stranger, a man who had no compunction about taking over her life. And she simply didn't care.

The kids started to argue upstairs and Jordan lifted his mouth. He was panting hard, his body shaking. His high cheekbones were slashed with aroused color, his emerald eyes burning. Heat poured off him.

In guttural tones that turned her limbs to butter, he

growled, "I'm so damn hard right now, one touch and I'd be in oblivion." He squeezed her tighter, pressed his erection hard against her. *"One touch, Georgia."*

It appeared he expected a reply to that. But she could barely think clearly enough to stay upright on the countertop, much less know what to say. She stared at his mouth, her own open in mute surprise at all she'd felt, at how incredible a kiss and a few simple touches could be. She'd been married nearly seven years, but she hadn't known, hadn't guessed....

He muttered a raw curse. "Don't look at me like that. You're killing me."

She sucked in air and tried to think.

"Say something, damn it."

Nodding, Georgia looked around her kitchen, at all he'd done, at all he still apparently expected to do. Not just to the house, but to her as well. She knew as soon as her thoughts cleared, she'd be mortified. She'd broken her own rules, she'd breached propriety. She'd shamed herself this time more than ever before.

She met his gaze and swallowed. "I'm supposed to work tonight. I...I can't go to dinner."

HE SHOULDN'T have been so angry, but his emotions had been in a whirlwind since the first moment he saw her, and he hadn't gotten a firm handle on them yet. How could he have done something so stupid as to practically take her in her own damn kitchen, with her kids upstairs? Not only was he disgusted with his own lack of restraint, but he was madder than hell at himself for upsetting her.

Once she'd really had a chance to settle down and get her wits together, she'd looked devastated. Jordan could tell she didn't blame him. No, Georgia blamed herself, and he couldn't stand it. He'd wanted to lighten her physical load, and instead, he had added to her emotional one. He could only imagine what she was thinking, but she wouldn't look at him, and that pretty much told it all.

What was between them was damn powerful, and neither of them were coming to grips with it very well. Rather than discussing it, though, she'd informed him she had to work. Again.

Jordan put up a good front for the kids, trying to shelter them from his black mood, a mood he was afraid was partially caused by jealousy. He'd never felt it before, so he couldn't be certain, but he did know that he hated it, hated the way his muscles refused to relax, the way his stomach knotted every time he pictured her on that stage. Hiding his rage wasn't easy, but he'd take a punch on the chin before deliberately upsetting her again, or making her children uncomfortable.

He must have been somewhat successful, because the kids were subdued, but far from silent. Georgia had explained to them about hospitals, so they were wide-eyed with respect for the sick people, and apparently oblivious to his turmoil.

Despite her near stomping, Georgia's soft-soled shoes made no sound as they walked the length of the long hospital corridor. He could feel her nervousness and he wanted to protect her. He wanted to devour her.

He didn't want her blaming herself for the uncontrollable chemistry between them. And he did not want her dancing on that goddamn stage again.

They rounded a corner, the silence between them a living thing, and then they both drew up short as they saw not only Sawyer standing there, but Gabe and Casey as well. Oh, hell. His entire family just had to turn out, didn't they? If Misty hadn't been sick, no doubt Morgan would have been here now, too.

They were likely enjoying his predicament. He'd always been different from them. More withdrawn. More self-

contained. Though he never doubted their love, he often
felt like an outsider; because of his father, there were things
he'd never be able to share with them. Like the pride of
their male parentage.

Knowing he'd gotten himself mired in an emotional con-
flict probably had them all rubbing their hands with glee.
They just loved it when he fell into the same traps that
grabbed them. It happened far too often for Jordan's peace
of mind.

Lisa, being a natural-born flirt, smiled widely at the sight
of Casey and took off at a run to see him. Casey grinned
and knelt down to catch her. Adam quickly followed suit,
but he was a bit more cautious, keeping one eye on Sawyer
and Gabe.

Georgia had come to a complete and utter halt. She just
stood there frozen, apparently as appalled as he felt. Jordan
could have told her it wouldn't do her any good.

Sawyer started forward with a wide smile and a warm
glint in his dark eyes. "Georgia?"

She nodded, staring up at him. Jordan heard her swallow.
"Yes?"

Sawyer, damn him, hugged her. He put his arms right
around her, as if she were a member of the family or something, and cradled her to his chest with a great show of
affection.

Jordan saw red and had to struggle not to huff like a
bull. Luckily Sawyer released her right away.

"It's so nice to meet you," Sawyer said. "Casey has
told me quite a bit about you."

Her eyes were still round, her expression awed. "You're
Casey's father?"

"Yes." Sawyer glowed with pride whenever he spoke
of Case. "I understand he'll be doing a spot of baby-sitting
today. We're all looking forward to it. Especially my wife.
Now that we have our own little one—six-month-old

Shohn—and with Morgan's daughter Amber, Honey's finding she really adores children. She's never had much chance to be around older children, so this'll be a real treat for her."

Jordan knew what his brother was doing, making it sound like a damn favor to him if Georgia didn't hesitate to let him take the kids. He'd told Sawyer on the phone that she hadn't quite agreed yet. But now, well...Sawyer's performance should clinch it.

He glanced at Georgia to see how she was reacting to Sawyer's long-winded introduction. He wasn't really surprised to see that her mouth was still open as she stared up at him. There was an innate compassion to Sawyer that drew women; they felt safe with him.

Then Gabe sauntered forward and Jordan thought she might faint. He cursed low even as he clasped her arm to steady her. Everyone ignored him.

"Hi, there," Gabe said, flashing her with his most engaging grin, and Georgia couldn't even blink. When Gabe waited, still smiling, she managed to lift one hand and flit her fingers in a feeble wave of greeting.

Jordan heaved a disgusted sigh. "Why are you all here?"

Sawyer shrugged. "I came because you asked me to. Gabe tagged along so you wouldn't have to leave Georgia here alone. He'll drive your car and drop me off to get Georgia's car, then we'll both be back. Casey is going to go ahead and take the kids to meet Honey, since she's practically bouncing with excitement."

Sawyer spoke as if the plans had all been finalized, attempting, no doubt, to head Georgia off at the pass, so to speak.

But at the mention of her offspring, Georgia came out of her stupor. "This is ridiculous. You're all going to so much trouble—"

"Not at all." Gabe winked at her, rendering her mute

again. He had that effect on all women, it seemed. Even his wife wasn't yet immune. He'd ask Elizabeth if she'd like mashed potatoes, and the woman would blush scarlet. It was uncanny.

"It's no problem at all," Gabe assured her. "And for the record, my wife is anxious to meet the kids, too. We don't have any of our own yet. Not that I'm above trying, you understand—"

Jordan stepped in front of him. "You know, Georgia, since Sawyer is here anyway, why don't we let him take a peek at your mother? He's a damn fine doctor. And that way, if she ever has any other problems, you can just give him a call. They'll already be acquainted."

Sawyer nodded. "I still make housecalls, if you can believe the convenience of that! But in Buckhorn, we're all real neighborly that way."

Jordan shook his head at the not-so-subtle suggestion that Georgia could be more neighborly herself.

She turned her back on them all, one hand to her head. "This is incredible." She appeared to be speaking to herself.

"Where did you move from?" Gabe asked.

Distracted, she waved a hand and said, "Milwaukee."

"Ah, that explains it. We do things differently here."

She turned back around, her eyes intent. "Are there any other brothers I haven't met yet?"

They said in unison, "No."

"Thank God for small favors." They all grinned at her, making her fall back a step before she caught herself. "All right, I want to see my mother. I won't really feel reassured until I have. She's on the third floor."

Casey spoke up. "I'll go on and head out. The squirts are anxious to see the lake. That okay?"

Georgia looked harried, but she nodded. "Yes, okay."

She pulled her children close. "You guys be on especially good behavior for Casey, all right?"

"We will!"

"We're always good."

Georgia smiled. "I know. I'm a very lucky mother to have you two."

The kids smothered her with hugs—quickly because they were anxious to be off—and she kissed each of them. "Jordan and I will be there soon. And be careful around that water!"

Casey put his arm around her shoulders and gave her a squeeze. "They'll be fine. Don't worry. We have a rule that no kids are allowed even on the shore without a life preserver on. I won't let them get hurt. I promise."

As Casey took both kids by the hand and walked away, Georgia got that shell-shocked look about her again.

Jordan gently maneuvered her into the elevator and pushed the third-floor button. In the crowded confines of the elevator, she stood closer to him than she had all morning. He assumed his brothers intimidated her because she was so damn small by comparison. Her curly golden brown hair would barely brush any of the male chins surrounding her, her shoulders were only half as wide as theirs.

Her petite build really emphasized her full breasts, he noticed. And once he noticed, he couldn't stop noticing. She wore a tailored yellow blouse buttoned to her throat and tucked into a long, trim denim skirt. There was nothing sexy about the outfit, and in fact, it was quite understated. But it did nothing to mask her appeal. He doubted a burlap sack could have managed that feat.

Jordan was lost in erotic fantasies better left to the privacy of his bedroom than a crowded elevator, when he felt her hand slip into his. He wanted to shout with the pleasure of it. She was warming to him, accepting him, even if reluctantly.

Then he saw that Sawyer had noticed it, too, and was whistling softly. He even nudged Gabe, who lifted both brows.

Jordan scowled at them. He could read their thoughts as clearly as if they were stamped on their foreheads. They liked it that he was exhibiting some male possessiveness. They'd reacted in a similar way when he'd had his first fight, ages ago. A few neighborhood bullies had been picking on an old dog, and when they'd thrown a rock and the dog had yelped, Jordan lost his temper. He'd been a young kid, but not too young to hate injustice and cruelty.

No one had been more shocked than he when he'd kicked butt on the older boys, but his brothers revelled in his loss of control. Since then, it had only happened a handful of times, but each and every time his brothers damn near had a celebration. It was as if they'd always known he could be ferocious, and loved seeing it firsthand.

Jordan had been disgusted with his loss of control then, just as he was now. Not that he would have done anything differently, but...

Before he could get truly annoyed with his brothers for being so smug at his predicament, the elevator doors opened.

Walking quickly now, Georgia made a beeline for her mother's room. Once there, she turned back to them as if not quite sure what to do with them. She glanced at Sawyer and Gabe, then to Jordan. "I might be awhile."

Jordan nodded. "Take your time. I'm in no hurry."

"Me, either," Gabe said, making her frown.

"Gabe and I will be on our way shortly," Sawyer promised her, "but I am interested in checking on your mother myself, if you're not opposed to it. It's not that I doubt the good care she's getting here. But with emphysema, any number of small ailments can come up. If you're comfortable with the idea, why then, I'm a whole lot closer than the hospital.''

Georgia looked so relieved by the repeated offer, Jordan wanted to kiss her. Anytime she was given genuine caring, she always seemed so surprised.

''Actually,'' she said, ''that would be wonderful. I worry so much about her. She says she won't overdo, but then something like this happens. She's so determined not to complain, to continue mothering me even when I don't need it, even though I'm twenty-three…''

Jordan nearly choked when she gave her age. Twenty-three? That had to mean she'd gotten pregnant at sixteen. Good Lord, that was a lot to expect of someone who was little more than a child herself. Had she finished high school? Gotten any college at all?

He again thought of her stepping onto that stage, and tried to imagine how she personally felt about it. She was so damn young, so driven by hard-nosed pride. Did she enjoy the work at all or was she taking the only job she could that would pay the bills?

''Most mothers are that way,'' Sawyer assured her while casting quick worried glances at Jordan. ''My own is as stubborn as a goat and twice as ornery.''

Gabe nodded to that. When Georgia looked at Jordan, appalled by what she took as an insult to their mother, he managed to laugh to cover the emotions she'd made him feel. ''You'd have to meet Mom to understand, sweetheart. We love her dearly, but—''

''But she did manage to raise the lot of you.'' Georgia shook her head. ''I suppose that takes great fortitude.''

They all laughed. ''Exactly.''

''Let me check on Mom and talk to her privately for a moment, to make sure she doesn't object to you coming in. I'll be right back.''

Georgia slipped silently into the room and the second

she was gone, Jordan began to pace. He could feel Sawyer and Gabe watching him.

"Any reason why you look so tormented?" Sawyer asked.

Jordan glared at him. "She's only twenty-three!"

"You thought she looked older?"

"No, Gabe, it's not that. It's just…damn she's young to do what she's doing."

Gabe asked, "What is it she's doing?"

Sawyer, having been apprised by Morgan, as well as Howard and Jesse who'd gotten a firsthand show, said, "I think he's talking about the dancing."

"Ah." Gabe caught Jordan's eye and gave him a wide, masculine smile. "You know, I was thinking of going to watch her act, myself. I haven't seen a live show in ages. Whadya think, Sawyer? You want to come, too?"

CHAPTER SEVEN

JORDAN TURNED so fast Gabe jumped in surprise. With his eyes blazing and his jaw locked, he growled, "Don't even think about it, little brother."

After biting his lips to keep from laughing, Gabe soothed, "All right. Don't get in a lather over it."

It took him a second, and then Jordan's eyes narrowed. He realized Gabe had just gotten him but good. And Jordan had made it disgustingly easy for him to do. Choking Gabe sounded better by the minute.

Georgia opened the door. She looked at Jordan's severe frown, then at Sawyer's exasperation and Gabe's innocent expression. Her own turned suspicious. "Am I interrupting anything?"

"Not at all." Sawyer stepped forward. "Am I allowed in?"

She didn't look convinced, but she let it go. "Yes. Mom said she'd like to meet you." Georgia glanced once more at Jordan, then turned away. She and Sawyer walked into her mother's room, Sawyer's hand at her waist.

Jordan was still looking at the closed door when Gabe murmured, "I see Morgan was right."

Jordan rounded on his younger brother again. He felt dangerously close to losing his edge. "You wanna tell me exactly what the hell that means?"

"Ho!" Gabe backed up, pretending fear. And this time there was no way for him to hide his amusement. "Don't bite my face off over a simple observation. If you're still worried that I might go to the bar, I promise I was just yanking your chain. You can quit snarling at me now. Besides, Lizzy would have my head if I looked at another woman and you know it. She's got a mean jealous streak.'' Gabe sounded immensely pleased over that observation.

"If you don't stop pricking my temper,'' Jordan rumbled, "you won't have to worry about Elizabeth. *I'll* have your damn head.''

Gabe laughed. "Honest to God, Jordan, I've never seen you in such a fury. It's kind of interesting.''

"You're on thin ice, Gabe.''

In his defense, Gabe said, "Hey, I'm justified. Don't think I've forgotten that you stole my wife from me!''

Georgia gasped behind them. When they both turned to her, she stammered, "Mom wanted a moment alone with Sawyer.'' She looked from one to the other of them. She appeared stricken, and embarrassed.

Gabe smiled as he explained. "My wife chose to work for Jordan in his clinic. Jordan knew that I wanted her with me, but he made up all these lame excuses and just swept her away.''

"That,'' Jordan said, watching Georgia closely, "is only Gabe's side of the story. Elizabeth has a knack with animals, a special rapport. She's much better suited to being my assistant than she is playing receptionist for Gabe. That's all he was referring to.''

Gabe shrugged. "Well, you did kiss her, too. Right in front of me.''

He snorted over that. "A brotherly kiss and you damn well know it.''

"Brotherly, huh? Well, in that case—'' Gabe reached for Georgia, who quickly took two startled steps away from him. But he'd barely moved more than a foot before Jordan caught him by his collar and hauled him back.

"Not in this lifetime, Gabe." The statement was low and mean, and made Gabe chuckle.

"That's what I figured." To Georgia, he said, "Can you believe he kissed my Lizzy? Not that I blame him. She's about the most beautiful woman in these parts and pretty irresistible. You'll see what I mean when you meet her. And luckily for Jordan here, I let him live because she turned right around after kissing him and agreed to marry me."

Georgia gave a nervous smile. "I see."

"No you don't." Jordan released Gabe and propped his hands on his hips. "Elizabeth had just helped me save all the animals in the clinic from a fire. It was a kiss of gratitude, no more."

"Uh-huh." Gabe pretended to think otherwise. "And what Morgan told me is that your Georgia here has incredibly pretty gray eyes. Now that I've seen her for myself, I agree. Very pretty."

He and Georgia spoke at the same time.

"She's not *my* Georgia."

"I'm not *his* Georgia."

Gabe said, "Oh, look. There's Sawyer."

They both turned and Sawyer nodded with a smile. "She's doing fine. Incredibly well, in fact. Her doctor is a good man. I've always liked him." Sawyer pulled out a card and handed it to Georgia. "Here's my home number. Once she's released, probably by the middle of the week, feel free to give me a call if you have any questions or if she has any problems, okay?"

Georgia's eyes softened to pewter. "Thank you. That's very generous of you."

"You might want to share that number with the children, too, so that if anything like this happens again, they can give me a call if you're at work."

She nodded as she tucked the card securely into her bag.

"They have my number at the bar, but Bill doesn't always answer the phone at night during the show. We've argued over that several times."

"I understand." Sawyer glanced at Jordan. "Perhaps a pager would be good?"

Jordan saw the guilt flash across Georgia's face and knew she couldn't afford one. He spoke quickly. "Gabe, don't you have an extra pager you're not using anymore?"

Gabe looked dumbfounded for only a second, then nodded. "Oh, yeah. Right." And with a grin: "Hey, it's even paid up for the next six months."

Georgia was already shaking her head, but Gabe slung an arm around her, which caused her to still immediately. "I insist. That's what friends are for."

She might have protested further, once she regained use of her tongue, but Sawyer chose that auspicious moment to tell Jordan, "Her mother wants to see you."

"Me?"

"Yep. She was rather insistent on it."

Georgia groaned. "Oh, God. She's so overprotective...."

Jordan peered at the closed door with deep reservation. He hoped like hell this wasn't the familial interrogation. At thirty-three, he was so rusty he had no idea if he'd know how to answer or not. Especially considering he hadn't yet figured out what he felt for Georgia. Lust certainly, and compassion. But if there was more...

Georgia started to follow him in, but Sawyer gently caught her arm. "She specified that she wanted to see Jordan, and only Jordan."

Jordan groaned in dread, mustered his manly courage and headed in. He wasn't a damn coward. He could face one disgruntled mother, with or without all his thoughts in order. But when he peeked around the curtain to the bed, he found Ruth Samson half-sitting up, very clear-headed, and more than a little disgruntled.

Good heavens, the woman looked as ferocious as Morgan on his most intimidating days.

"Ms. SAMSON?"

Her eyes, the same blue gray as her daughter's, locked onto him and without preamble she stated, "My daughter has whisker burns this morning."

Jordan gulped, and before he could stop himself he ran a hand over his now smooth-shaven jaw. Deciding to brazen it out, he said, "I only kissed her."

"Must have been one heck of a kiss." Ruth looked nothing like the frail, ill woman of yesterday. In truth, she appeared ready to get out of bed and whup Jordan's backside. "Georgia couldn't quite look at me without blushing."

Against his better judgment, Jordan grinned. "Georgia does seem prone to a pretty blush now and then."

Ruth sighed, and all the vinegar seemed to leave her from one second to the next. "It's incredible, but regardless of all she's been through, she's still so sweet. Not that I want her to toughen up. She's a wonderful daughter and a wonderful mother to my grandchildren." Once she said it, Ruth glared, daring him to disagree.

Jordan nodded. "She amazes me, if you want the truth."

"Yes. She's amazing." Her eyes sharpened and she asked, "Exactly how much do you know about my daughter?"

"Very little. I only just minutes ago found out she's a mere twenty-three."

"That bothers you? Well it shouldn't. Georgia is very mature for her years."

Jordan had no idea how to reply to that. "I also know that she works in a pretty disreputable bar."

Ruth laughed. "And of course, you don't approve?"

Jordan matched her stare without hesitation. "No, not at all."

"Good." She nodded in satisfaction. "Neither do I. But she has few choices."

"Georgia mentioned that to me."

Ruth looked surprised. "She did? That's interesting. She usually won't give a man the time of day. And believe me, plenty of them are after her."

Jordan ground his teeth together. "I believe it."

"I can tell there's still a lot you don't know. Pull up a chair and I'll fill you in. But we better be quick because if I know my daughter, we maybe have about two minutes more before she barges back in."

Jordan obediently pulled up a chair. He was anxious to learn more about Georgia, to find out how she'd ended up in these circumstances. She and her mother both felt she had few options, but Jordan intended to give her several, and they all had to do with her staying off that damn stage.

Ruth's first burst of indignant anger had faded and had left her looking decidedly limp. She was now pale, her hands shaking. Jordan reminded himself that the woman had been extremely ill only the night before, and that he had to make certain she didn't overdo. He had the feeling she'd push herself, given half a chance, to defend her daughter. *Against him.*

"Ms. Samson," he said, hoping to reassure her, "you don't have to worry about me being with Georgia. I only want to help."

She sighed wearily, then started in coughing. Jordan was ready to call for a nurse when she waved him back into his seat.

She had to use her oxygen for a moment, taking slow shallow breaths, and afterward she took quite a bit of time resettling her blankets around her. Finally she said, "I seriously doubt Georgia wants your help."

"Well, no, she doesn't."

"But you're insisting?"

"Yes, ma'am."

She nodded, apparently pleased by that. "Georgia got pregnant when she was only sixteen."

Since he'd already done the math, Jordan didn't show a single sign of surprise.

"My husband was an old-fashioned man. A sour, undemonstrative man who never really understood Georgia. We had her late in life. I was nearly forty, and my husband was eleven years my senior. We'd thought we were past the stage of having children. So she took us both by surprise."

"A pleasant surprise?"

"Oh, surely. But adjusting wasn't easy. Avery was set in his ways, and part of those ways was being miserly to the point of wanting Georgia to wear secondhand clothes, and insisting we drive our old Buick forever, and that we make do with one old black-and-white television. It had never mattered much to me. But I hated seeing Georgia do without. She didn't fit in with the other kids because of how we lived, and it wasn't even necessary. We could have afforded better for her, but I'd always been a housewife, and Avery had always controlled the money."

Jordan nodded. "I understand." And he did. He knew plenty of older women like Ruth, women who'd been raised to believe that wives were meant to stay at home, to cater to their husbands. He could only imagine how a child thrown into the mix might have complicated things.

"Well, I don't. I could have done more. And I could have done it sooner." Ruth looked past Jordan's shoulder, her eyes so sad. "We argued endlessly over Georgia, which was probably harder for her than the divorce. I was a coward, and the idea of being on my own was terrifying. But I finally did it. I should have left him years earlier, but I kept thinking that I needed to keep our home intact. I didn't want Georgia to have to start over in a new school system just because I couldn't afford the area anymore. Then, when she started dating Dennis Peach I wished like crazy that I *had* moved.''

"She got pregnant?''

"Yes. Dennis was every young girl's dream. He was good-looking, athletic, nice. He took her to all the dances and the parties, places she hadn't been before. Georgia went head over heels in love with him almost overnight.

"We were still hashing out the divorce when Georgia eloped. I couldn't believe it. But to give her her due, she made things work for awhile there.''

Jordan imagined that Georgia had enough sheer will and determination to make anything work when she put her mind to it. He thought about her at that age, so young, so innocent. At sixteen, he'd been into more mischief than his mother ever guessed, but he'd been careful, with himself and the girls he'd been with.

He resolved to have another talk with Casey real soon. It wouldn't hurt to drive the point home one more time.

"Dennis wasn't too bad,'' Ruth said. "They lived like paupers, but then Georgia was used to that. And she seemed so happy, especially after Lisa was born. My gosh, she adored that baby. She took to mothering as natural as could be.''

Jordan didn't want to hear about how happy she'd been with her husband. He was glad the man was long gone from the picture. "So what happened?''

"Her in-laws happened. They made life as tough for Georgia as they could. While she was willing to make sacrifices for the marriage, Dennis wasn't used to living without. They coddled him something awful, and ignored Lisa—even to the point of questioning whether or not she was his. I tried to help out as much as I could, but I was dealing with the issue of my divorce and somehow Georgia ended up helping me.''

Ruth looked so wretched over that admission, Jordan reached out patted her hand. ''Your daughter loves you very much.''

''I know.'' She spoke barely above a whisper. ''My husband had always smoked and right after the divorce I started getting sick. I tried to find a job, but I had no experience and I'd get winded so easy. More so than most people, I'm prone to getting bronchitis and even pneumonia. That's when they found out how bad my lungs are. Only by then, I didn't have any health insurance because I'd been covered under my husband's policy. I was so, so stupid not to think of that.''

Jordan wondered if Georgia was paying for insurance for her mother. He frowned with the thought, mentally adding up all her responsibilities.

''I was a burden to my daughter at a time when she needed me most.''

''No.'' Jordan shook his head, knowing exactly what Georgia would have to say about that. ''That's not true. Family helps family. Period. She was there for you, just as you're here for her now. She's told me several times how much you contribute.''

Ruth tilted her head. ''You sound like a man with a close family.''

''Yes. Like you, my mother is divorced.'' His mother, however, had always been one of the strongest, most independent women he knew. Of course, she'd had a fabulous first husband who'd shown her exactly what marriage should be. And that had thankfully gotten her through her marriage to Jordan's father.

Jordan forced a smile for Ruth's benefit. ''She's also happily remarried. Through it all, we've stayed a very close family.''

"I like you, Jordan."

She said that as if he'd passed a test. "I like you, too."

"And you like my daughter?"

When he hesitated, not quite sure how she meant it and afraid of committing himself to her, she laughed. "That's all right. I didn't mean to pressure you. But I will tell you that it's not going to be easy."

"I already figured that out."

She laughed again. "The end of this long tale is that shortly after Georgia got pregnant with Adam—an accident, and a blessing from God—Dennis's parents convinced him that he was overburdened, that Georgia had gotten pregnant on purpose just to chain him down." Under her breath she muttered, "As if a broken condom was her fault."

That was *definitely* not an image Jordan wanted haunting his brain. He frowned.

"Dennis had always been pampered, and as their bills started to pile up and things got tougher and tougher, he got more and more distant, more willing to run home to his parents. And unfortunately, more willing to run up additional bills. Their combined incomes just weren't enough, and one day he went home to his folks and never came back."

Jordan nodded in satisfaction. "So she divorced him?"

"Yes. Georgia was really hurt. She loved him and yet he just walked away. She agreed to a peaceful divorce, and allowed the courts to divide the bills down the middle even though many of them had been his recent purchases. She wanted to make the transition as easy on the children as she could. But the really sad part is that Dennis agreed to it all, wished Georgia well, then stole several thousand dollars from his parents and took off. Not only did he not pay his half of the bills, he's never paid a dime of child support."

"He doesn't see the kids?"

"No. No one's heard from him since he left. His parents blamed Georgia, and added to her burden—until I told them I'd have the police after their precious son for skipping out on his responsibilities."

She looked downright feral again, and Jordan nodded. "Good for you."

"No, it was an error in judgment. His parents apologized and promised to pay Dennis's share of things. Georgia argued with them. They were Dennis's bills, not his parents. But they insisted, and she believed them. She...trusted them. In the end, they were only biding their time until they could petition the court for custody of Adam and Lisa. They even tried to accuse Georgia of being an unfit mother."

Rage churned forth in Jordan, taking him by surprise. In a voice of icy rage, he said, "They obviously failed in their efforts."

"Yes. But not without a lot of cost and heartache to my daughter. And they didn't give up. They dogged her steps everywhere she went, making her lose jobs, constantly posing a threat to her peace of mind. Not once have they ever shown genuine concern or caring for the children. The few times they visited them, they tried to fill their heads with poison, bad-mouthing Georgia while making Dennis sound like a saint that she'd run off. Can you imagine? Their own blood kin, yet all they're interested in is using the kids to try to hurt Georgia."

"They're beautiful children," Jordan said with sincerity. He'd been surprised at how much he'd enjoyed making pancakes with them that morning. Lisa and Adam were lively and bright and polite. "She's done a good job with them."

"Yes, she has. And she'd die before letting anyone hurt

those kids. So finally we thought it was best to simply move away. It makes me so mad, I want to spit.''

Jordan could easily see where Georgia got her backbone. He patted Ruth's hand and tried to calm her. ''Don't get yourself all riled up. You'll get winded again and the doctors will throw me out.'' He smiled. ''Besides, Georgia is here now, away from them, and the kids seem very happy. I wish she hadn't gone through so much, but all in all, I admit I'm pleased with the outcome.''

''Moving here was a blessing,'' Ruth agreed. ''And you know, it was my ex-husband who made it possible.''

Jordan raised a brow. He hoped the man had somehow redeemed himself, had supported his daughter and her decisions—mistakes included—after all. ''How's that?''

''He died.''

Not the happy ending he'd been looking for. Jordan sighed, wishing Georgia had been able to resolve things with her father before his death, but he had the feeling even that had been denied her.

''He hadn't ever gotten around to changing his will. He had money that he'd hidden during our divorce. It all came to me. Not that there was a fortune or anything. But it was enough to finance the move and put a down payment on the house. I just hate seeing Georgia work so hard to keep it all together.''

''I intend to help her with that.''

Ruth shook her head. ''She won't like it. Everyone she's ever relied on has let her down. Her father, her husband, her in-laws. She's determined to be totally independent this time.''

''You never turned your back on her.''

''No, but I made some awful mistakes.''

Jordan pushed to his feet, anxious to see Georgia again now that he had a better understanding of her. ''Making mistakes is the name of game. We're human, so it happens. Trying to atone for mistakes is what makes you a mother.''

She grinned at that. "True. So what are you going to do?"

"I don't know yet."

"One thing, Jordan, before you leave."

"Yes?" He turned to face her.

"If you think there's any chance at all you might hurt her, it'd be better if you walked away right now."

Jordan stared down at his feet. He didn't want to hurt her. Ever. But even more than that, he didn't want to walk away. He wanted to gather her closer, much closer. He wanted to bind her to him in some undeniable way.

He made plans for the coming weeks, how he'd ingratiate not only himself, but his best selling tool—his family. They were irresistible, and once Georgia got comfortable sharing with them, relying on them and letting them rely on her, she'd soften. She had to.

Jordan shook his head. No doubt about it, he was in over his head. But damned if he wasn't starting to like it.

CHAPTER EIGHT

WITH AN OUTRAGED and appalled gasp, Georgia slapped the stage curtain back into place. "Damn him!" Her heart felt lodged in her throat, and with a lot of trepidation, she looked down at her costume.

"Oh, God." It looked worse than she'd first thought, given that Jordan was about to see her in it. Again she pulled the curtain aside and peeked out. But Jordan was still there, sitting at a front-row table as had become his preference, scowling at every other man in the room. He resembled a dog guarding a bone.

What in the world was wrong with him? She should have been able to ignore him, and in fact, when he'd first shown up as part of the audience, she hadn't even realized he was there until she'd almost finished. She made it a point not to look at the men in the audience; it was the only way she could get through putting herself on display that way. But she'd felt something different that night, something that had affected her deep inside. Against her will her gaze had sought out the source of her discomfort—and clashed with Jordan's hot green stare.

She'd missed a step and nearly fallen on her face. He'd looked as menacing as Morgan ever had. Of course, now that she knew Morgan better, she knew most of his dark countenance was bluster. Not so with Jordan. His brothers insisted on telling her—in private little whispers—that Jordan was the most even tempered one, the pacifist, the gentlest of men. Ha! Twice now, he'd almost started another fight.

Bill had threatened to ban him from the bar and Georgia had silently prayed that he'd follow through. But then Jordan had slipped her boss a twenty, and Bill had grinned and walked away. Curse him.

The music was getting louder, her cue had come and gone, and she could hear the rumble of impatient voices out front. If she didn't get going, she'd have to start the CD over.

She lifted her chin. So what if this particular costume left her stomach bare? That you could see her navel? So what that more of her backside showed than was covered? All that meant was that her tips tonight would be especially good and she'd finally be able to afford the electrical work needed on the house. If Jordan didn't like what she wore…well, too bad. She wasn't too crazy about him right now anyway.

Determination masking her churning nervousness, Georgia thrust the curtain aside and made an entrance onto the stage. She had every intention of ignoring Jordan completely.

Of course, that was before he fell off his chair.

He took one look at her, dropped his cola and toppled. Luckily no one seemed to pay him any mind as he hauled himself back up and into his seat.

Georgia deliberately turned her back on him—and heard a roar of applause along with some loud wolf whistles, likely because the bottom of her costume was no more than a thong. Embarrassment washed over her, so hot she felt light-headed and couldn't see beyond the fog of shame. She knew she was blushing. *Everywhere*. The dance steps that normally came so easily to her now felt forced and awkward; she had to concentrate hard to keep to her rhythm.

At least, she told herself as she executed a high kick, her

top was more concealing. It had midlength sleeves and a V-shaped neck with lapels. The whole outfit was stark white, including the stupid little hat that Bill had insisted on. She wore white gloves, white high-heel sandals, and garters with black velvet ribbons.

It looked cheesy, like something out of a fetish catalogue. But already money landed at the front of the stage. Georgia moved farther back, being careful not to lose her footing on the scattering of bills.

By the time she finished her number, she figured there had to be a good three hundred dollars at her feet. Not bad for a night's pay. She almost smiled. *Almost.*

And then she accidentally caught Jordan's eye.

He looked livid, with his eyes sort of red and unfocused. Georgia frowned at him. How such a dominating, stubborn, pushy man could have such nice relatives was beyond her.

With one last bow, she turned and ducked behind the curtain. Her changing room was really a cleaning closet overflowing with supplies. Next to her street clothes hanging on a metal hook, rested a mildewy mop and several stained rags. One bare bench, raw enough to leave splinters in her behind if she was ever foolish enough to sit on it, occupied the space next to the door.

Georgia tossed the foolish hat aside, then leaned against the wall and struggled to catch her breath. Dancing, even at the bar, always left her exuberant. She loved to dance, to feel her movements become fluid like the music. And thanks to Jordan, she no longer had to go on stage in a state of exhaustion. He and his family had forced so much help on her, had been so supportive and friendly and accepting, she'd gotten plenty of rest the past few weeks.

But while she was grateful, she was also resentful because it was Jordan's fault that she hesitated to answer tonight's screaming applause with an encore. She just couldn't make herself go back out there. Not with Jordan watching.

Bill pounded on her door. "Front and center, damn it! They're calling for you."

Georgia stared at the closed door. She could probably convince Bill that it was better to leave them wanting more....

Then Jordan's voice intruded. "If she doesn't want to go back out there, then leave her alone."

She gasped in outrage. How dare he confront her boss? Was he trying to get her fired?

She answered her own question with an obvious, resounding yes. Not once had Jordan tried to hide his disdain of The Swine. This time, however, he'd stepped completely over the line.

The door bounced hard against the wall when she threw it open. Both Jordan and Bill jumped, but Georgia stomped right past them to the steps leading up on stage. It was uncanny, but she could actually feel the searing heat of Jordan's gaze on her exposed rump.

The second she opened the curtain, the men bellowed their appreciation. More money came flying her way and Georgia, with grim resolve, submitted to the attention.

After three encores she was finally left in peace.

For all of one minute.

She'd just stepped out of her high-heel sandals and started to relax when Jordan walked in without knocking. His gaze did the quick once over, scaring her from head to toes and everywhere in-between. Georgia glared at him. "What are you doing here?"

Despite his heated expression, his tone sounded mild enough. "I was already out."

She didn't buy it for a second. "Try again, Jordan."

"All right." He didn't appear the least put off by her hostile attitude. But then, she'd already realized how pigheaded he could be in his determination. "I stopped by to see your mother. She had the kids in bed, so I missed visiting with them. We took tea in the patio room, and when she started yawning, I told she should turn in, too. Though she's doing so much better, Sawyer says she should continue to get plenty of rest."

His words were easy and rehearsed. But his gaze burned over her, lingering in places that always felt too sensitive whenever Jordan Sommerville was in the vicinity.

Realizing she still wore the stupid gloves, she jerked them off and stuffed them into her bag. Jordan leaned against the wall, crossed his arms over his chest, and watched her every movement with an intensity that set her stomach to roiling. She couldn't very well finish changing with him standing there.

"It's rude to stare," she grumbled.

"Honey, the whole point of that getup is to make men stare."

She lost it, stepping forward and poking him hard in the chest. "Not *you!* Other men, okay, men who want to watch me dance, men who—"

Rubbing at his chest and frowning at the same time, Jordan interjected, "I came to watch you dance."

"No, you came to watch everyone else watch me dance!" Her head pounded, keeping time with her heart. She felt ready to burst into tears, to scream. He and his family were so wonderful, so giving, they made her feel terrible in comparison. All her life she'd screwed up. Having Jordan around only emphasized that, and weakened her resolve to learn independence. But she needed to know she could protect her children now, and in the future.

"You," she said in a tone nearing a snarl, "came to make sure no one did anything improper like *speak* to me."

Jordan took his own step forward. "Are you telling me you *want* to converse with these yahoos?"

"I'm telling you it's none of your damn business what I do!"

Jordan stalled, then in a voice as soft as warm velvet, he whispered, "I want it to be my business, though. Keeping my hands off you the past few weeks has been torture. Hell, Georgia…"

Her heart slammed into her ribs. He reached for her, touched her face with a gentleness she'd never known, and her knees went weak. "Jordan?"

Even to her own ears, his name sounded like a plea. The past few weeks had been hell, with the memory of his touch haunting her. She'd dreamed about that morning in the kitchen, and every night the dreams got hotter, more real.

Jordan cupped her jaw. "Don't ask me to go away, sweetheart. And don't ask me not to care."

Georgia watched his eyes darken, now so close to her own since he loomed over her. She exhaled on a trembling sigh. "You're making me crazy," she admitted. "I don't even know what I'm thinking or saying anymore."

His gaze flickered, becoming more intimate, hotter. "I don't mean to upset you."

"I know that." She almost laughed, it was so absurd. Jordan and his family had irrevocably changed her life— all for the better. Casey cut her grass, Gabe fixed her leaky pipes, they all doted on the children and on her mother. And on her.

But what if she came to depend on them, if she let her children start to love them, and then they went away? What would she do then? She'd be no better off, and she'd have the memories to torment her.

She squeezed her eyes shut, but quickly opened them again when Jordan's big thumb teased at the corner of her mouth. "Jordan," she said, hoping to make him understand, "dancing on that stage is hard enough for me. Especially in this getup. I do what I have to do, but I don't like it. When you're here, passing judgment and waiting to condemn, well…it only makes me more nervous.''

Jordan shook her gently. "I'm not condemning *you*. How could you even think that?"

"You condemn all this." She'd learned so much about him from his family. Her visits with them had started out strained, but Honey wasn't a woman who left anyone feeling uncomfortable, and his brothers were too outrageous to be kept at an emotional distance. They treated her with all the teasing irreverence normally reserved for a little sister. And she loved it.

Where Jordan tended to close up about anything personal, his brothers took delight in sharing his deepest darkest secrets. Gabe had told her that Jordan never drank. And Morgan had told her because of his father, he protested any abuse of alcohol.

Georgia shook her head. "You may not condemn me specifically, but the bar, the men here, the atmosphere… And I'm a part of it, Jordan." She hesitated, unsure how much she wanted to push him, especially in a damn closet, but she just couldn't take it anymore.

She stepped away from him and concentrated on what she had to say while putting away her high heels. "You've done so much for me. I never would have gotten through the past weeks without your help."

"Nonsense. You're about the most resourceful woman I've ever met. I have no doubt you'd have managed just fine. But you know I wanted to help."

His praise made her feel more vulnerable than ever. "And I appreciate it more than I can say. You're…well, you're wonderful."

Jordan stared at her hard. "But?"

She drew a deep breath, forcing herself to say the words. "But I want to make it on my own. It's important to me. I've made some really dumb mistakes in the past, mistakes that have hurt me, my children and my mother. I'm trying to fix all that.''

''You can't fix the past, sweetheart. All you can do is make the future different.''

She nodded. ''I know. And that's what I'm going to do. My mother insists she's feeling as good as ever, and I've cut back on the hours I work during the day so she's not overburdened with the kids. And thanks to Bill's stupid costume choices, I'm making more money in the evenings so my budget is more sound than ever. I'm managing, Jordan, and that's what I want to concentrate on.''

Jordan gave her a long, considering look. As if she hadn't just spilled her guts to him, he said, ''Your mother likes me.''

Georgia had no idea how to respond to that. Truth was, her mother adored him.

''Your kids are crazy about me.''

She smiled. ''I know. They're also crazy about your family. Honey has been promoted to honorary aunt. Morgan, that big ox, astounds me every time he manages to be so gentle with them. And Sawyer and Casey...'' She shook her head. ''They're incredible men.''

Jordan stepped closer until his chest brushed her breasts. ''We're your friends now. You can't just expect us all to go away.''

''I wouldn't want that!'' It was so difficult to think clearly with him this close. She wanted to wrap her arms around him, to ask him to hold her. But he hadn't touched her sexually since that morning in her kitchen, and she knew that was for the best.

''My children,'' she said slowly, measuring her words, ''have never had enough people in their lives who cared about them. My ex-in-laws...'' She shook her head, not willing to go into details. ''They weren't nice people. They've never really cared about Lisa or Adam.''

"They must be idiots, then, because your children are very lovable."

Anyone who loved her kids automatically got her love as well. And that fact scared her to death.

Feeling almost desperate, she put a hand on his arm and explained, "I want to keep the friendship." She wanted that so badly her stomach felt like lead whenever she thought of losing it. As a child, she'd craved friendship so badly, always watching from the sidelines as someone else got picked for tag, as other girls gathered in clusters to giggle, excluding her. As a teenager, she'd put everything into her dance, detaching herself from the hurt, telling herself that she didn't care. She'd gone from being almost totally isolated from friends, to being Dennis's wife, then to being on her own again.

Gaining friendship only to lose it once more would be unbearable. "I just...I just don't want you here at night, watching me. I don't want it to go beyond friendship."

Jordan cradled her face between his large hands. She felt helpless against the drugging pull of his nearness, the warmth of his body, his scent. Everything he'd ever made her feel came swamping back with his first gentle touch.

"I'll tell you what I think." His sensual tone made her heart race. "I think everything you've just said is bullshit."

She stared at him, appalled, wondering if he could really see through her so easily.

"I think," he growled as he pulled her into the hardness and heat of his body, "that you want me every bit as much as I want you. Friends? Hell yes, we'll be friends. And a whole lot more."

She wasn't at all surprised when he kissed her.

JORDAN WANTED to devour her. The need she created just by being close nearly made him crazy. It was a live thing, a teeth-gnashing hunger that he had no control over. He groaned, sucking her tongue into his mouth and stroking it with his own.

Georgia's arms slipped around his neck, her soft breasts nestling into his chest. Her costume top was skimpy and he slipped his hands beneath it to feel the warm skin of her back, then couldn't resist sliding his hands down to her sweetly curved ass. His body pulsed with need, his erection growing painfully. Her bottom was bare except for the thong and her cheeks were hot, soft. He traced the thin line of material with his fingertips as deeply as he could, and took her rough groan into his mouth.

She went on tiptoe against him, pushing into him. Her nipples were hard and he used his other hand to explore her breasts. He wanted her naked. He wanted to see her nipples, to taste them.

He kissed her neck as he brought both hands up to the lapels on her top and pulled them open. The low vee of the costume made it easy to expose her and the second her breasts were freed, pushed up by the material bunched tightly beneath them, Georgia gasped. Jordan didn't give her time to pull away. He dipped his head down and licked one dark rosy nipple.

Her fingers clenched in his hair. *"Jordan."*

"Shhh." Even with his blood roaring in his ears, Jordan cautioned himself to go slow, to tease her, to make her admit to the incredible passion between them. All the well-grounded reasons to give her more time, to avoid sexual interludes, were chased away by the sight of her.

Her nipples were large, tightly puckered. He licked again, then again, using the rough tip of his tongue to torment her. Tantalizing sounds of hunger escaped her. He caught her with his teeth and nipped gently, then not so gently. Georgia trembled. When she tried to pull him closer he sucked her deep into the heat of his mouth.

"Jordan..." she whispered on a vibrating moan.

"I know, sweetheart, I know."

He cupped her between her legs. She was so hot, and she pushed against his probing fingers, her thighs opening without his instruction. He could feel her swollen flesh, feel the dampness of her even through the material. The bottoms were tight but he insinuated his fingers beneath the right leg opening and found her wet and ready—for him. He straightened and held her tightly with his free arm.

Her hips moved with his fingers, seeking more of his touch. Jordan felt swollen and thick, achingly hard. The damn saloon could have blown up and he might not have noticed. He was only aware of the feel of her, her scent, now stronger with her excitement.

"Come on, sweetheart," he encouraged roughly, seeing that she was already climbing toward a climax. Her eyes were cloudy, unfocused, her lips parted as she panted for breath. His fingers moved more deeply, stroking, sliding insistently over her slick flesh then up to her swollen clitoris. Delicately now, he touched her, light, rhythmic touches.

Georgia groaned and squeezed her eyes closed. Jordan watched her face, saw her skin flush darkly, her lush mouth tremble. Her pulse raced in her throat, and her hands bit into his upper arms, caught between pulling him closer and pushing him away.

"Come for me, Georgia," he groaned, knowing he, too, was perilously close to the edge. "I want to see you come."

Her beautiful breasts heaved, her throat arched, and then she bit her bottom lip and groaned harsh and low and Jordan supported her, mesmerized as she jerked and shuddered and it went on and on. He felt so much a part of her that he knew nothing would ever be the same again.

Long seconds passed. Gently, he pulled his fingers from her. Her eyelashes fluttered and she looked at him, still slightly dazed. Her forehead and temples were dewy, her breathing still labored. Jordan met her gaze, held it as he lifted his fingers to his mouth and sucked them clean.

Georgia shuddered. She clung to him with a rough tenderness he'd never known before. She was pliant, accepting of his will.

He gave her a kiss of lingering need and apology. Holding her, seeing her like this, brought him back to reality. The very last thing she wanted or needed was to be taken quickly in a damn saloon closet. Not that he regretted giving her pleasure. How could he?

"We have to stop." Jordan couldn't quite believe the words came from his own mouth. Not when he wanted her so badly. But the past few weeks had been a carefully wrought campaign to win her over, and he wouldn't blow it now. If he made love to her here—and he was about a nanosecond away from doing just that—her embarrassment would drive a new wedge between them.

He took a deep breath and said, "I can't take you here, sweetheart." He kissed her damp, open mouth in quick little pecks, hoping to soften his next words. "Let's go somewhere else."

The slumberous, sated look left her eyes. Her cheeks, warmly flushed only seconds before, went pale. He knew before she answered that she'd refuse.

Georgia pushed away from him and covered her face with both hands. In a tone more startling for the lack of emotion, she whispered, "I can't believe I just did that."

Alarmed, Jordan smoothed her hair away from her face with trembling hands. "I can't believe I stopped."

She looked up at him. "You must think I'm awful."

"No." She started to say something more, but he didn't let her. "Shh. It's okay." Even with her heavy stage makeup, she looked precious to him. "Actually, it was better than okay. Much much better."

"But you didn't—" She glanced down at his very visible erection.

"Believe me, I know." Jordan ran a hand through his hair and tamped down his sexual frustration. He met her wary, shame-filled gaze, knowing his own was hot, piercing. "The thing is," he said, his voice sounding like sandpaper, "making you come was a helluva fantasy. And I wasn't disappointed."

"It was wrong."

"No. Hell, no. Nothing wrong can feel that right and you know it." He shook her gently. "Don't ask me to apologize, Georgia. We've both been on the ragged edge since first meeting and it was only a matter of time before this—and more—was bound to happen."

She attempted to turn away. "Please, don't come here again. I can't trust myself around you."

She asked the impossible. The first time he'd sat there and watched her dance, he swore he'd never come back. It ate him up to see all those men drooling over her, to know what they were thinking, that she was the center of so many drunken, lurid fantasies.

But he'd discovered that staying away was even harder. He couldn't sleep for wanting her; she occupied his thoughts both day and night. The few times he managed to get her out of his mind, he found himself thinking about the kids instead, smiling, missing them. And Ruth, too. She was such a gutsy woman, altering a lifetime of social conformity to stand up for her daughter.

"I'm not just here because of you." The second the words left his mouth, Jordan felt hemmed in by his own deceptions. He came because of Georgia, but he did have another purpose.

He truly detested the place, the smells of sour alcohol, sweat and dirt, the foul language and the overall atmosphere of depression. He considered The Swine a major nuisance, perhaps even a threat to the peace. It wasn't a quaint small-town saloon. It didn't provide lively conversation or a relaxing ambiance.

It was run-down, dirty and bred trouble because of a distinct lack of conscience on the owner's part. It didn't matter how staggering drunk the patrons might be, they could always get one more drink.

But because of Jordan's personal bias against alcohol, he'd have left others to deal with the bar if it hadn't been for Georgia. With her working at night, dressed so provocatively, he couldn't bear the thought of any of his friends or acquaintances seeing her.

Georgia looked shaken to her soul. She turned away and began pulling on her clothes over the costume. "If...if you're not here because of me, then why?"

"I'm here," he said gently, trying to ignore the demanding throb of his body, and the pleasant buzz of satisfaction despite his still raging lust, "because the Town Advisory Board had another meeting."

She turned to him with open anxiety.

"After Zenny and Walt and the others told them what they'd seen that first night, they've been outraged about the whole thing."

"Zenny and Walt?"

Jordan nodded. "I told you I was here with other men that first night? Well, they're the elders of the town, fairly set in their ways, too. When the trouble started they didn't even wait around to see how it'd turn out. They took off and by that next morning everyone in Buckhorn knew what had happened."

Her mouth opened and she breathed deeply. She stared at the far wall. "They know about me dancing?"

He nodded. "That, and the fact the police were called. I'd say folks are suffering equal parts of morbid fascination and outrage."

Georgia closed her eyes on a grimace.

He wanted to protect her from the opinions of others, but she deserved to know what was going on. Given a choice, many of the townsfolk would prefer the bar be shut down. That'd put Georgia out of a job, and into one hell of a predicament. "Sawyer and I cautioned them not to get up in arms, but then last night Morgan arrested two men who were menacing a mule."

Georgia's eyes snapped open again. "Menacing a *mule?*"

"That's right. They drove straight into a pasture, knocking down fence posts and tearing up the ground. The mule is a gentle old relic, but those bastards drove around with their horn blaring and their bright lights on, chasing her and scaring her near to death."

His fists clenched. He couldn't abide cruelty of any kind, but especially cruelty against women, children—or animals. "They're lucky Morgan found them instead of me. I'd have been tempted to teach them a better lesson than a night in jail, three-month suspension of their licenses, and a large fine."

Georgia's gray eyes were soft and sympathetic. "I thought you were the least militant one in the family."

"They were chasing a poor mule, Georgia, and they destroyed a good deal of property. Of course I'm feeling militant."

She touched his chest, her small hand gently stroking. Since his lust was unappeased, she nearly sent him into oblivion. "They had been drinking here?"

"That's right." Jordan felt far too hot. He wanted her hand on his bare skin. And he wanted it a good deal south of his chest. Just the thought of her slender fingers curling around his hard swollen flesh made him quiver like a virgin. He hurt with wanting her. "Your boss," he rasped, "knew they were drunk when they left here."

She nodded. "Bill could care less as long he's getting paid.

Jordan struggled for breath. He flattened his own hand over hers, stilling her caressing movements. "Morgan is meeting with the sheriff here. He thinks they might hit the bar with a heavy fine." Jordan braced himself against her reaction and admitted, "A lot of people are pushing for it to be shut down."

With an embarrassed little shrug, Georgia said, "I understand." Then she moved away from him. "I need to get going. It's late and I'm tired and I've got some things to do when I get home."

He hated seeing her withdrawal. "Georgia…" He was uncertain what to say. "I don't mean to hurt you."

"I know. But if I lose this job…I don't know where I'll be able to make as much money." She went about pulling on her shoes and slipping on her lightweight jacket. Jordan watched her movements with barely leashed possessiveness.

"You could work for me." He didn't really need more help, but he'd hire her in a heartbeat. In fact, he really liked the idea once he said it out loud.

Her eyes looked silver rather than gray in the dim light. "I'm sure Elizabeth will have something to say about that."

"She'd be glad for the help."

"Nonsense. You bragged to me yourself that she keeps everything running smoothly." With her purse and her bag hanging from her shoulder, Georgia clasped her hands together and silently requested that he stop blocking the door.

Even in his wildest dreams, Jordan couldn't have imagined how badly he'd dread leaving a damn closet. But he had no reason to keep her inside now that she was ready to go. He opened the door and stepped out. "I'll walk you to your car."

"I would object, but I suppose you'd start insisting?" In spite of all that had just happened, she sounded shyly teasing, and Jordan smiled in relief.

"Of course."

Because they were looking at each other rather than where they walked, they almost bumped into Honey and Elizabeth.

"Hey," Elizabeth said. "Great show, Georgia!"

Jordan gaped at them. His sisters-in-law? In The Swine? He said, "Uh…"

Honey pulled Georgia—who was speechless with astonishment—into a tight hug. "I had no idea you were so talented. And I love the costume!" In an audible whisper, she said, "No one would ever guess you'd had two kids. You looked fantastic." Then in a further confidence, she added, "Sawyer would keel over dead if I wore anything that sexy."

Elizabeth laughed. "Gabe would probably faint. *After.*"

"After?" Georgia asked, still looking bewildered.

"Yeah, after he wore himself out." She chuckled. "The man does like to—"

Jordan said again, "Uh…"

"Oh, relax, Jordan," Honey told him, patting at his chest. The touch didn't feel at all the same as when Georgia did it.

He caught Honey's hand and gathered together his wits. "What are you two doing here?"

In unison, they said, "We came to watch Georgia dance."

"I…I didn't see you," Georgia told them, glancing nervously at Jordan.

Jordan felt poleaxed. When his brothers found out, there'd be hell to pay and somehow he'd probably get blamed. "Neither did I."

"Well, we didn't just sit out in the open, silly." Honey

looked at him as though he should have figured that one out on his own. "We didn't want to make Georgia nervous. We were in the back corner booth. The bouncer—what was his name, Elizabeth?"

Elizabeth smiled. "Gus."

"Yes, Gus made sure no one bothered us."

Jordan glanced at the big no-neck ape who he'd tangled with that first night, and got a sharp nod. Jordan nodded in return. Good grief.

"Anyway," Honey said, waving away the remainder of that topic, "I was positively amazed how well you dance. It's incredible. Even when Jordan fell off his chair, you barely missed a beat."

Elizabeth snickered.

His face red and his temper on the rise, Jordan asked, "Where does Sawyer think you are?"

"At the movies."

His grin wasn't nice. "Not for long."

Honey gasped. "Don't you dare tell! You know he'll have a fit."

"Rightfully so."

Elizabeth shrugged. "I don't care if you tell. Gabe's not my boss."

Honey considered that, then shrugged, too. "Well, Sawyer's not my boss, either, but he is somewhat overprotective."

"Somewhat? Ha!" Elizabeth flipped her long red hair over her shoulder then leaned toward Georgia. "Before you get too involved with this family, you should know that they're autocrats. All in different ways, of course, but they sure do like to hover, if you know what I mean."

Jordan couldn't wait to deliver Elizabeth back to Gabe. "I do *not* hover."

Elizabeth raised an auburn brow and gave a pointed look at Jordan's arm squeezing Georgia's shoulders.

Muttering to himself, he asked, "Instead of debating this now, why don't we get the hell out of here? Bill's not too happy with me tonight anyway."

"He's not?" asked Georgia.

Jordan didn't want to explain exactly what her boss had said about a drinking limit, or how Jordan had reacted to his apathy. Luckily Honey saved him.

"He's a smarmy one, isn't he?" Honey asked.

Jordan stopped dead in midstep. In lethal tones, he asked, "Did he say something to you? Did he insult you?"

Both Honey and Elizabeth rushed to reassure him, patting his chest and shaking their heads. "No, of course not. He just looks like a weasel."

Georgia laughed. She looked at each of them, saw that they had no idea what she found humorous, and laughed some more. Jordan smiled, too. The ways that she affected him were numerous. Georgia breathed and he got aroused. But what her laughter did to him was enough to cause spontaneous combustion.

Still chuckling, she said, "I really do like your family, Jordan."

Elizabeth and Honey grinned widely.

The moist night air was very refreshing after being in the stale bar. A light breeze teased through the trees, ruffling Georgia's loose curls. She lifted her face into the breeze, breathing deeply. Jordan watched her, wanting her more than ever.

When they reached the parked cars, he played the consummate gentleman. He opened car doors and kissed cheeks and when his sisters-in-law were finally ready to head home, he cautioned them to drive safely.

Elizabeth rolled her eyes. Honey told him to do the same. They waved to Georgia and drove off.

When Jordan looked down at Georgia, there was still a small, very sweet smile curving her mouth. He tipped up her chin with the side of his hand. "Do you know how badly I want to kiss you right now?"

"You're incorrigible."

"And you're breathless, which means you want me to kiss you, too. Don't you?"

"I'm breathless," she said somewhat smugly, "because Honey and Elizabeth were so complimentary. It's been a long long time since anyone praised me for my dancing skills. And no, don't you dare say anything. The way men view what I do on stage has nothing to do with my actual talent."

Jordan blinked at her. An idea bloomed in his mind, growing, gaining momentum. "Where'd you learn to dance?"

"I took lessons as a child. All the other kids made fun of me for it, but I loved it. I've always enjoyed moving to the music. By the time I was a teenager, I was helping to teach the rest of the class. It's something that's always come naturally to me."

Jordan caught her shoulders and pulled her to her tiptoes. He kissed her soundly before she could object. For the first time since meeting her he felt like he had the upper hand. He could help her while helping himself to get closer to her. He pulled Georgia into his arms and spun her around, lifting her off her feet.

Georgia laughed in surprise while clinging to his shoulders. "What are you doing?"

"Dancing with you." She started to say something more, but he stopped and asked, "You won't forget about this weekend, right? The cookout? Honey has been planning it all month and the kids are looking forward to it. Sawyer has promised to make them his famous fruit salad with melon balls—kids love melon balls—and Casey intends to take them boating."

She ducked her head and said, "We'll be there."

Tipping her chin once again, Jordan asked, "You don't sound very happy about it. What's wrong?"

She shook her head, refusing to answer. But then, he didn't really need her to. He knew she resisted their growing closeness and the need that got harder and harder to ignore. She was afraid if she relied on him, he might let her down. Jordan smiled, remembering that she wanted options.

He'd start working on that first thing in the morning.

CHAPTER NINE

THE KITCHEN was filled to overflowing with meddling relatives when Jordan walked in for breakfast. Even though
Morgan and Misty now lived up on the hill, they often
came down for breakfast. Honey insisted on it. And since
Gabe and Elizabeth were still living downstairs in the renovated basement of the big house, they were always there
in the mornings, too. The women generally helped each
other out, cooking, watching babies, laughing and provid-
ing a nice feminine touch to what used to be a totally masculine gathering.

Casey, he noted, wallowed in all the attention. The
women doted on him shamefully.

Jordan saw everyone look up when he closed the kitchen
door. His own apartments were over the garage, converted
years ago when he realized he was a little different than
the others, that he wanted and needed more privacy than
they did. "Morning."

Morgan, with his daughter Amber perched on his lap,
leaned back and grinned. "I hear you're checking into
property around town. You thinking of moving?"

"No!" Honey put down the spatula she'd been using to
turn eggs and turned to Jordan with a horrified expression.
"It's bad enough that Gabe and Elizabeth are planning to
move. I *like* having you all here!"

Misty picked up the spatula and took over for her sister.
"He's been looking at warehouses, not homes."

"Oh." Honey seemed so relieved that Sawyer walked

up to her, put his arms around her from behind and began kissing her nape.

"You can't keep them all underfoot forever, sweetie."

She looked dreamy for a moment—a common occurrence when Sawyer kissed her or touched her—then scowled at him over her shoulder. "Don't say that. You'll have them thinking we want them to leave."

"My brothers know they're always welcome."

"And their wives."

Sawyer nodded. "I think I hear Shohn."

He left the room, oblivious to Casey's chuckles. "How the heck does he hear Shohn," Casey asked, "when no one else does? What'd the baby do? Burp?"

Everyone laughed except Honey. She, being as attuned to the baby as her husband, said matter-of-factly, "No, he yawned."

Morgan brought the conversation back around just as Jordan sprawled into his seat. "So why are you checking out warehouses?"

Jordan tried to stare him down before everyone started questioning him, but it didn't work. Amber reached up and pulled on her daddy's nose, and Jordan had to smile. He adored kids and Amber was a real cutie. Luckily, she looked just like her mother.

He wondered how they'd found out about his property inquiries so soon. Granted, he'd started checking into it yesterday morning, right after the idea had come to him the night before. But he'd barely called five places. Half the time he thought his family had radar.

Misty, long since recovered from her bout with the flu, jumped in, saying, "According to what Honey and Elizabeth told me about Georgia's talent, I bet he's thinking of putting together a dance studio. Buckhorn doesn't have anything like that, you know. A little culture wouldn't hurt anyone."

If he'd been prepared, if he'd had any forewarning at all that Misty might guess so close to the truth, Jordan could have blustered his way out of it. But he didn't. He simply stared, in awe of Misty's ability.

She felt him looking at her and glanced back. "What? Am I right?"

Morgan laughed. "Damn, you're good, sweetheart! And Jordan, I personally think it's a helluva idea."

"Helluva idea," Amber said, and Morgan quickly tried to hush her, but not quick enough. Misty glared at him with one of her you're-in-trouble looks.

"Amber, sweetie," Misty said, "Daddy's got a nasty mouth and says things he shouldn't. You can't always copy him or people will say you have a nasty mouth, too."

Amber pursed her cute little rosebud mouth and nodded. "Daddy's nasty."

"That's right." Misty kissed her daughter, who kissed her nasty daddy, just to make him stop looking so guilty.

Sawyer walked back in with Shohn on his shoulder. The baby still looked sleepy and had a soft printed blanket clutched in his chubby fist.

Honey said immediately, "Jordan is going to buy Georgia a dance studio."

Sawyer drew up short. "He's going to what?"

Jordan leaned forward, put his head on the table, and covered it with his arms. Amber patted his ear.

"A dance studio?"

"Yes." Honey took the baby and snuggled him close. "Georgia would be a wonderful dance instructor."

"How do you know?" Jordan asked, his voice muffled because he hadn't sat up yet.

A heavy pause filled the air. Everyone looked at Jordan. He sighed and propped his head up on his fist. "What makes you think she'd be a good instructor?"

Knowing his ploy, Honey lifted her chin and said, "Because I watched her dance two nights ago, as you very well know.''

Jordan couldn't have been more amazed by her admission than if she'd thrown an egg at him. ''You told him?''

She nodded. He glanced at Elizabeth who sat in Gabe's lap. ''Of course we told.''

Jordan stared at his brothers' red faces. ''And neither of you are angry?''

''Damn right I'm angry,'' Sawyer admitted. ''I told her she should have told me if she'd wanted to go and I would have taken her.''

''Damn right,'' Amber said. When Sawyer groaned, she asked, ''Unca Sawyer nasty, too?''

''Yeah,'' Morgan answered. ''Nastier than me.'' He kissed Amber's belly and made her laugh.

Gabe made a face. ''I had fully intended to impress upon Elizabeth the error of her ways, but it didn't work out quite as I had intended.''

Morgan covered Amber's ears and said with remorse, ''I know what you mean. You plan on giving a woman a good swat, but once you've got her pants off, you forget what you're doing.''

Misty pinched Morgan for that bit of impertinence. Elizabeth just laughed, knowing it was all bluster. It was the truth not a one of them would ever lay a harsh hand on a female and their wives more than understood that.

Jordan laughed. God, he loved the lot of them. They were all nuts and overbearing and intrusive, and he had no idea what he'd do without them. The phone rang so he decided to excuse himself from the chaos.

He went into the family room and when he picked up the receiver and said, ''Hello,'' he heard a long pause before his mother asked, ''What's wrong?''

Jordan stared at the phone. ''Mother?''

"Of course it's your mother. Now tell me what's wrong."

Of course it's your mother? Jordan held the receiver away from his ear to stare at it. His mother and Brett now lived in Florida. She'd called last week, but he'd been at Georgia's and missed her.

Because he wasn't sure how much she knew, Jordan hedged. "What makes you think anything's wrong?" Though he'd just been entertaining softer thoughts about his family, he now considered knocking all their heads together. If one of his damn brothers had been tattling, upsetting their mother, he wouldn't be pleased.

"I can hear it in your voice," she explained. "You've always had the most betraying voice. Even when you were a baby, I could tell by your gurgles what you were thinking and feeling."

Jordan dropped onto the edge of the couch and without giving himself time to plan out his reply, he said, "I think I'm in love."

Another pause, then softly: "Will you tell me about her?"

Even as he considered his words, Jordan smiled. "She's beautiful."

"Of course."

"But that's not what got to me." He frowned. "She has two kids. Lisa, six and Adam, four. They're incredible."

There was a smug note in his mother's voice when she said, "Then obviously *she's* incredible."

"She is. And gutsy. She's made a few mistakes, I guess. And…" Jordan hesitated. "In a lot of ways, she's like you."

Another pause. "How's that?"

Jordan looked toward the doorway, saw no one was lurking, and said, "She'll do anything necessary to see that her kids are taken care of."

His mother laughed. "What in the world did I ever do to warrant that comment? You make it sound like I worked in the coal mines to feed you or something."

Jordan considered all the things she had done, the sacrifices she'd made, how hard she'd always worked to make them happy. But the one thing that really stood out in his mind, the one thing he'd always hated, slipped out without his permission. "You married my father," he said, "hoping to make a complete home for Sawyer and Morgan."

"Jordan!" She sounded incredulous that he'd come to such a conclusion. "I married your father because I loved him!"

Jordan heard a muffled shout in the background and his mother said, "No Brett, it's not Gabe. It's Jordan." And then: "Yes, I can see how you made that assumption."

Jordan chuckled. He could just imagine what Brett, Gabe's father, was thinking right now. "Tell Brett I said 'hi.'"

"Later. Right now I have something that I want you to understand. Do you have your listening ears on, Jordan?"

"My listening ears?" She hadn't used that term on him since before he'd become a teen.

"Don't get smart, son. Just pay attention."

He grinned even as he said, "Yes, ma'am."

"I have never regretted marrying your father. How could I when I have you?"

"He was a damn drunk."

"He was human. He made mistakes and in my mind, he's paid dearly for them. He lost me, and he lost all of you. Surely there couldn't have been a worse penalty."

Jordan gripped the receiver hard. "He was irresponsible, selfish—"

"No, sweetheart, he was just an alcoholic." She sighed, then continued. "We humans are prone to screwing up our lives on occasion. Most of the time we're given the chance to make amends. Your father was a wonderful man when I met him. Things happened that he couldn't deal with, and he...well, he wasn't strong enough to cope. If you ever get to meet him, I hope you keep that in mind.''

Jordan didn't want to meet him, ever. But to appease his mother, he said, ''I'll think on it.''

''Now tell me about this young lady you're going to marry.''

He choked on his own indrawn breath. ''I didn't say anything about marrying her! I haven't even known her that long. It's just...''

''It's just that you love her. So why wait?''

''Well, one good reason might be that she doesn't want to marry me. In fact, she doesn't even want to see me.''

''That's ridiculous! Why wouldn't she? There's no finer man than you.''

Jordan got an evil grin when he said, ''I'll tell the others you said so.''

Laughing, his mother replied, ''You're all equally fine men. And I can tell them myself this evening.''

''There's no need to call back. Everyone's here for breakfast.''

''That's not what I meant. Brett and I are flying in tonight. We should make it to the house by about five.''

Jordan froze. ''You're coming here? Tonight?''

''Now, Jordan, if I didn't know better, I'd say you didn't want to see me.''

Jordan quickly reassured her otherwise. But in his mind, he was thinking of the cookout, the fact that Georgia would be there with her kids. He'd hoped to tell her about the studio, but until he knew for certain that there was a building that'd work, he didn't want to mention it.

His mother again told him that she loved him, and Jordan reciprocated. It'd be good to see her, and the babies would love it, not to mention how Casey would feel. But with his mother there, he didn't know if he'd be able to get a single moment alone with Georgia.

And that's what he wanted, because he was through with waiting. He'd planned to cement their relationship in the oldest way known to mankind.

Now that he'd seen firsthand how she responded to him, he knew it would be so damn good, so explosive, she'd never be able to deny him again.

RUTH WAS in the kitchen baking when Georgia walked in. She paused, watching her mother for a moment before announcing herself. Ruth looked pretty in a matching nightgown and robe decorated with small sprigs of yellow flowers. Her light brown hair, now slightly streaked with gray, was twisted at the back of her head in a loose knot. She was humming as she put a new sheet of cookies in the oven.

"Morning, Mom."

Ruth turned with a smile and then went to Georgia to kiss her cheek. "You're up early!"

Georgia grinned. "So are you. And baking already?" She made a beeline for the coffeepot, as usual. Now, whenever she drank a cup, she thought of Jordan—and remembered everything he'd made her feel.

"I wanted to bring something to the cookout today. I'm looking forward to it."

Georgia's heart swelled. The kids had talked about little else for the past few days and her mother's eyes glowed with just the mention of the gathering. Georgia hadn't realized how isolated, how withdrawn from society she'd kept them all. Between working so much, both at the bar and on the house, there'd been little time for playing. It seemed every day she found another way that she'd failed the ones she loved most.

"I'm sorry. I hadn't thought about how lonely you might have been."

Ruth shook her head. "Or how lonely *you've* been?"

She started to deny that, but Ruth took her coffee cup and set it aside, then clasped both of Georgia's hands and squeezed them. "Georgia, it's okay to admit it, you know." Her mother met her gaze squarely and stated, "It's also okay to want a man."

"Mother!" Georgia felt a hot blush begin creeping up her neck.

"Oh, don't give me that tone." Ruth paid no heed to her daughter's embarrassment. "I'm older, not dead. I know how it is. And Jordan is...well, he's a potent male. Personally I think you're downright foolish to keep putting him off."

Georgia thought she might fall through the floor with her mother's words. "He *is* potent, and that's what scares me." In a softer voice, she admitted, "It'd be so easy to love him."

"So?" Ruth sounded totally unconcerned with her plight. "The kids and I love him, so you might as well, too."

Georgia shook her head. "It isn't that easy, Mom. I thought I loved Dennis—"

"You did love Dennis. And I think he honestly loved you. He was just young, Georgia. Young and foolish." Ruth hesitated, then said, "Let's sit down. I want to tell you something."

Georgia agreed, but she also snatched back her coffee cup. No way could she handle all this without some caffeine. Luckily the kids were still sleeping soundly, giving them some quiet time alone.

As Georgia refilled her cup, she looked around her home. Everything was in order now. Oh, there were still plenty of repairs to be made, but nothing crucial. She could finally see the end of the tunnel. And beyond the material things, her children were more lively than they'd ever been.

They'd flourished under all the added attention from Jordan and his family.

Morgan had dubbed them "official deputies" and given them both badges to wear. Casey took them swimming and boating and taught them both how to fish. Saywer had let them listen to their own heartbeats with his stethoscope. The women had praised Lisa for helping with the babies and had convinced Adam that he was the handsomest guy in Buckhorn, even more so than Gabe—which made her shy son start strutting.

And Jordan…Georgia sighed just thinking about him. It amazed her that one man could truly be so wonderful. He'd gone with them to find salamanders in the woods behind the house. One day he had even paid them to help him at his office, though Georgia knew they'd been in the way more than not. Still, he never seemed to mind. They started the day talking about him, and often wanted to call him in the evening to tell him good-night.

"Georgia?"

She hadn't realized that she'd stopped in the middle of the floor and was just standing there. She looked at her mother, saw her caring and love and acceptance, and she burst into tears.

Ruth didn't cry with her. As she got out of her seat to embrace her daughter, she gave a sympathetic chuckle. "Love is the damndest thing, isn't it?"

Georgia tried to mop her eyes and hold on to her coffee at the same time. "I don't know what I'm going to do."

"You're going to tell him." Ruth held her away so she could see her face, and nodded when Georgia shook her head. "Sweetheart, don't make the same mistakes I made. Don't waste your time being afraid. Sometimes you just have to take a few chances, and I think Jordan's worth the risk, don't you?"

With a shuddering breath, Georgia reached for a napkin

off the counter and blew her nose. She whispered, "He's never said anything about loving me."

"So? Your father dutifully told me every night that he loved me. But it would have meant so much more if he'd shown me instead. If he'd cared when I was tired or sick. If he'd held me when I was upset."

Georgia stared at her mother. *If he'd given her foot rubs and held her when she was afraid and loved her children....* Her father had never really loved her, not the way she loved Adam and Lisa.

As if she'd read her thoughts, Ruth nodded. "Jordan has shown you that he cares in more ways than I can count."

"Oh, God." Her mother was right. From the moment she'd met Jordan, she'd known he was different. True, he was pushy and arrogant and determined—but according to his family, he only behaved that way when he really cared about something. Or someone. She didn't want to rely on him, but...maybe it would be okay. Maybe depending on him to share with her, to give and let her give, too, wouldn't be so bad. If she could only balance her independence against what he made her feel....

But she knew she'd always hate herself if she didn't at least give him a chance. "I'll tell him today."

Ruth laughed out loud. "That's wonderful!" She hugged Georgia again before gently pushing her into a seat at the table. "Now, how about a cookie to celebrate?"

From the doorway, Adam and Lisa said, "I want one, too!" and as Georgia opened her arms to her children, still sleepy warm from their beds, she thought that she had to be the luckiest woman alive. Perhaps after today, she'd also be the most fulfilled.

JORDAN HEARD her car pull up and walked around to the front of the house. People had been arriving all afternoon, and he'd been anxiously waiting for her. He'd found a studio, and he could barely wait to discover her reaction to that.

The moment they saw him, Adam and Lisa jumped out and came running, followed by Ruth. Jordan was barely able to swallow down his emotion as he embraced both children. They chatted ninety miles a minute, telling him about all the cookies their grandma had made and about the pictures they'd colored for him to decorate his office, and about a frog they'd found in the backyard.

"Jus' like you tol' us to, we played with it and then turned it loose."

Jordan stroked Adam's downy hair, warmed by the sun. "I'm sure the frog appreciates it. They're not meant to be pets."

Lisa nodded. "We remembered." Then she leaned forward to whisper, "'Sides, Grandma hates frogs."

Jordan was still chuckling when Ruth and Georgia reached his side. Ruth gave him a hug, though Georgia looked shyly away, prompting him to curious speculation. Following the lead her mother and children had set, Jordan pulled Georgia close for a hug. To his surprise, she briefly nuzzled her nose into his throat and sighed.

Just that easily, he was aroused. Of course, he stayed semiaroused around her anyway.

Trying to discern her mood, Jordan studied her and only vaguely heard Ruth announce that she and the kids were taking the cookies to Honey. Georgia waited until she'd gone, then licked her lips in a show of nervousness.

Jordan touched her hair, teased by the warm afternoon breeze. He loved how the golden-brown curls framed her face and how the sunlight glinted in them. "Georgia?" His voice was husky, affected by more than his sexual need of her. He wanted her, all of her. Forever. "Is something wrong?"

He took her arm and started her toward the back of the

house where everyone was gathered. He could feel the tension emanating from her and sought to make her more at ease by rubbing her back.

Her eyes closed and she moaned softly, then suddenly blurted, "I have something I want to tell you."

Jordan tensed. He could tell by her expression that she wasn't completely comfortable with what she had to say. If she thought to try pulling away from him, after they were finally getting so close, she could damn well think again. He took her hand in his and laced their fingers together. Jordan could hear the others chatting in the backyard as they rounded the house, though Georgia seemed oblivious.

"I've been going over everything you said." She peeked a look at him, then frowned in concentration. "That last night at the bar, I mean."

Jordan nodded. "I want to talk about that, too." He now had options for her, viable options. He hoped she'd be pleased.

She stared at him in sudden horror. "You've changed your mind? You don't want me anymore?"

"*What?*" Jordan jerked around to stare at her. "No," he said, his frown deepening. "Hell, no. Where'd you get that crazy idea?"

"I thought—" She shook her head and started walking again. "I thought maybe, because I pushed so hard, you'd decided to leave me alone now."

"Georgia." How could she possibly think such a thing? Leave her alone? He couldn't even stop thinking about her, so how would he keep away?

They had just stepped into the backyard when she drew a deep breath and said, "That's good, because...I want you, too." She looked up at him, her eyes so pale in the sunlight. "Jordan, I don't think I've ever wanted any man as much as I want you. What...what you did to me the other night? That was wonderful and I loved it. I haven't been able to think of much else. But I want more than that." She stared him right in the eyes and whispered, "I want to feel you inside me and I want to watch your face when you come, and I want to hear your voice and hold you. I want that so badly I can't stand it anymore."

Jordan sucked in a huge breath of air, but it didn't help. Just that quickly he had an erection that threatened the seams of his jeans. Every muscle in his body shook.

And then the sound of conversation intruded and he looked around, seeing himself surrounded by family and neighbors. Luckily no one was paying them any attention.

He groaned aloud. Georgia finally admitted to wanting him, and there wasn't an ounce of privacy to be found. "Sweetheart, you really know how to make a man crazy."

She stared up at him, her eyes full of questions. And invitation. "It's fair. You've certainly made me nuts." She reached up and touched his face. "Can I ask you something?"

Jordan put his arm around her and led her to the side of the yard, as far away from the others as he dared to go without drawing a lot of attention. "You can ask me anything, Georgia. Don't ever forget that."

Her smile was so sweet and gentle. He loved her mouth. Damn, how he loved her mouth.

"If," she said, looking uncertain once again, "I didn't want to be involved with you. If I made it clear that I had no feelings for you at all—"

"Then I'd respect your wishes, even if it killed me."

She went on tiptoe to give him a quick kiss. "I already knew that. You're not a man to ever force a woman in any way."

Jordan laughed at her assumptions. "I'd do my damndest first to convince you."

"You already have. Done your damndest *and* convinced me. But you're such a seducer with that sexy voice—" she touched his mouth with one fingertip "—it wasn't that hard."

The way she touched him, how she looked at him, took him to the edge. In a rasp, he said, "Speak for yourself."

She understood his meaning and glanced down at his fly. "Oh." Warmth colored her cheekbones, making him nuts, but when he went to kiss her, she said, "Jordan, it was something else I was going to ask."

"Tell me."

"If we had no personal relationship, would you still want to see my kids? Or would you suddenly disappear from their lives?"

Jordan didn't give a damn if everyone in Buckhorn saw him. He cupped her face in his hands and took her mouth in a kiss meant to offer reassurance and so much more. When he lifted away, she clung to him, as unconcerned with their audience as he was. "I love your kids, sweetheart. I'd never do that to them."

Tears glistened on her lashes. "That's what I thought."

Jordan knew what she was getting at. Their own father had walked away, just as his had. For whatever reason, her ex had been able to give up his own two offspring, never knowing if they were all right, if they needed him or not.

But Jordan was different. He'd never before realized exactly how different until that moment. "I used to worry about my father," he said. "Not about his well-being, but whether or not people would associate me with him. Like your ex-husband, he split after the divorce and no one has seen him since. Not a single phone call, not even a card. If I died, I'm not sure he'd know, or even care."

Jordan shrugged and admitted, "There've been times when I hated him because I felt so ashamed. Not because he wasn't here, but because my brothers had respectable, honorable, loving fathers and yet my father was a huge mistake."

His throat felt raw as he told her things he'd never said to another living soul. "I wanted to hold myself to a higher standard, to prove to myself and to everyone else that I was better than that, better than him."

Georgia put her arms around him and rested the side of her face on his chest. He cupped the back of her neck, tangling his fingers in her soft curls.

He smiled when she said, "You're the best person I've ever met." But then she added, "You make me feel so inferior."

Jordan abruptly pushed her back so he could scowl into her face. "What the hell are you talking about?"

She lifted her shoulders in a slow shrug. "I know it probably bothers you to want me. I got pregnant at sixteen, I've already been divorced and I dance in a bar." Her smile was sad and fleeting. "I'm hardly anybody's idea of a 'higher standard.'"

Rage washed over him, making him break out in a sweat. His vision narrowed to her face, a face he loved. He gave her a quick, sharp shake. "Don't you *ever* say anything like that again!"

"Jordan!" She glanced around, reminding him that they weren't alone. "Someone will hear you."

It took all his concentration to lower his voice, to temper his fury. Tears filled her eyes again, slicing into him like the sharpest blade. It was her vulnerability that gained him some control. He pulled her into his chest and held her tight. "I never thought," he whispered against her forehead, "that I'd meet someone as beautiful as you. Do you know what I see when I look at you, Georgia?"

She shook her head.

"I see a woman who will do anything she has to in order to take care of the people who depend on her. A woman with enough strength and courage and honor to beat the odds, and still be so incredibly sweet that it breaks my heart just to look at her.''

Georgia's self-conscious laugh teased along his senses. He felt her wipe her eyes on his shirt and wished he was alone with her. She filled him with lust, broke his heart with her gentleness and humbled him with her strength.

"You make me sound like a conquering Amazon,'' she whispered.

He put his mouth close to her ear. ''From the moment I saw you,'' he breathed, relishing her scent and her softness, ''I was so hot to have you I nearly ground my teeth into powder. That's never happened to me before. I stay so aroused I ache, but I only want you.''

Her hands fisted in his shirt. ''Me, too. I want you so much, it scares me.''

He didn't want her to fear him, but he'd explain that to her later. ''I think you're the sexiest woman I've ever met. And the more I got to know you, the worse it became, because your sexiness is earthy. It isn't just about your gorgeous body, or the way you move or how you look at me. It's you. Everything about you, Georgia. Do you understand?''

She nodded. ''All right.''

Jordan suddenly felt someone behind him. He jerked around and found Morgan and Gabe both breathing down his neck.

"Hey,'' Morgan said, as if he hadn't just intruded. ''You two are embarrassing everyone, me included. Why don't you find a room somewhere?''

Gabe shoved Morgan. ''You're so crude.'' Then to Georgia: ''Put him out of his misery, sweetheart. Jordan isn't used to this kind of excitement. Sawyer says it isn't good for his heart.''

Georgia covered her face and laughed. Jordan thought about tossing his brothers into the lake. But then Morgan whispered, "You know, the gazebo is real private. Everyone is getting ready to eat and I can keep the kids occupied if you two want to go…talk things over."

Jordan looped his arm around Georgia and pulled her to his side. He peered around the yard. Zenny and Walt and Newton waved to them. Georgia groaned, but waved back. Howard and Jesse were arguing—as usual.

Morgan's enormous dog, Godzilla, had the kids well occupied. Lisa, Adam and Amber were all petting him and Godzilla rested on his back in doggy bliss, his tongue hanging out of the side of his mouth. Godzilla looked more like the missing link than a pet, but he was about the sweetest creature Jordan had ever seen. Even Honey's calico cat liked the dog. She sat next to Lisa, getting her own pet every now and then and rubbing her head against Godzilla's hip.

"Will you look at my mother?" Georgia said in awe.

Jordan followed the direction of Georgia's gaze and found Ruth in animated conversation with Misty's and Honey's bachelor father. Damned if there wasn't a bright blush on her face, too. Well, well, Jordan thought. He wasn't crazy about the man, despite how he'd softened since his daughters had joined the family, but whatever he said to Ruth must have been complimentary because she hadn't stopped smiling once.

He heard a laugh and noticed Casey was sitting beneath a shade tree, surrounded by female admirers. Gabe nodded toward Casey, chuckling. "They've been after him all day. He can't get himself a cola without them all trailing behind."

Even as Gabe spoke, Emma walked up to group. She wore another halter top that showed more than it concealed and shorts that should have been illegal. She was barefoot, carrying her sandals, and Casey made an obvious point of not looking at her, at completely ignoring her existence—

until two of the girls said something obviously snide. Emma, head bowed, started to walk away and within two heartbeats Casey was at her side. They appeared to disagree on something for just a moment, then Casey shook his head, slung his arm around her shoulders, and practically dragged her off.

A lot of feminine complaints ensued as Casey and Emma disappeared around the side of the house.

Georgia sighed. "I really adore your nephew."

Morgan laughed. "We're rather fond of him, too." Under his breath he added, "But what the hell is he up to?"

"You two should get going," Gabe said. "But I'd take the long route if I was you. Casey's not the only one with disgruntled females hunting for him."

Georgia frowned over that, looking around the yard with an evil glint in her eyes. Jordan appreciated her mild show of jealousy; she'd admitted to wanting him and now she was acting possessive. All he needed was a quiet spot to show her how much he cared.

Morgan suddenly laughed. "Too late. You should have fled when you had the chance."

"What are you talking about?" Jordan demanded, not in the least amused by the possibility of yet another delay.

"She's here." Morgan tipped his head toward the back-door of the house. "And you know there's no way in hell she'll let you slink away."

Georgia's frown turned ferocious. "She *who?*"

Gabe, too, looked at the house, then started to laugh. "Our mother. Prepare yourself, Georgia, she's making a beeline this way."

All three brothers smiled and started forward; Jordan pulled Georgia along with him. They met Sawyer on the path and before Megan Kasper could descend off the back stoop, she was enveloped in masculine hugs that kept her completely off her feet for a good five minutes.

CHAPTER TEN

"YOUR CHILDREN are wonderful."

Georgia smiled at Megan as she stroked Lisa's hair. "Thank you."

Lisa sent Megan a big grin, worshiping her. Of course, she and Adam had both been amazed by this tiny woman who ruled her gigantic sons with an iron fist. The men jumped at her slightest whisper, and did so with grins on their faces.

Georgia had heard so many stories about Megan's stubbornness, her strong will, she'd certainly expected some-one...bigger. But while Megan was small in stature, she had an enormous smile and an innate gentleness and she loved to laugh.

It tickled Georgia to see how her sons fawned over her. When Megan had first arrived several hours ago, she'd been passed from one strong set of arms to another. How such a small woman could mother such colossal men was beyond her. When one of the neighbors had commented on it with a smile, another had said that Megan always gravitated to the "big guys." Seeing her husband, Georgia understood.

Brett Kasper had stood there looking pleased and smug and adoring over everything Megan did. He resembled his son Gabe quite a bit, in that they were both drop-dead gorgeous, they both liked to pet on their wives, and they were both strongly built. Once the brothers had finished with Megan, Brett had been treated to a round of bear hugs himself, with no preferences shown. He was, obviously, very well loved.

"I'm going to skin Casey when he gets here."

Georgia laughed at that, knowing Megan was anxious to see him again. Georgia leaned forward and said, "He went off with a girl."

"I never doubted it for a moment." Megan frowned at Jordan, sitting beside her in a lawn chair, and said, "He's far too much like his uncles *not* to be with a female."

Lisa thought that was funny and giggled, but when she saw Adam go by chasing the dog, she ran after them. Georgia watched her go, feeling so incredibly at peace.

Jordan shrugged. "He's a little like Gabe, with the girls after him. And a little like Sawyer, being so compassionate. I'm just not sure what's motivating him today." As he spoke, he lifted one of Georgia's feet, pulled off her sandal, and started another foot rub. She gawked at him, but Megan only smiled and Jordan didn't even seem aware of what he was doing. "I think Emma has him on the run."

Both Megan and Jordan ignored Georgia's struggle to retrieve her foot. *"Jordan…"*

He smiled at her, then said to his mother, "Georgia's a dancer, you know. In high heels."

"Ah." Megan did her best to hide her amusement as Jordan caught her other foot also. "I suppose that explains it."

Georgia thought she might die of embarrassment, but instead she ended up groaning. Everyone talked about Jordan's magical voice; why hadn't anyone warned her about his magical hands?

Megan stood. "I see Ruth and Misty calling the kids in. Sounds like they're going to make popcorn. I think I'll help."

Sure enough, Amber led the way with Lisa and Adam following, trailed by the dog and cat. Misty held Shohn in her arms while Ruth kept the door open for the parade. Georgia was amazed at how the kids were so accepted by everyone. They didn't deliberately take turns that she'd noticed, but somehow it worked out that way. Earlier she and Jordan had taken them all on an expedition to the lake where they'd lifted stones along the shore and found not only crawdads, but minnows and rock bass. Amber, strangely enough, had been the most daring at grabbing for the creepy-crawly creatures. But then Jordan explained that she'd been in or near the water since her birth, thanks to Gabe. Adam and Lisa professed to love it, too, so Jordan had promised to get Gabe to take them to the dam very soon.

They were all so giving and so accepting. Her children had found a family here. And that made her full to bursting with happiness.

Since Georgia couldn't stand, given that Jordan had both her feet held firmly in his lap, Megan bent down to her instead. After a tight hug and a kiss on the cheek, she said, "I'll be in town for awhile this trip. Do you think we could get together for lunch or something? I'd love to visit more."

Georgia glanced at Jordan, saw his small smile, and agreed. "I'd enjoy that. Thank you."

Next Megan clasped Jordan's face between her hands and said, "I love seeing you so happy."

Jordan chuckled. "I'm rather fond of the situation myself."

She kissed him soundly and then took herself off. She'd barely gone ten feet when a rubber-tipped dart hit her in the backside. Megan jumped, whipped around, saw Gabe hiding behind a tree and started after him. Gabe ran for his life as Morgan and Sawyer, standing together at the back door, doubled over in laughter.

Georgia couldn't help but laugh, too. Then she looked up and locked gazes with Jordan. He looked...serious.

"Jordan?"

His fingers continued to work over her feet, only now his touch felt more sexual, more exciting. She let out a small, breathy moan, imagining those hands in other places.

"Do you know," he whispered, his eyes so hot she felt scorched, "that I'm about to die from unsated lust? I want you so bad right now I'm close to—"

"Ho!" Sawyer slapped him on the back, nearly knocking Jordan out of his lawn chair. "Hold that thought until I'm a safe distance away."

Jordan's growl was feral. "*Damn it*, will you guys stop sneaking up on me!"

Sawyer bit back a laugh. "Mom has decided to do a sleepover, just like she used to when we were young." In a stage whisper he added, "It's possible she's hoping to give you a helping hand."

Then to Georgia, "Honey's already dragging the family-room furniture around, making space for the tent, but Mom said she wants your permission to invite Adam and Lisa to spend the night, too."

Jordan closed his eyes and ignored Sawyer.

Georgia, a bit shaken by the interruption and her own repressed desire, said dumbly, "A tent?"

"Yeah. Kids love making tents out of blankets and stuff. They'll sleep on the floor and Mom and Brett will sleep on the couch." He shrugged. "It's her way of giving everyone a night off. Except me because Honey is still breast-feeding, but we're claiming tomorrow afternoon." He grinned shamelessly with that admission.

Jordan came to his feet in a rush, cupped the back of Georgia's head, and gave her a hard kiss. "Say yes."

She looked into his eyes, saw all the promise there, and nodded. "Yes."

Jordan's eyes flared with satisfaction. "Let's see if I can keep you in such an agreeable mood," he murmured.

Ten minutes later Georgia found herself being hustled across the yard to Jordan's apartments over the garage. Her kids had kissed her goodbye and good-night without a qualm. They knew she'd be close if she was needed. Ruth had been invited to 'camp out' with them and had accepted, especially when Mr. Malone had done the same.

Jordan paused beside the steps leading to his front door.

"What is it?" Georgia asked, a little breathless from the idea of what they were about to do.

"I thought I heard something." Jordan frowned, looked around the yard, then shook his head. "Nevermind. It doesn't matter." He put his arm around her shoulders and together they practically ran up the steps. No sooner did Jordan have the door closed than Georgia found herself in his arms.

"God, I need you," he whispered and his rough velvet voice stroked over her as surely as his hands were doing. "Let me love you all night."

She would have said yes, but his mouth covered hers and his tongue thrust inside, hot and wet and hungry and all she could do was moan. Jordan must have understood; one of his large hands settled on her breast, softly kneading, and the other curved around the front of her thigh. He pressed into her, all hard, tensed muscles and trembling need. She felt his erection against her belly and rubbed herself against him.

In that instant, he lost it.

CASEY CHUCKLED as he saw the light go out in the rooms overhead. Jordan was a goner—and Casey had never seen him happier.

He was behind the garage in the darkest shadows, Emma

clinging to his side. Very gently, he eased her away. "We should join the others."

"No." Her hand, so small and soft, stroked down his bare chest, but Casey caught it before she reached the fly to his jeans.

It took more control than he knew he had to turn her away. "Emma," he chided, and hopefully he was the only one who heard the shaking of his voice. He'd started out befriending her, but Emma wanted more. She was so blatant about it, so brazen, it was all he could do not to give in. But more than anything Emma needed a friend, not another conquest. And beyond that, Casey didn't share.

"Are you a virgin?" she taunted, and Casey laughed outright at her ploy.

"That," he said, flicking a finger over her soft cheek, "is none of your business."

She shook her head in wonder. "You're the only guy I know who wouldn't have denied it right away!"

"I'm not denying or confirming."

"I know, but most guys'd lie if they had to, rather than let a girl think—"

"What?" Casey cupped her face and despite his resolve, he kissed her. "I don't care what anyone thinks, Emma. You should know that by now. Besides, what I've done or with who isn't the point."

"No," she agreed, her tone sad. "It's what I've done, isn't it?"

He repeated his own thoughts out loud. "I don't share."

"What if I promised not to "

"Shhh. Summer break is almost over and I'll be leaving for school. I won't be around, so there's no point in us even discussing this."

Big tears welled in her eyes, reflecting the moonlight, making his guts cramp. "I'm leaving too, Casey."

"And where do you think to go?"

"It doesn't matter." He could see her soft mouth trembling, could smell her sweet scent carried on the cool evening breeze. Boldly, she took his hand and pressed it to her breast. She was so damn soft.

With a muttered curse, Casey pulled her closer and kissed her again. It didn't matter, he promised himself, filling his hand with her firm breast, finding her nipple and stroking with his thumb. He was damned if he did, and damned if he didn't. And sometimes Emma was just too much temptation.

But it wouldn't change anything. He told her so in a muted whisper, and her only reply was a groan.

"I WANTED to go slow," Jordan ground out as he jerked Georgia's T-shirt high, pushed her bra aside and bared one breast. He had very large hands, but even for him she was lush and full. "I wanted to make this last."

"Don't you dare go slow," she gasped, and gripped his head as he closed his mouth over one taut straining nipple. *"Jordan."*

He pulsed with incredible need, his heartbeat wild and uncontrolled. She tasted even better than he remembered, ripe and hot. With a low groan, she parted her thighs and she pushed against him, using her body to stroke his erection, her movements sinuous and graceful, making him think of all the fantasies he'd had when watching her dance.

He sucked her nipple deep, drawing on her while with his other hand he teased the crease of her behind. "Do you know what I want?" he growled, and switched to her other breast. The nipple he'd just abandoned was wet and so tight he ached just seeing it. He pinned her against the wall, knowing if he didn't slow her down he'd be gone in under three seconds.

Georgia gave a breathy, barely-there laugh. "It's obvious

what you want." Her small hand pressed between them and curled around his hard-on. "This is a dead giveaway."

Jordan squeezed his eyes shut and concentrated on holding back his orgasm. "Don't do that." He stepped away, putting an arm's length of distance between them, staring at her through a haze of lust. "I'm not sure how you manage it, but you set me off and I don't want to end this too quick. Not for me and not for you."

Georgia looked at him while using the wall for support. Her chest, bared from his petting, rose and fell with deep breaths and quick pants. Her legs were still parted, her hands flat on the wall beside her hips. She looked enticing and tempting and Jordan wanted to drag her down to the carpet and bury himself inside her until they both screamed with the pleasure of it.

Slowly she gathered her wits and a small, seductive smile curled that sexier-than-sin mouth. Her eyes were dark and inviting. "Tell me what you want, Jordan."

He didn't hesitate. "I want you to ride me. Hard. I want to lie on my back and watch you while you take your pleasure. I want to see all those sensual movements you make when you dance, only I want them for me and me alone." Her lips parted, her breath came faster. He added in a whisper, "And I want it all while I'm deep inside you."

She came away from the wall in a rush, grabbing him and kissing him—his mouth, his throat, his chest. Jordan palmed her backside, lifted her and started for his bedroom. When her legs wound around him he had to stop for just a moment and kiss her deeply, but he could feel his passions on the boiling point, ready to erupt.

He tripped over a pair of slacks on his bedroom floor, stumbled to the bed and dropped there with Georgia still in his arms. "Don't move," he rasped.

She ignored him, grabbing his shirt and trying to yank it off him. He did that for her, then wrestled her own shirt over her head, leaving it and her bra twisted around her arms to try to hinder her movements just a bit.

"You're pushing me, sweetheart and I can't take it."

"Damn it, Jordan..." She struggled with the shirt and bra and by the time she had her arms free he'd already yanked her shorts and panties off.

Sitting back on his heels between her wide-spread legs, he whispered, "I could come just looking at you."

She moaned.

"Don't move now. I mean it." And before she could ignore that edict, he caught her hips in his hands, lifted her, and stroked with his tongue. She was already wet and hot and he grew voracious in his need to take as much of her as he could. "You taste so sweet."

Like a wild woman, she writhed and squirmed and cried out. Jordan loved it all, just as he loved her. His fingers bit deeply into her cheeks and he used his thumbs to open her further, stroking with his tongue and teasing with his teeth and breathing in her heady, musky scent.

His erection throbbed and strained against his fly, but he wanted her pleasure first because he wasn't at all certain how long he'd last once he got inside her. He'd meant to seduce her, but he forgot everything he knew about women and what they enjoyed. He acted solely on instinct, but it must have been enough. After several minutes of reacting to her moans and her small movements and her breathless encouragement, Jordan felt her climax start.

Her hips jerked, her thighs trembled and she groaned, long and low and real, pressing herself against his mouth to take everything he could give her. He held her closer, used his tongue to stroke her deeper, faster, and she came with all the energy she gave to her dance.

When she quieted, her harsh breathing the only sound in the room, Jordan rested his face against her thigh. Her completion, as if it had been his own, had helped to calm him.

Idly, he traced his fingers over her slick flesh, her soft brown curls, making her twitch and moan.

He grinned. "This," he whispered, softly stroking her swollen folds before slowly, carefully pushing one finger deep, "was worth the wait."

She moved to his touch, lazy, sated movements. He loved seeing her spread out naked on his bed. When he pulled his fingers away, she heaved a long, shuddering sigh, and he decided he'd better not stall any longer or she was liable to fall asleep on him. And he knew firsthand how difficult it was to get her awake again.

Jordan stood beside the bed and stripped off his jeans. Georgia watched him through heavy, slumberous eyes— until he was naked. Then her cheekbones colored with renewed heat and her lips parted.

She took him completely off guard when she whispered, "I love you, Jordan."

An invisible fist squeezed his heart. Every bit of calm he'd just achieved shot out the ceiling.

He barely had the sense or patience to find a condom and put it on, especially when the second he sat on the mattress she pushed him to his back. Jordan dropped flat, more than willing to give her control. Without hesitation she straddled his hips. For a brief moment she cradled his testicles, testing his long-lost control, her small soft hand making him crazed. Holding back became torture, and he told her so.

She clasped his penis in her hand and thankfully guided him into her body.

Jordan watched as she slowly slid down to envelop him, and he groaned deeply. With only that initial stroke he felt his body drawing tight in prerelease. *"Georgia."*

She seated herself completely. He held her hips and pressed her down farther; he was so deep inside her, her inner muscles gripped him and she caught her breath on a gasp. When Jordan started to lift her away, unwilling to hurt her, she shook her head and braced her hands on his chest. Her gaze was cloudy with a mix of discomfort and incredible pleasure. "I want all of you."

Jordan locked his jaw and concentrated on not coming. Georgia didn't make it easy on him. At first, she held perfectly still and Jordan, teeth clenched and thighs tensed, did all he could to keep from rushing her.

Her thumbs found his nipples beneath his chest hair. "You are, without a doubt," she murmured, "the most gorgeous, sexy man I've ever seen."

His heels pressed into the mattress and his hands fisted in the sheets.

Her small palms, cool against his burning flesh, coasted over his shoulders, down his biceps then to his abdomen. "You're all hard muscles and lean strength and I've wanted you since the first time I saw you in the audience."

Jordan felt himself jerking, knew the end was near for him. "Move, damn it. *Move*."

With a feminine laugh of sheer power, she did as he asked, lifting with torturous slowness, then dropping hard. It took a mere three strokes, three times of watching her beautiful body slide up and then down again on his rigid shaft for Jordan to go mindless.

He cupped her breasts, arched his back, and exploded like a savage. To his immense surprise and pleasure, just as he began to regain sanity he heard Georgia sob and opened his eyes to watch her take her own pleasure. He was still hard, still buried deep inside her. She rocked her hips, her breasts bouncing, until she threw her head back and groaned out her second orgasm.

When she collapsed on his chest, Jordan put his arms around her and held her tight. He loved her so much it hurt, but when he decided to tell her, he heard her breathing even into the deep rhythm of sleep.

Pushing her hair from her face he studied her features. Her temples were damp from her exertions, her lips swollen and rosy, her cheeks still flushed. He kissed her forehead and the bridge of her nose. "I love you," he whispered, and though she didn't reply she did snuggle closer.

Smiling, Jordan eased her to his side so he could remove the used condom and find the blankets. It took him scant minutes and then he was back, pulling her onto his chest again, determined to keep her as close as possible. Forever.

Her heartbeat echoed in his chest, and with his mind at peace, Jordan dozed off.

GEORGIA WOKE the next morning to an empty bed. She automatically reached for Jordan, but he was gone. Then she heard him singing in his low, sexy voice, and with a smile, she climbed out of bed and wrapped the sheet around her.

His apartment was fabulous. Located over the three-car garage for the main house, it was open and spacious. The bedroom and private bath were the only doorways. The kitchen, breakfast nook and wide living room all flowed into each other. Since the bedroom door was open she could see Jordan at the kitchen sink, measuring out coffee. His broad naked back made her body feel liquid and warm. He wore only a pair of faded jeans riding low on his narrow hips, and even his bare feet looked sexy. Of course he was making coffee, and she smiled.

She'd told him she loved him.

Georgia remembered her declaration with a touch of embarrassment, but decided it didn't matter. So what that he hadn't responded in kind? She knew he cared for her, and he and his family were so wonderful....

The phone rang and as Jordan turned to answer it he caught sight of her. Immediately, he forgot about the phone and started toward her with a male determination that had her blushing. "Morning," he murmured in a suggestive way.

Oh, that sexy just-up voice! Her heart picked up speed and a wave of warmth shook her. "Good morning."

His smile was so gentle. Combined with a mostly naked superior male body, Jordan Sommerville was very potent! Georgia cleared her throat. "Aren't you going to get the phone?"

"The answering machine will pick up."

No sooner did he say it than it happened. Georgia missed the beginning of the message because Jordan kissed her while slowly unwinding the sheet from her body. He held it out to her sides and looked at her in the bright morning sunlight cascading through the kitchen windows.

"You're so beautiful."

She thought to tease him about needing glasses, since she knew her hair was tangled and her makeup smudged, but then the person on the phone said, *"So as of a few hours ago, the bar is officially shut down. Who knows how long it'll last, but I knew you'd be happy to hear it. Serving minors is a serious offense, and about the quickest way around to lose your licence. I think we can probably keep him shut down. Anyway, give me a call when you can and I'll fill you in on the rest of the details."*

They were both frozen, Jordan in what appeared to be satisfaction, Georgia with dawning horror.

She was unemployed.

She yanked the sheet away from Jordan and held it to her chin to cover her nudity. She felt lost and vulnerable and scared. What would she do now? Good God, she couldn't make the bills without that job! In a daze, Georgia swallowed hard and turned away from Jordan.

He caught her shoulder, and his voice sounded a bit harsh. "Where are you going?"

Blankly, her mind in a muddle, she stared at him. "I

have to go find a job. I have to…I don't know. I have to do something." Then, before she could stop herself, she whispered, *"Jordan, what am I going to do?"*

His expression softened, and she wondered if what she saw in his eyes was pity. Details whipped through her mind with the speed of light. Scheduled dental checkups for the kids. The premium on her mother's health insurance. The gas and electric, the mortgage…. She hadn't had a chance to save up much money yet. She'd been too busy making repairs. And now…

The sheet fell to the floor, forgotten as she covered her face with her hands, knowing she'd failed yet again. "I have to find a job." She said it once more, hoping to make herself understand. But she'd already looked everywhere before accepting the work at the bar. Nowhere else had paid enough. For a high school dropout who could only work certain hours because of being a mother, she wasn't exactly prime employment material.

Jordan's hands curved around her shoulders, caressing, comforting. "It's too early to do anything right now. I'll call the sheriff back in a bit and get all the details, okay?"

The sheriff? Not his brother, so it must have been the one who'd wanted them arrested. She'd known he was watching the bar, that he was fed up with the nightly problems that seemed to erupt….

Jordan interrupted her thoughts. "I have a few solutions, sweetheart. Will you listen to me?"

Georgia realized she'd put her worries onto him; she'd come to depend on him whether she wanted to admit it or not. How had she let that happen?

He'd once offered to let her work for him, but that would be no more than charity and she didn't think she could stand it. She shook her head as she tried to pull away.

"You *will* listen," Jordan stated, and urged her toward his sofa.

"What is there to say? I won't work for you—"

"You don't have to." Jordan gently pushed her into the seat, then plucked up the sheet and handed it to her. Georgia wrapped it around herself; she had all but forgotten she was nude.

"Now just listen." He caught both her hands and held tight. "You said you wanted options, well here're two." He drew a deep breath. "You can marry me." He waited, watching her closely, and when she only stared at him in shock, his expression hardened. "Or you can teach dance at your own studio."

That was every bit as confusing as his proposal. Only… he hadn't really proposed. Not once had he ever said he loved her, only that he wanted her. And last night he'd admitted to respecting her, admiring her…

"Georgia, are you listening to me?"

She blinked. "Yes, but…I don't have a studio."

Jordan seemed to be getting angrier by the moment. "I found you one. It's in the center of town. It used to be a novelty shop, but the owner is retiring and the place is wide and airy and with a little renovation it'd be perfect."

She sat there, naked but for a sheet, confusion weighing her down. "A novelty shop?"

Jordan grabbed her chin and kissed her hard. He actually trembled he was so furious. "I already agreed to buy the building so you might as well agree." When she still hesitated, he barked, "You said you enjoy teaching dance, and Misty and Honey assure me there'll be—"

Incredulous, Georgia shot off the sofa to stare down at him. "You bought me a *building?*"

He didn't stand, but instead sprawled back in his seat and put his arms along the sofa back. Every single muscle in his arms and chest and shoulders was defined. "Yes."

"Ohmigod." She paced away, but had taken no more than ten steps when she whirled back around to face him.

"How can you buy me a building? Nobody buys someone else a building!"

His eyes narrowed. "I also asked you to marry me."

"No." Wildly, she shook her head. "You told me I *could* marry you. It's not at all the same thing."

"You want all the fanfare? You want me to go down on one knee?"

"No!" Her head had started to pound and she felt queasy. It would be so easy to marry him, to let him fix everything, but she'd sworn she wouldn't do that again. She felt wetness on her cheeks and realized she was crying. Her heart ached and she said on a near wail, "I can't marry you, Jordan. Why would you even suggest such a thing?"

His eyes closed briefly; he rubbed a hand over his face. "You said you loved me."

"I do, but…you have everything. You have a wonderful supportive family and a great job, an education and respectability, a home and money and—"

He came to his feet so quickly, she yelped and nearly tripped over the trailing sheet. Jordan gripped her arms.

"So that's what you love about me?" he roared, scaring her half silly. "What I can give you?"

She'd never seen Jordan like this. She'd watched him easily subdue a man twice his size. She'd watched him face off with his brothers. She'd seen Jordan angry and frustrated and deliberately provoking, but she'd never seen him in this type of rage. Oddly enough, though he'd startled her, she wasn't afraid of him.

"No." She emphasized that with a tiny shake of her head. "I love you," she said very quietly, choking on her tears, "because of who you are."

He stepped up to her until she had to tip her head back to see his face, until his bare chest brushed her knuckles clutching the sheet and his feet were braced on either side of hers. He surrounded her and overwhelmed her and then he whispered, "That's why I love you, too."

More tears blurred her vision and she rubbed them away, sniffing and gulping and sounded horribly like a frog. "But I—"

"You're going to really piss me off," he informed her, "if you put yourself down again." She hiccuped on a laugh. Jordan raised one hand to gently smooth her cheek. "Weren't you listening last night, baby? I love you. I'm crazy nuts about you. My whole family knows it, even my mother. Yes I have all the things you mentioned, but I don't have you. And without you, I'm not going to be happy."

"Oh Jordan." She swallowed hard. "You really love me?"

He shook his head. "What did you think? That I just enjoy giving foot rubs?"

She lost what little control she had on her emotions and dropped the sheet again to throw herself into his arms. "I love you so much."

"I do, you know," he whispered. "Enjoy rubbing on you, I mean." She laughed as he cradled her close. He slid his hands down to her backside and lifted her. "Marry me, Georgia. Let me have you. Let me make your family my own and give you mine and we can both be happy."

"It…it doesn't feel right to take that much from you."

He rocked her into his erection. "Does this feel right?" When she nodded, he kissed her gently. "And this?"

"Jordan…"

"And this?"

Georgia had known from the start that he could seduce with just a few whispered words. Now she had firsthand proof.

EPILOGUE

"HEY DAD!"

Jordan looked up from making salad as Lisa came barreling through the front door, followed closely by Adam and two dogs, one a mixed-breed puppy and the other an ancient dachshund. They'd all been outside playing and smelled of sunshine and fresh crisp air. Between the children laughing and the dogs barking, the house was always filled with excitement.

Jordan knelt down and caught the children to him, hugging them fiercely. Life, he thought, was pretty damn good. "Mommy's home," Lisa told him, after a loud wet kiss to his cheek.

Seconds later Georgia strolled in. Under her coat, she wore her workout clothes of leotard and tights, guaranteed to make his blood boil. Seeing the skintight outfits affected him more strongly than her stage costumes had.

Of course, nothing affected him as much as her bare, beautiful skin.

He stood, and with the kids still close to his side and the dogs jumping between them, he gave her a long, thorough kiss. "Hi," he whispered and she smiled back.

Her smiles, he decided, were downright lethal.

"What time is everyone due to arrive?"

Jordan took her coat from her and hung it on the back of an oak chair. Thanks to Gabe's handyman skills, the remodelled kitchen had become a favorite hangout for everyone. "You have time to shower, if that's what you're wondering."

"Can I do anything to help you first?"

Jordan went back to preparing his salad. "The sauce you made yesterday is already heating, and the spaghetti will go on as soon as the water starts to boil." He glanced at the kids. "My assistant chefs can wash their hands and start to work on the garlic bread."

Lisa grinned up at him. She'd lost another tooth and her words now whistled when she spoke. "Grandma said she's bringin' dessert."

Jordan shook his head. Grandma, he knew darn good and well, was smitten with Mr. Malone, who would also be in attendance. Ruth had moved into his vacated apartments over the garage. Neither he nor Georgia had wanted her to, but she'd insisted on giving them time to be alone. When Misty and Honey had begged her to stay close since the babies loved her so much, she'd agreed. She was now a paid housekeeper/sitter with her own measure of independence, which she loved.

She also loved the way Mr. Malone hung around on the pretense of visiting his daughters, though Sawyer and Morgan were both quite disgruntled by that situation. Jordan sympathized with them. He didn't understand the attraction at all. Ruth was so sweet and open and loving, but Mr. Malone—they'd known the man for ages and still called him mister—was so detached. Ruth claimed he was softening and that he wasn't at all detached when they were alone. He wasn't detached with any of the kids, either, and he was openly impressed with Casey.

Georgia touched his cheek. "You've got that protective look about you again."

Jordan grinned at her. "Do you know how many people will be here tonight?" When she shook her head, sidetracked just as he'd hoped, he said, "Fourteen, if we include all the kids. When you add the four of us, that's a lot of confusion. Are you sure you're up to this after working all day?"

Adam crossed his arms in the same pose Jordan used. "We'll need lots of garlic bread!"

Georgia laughed. "Yes, I'm up to it, and yes, we'll need lots of bread." Then to Jordan, "You know dancing doesn't tire me. Just the opposite, I always feel energized after a class."

In the two months since their small, quiet marriage, Georgia had gotten her studio set up and filled to the maximum with students. She taught not only dance classes for the fun of it, but also aerobics. She had people of all ages coming throughout the day. And true to her word, she was always bursting with energy.

Especially in the bedroom.

Jordan had to pull his thoughts away from that direction or he'd never survive the massive family gathering. Georgia left to shower and dress and a few minutes later all the relatives started to arrive.

He wasn't surprised to see Casey with yet another beautiful young lady. He seldom saw the same girl twice these days, and other than a few surprise meetings, Emma hadn't been around.

At her first bite of dinner, Georgia smiled at Jordan and said, "Delicious. You really are perfect at everything, aren't you?"

Jordan grinned. He was used to her saying that, but obviously his family wasn't.

Morgan choked on his spaghetti, then doubled over laughing. "Maybe perfect for you," he laughed, "but I think old Jordan is plenty flawed. Now Malone, she prefers men with a little more steel, don't ya, sweetheart?"

Misty pretended she hadn't heard him, though everyone

could see her trying not to smile. Amber said, "Daddy's nasty."

Sawyer shook his head. "Can't you control him, Misty? He gets more outrageous by the day."

"Look who's talking!" Morgan said.

Sawyer was trying to eat and love on his wife and son at the same time. His mother took Shohn so she and Brett could spoil him just a bit, and Honey found her chair bumping up against her husband's.

Gabe tipped Elizabeth's chair toward him and kissed her hard. She didn't even try to fight him off. Adam mimicked their smooching sounds until everyone laughed. Lisa announced to the table at large that her grandma and Mr. Malone were playing footsie beneath the table.

CASEY SAT BACK in his seat and watched them all with an indulgent smile. Things sure had changed over the past few years, and he loved it. He missed having Jordan so close, but they visited often, and it was obvious Jordan was as happy as a man could be. His father and uncles had all found the perfect women for them.

The girl beside Casey cleared her throat. She was uncomfortable in the boisterous crowd, but it didn't matter. He doubted he'd see her again anyway. She was beautiful, sexy, and anxious to please him—but she wasn't perfect for him. Though he was only eighteen and had quite a bit of college ahead of him, not to mention all his other plans, Casey couldn't help but wonder if he'd ever meet the perfect mate.

An image of big brown eyes, filled with sexual curiosity, sadness, and finally rejection, formed in his mind. With a niggling dread that wouldn't ease up, Casey wondered if he'd already found the perfect girl—but had sent her away.

Then he heard Georgia talking to his date, and pulled himself out of his reverie. No, she wasn't perfect, but she didn't keep him awake nights, either. And that was good, because no matter what, no matter how he felt now, he would not let his plans get off track. He decided to forget all about women and the future and simply enjoy the night with his family.

It was late when Casey finally got home after dropping off his date, and he'd just pulled off his shirt when a fist started pounding on the front door. He and his father met in the hall, both of them frowning. Honey pulled on her robe and hustled after them.

When Sawyer got the door open, they found themselves confronted with Emma's father. He had his daughter by the arm, and he was obviously furious.

Casey's first startled thought was that Emma wasn't gone after all. Then he got a good look at her face and he erupted in rage.

He'd been wrong. His plans would change after all. In a big way.

Bestselling author Lori Foster takes you back to Buckhorn County!

Sawyer's son Casey has grown up. And he's about to be reunited with the *one* woman he could never resist—Emma Clark

In December 2002 look for *CASEY,* the final story in the sexy, compelling Buckhorn Brothers series!

Here's an excerpt.

CHAPTER ONE

AS IF FROM A DISTANCE, Emma heard the knock on the thin motel-room door. She forced her head from the flat, over-starched pillow and glanced at the glowing face of the clock. It was barely six-thirty and her body remained limp with the heaviness of sleep. She'd been in bed only five hours.

After Damon had finally returned and they'd transferred everything from her car to Casey's and gotten to the Cross Roads Motel, it had been well past one o'clock. She hadn't unpacked, had only pulled off her shoes, jeans, bra and sweatshirt, and dropped into the bed in a T-shirt and pant-ics. She'd been so exhausted, both emotionally and physi-cally, that thoughts of food or a shower had disintegrated beneath tiredness.

Why would anyone be calling this early?

B.B. snuffled around and let out one warning "woof," but Emma patted him and he resettled himself with a mod-icum of grumbling and growling. Stretched out on his side, he took up more than his fair share of the bed. "It's okay, boy. I'll be right back."

Probably Mrs. Reider, she thought, ready with a com-plaint of some kind, though Emma couldn't imagine what it might be. They'd been very quiet coming in last night and hadn't disturbed anyone as far as she knew.

B.B. was atop the covers, so Emma grabbed the bed-spread that had gotten pushed to the bottom of the bed. She halfheartedly wrapped it around herself and let it drag on the floor.

Without turning on a light, she padded barefoot to the door, turned the cheap lock and swung it open. The room and been dark with the heavy drapes drawn, but now she had to lift a hand to shield her eyes against the red glow of a rising sun. She blinked twice before her bleary eyes could focus.

And there stood Casey.

His powerful body lounged against the door frame, silhouetted by a golden halo. In the daylight he looked more devastatingly handsome than ever. Confusion washed over Emma and she stared, starting at Casey's feet and working her way up.

Laced-up, scuffed brown boots showed beneath well-worn jeans that rode low on his lean hips and were faded white in stress spots—like his knees, the pocket where he kept his keys. His fly.

Emma blinked at that, then shook her head and continued upward. With the casual clothing, he'd forgone a belt, and in fact, two belt loops were missing from the ancient jeans.

In deference to the heat, he wore a sleeveless, battered white cotton shirt that left his muscular arms and tanned shoulders on display. Mirrored sunglasses shielded his eyes, and his mouth curled in a lopsided, wicked grin. "Morning, Emma."

Her tongue stuck to the roof of her mouth, making speech difficult. "What are you doing here?"

Lifting one hand—which caused all kinds of interesting muscles to flex in his arm—he showed her the smallest of her suitcases. "You forgot this in the trunk of my car. I thought you might need it today."

"Oh." She looked around, not sure what to do next. She did need the case, seeing that it held her toiletries and makeup. But she could hardly invite him in when she wasn't dressed. Loosening her hold on the spread, she reached for the case. "Thank you…"

Casey removed the decision from her. Lifting the case out of reach, he stepped inside just in time to see B.B. bound off the bed and lunge forward with a growl. When he recognized Casey he slowed and the growl turned into a tail-wagging hello. Casey greeted the dog while eyeing the bed he'd just vacated. Being a double, it provided just enough room for one woman—and her pet.

He quirked a brow at Emma as realization dawned.

She hadn't slept alone, so he couldn't accuse her of lying. But she hadn't slept with a man, either, which had been his assumption.

Casey grinned and reached down to pat the dog. "You've sure got the cushy life, don't you B.B.?"

The dog jumped up, putting his paws on Casey's shoulders. Casey just laughed. "Yeah, sleeping with a gorgeous broad would put any guy in a good mood."

Left standing in the open doorway, Emma hadn't quite gathered her wits yet. Too little sleep combined with Casey Hudson in the morning could rattle anyone. She certainly wasn't up to bantering with him. "He's always slept with me. It's one reason I bring him along wherever I go."

"Gotcha." Casey looked around again, and his grin widened. "So. Where's Damon?"

He tried to sound innocent, but failed. Knowing the gig was up, Emma scowled at him. Would he now consider her fair game, since she wasn't involved? What would she say to dissuade him, if he did?

Did she really want to dissuade him?

The connecting door opened and Damon stuck his dark head out. With only one eye opened, he demanded, "What the hell's going on?" Then he saw Casey, and that one eye widened. "Oh, it's you. I should have known."

In his boxers and nothing more, Damon pulled the door

wider. Emma wasn't uncomfortable with his lack of dress. More often than not, Damon acted like her brother.

Casey took in the fact of the separate rooms with a look of deep satisfaction. "Morning, buddy."

"Yeah, whatever." Damon yawned, leaned in the doorway and crossed his arms over his naked chest. His blue eyes were heavy, his jaw shadowed with dark beard stubble and his silky black hair stuck out in funny disarray. "You country boys like to get up early, I take it?"

"Country boys?" Casey didn't sound amused by that description.

Undisturbed by Casey's pique, Damon lazily eyed him, taking in the old snug jeans and the muscle shirt. "Brought it up another notch, I see."

Casey's scowl darkened. "What?"

Damon just shook his head and glanced at Emma. "Give me a minute to get dressed."

She didn't want to turn this into a damn social gathering, and besides, both men were bristling, which didn't bode well. "That's not necessary."

"No?"

"*No!*" Emma saw Damon's surprise and rubbed her forehead. He looked as tired as she felt, so why didn't he just go on back to bed so she could deal with Casey in private? She moderated her tone. "It's fine, Damon. Get some more sleep."

He didn't budge. "You turned willing overnight?"

Her moderation shot to hell, Emma ground her teeth together. "Damon…"

"Was it the macho clothes that turned the trick?"

Casey shifted his stance, but Emma growled, causing both B.B. and Damon to watch her warily.

Damon straightened in the doorway with dawning suspicion. "Have you had your coffee?"

Emma slowly looked up at him. A long rope of tangled hair hung over her bloodshot, puffy eyes. She wore only her T-shirt and a bedspread. Curling her lip, she asked, "Do I look to you like I've had coffee?"

"Shit." He turned to Casey with accusation. "So where is it?"

Casey frowned in incomprehension. "Where is what?"

As if speaking to an idiot, Damon enunciated each word. "The coffee."

Casey shrugged, but offered helpfully, "They keep a pot brewing in the lobby."

"Right. In the lobby. And here I had the impression you knew something about women." Shaking his head at Casey in a pitying way, Damon turned back to Emma. "Just hang on, doll. I'll run down and snag you a cup."

On a normal day Emma would have thanked him and dropped back into bed. But this wasn't a normal day. Today Casey was standing in her temporary bedroom looking and smelling too sexy for a sane woman's health and she wasn't properly dressed. "It's okay. B.B. needs to go out, too, so I might as well get it myself." And then she wouldn't be left closed up in the motel room with Casey.

Apparently stunned, Damon blinked at her. "Are you sure?"

"I'm sure I'm going to smack you if you don't stop pushing me."

"All right, all right." Damon held up both hands, which should have been comical given that he wore only print boxers. "Hey, what do I know about a woman's needs? They're ever shifting and changing, right? One day coffee is a necessity before she can open her eyes, the next—no problem. She'll get it herself."

Emma turned away and stomped to the dresser to snatch up her jeans. Ignoring both men, she trailed into the bathroom and shut the door. She didn't exactly slam it, but her irritation definitely showed.

She heard Casey whistle low. "Wow. Is she always like that in the morning?"

"Be warned—*yes*."

Casey chuckled, but Damon, clearly disgruntled, said, "I wouldn't laugh if I was you. What you just saw is nothing compared to how grouchy she'll get if she doesn't get a cup of coffee real soon."

"I'll keep that in mind."

"You do that."

Emma brushed her teeth while praying that Damon would now go back to bed. He did—but not without a parting shot.

"I usually fetch her a cup before I wake her up, especially when she hasn't had enough sleep. But since you did the deed this morning, and at such an ungodly hour, at that, you can deal with the consequences alone."

She heard Damon's door close, then heard Casey mutter to B.B., "You won't let her hurt me, will you, buddy?"

B.B. whined.

In desperate need of caffeine, Emma left the bathroom. She slipped her feet into her sneakers, latched B.B.'s leash to his collar and stepped around Casey to head out the door. Obedient whenever it suited him, B.B. followed, and without a word Casey fell into step behind him. She'd gone down only three steps, her destination the lobby where fresh coffee waited, when she heard Casey begin humming some tune she didn't recognize.

He knew she slept without a man; Emma wondered what he intended to do with that knowledge, because she knew Casey too well to mistake him now. He was up to something, and she dreaded the coming battle.

It was herself she'd have to fight, of course. She'd never been able to resist Casey, not then, and not now.

BEFORE SHE COULD head for the lobby, Casey caught Emma's arm. "Take B.B. to the bushes, then park yourself at the picnic table. I'll get the coffee."

She looked ready to argue and Casey continued. "You can't take the dog inside, and he's starting to look desperate. Really, fetching you a cup of coffee won't tax me. I'll even get one for myself. Okay?"

She glanced at the dog, whose need did indeed appear urgent, then nodded. "All right. Lots of sugar and a smidgen of cream."

"Got it." Casey sauntered away with a smile on his face. He'd spent the night thinking about Emma, and being sexually frustrated as a result. He couldn't say what he'd expected this morning when he'd knocked on her door, but the picture she'd presented had taken him by surprise.

Soft. That was the word that most came to mind when he thought of Emma. Soft eyes, soft heart, soft breasts and hips and thighs…

This morning, still sleepy and wrapped in a bedspread, she'd been so soft she damn near melted his heart on the spot, along with all the plans he'd so meticulously devised throughout the long night. He'd taken one look at her and wanted to lead her right back to bed.

It had been doubly hard to give up that idea once he knew Damon had a separate room.

Seeing her sleek, silky hair tangled around her shoulders, her cheeks flushed, her eyes a little dazed had made him think of a woman's expression right before she came. Emma's very kissable mouth had been slightly puffy, and her lips had parted in surprise when she saw him at the door, adding to the fantasy.

Her legs…well, Emma had always had a killer ass and gorgeous legs. That hadn't changed. As a perpetually horny teen, he'd found resisting her was his biggest struggle.

As an adult, it wasn't much easier. In fact, he had no intention of resisting her now.

Unfortunately, she'd pulled on jeans rather than the ultrashort shorts he remembered in their youth, and her legs were now well hidden. But she hadn't bothered with a bra yet. With each step she took, her breasts moved gently beneath the cotton of her T-shirt, and the faintest outline of her nipples showed through.

Casey's muscles tightened in anticipation of seeing her again and he snapped lids on three disposable cups of coffee, then plucked up several packets of sugar, two stirrers and some little tubs of creamer. He stuffed them in his pockets. Balancing the hot cups between his hands, he shouldered the door open and started back to Emma.

In limp exhaustion, she rested at one of the aged wooden picnic tables that had always served as part of Mrs. Reider's small lot. Guests used the tables often, but this early in the day no one else intruded. Casey didn't make a sound as he approached, and Emma remained unaware of him.

She'd kicked off her shoes and her legs were stretched out in front of her with her bare toes wiggling. Sunlight through elm leaves, shifting and changing with the careless breeze, dappled her upturned face.

The air this time of morning remained heavy with dew, rich with scents of the earth and trees. Emma sighed, and her expression bespoke a peacefulness that made Casey smile from the inside out. He liked seeing Emma at peace. When she'd been younger, so often what he'd seen in her eyes was uncertainty, loneliness, even fear.

She spoke a moment to B.B., who sprawled out in the lush grass at her feet, then she reached up and lifted her hair off her nape. Casey stalled in appreciation of her feminine gesture. Even from her early teens, Emma had displayed an innate sensuality that drove every guy around her wild. She stretched her arms high, and her hair drifted free to resettle over her shoulders.

Damn. He absolutely could not get a boner in Mrs. Reider's motel lot.

Neither could he allow Emma to affect him this strongly. He had to remember that despite her appeal and everything he'd once felt—still felt, dammit—she'd walked out on him and hadn't bothered to get in touch in eight long years. She hadn't come back for him. If her father wasn't so sick, she wouldn't be here now.

"Here's your coffee." His emotions in check, Casey took the last few remaining steps to her and set the cups on the tabletop. "I hope you haven't chewed off any tree bark or anything." He scattered the sugar packets and creamer beside the cups.

Her eyes scrunched up because of the sun, Emma turned to him with a frown. "Damon exaggerated. I'm not that bad."

"If you say so." He smiled at her. "But remember, I witnessed you firsthand. For a minute there I expected to see smoke come out of your ears."

She looked ready to growl again, but restrained herself. "I hadn't had much sleep."

"I'm sorry I woke you."

"You don't look sorry."

Casey shrugged—and continued to smile.

Emma considered him a long moment, then took the coffee and quickly doctored it to her specifications. The second she tipped the cup to her mouth, she moaned in bliss. "Oh, God, I needed that." She took another long drink. "Perfect. Thank you."

Casey sipped at his own coffee, prepared much like hers. "Not a morning person, huh?"

She shook her head. "I'm barely civil in the morning. I've always been more a night owl."

She didn't say anything else, made no effort toward casual conversation, and Casey felt provoked. She sat with him, drank the coffee he'd bought to her, but she kept him shut out.

To regain her attention, he touched the back of her hand with one fingertip. "I still think waking up with you would be fun."

Immobilized by that comment, Emma froze for a good five seconds. Then she abruptly drained the rest of her cup and stood. She didn't look at him. "Thanks again...for everything." She started to step away.

Casey moved so fast, she gasped. In less than a heartbeat he'd reached over the table and snatched her narrow wrists, shackling them in his hands. He stared into her mesmerizing, antagonistic brown eyes until the air around them fairly crackled.

"Don't go." Two simple words, but his heart pounded as he waited.

She looked undecided.

"I brought you another cup." Casey stroked the insides of her wrists with his thumbs, kept his tone easy, persuasive. "Sit with me, Emma. Talk to me."

He ignored the rise of her breasts as she slowly inhaled. Her hesitation was palpable, forcing him to think of more arguments, other stratagems, and she said, "Why?"

Sensing that she'd just relented, Casey relaxed. "Sit down and I'll tell you why."

With enough grumbling to wake the squirrels, she dropped into the seat. This time she slid her legs under the table and faced him with both elbows propped on the tabletop to hold her chin. "I'm waiting."

Casey took in her belligerent expression and swallowed his amusement. Not once in all the time he'd known her before she'd moved away had Emma ever shown him disgruntlement. She'd shown him adolescent lust, feminine need, a few flirting smiles and occasionally her vulnerability.

It didn't make any sense, but he felt as if he'd just gained three giant steps forward. "Yeah. Ya know, I think I'll feel more secure if you drink the other cup of coffee first." He prepared it as he spoke, and now he handed it to her with a flourish.

She slanted him a look through her thick lashes. "With the way you've acted so far, you're probably right." She accepted the coffee and sipped. "You've been deliberately provoking."

Casey waited until she swallowed before he spoke. "There's still something between us, Emma."

She promptly choked, then glared at him before searching in vain for a napkin. Casey offered her his clean hanky. "You okay?"

She brushed away his concern. "Something, huh?" Her voice was still raspy as she wheezed for air. "Well, I can tell you exactly what that *something* is."

Casey tilted back. "That right?"

"Sure." She finally regained her breath. "I'm not dead. I felt it, too."

Her mood was so uncertain, he couldn't decide how to handle her. "You know, you're a lot more candid when you're crabby."

Without another word she dropped her head to her folded arms. He didn't know if she was laughing, but he was certain she wasn't crying.

Casey wanted to touch her, wanted to feel the warmth of her skin. Her light brown hair fanned out around her, spilling onto the table. The sun had kissed it near her temples, along her forehead, framing her face with natural golden streaks. It looked heavy and soft and shiny. The length of her spine was graceful, feminine. Her wrists, crisscrossed under her head, were narrow, delicate.

Everything about her turned him on. At the first hint of her perfume, the natural scent of warm woman fresh from her bed, he got excited. Around her, he felt things more acutely than he had for years.

Making an abrupt decision, he stroked one large hand over her head, down to her nape. "I want you, Emma."

Her silent laughter morphed into a groan.

Casey waited, content to smooth her hair and rub her shoulder. Content to touch her. For now.

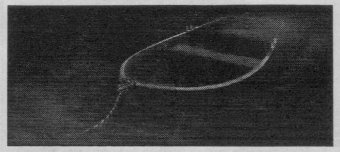

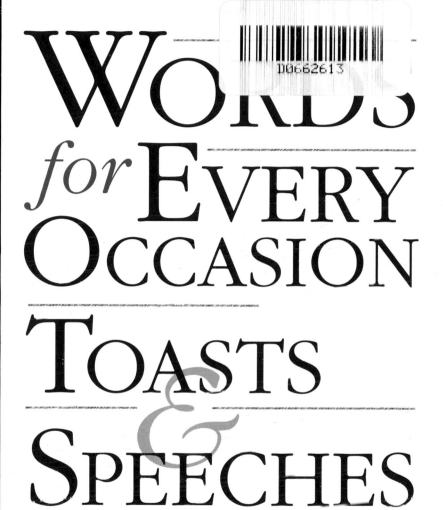

WORDS *for* EVERY OCCASION

TOASTS & SPEECHES

WORDS
for EVERY
OCCASION

TOASTS
&
SPEECHES

hinkler

Published by Hinkler Books Pty Ltd
45–55 Fairchild Street
Heatherton Victoria 3202 Australia
www.hinkler.com.au

© Hinkler Books Pty Ltd 2013

Author: Sarah Russell
Design: Sam Grimmer
Typesetting: MPS Limited
Prepress: Graphic Print Group

Images © Shutterstock.com: Monarch Butterfly Released © Katrina Brown; Shifting
the red curtain © italianestro; Fireworks of various colors © Carlos E. Santa Maria;
Champagne © Subbotina Anna; Girl holding present © chaowalek julaketpotichai;
Thumbs Up © Brian Goff; Businessman offering handshake © Maryna Pleshkun.

ISBN: 978 1 7436 3388 5

Printed and bound in China

Contents

INTRODUCTION

Be sincere; be brief; be seated.

Franklin D. Roosevelt

Saying a Few Words

On many special occasions, someone will give a speech. Whether it's a wedding or a retirement party, an eightieth birthday or a twenty-fifth wedding anniversary, we pause to listen to someone say a few words in honour of the occasion and more often than not make a toast. Even though we use modern technology help us to stay connected, giving a speech is still something most of us will be called on to do at some stage in our lives.

This book is for you when you are asked or volunteer to make a speech at a special event. The kind of the event may differ, but there are some basic things you should know when you're giving a speech.

A speech is delivered in front of an audience. For many people, this is a really terrifying thought! But, being prepared will help you overcome those nerves. And if you know the purpose of your speech and the audience who you'll deliver it to, you're halfway there. It also helps to write down what you want to say before you say it and to rehearse. As Franklin D. Roosevelt said, 'be brief' and speak from your heart.

Purpose and Audience

To prepare your speech, you need to know your purpose and audience. Everything you say should help you achieve your purpose and engage your audience. And remember that you may not have very long to get your message across, especially if there will be other speeches. So being brief is essential to help you achieve your purpose.

If your purpose is to farewell someone who is leaving a job, but not to roast them, it wouldn't be right to tell funny stories that show the person in a bad light. However, if your purpose is to roast, you can include those stories. A roast is a kind of speech that is usually given at birthday parties, retirements and weddings. Instead of just honouring the person, it also makes fun of them. But

it's a question of degree. Although the purpose of a roast is to embarrass the person, you don't want to make them cry!

If you're speaking to an audience you know well about a topic they know nothing about, don't spend too long introducing yourself. Instead, present some basic information about the topic at the beginning of your speech. Alternatively, your audience may know the subject of your speech very well, so you will need to do your research thoroughly.

To Roast or Not?

Whether or not to roast depends on the purpose of your speech. Is your purpose to 'name' a new baby or to farewell an employee who is retiring? If your purpose is the former, you wouldn't want to 'roast' the baby's parents. However, if you're giving a speech at a retirement party, your audience will no doubt enjoy a few funny stories about the retiree.

Showing respect for others is always important, so knowing when to stop is wise. And don't forget to include some genuine tributes in your speech as well – after all, you're all friends and you want to leave your listeners with a good impression.

More information is provided about roasts in the sections about giving a speech at a friend's birthday party on pages 49–50, at a retirement party on pages 82–84 and at a wedding on pages 124–127.

Writing and Practising Your Speech

After you've have worked out your purpose and audience, it's time to do your research. This might mean searching through books, newspapers and websites, or chatting to friends and family. Remember to take notes about who said what and where you found bits of information, because you may need to acknowledge your sources.

Next you need to organise your material in order of importance. At this point, it's wise to come back to your purpose: why are you giving this speech? This should help you to decide which information is most important.

Now you need to sit down and write. Start with your introduction, which might be a friendly welcome, a dramatic statement or a joke. Then write a first draft, including all of the material you think is important. The next step is to practise your speech in front of another person.

Knowing the size and shape of the room where you will give your speech will help you practise it. For example, if you're going to be in a small space, practise getting close to your audience. You may like to incorporate changes in volume, such as whispering, for dramatic effect. However, if you're going to be in a huge hall, practise projecting your voice and using gestures that a large audience will be able to see.

After a first practice, it's time to refine your speech. It can be hard, but it's a good idea to take on board comments from the person who watched you practise your first draft. You may even need to write a second draft. Then you'll need to practise again, preferably in front of the same person. This time think about adding some visual aids or props to liven up your speech.

Finally, it's a good idea to practise your speech with a stopwatch. If it's too long, now is the time to make cuts. If it's too short, you can go back through your material and add in extra points or examples.

Dealing with Nerves

A recent study revealed that the number-one fear among Australians was death, then public speaking. A famous US study in the 1970s showed that most of the people surveyed feared public speaking more than death!

Making a speech can be quite scary, but there are ways to overcome your nerves before the big day. A sure-fire way to deal with nerves is to be prepared, to know your purpose and audience, and plan your speech. The next most important way to overcome nerves is to practise.

It may seem obvious, but the more you practise, the better your speech will be. Once you have written a number of drafts, cut or extended your speech and timed it, practise as many times as

you can before the big day. Practising in front of a mirror is a good idea. You can check how often you make eye contact and when you smile. Practising in front of someone else is even better – you can receive feedback instantly.

Another way to deal with your nerves is to have confidence in yourself and in what you have to say. Remember that you have a unique point of view, and people will be interested in what you have to say. Theodore Roosevelt said, 'Believe you can and you're halfway there.' Tell yourself that you can deliver this speech and it will be a huge success. Imagine yourself giving it, and receiving lots of clapping and whistling! The more you visualise yourself doing well, the more likely you are to do so.

To Toast or Not?

Before delivering your speech you need to decide whether or not you should also make a toast. Today, the etiquette about the occasions to make a toast and how to make it is very relaxed.

Traditionally, a toast was always offered at celebrations and commemorations, as well as at some festivals, such as New Year's Eve festivals. So, weddings, funerals and retirement parties were typical occasions when a toast was made. The toast was usually made by the host and was offered standing, with the right arm outstretched holding a glass containing alcohol, generally champagne or a sparkling wine. There was in fact a strict protocol for toasts at weddings.

Today, it's generally accepted that anyone can make a toast at an event, and it doesn't need to be made with alcohol. Occasionally, at weddings, the bridal couple may decide to follow the strict protocol, but it's unlikely that anyone is going to be offended if the protocol isn't followed to the letter.

When you're asked to give a speech, the best thing to do is to ask if you should make a toast. The answer will usually be yes, because it's a nice gesture to offer a toast.

For more information about toasts, see pages 108–112.

Warming Up

It may sound silly, but it's a good idea to warm up before giving your speech. Even if the occasion isn't very formal, it still helps to breathe deeply about five times before speaking. This way, you'll feel calm and relaxed.

If the occasion is formal, like a wedding or a retirement party, taking the time to warm up your body and voice will help you speak better and conquer those nerves. There are various ways to warm up your body and your voice together. Here are some tips on warming up.

• Before the event, check if you'll be using a microphone. If so, that's good – using a microphone means you won't have to yell to be heard. If not, you can always ask if one is available. If a microphone isn't available, don't worry – warming up properly will help you project your voice.

- The day before your speech, rest your voice as much as possible by trying not to talk. Also sip water that's at room temperature to stay hydrated.

- On the big day, stay hydrated by sipping water. Then, when you arrive at the venue, see if you can set aside about 15 minutes for your warm-up. Start by doing five deep breaths, have a rest, then do five more. The aim of breathing deeply is to bring your heart rate down. You should feel calm and relaxed.

- Next, focus on your body. Stretch your neck by doing five slow head rolls, have a rest, then do five more. Hunch your shoulders five times, have a rest, then do five more.

- Then, focus on your face and jaw. First, with your fingertips, massage the muscles in your face while opening and closing your mouth. This will help release all of that tension in your jaw. Second, smile in an exaggerated way and hold, then release. Do this five times, have a rest, then do five more.

- Now, focus on your mouth. Stretch your mouth open wide and stick out your tongue. Wiggle your tongue from side to side. Do this five times, have a rest, then do five more.

- If you've got time, the next step is say a few tongue twisters. Enunciate every word so your lips are really moving. Alternatively, you can repeat a word, such as 'ha'. If you prefer to say 'ha', repeat it five times in a row, have a rest, and then repeat it another five times. And, finally, if there's time, sing a favourite song because singing will make you feel good and help calm your nerves.

If there isn't time to do all of the steps, just do some deep breathing and make sure you're hydrated.

There are lots of websites where you'll find information about warming up, so if you've got time, check them out. You may find something that really works for you.

Giving Your Speech

Well, here you are, on the big day. You've got five minutes to go before giving your speech.

Instead of giving in to the nerves that threaten to overwhelm you, use these last-minute ideas to stay calm and ensure you give a great speech.

- Breathe deeply three or four times.

- Keep in your mind an image of yourself giving your speech well.

- If your name will be announced, listen carefully so you don't miss your cue to begin. If not, wait till the right moment arrives before beginning. The right moment is when there's a lull in the conversation.

- Finally, speak clearly and take your time. Everyone's really keen to hear what you've got to say!

Using This Book

This book will provide you with inspiration when you set out to write your speech. The first section has given you information about speech writing and speech making in general. It has also offered some ideas about dealing with nerves, warming up and actually giving your speech.

The rest of the book is divided into different sections that relate to situations when a speech may be called for. Within each section is a range of people for whom you may give your speech. There is also some general information about each situation that will help you know what to say and how to say it. In the example speeches, he/she, him/her and his/hers have been used interchangeably.

You will then find text and quotations that you can incorporate into your own speech or use as inspiration. It may be that you can take parts of several texts or even text from different sections to make your own speech. By all means, use the text provided in whatever way works for you to make your speech the best it can be.

SAYING HELLO

From small beginnings come great things.

American proverb

General

Beginnings are wonderful, aren't they? They're a chance to say hello to a special new someone. We all love receiving news of a beginning, such as a birth, the creation of a new family or a new job. Today, it seems as if celebrating a beginning is more important than ever. Perhaps because we lead such busy lives and don't catch up with family and friends often, many people use these occasions as a chance to have a party or get-together.

In this section, you'll find examples of speeches you can use at an occasion celebrating a beginning. There are some quotations that you might like to include in your speech. And remember that it's a lovely idea to toast a beginning, so for more information about toasts, see pages 108–112.

Births

The most obvious beginning is of course a birth. The beginning of a precious new life is such a happy occasion and rarely passes without a celebration. Today, many parents celebrate the birth of a new baby with a special ceremony in which the baby is 'named'. This ceremony can take many forms and may be religious or non-religious.

Religious Naming Day

After the religious ceremony, many families have a party or reception at home where someone important to them, such as a godparent, close friend or member of the family, will say a few words. Alternatively, the father or mother may decide to make a speech. For this kind of speech, you need to know all of the details, such as the baby's name and how to pronounce it, Mum's and Dad's names and names of siblings, if any, and perhaps also grandparents' names.

On this very special day, we've welcomed you, [baby's name], into [deity's name]'s family. We wish you and your Mum, [name], Dad, [name] and [brother/sister], [name/s], many blessings. May your life be filled today and all days with love, happiness, peace and faith. It's such a joy for all of us here to share in this very special occasion.

Thank you for allowing all of us to share in [baby's name]'s ceremony today, [mother's name] and [father's name]. We hope that [baby's name] will always be surrounded by love and happiness. May [deity's name] protect [baby's name] always and fill his heart with joy and faith.

It's such a privilege to be here today at [baby's name]'s [name of ceremony]. Please accept my congratulations on this very special day. May [deity's name] bless [baby's name] and her family, and watch over all of you today and always.

Quotations to Use

'A sunbeam to warm you, A moonbeam to charm you, A sheltering angel, so nothing can harm you.' – Irish Blessing

'A baby is God's opinion that the world should go on.' – Carl Sandburg

'... a little child, born yesterday,
A thing on mother's milk and kisses fed ...' – from 'Hymn to Mercury' (one of the Homeric Hymns), translated from Greek by Percy Bysshe Shelley

Non-Religious Naming Day

Today, some parents decide to celebrate the birth of a new baby with a non-religious ceremony, such as a naming day. If you're asked to give a speech at a naming day, including 'naming' the baby, there are some simple things to remember. The 'namer' welcomes the baby into the world and says the baby's full name, the names of the baby's parents and siblings, godparents, if any, and perhaps grandparents.

I'm proud to stand here before you all to welcome [name] into the world and into this loving community of family and friends. He was born on [day and date] to parents [mother's name] and [father's name]. His parents have decided to name him [provide baby's full name]. He joins [sibling/s] [name/s].

I invite godparents [name] and [name] to share with me in welcoming [name] to the world and to watch as he grows, learns, loves and plays.

Welcome to the world, little [name]! We are delighted to meet you at last. We have been looking forward to meeting you for a long time. We have watched as you have grown over the months and wondered what you would look like. And now you're finally here!

We'd like to congratulate your Mum, [name], and Dad, [name], on your safe arrival. We can report that you arrived on [day and date] weighing [weight]. We're sure that [sibling's name/s] are excited that you're now here. They must be looking forward to playing and laughing with you.

Congratulations, [mother's name], [father's name] and [sibling's name/s], on the birth of your precious daughter and sister, [name], on [day and date]. We know you are overjoyed to welcome [name] into your family. And isn't she lucky to have such a wonderful family to look after and love her?

Weighing in at a healthy [weight], we know that [name] will be loved and cherished always. We're so happy for you all and wish you a lifetime of happiness and love as you watch [name] grow. Well done!

Quotations to Use

'Babies are such a nice way to start people.' – Don Herrold

'Children are one-third of our population and all of our future.' – Select Panel for the Promotion of Child Health, 1981

'Babies are always more trouble than you thought – and more wonderful.' – Charles Osgood

Welcoming Ceremony

In recent years, some families have held a unique type of ceremony called a welcoming ceremony as an alternative to a naming day for a baby, and also to welcome a 'new' family. A 'new' family may be formed when a couple, each with their own children, enters into a new relationship or gets married. Often, a welcoming ceremony will follow a marriage or a renewal of vows. Welcoming ceremonies are also held by couples who adopt a baby or a child.

If it's your job to say a few words at a welcoming ceremony, you need to know the names of the new family members, especially the surname.

I'd like to take this opportunity to present the [surname] family. Today, they have affirmed their commitment to each other as a new family. We welcome [parents' names] and [child/children's name/s], who have come together as a brand new family. We wish all of you a long and happy life together.

Please join with me in welcoming [name] to the [surname] family. I know that everyone here is overjoyed that [names'] wish of having a family has been fulfilled. They now have their precious son to complete their family. We know that [name] will be cherished. We all look forward to watching him grow as a member of the [surname] family.

Welcome to the [surname] family! We're so happy for you that you've taken this huge step and come together as a new family. And thanks for having us here today to celebrate. I know we all look forward to lots more happy times together with you as a new family!

Quotations to Use

'Every child begins the world again ...' – Henry David Thoreau

'Adoption is when a child grew in its mummy's heart instead of her tummy.' – Author unknown

'Aside from new babies, new mothers must be the most beautiful creatures on earth.' – Terri Guillemets

Welcome to a New Job

Another type of beginning is a new job. At many workplaces today, new employees are welcomed and introduced to other staff. Such an introduction can be a big help not only for existing staff, but also for the new employee. It's a great way for the new employee to put names to the faces of the people he or she will be working with and to feel part of the team.

I take great pleasure in welcoming [new employee's name] to [name of workplace]. [Name] will take on the role of [name of job]. She comes to us with a strong background in [area of expertise], having studied [subject] and worked with [name/s]. We are delighted to have [name] join us, and I'm sure you'll all make her feel welcome. We look forward to working with [name] in the coming months.

I'd like to introduce you all to [new employee's name]. He comes to us fresh from [name] with lots of experience in [area of expertise]. It's going to be fantastic having him around because he is great at [area of expertise] and really knows his stuff. I know you'll make [name] feel welcome.

I'd like you to welcome [new employee's name] who will be replacing [name]. [Name] has lots of experience in [area of expertise] so it's going to be great to have her here. Please make her feel very welcome.

Quotations to Use

'Find a job you like and you add five days to every week.' – H. Jackson Brown

'When people go to work, they shouldn't have to leave their hearts at home.' – Betty Bender

'Choose a job you love, and you will never have to work a day in your life.' – Confucius

SAYING HAPPY BIRTHDAY

Every year on your birthday, you get a chance to start new.

Sammy Hagar

General

The birthday of a friend or family member is the perfect time to reconnect if you haven't been in touch for a while and to tell them how special they are to you. Today, it seems as if celebrating a loved one's birthday is more important than ever. Many people use a birthday as an opportunity for a party or a special dinner.

In this section, you'll find examples of speeches you can use at birthday celebrations. A birthday speech doesn't need to follow a set formula, but it's a good idea to include the following:

- an opening comment that grabs the audience's attention

- a thank you to the host, if there is one, and to everyone for coming

- a story or two about the birthday boy or girl

- a salutation to conclude with, such as 'Happy birthday!'.

There are also some quotations that you might like to include in your speech. And don't forget that you can conclude your birthday speech with a toast, so see pages 108–112 for more information about toasts. Also, it's not uncommon to roast a birthday boy or girl, so information about roasting at a birthday party is provided on pages 49–50.

Friends

Today, many people celebrate their birthday with friends over drinks or dinner. It's not uncommon for someone to make a speech about the birthday girl or boy. If you decide or are asked to say a few words, keep in mind that your friend may not want to reveal their age, so don't make any reference to age, unless you're sure they won't mind.

Welcome everyone to this celebration for [name]'s birthday. [Name], I know everyone shares with me in wishing you a very happy birthday! We hope today is the beginning of another year of happiness and love. Have a wonderful day and thanks for the excuse for a chance to catch up and enjoy a great night. Happy birthday!

[Name], we hope this day will be the start of a year of happy times and lots of laughs. We all look forward to sharing it with you. Happy birthday!

Happy birthday to our great friend, [name]. Well, here we are again, another year older and another year wiser! Here's hoping you have a fantastic year and a wonderful night. Well done for bringing us all together to celebrate. Happy birthday!

Quotations to Use

'Age is strictly a case of mind over matter. If you don't mind, it doesn't matter!' – George Bernard Shaw

'A birthday is just the first day of another 365-day journey around the sun. Enjoy the trip.' – Author unknown

'Believing hear, what you deserve to hear:
Your birthday as my own to me is dear ...
But yours gives most; for mine did only lend
Me to the world; yours gave to me a friend.' – Martial

Roasting a Friend

If you're giving a speech at a friend's birthday party, you may like to turn some of your speech into a roast. However, while it's lovely to catch up with friends, it's not so lovely to be embarrassed in front of them! So, unless you know your friend won't mind, keep your stories about your friend's outrageous antics to yourself.

If your friend can laugh at themselves and would enjoy a roast, common topics to talk about include past relationships, sporting prowess, funny travel mishaps and previous nights out. But do avoid mentioning situations that bring up painful memories, and don't just tell inside jokes that only you and your friend will get.

If you plan to roast a friend, use one of the speeches on pages 47–48 and insert your roasting comments where appropriate. A few examples of how to begin a roast are included.

Welcome everyone to this celebration for [name]'s birthday. [Name], I know everyone shares with me in wishing you a very happy birthday! We hope today is the beginning of another year of happiness and love. [Insert roasting comments here before concluding.]* Have a wonderful day and thanks for the chance to catch up and enjoy a great night!

* Now, did I ever tell you about the time [name] and I went to [name of destination]? No? Well, even before we got there, [retell funny story].

* Now, I'd like to share a little secret with you all. I know [name] won't mind! Once, we went to [name of destination] and we met [name] and [name]. Well, [describe what happened].

Milestones

There is a tradition of celebrating twenty-first and fiftieth birthdays, but it's become the norm to celebrate other 'milestone' birthdays as well. The first, eighteenth, thirtieth, fortieth, sixtieth, seventieth, eightieth, ninetieth and one-hundredth birthdays are now also seen as special occasions, and serve as an excuse for a party and of course a speech or two.

There is no set formula for what to say on a milestone birthday. However, it's important to remember that yours might not be the only speech, so be brief. You also need to mention the person's age, no matter how much the birthday girl or boy cringes!

Happy first birthday to our beautiful daughter. We remember with love this day one year ago when you came into our lives. It has been a pleasure to spend each day since with you. And thanks everyone for coming and sharing this special day with us. Happy birthday, little one!

Dear [name], happy [eighteenth/twenty-first] birthday! Here you are – all grown up. We couldn't be any prouder of you and we love you more today than ever. We hope you have a fantastic day and, in the coming years, may all of your dreams and wishes come true.

Happy thirtieth birthday, [name]! As you embark on your fourth decade, we offer you our best wishes for a wonderful birthday and many more to come. We hope this decade sees all of your dreams come true!

Happy fortieth birthday, [name]! This brand new decade sees you reach an age where you can be the person you want to be. Enjoy all that life has to offer and know that we wish you all the best for a very happy birthday and many more to come.

Happy fiftieth birthday, [name]! Today we come together to celebrate your birth fifty years ago. Fifty is truly the new forty, so embrace life and do everything you've always longed to do. May the next fifty years be as wonderful as the first fifty!

Happy sixtieth birthday, [name]! May today be the start of a decade of fun, love and happiness. We want to thank you for sharing the first sixty years with us and we can't wait to share many more fun-filled years with you. Have a wonderful day.

Happy seventieth birthday, [name]! To a truly inspirational person, we say thank you for every day we have spent together and we look forward to more wonderful years together. May your special day be truly wonderful!

Happy eightieth birthday, [name]! Today we give thanks for you and all you have achieved. You have been an inspiration in our lives. May today be filled with every joy as you reflect on everything you've done. Our very best wishes for a sensational birthday!

Happy ninetieth birthday, [name]! What a milestone we're celebrating today. I'm so proud to stand here before you on [name]'s ninetieth birthday. How lucky are we to have our [name of relationship] still with us, inspiring and guiding us with his wisdom. You are truly our inspiration. So, happy, happy birthday and here's to many more wonderful memories!

Happy one-hundredth birthday, [name]! Wow, one-hundred years – a whole century. We're so happy to share this amazing milestone with you today. You are truly our inspiration and guide for how to live a happy, healthy and joyful life. Have a wonderful day and know how much we love you!

Quotations to Use

'You're not 40, you're eighteen with 22 years' experience.' – Author unknown

'Our birthdays are feathers in the broad wing of time.' – Jean Paul Richter

'The old believe everything; the middle-aged suspect everything; the young know everything!' – Jack Benny

'We know we're getting old when the only thing we want for our birthday is not to be reminded of it.' – Author unknown

'May you live to be a hundred years With one extra year to repent.' – Author unknown

'Birthdays are good for you. Statistics show that the people who have the most live the longest.' – Larry Lorenzoni

'Inside every older person is a younger person wondering what happened.' – Jennifer Yane

'Wisdom doesn't necessarily come with age. Sometimes age just shows up all by itself.' – Tom Wilson

Partners

Your partner's birthday is a perfect time to tell them how much they mean to you. It's a great opportunity to spoil that special someone in your life. You can share special moments enjoying or recapturing the love you share. It's also a chance to have a party or dinner with family and friends to celebrate your loved one and show them how much they mean to you.

[Name], I'm so happy to be sharing this special day with you, my favourite person in the whole world. I hope that the coming year is filled with all of the love and happiness you so richly deserve. I love you more today than ever before – if that's possible. Happy birthday!

Wishing you, [name], a very happy birthday! I just want you to know how much I love you and value all our life together. I hope the coming year makes you smile and brings you nothing but good things. Happy birthday!

To my beautiful [name of relationship], wishing you the very happiest of birthdays! I want you to know how special you are to me and how much I treasure our life together. May today be the start of another wonderful year together. Happy birthday!

Quotations to Use

'A diplomat is a man who always remembers a woman's birthday but never remembers her age.' – Robert Frost

'A hundred hearts would be too few To carry all my love for you.' – Author unknown

'Love does not consist of gazing at each other, but in looking together in the same direction.' – Antoine de Saint-Exupéry

Parents

It's a lovely idea to hold a special dinner or party for a parent's birthday, even if it isn't a milestone birthday. Again it's a way to reconnect with family and friends you may not have seen for a while and to say a few words to celebrate the life of a very special person. This may be an occasion when the birthday girl or boy doesn't wish to reveal their age, so it's wise to check this beforehand.

To my amazing [Mum/Dad], I wish you the very happiest of birthdays today and hope there will be many more to come. Thank you for all you've done for me. As you know, the list is endless, but I just want you to know that I appreciate everything you do and love you for just being you. Happy birthday!

[Mum/Dad], we want to wish you a very happy birthday. Enjoy this special day that belongs only to you because you've earnt it. We couldn't wish for a better [mum/dad] and are proud to be your kids. Happy birthday!

Happy birthday, [Mum/Dad]. We hope you have a wonderful day being spoilt rotten. We just wanted to say thank you for being the best [mum/dad] in the whole world and we love you so much. Thank you for everything you do. Happy birthday!

Quotations to Use

'I can no other answer make, but, thanks, and thanks.' – William Shakespeare

'I would thank you from the bottom of my heart, but for you my heart has no bottom.' – Author unknown

'We can only be said to be alive in those moments when our hearts are conscious of our treasures.' – Thornton Wilder

Children

It used to be that children's birthdays were celebrated quietly at home without much fuss. Today, it seems the opposite occurs! Each year, many families hold a birthday party with lots of friends and family, and sometimes even an entertainer for their child or children. Perhaps again this is because we don't see our family and friends as often as we used to and a child's birthday is a perfect excuse for a party.

If you're making a speech at a child's birthday, this is one occasion when you definitely need to mention the age of the birthday boy or girl in order to celebrate just how grown up they are.

Happy, happy birthday to our special daughter, [name]. We are so proud to be celebrating your birthday today and can't believe how much you've grown. We hope that your special day is magical and that all of your dreams come true! And we wish to thank everyone for coming to help us celebrate [name]'s birthday today.

Wow – look at you, all grown up! Happy birthday to a fantastic boy. Here's hoping you have a magical day and a wonderful year. I hope all your dreams come true!

Today we're celebrating the day you came into the world and changed our lives forever! Happy birthday to a fabulous girl. We hope that you have a wonderful day and an even better year. Happy birthday!

Quotations to Use

'So mayst thou live, dear! many years,
In all the bliss that life endears, ...' – from 'To My
Daughter, On Her Birthday' by Thomas Hood

'Children make you want to start life over.'
– Muhammad Ali

'Every child comes with the message that God is not
yet discouraged of man.' – Rabindranath Tagore

SAYING GOODBYE

May the **road rise up** to meet you, may the wind be ever at your back. May the **sun shine warm** upon your face and the rain fall softly on your fields. And **until we meet again,** may God hold you in the hollow of his hand.

Irish blessing

General

Unlike beginnings, endings are often sad occasions. But it's important to say goodbye when an ending has occurred – we usually feel better for having done so. And an ending does offer another chance to connect with those people who are important to us.

In this section, you'll find examples of speeches you can use at an occasion when you say goodbye. There are also some quotations that you might like to include in your speech. A toast can be a fitting way to end a goodbye, so for more information about toasts, see pages 108–112. And at some goodbye occasions, such as a retirement party, it's not unheard of to roast someone, so information about roasting is provided on pages 82–84.

Funerals and Memorials

General

When someone you love dies, it can often be very difficult to find the right words to say. There is no set formula for a tribute or a eulogy – it really is up to you. But, typically, eulogies are written in chronological order, so that can help to give you a structure. And keep in mind that your eulogy may be one of several at the funeral. There may be one from a child or close family member, another from a close work colleague and the final one from a best friend. Your relationship to the deceased will help you know what to say.

Following a process for writing your tribute may help you too.

- First, collect information about the deceased. This may take the form of memories, letters or other documents, or photos. You may find it useful to talk to other people as well.

- Next, organise all of the information into sections, which may follow chronological order or some other order, such as the deceased's interests, your memories and how you will remember the deceased.

- Then you need to write a draft. Once you've got something down on paper, you need to practise. The best way to practise a speech is in front of someone else, who can give you instant feedback.

- You may need to redraft and practise again.

On the next pages, you'll find some examples of eulogies you can use to write your own. Here are two general eulogies to get you started.

Thank you so much for coming today to farewell [name]. We value your presence greatly as we say goodbye to our cherished [name of relationship]. [Name] was one of [number of children] and was born [birth date] in [birth place] to [parents' names]. He was [provide biographical details about childhood and young life]. He had [provide details about the deceased's work life, if appropriate, and subsequent family life, if relevant].

[Name] leaves behind [provide name of partner, if appropriate, and number and names of children, grandchildren or great-grandchildren, if any], all of whom loved him and valued his wisdom and love. We remember him as a [provide details] and will always miss his [provide details]. We invite you to join us after the memorial at [place] for some refreshments.

It makes me very happy today to see so many friends and family here to farewell [name]. [Name] was my [describe relationship]. She was a kind, hard-working woman with a positive attitude to life. She leaves behind [list family members], and we'll all miss her smile and warmth very much.

[Name] loved [describe interests]. She spent a lot of time [describe activity]. She also loved [describe another interest] and was never happier than when [describe activity]. I remember when [tell what happened]. These special memories of [name] will live in my heart forever.

No matter the situation, [name] was always [list quality/ies]. I know we'll all remember when she was faced with [tell what happened]. But it was her [list quality/ies] that won through.

I will miss [name] very much, but her [list quality/ies] and memory will live in my heart forever. Thank you all so much for coming today to remember her, and please join us afterwards at [place].

Quotations to Use

'Don't be dismayed at goodbyes. A farewell is necessary before you can meet again. And meeting again, after moments or lifetime, is certain for those who are friends.' – Richard Bach

'Every parting is a form of death, as every reunion is a type of heaven.' – Tryon Edwards

'Great is the art of beginning, but greater is the art of ending.' – Lazurus Long

'Never part without loving words to think of during your absence. It may be that you will not meet again in this life.' – Jean Paul Richter

'Don't cry because it's over. Smile because it happened.' – Author unknown

'Our death is not an end if we can live on in our children and the younger generation. For they are us, our bodies are only wilted leaves on the tree of life.' – Albert Einstein

'Let life be as beautiful as summer flowers and death like autumn leaves.' – Rabindranath Tagore

'As a well-spent day brings happy sleep, so a life well used brings happy death.' – Leonardo da Vinci

Family Member

When a close family member, such as a mother, father, partner or child dies, you may like to include biographical details about the person. You can also provide special memories of your loved one, before inviting attendees to join the wake. You may even discuss with other family members which memories to share – that way all of the family has contributed to the eulogy.

Thanks to all of you for coming today to remember [name], my [describe relationship]. [Name] was born on [birth date] in [birth place] to [parents' names]. He was one of [number of children] and was [provide biographical details about childhood and young life]. He [provide details about the deceased's work life, if appropriate, and subsequent family life, if relevant].

[Name] had [provide name of partner, number and names of children, grandchildren or great-grandchildren, if any], all of whom loved him and valued his guidance and love. We remember him as a warm, loving father who gave of himself generously. I recall when [provide a specific memory]. I'll always smile when I think of [provide another specific memory]. I'll never forget how [name] [provide another specific memory].

We will always miss [name] and hold his memory in our hearts always. Please join us now at [place] for some refreshments.

Friend

If you are a very close friend of the deceased, you may already have in mind what you would like to say about them in a eulogy. This will help you organise your thoughts at a difficult time. A tribute by a friend can really take any format – it's up to you. Generally, friends know things about us that family members and work colleagues may not, and it's these special, possibly unusual things that you may wish to share about your friend.

You won't need to provide all of the biographical details about your friend – that's the family's job. Feel free to be creative and to say as much or as little as you feel able. Remember there are only two important considerations – first, pay tribute to your friend, and second, thank the family for the opportunity to contribute.

I'm here today to remember my dearest friend, [name], and want to thank [name] for allowing me to do so. [Name] was so full of life that it's impossible to believe she is gone. As I look back on countless happy times together, I can't believe how much we fitted into a lifetime. I remember this one time when we [tell what happened].

[Name] lived life to the fullest, and her legacy of kindness, generosity and friendship will never be forgotten. In particular, I remember how [name] [tell what happened]. I want to thank [name] for the many years of friendship we shared. I will always carry her memory in my heart.

Colleague

Again, there really is no set formula for a tribute or a eulogy by a colleague. But, if you're delivering the work tribute, chances are yours might be the last one delivered. Generally, the family comes first, followed by the friend. So this is one situation when it really is wise to be brief. As with any tribute, your speech will sound more natural if you speak from your heart.

Also, don't forget to introduce yourself, explain your connection to the person and include details about when he or she started work with you and the positions held. Include one or two anecdotes and some special memories, and then conclude by expressing your gratitude for having been given the chance to speak about the person.

My name is [name], and I worked with [name] for [number of years] at [workplace]. I remember how [name] just fitted in perfectly with the whole team. [Name] held various positions during his time at [workplace], including [name]. Every day, he put one-hundred per cent effort into the job. I remember one time when we were [tell what happened].

[Name] contributed so much to the job. We just couldn't have done it without him. I'll never forget when [name] helped us with [tell what happened]. He did such a great job. We'll never be able to replace him.

I'd like to thank [name] for giving me this chance to speak about [name]. It's an honour to speak about him. We'll remember [name] always.

Retirement

The ultimate goodbye at work is when someone retires. Retirement is a unique occasion because the person isn't only leaving their workplace, they are leaving work behind as well – although, today, some people have another successful career after retirement!

If it's your job to do a speech or one of the speeches when an employee retires, remember that it's natural for most retirees to be reflecting on their career. Retirement can be a bittersweet occasion – it might be a time when people ponder what they've achieved. So, unless your brief is to roast a retiree, don't! Instead, focus on the person's valuable contribution, and provide a few examples.

Following the formula for a speech when an employee is leaving will ensure you cover the basic details. Then you can add those special examples showing how significant the person's contribution was.

As you know, we're saying farewell to [name] today, who is retiring. I'd like to say a few words about her. [Name] started working here in [year] in the position of [name]. She worked on [name] with [names]. Without [name], we couldn't have achieved everything we did and we want to thank [name] for everything she has done over the years. [Insert specific contribution example here.]*

We wish you all the very best for the future, whatever it may hold. Please don't be a stranger – come in and say hello and tell us how great retirement is. We'll miss seeing you around. Happy retirement!

Well, the time has come to say goodbye to [name], who leaves us today on the big adventure called retirement. I can remember when [name] started working here as a [name of position]. [Name] has done a fantastic job over the years, and we couldn't have achieved everything we have without his contributions. [Insert specific contribution example here.]*

So, from all of us here, we say thank you to [name] and farewell. But don't forget us – please visit and let us know what you're up to. We'll miss you.

* [Name]'s sense of humour helped us all keep going when things became very tough. I remember when [tell what happened].

* [Name]'s determination to deliver one-hundred per cent every time inspired all of us to work harder. Did you know it was [name] who [tell what happened]?

* Without [name], we wouldn't be where we are today. I know you all remember when [name] [tell what happened].

Quotations to Use

'The trouble with retirement is that you never get a day off.' – Abe Lemons

'Life begins at retirement.' – Author unknown

*'O, blest retirement! friend to life's decline –
How blest is he who crowns, in shades like these,
A youth of labour with an age of ease!' – Oliver
Goldsmith*

Roasting a Retiree

If your brief is to roast a retiree, you can tell those funny stories that are guaranteed to get a laugh. It may even be possible to find a common theme within the stories that you can exploit. Perhaps the retiree always uses the same funny expression, tells bad jokes or talks loudly on the telephone. If your stories are a little more controversial, it may be wise to clear your speech in advance. Talk to your manager.

If you plan to roast the retiree, you can use the same speech as for an employee who is leaving, but after mentioning some examples of the person's valuable contribution, insert a few funny stories. Some opening lines have been provided. Remember, though, to conclude on a good note.

As you know, we're saying farewell to [name] today, who is retiring. I'd like to say a few words about her. [Name] started working here in [year] in the position of [name]. She worked on [name] with [names]. Without [name], we couldn't achieved everything we did and we want to thank [name] for everything she has done over the years. [Insert funny stories here if you are roasting as well.]**

>** Now, I know I won't miss when [name] does [describe activity]. In fact, I remember a time when [tell what happened].

>** Does anyone remember when [name] did [describe activity]? Yes? Well, you may not know that once [name] was found [tell what happened].

** Did you know that [name] can do [describe activity]? Well, let me tell you about the time we found [name] [tell what happened].

** Have you heard the one about the employee who did [describe activity]? Well, believe it or not, that was [name]! And that's not all she got up to. I remember when [tell what happened].

Leaving a Job

Just as new employees are welcomed at work, employees who leave are farewelled. A farewell will often take place at the end of the working day and involve other employees gathering together to say goodbye. There may be a number of speeches at a work farewell, so be brief if you're giving a speech.

The basic format for a speech to farewell someone leaving a job is as follows:

- Say why you've all gathered and how many months or years the person has worked at the workplace.

- Say what the person will be doing when they leave.

- Thank the person for their great work.

- Finally, wish them all the best and, if appropriate, introduce the person who will replace them.

It's with much regret that I'm here before you to say a few words about [name], who is leaving today. [Name] began work here in [year] in the position of [name]. He leaves to take up a position at [name]. We wish [name] all the very best in the future and will miss seeing him around here. And welcome to [name] who will be filling [name]'s position. Please make her welcome.

We all know why we're here today – to say goodbye to [name]. She came to us fresh from [name] and has been here for [number of months/years]. Now, she is leaving to do [name new position or reason for leaving]. Thank you to [name] for doing such a great job. It's just not going to be the same without you here, so please keep in touch.

I'd like to say goodbye to [name], who's been here for [number of months/years]. [Name] has done such a great job over the time he has been here, and we want to thank him very much for everything he has done. He is leaving us today to do [name new position or reason for leaving], and we wish him all the best in his new role. And please make [name] welcome as she will be replacing [name].

Quotations to Use

*'Promise me you'll never forget me because if I
thought you would I'd never leave.' – A.A. Milne*

*'How lucky I am to have something that makes saying
goodbye so hard.' – Carol Sobieski and Thomas
Meehan,* Annie

*'The world is round and the place which may seem
like the end may also be the beginning.' – Ivy Baker
Priest*

Moving Away

These days, it seems many people move home more often than in the past. Perhaps it's for work, to be closer to family or for better schools. The people who make up your neighbourhood may change every few years. If you're saying a few words when neighbours or friends move away, keep your speech short if you fear you may get upset. Focus on the positives, such as the wonderful new opportunities this move offers and that it's easier these days to stay in touch.

I'd like to farewell our special friends, the [name] family. They have lived in this neighbourhood for [number of years], and we've all enjoyed their company. It just won't be the same here without you, but we know this is a fantastic opportunity for you all. All the best and let's keep in touch.

Well, here we are saying goodbye to [name], who's moving to [name of place]. What are we going to do without you? Our catch-ups just won't be the same without you. But you'll have to stay in touch and tell us how it's going. We're really going to miss you, but we wish you all the best for the big move!

We're so sorry to see you go, but we know this is a fantastic opportunity. We wish you the best of luck for your move and hope that the new [house/job/school/country] is everything you wish for. Goodbye and good luck!

Quotations to Use

'Love is missing someone whenever you're apart, but somehow feeling warm inside because you're close in heart.' – *Kay Knudsen*

'Nothing makes the earth seem so spacious as to have friends at a distance; they make the latitudes and longitudes.' – *Henry David Thoreau*

'Goodbyes are not forever.
Goodbyes are not the end.
They simply mean I'll miss you
Until we meet again!' – *Author unknown*

Going on Leave

Many school leavers today take a 'gap year' before they start further study or work, and it's not uncommon for retirees to set off on holidays for six months. If you're farewelling someone who's off on a long trip, remember to focus on the positives so you don't get too upset.

Good luck on your travels! We hope you have a truly wonderful time away, enjoying new cultures, sights and sounds. Make the most of every minute and don't forget your camera. We'll be waiting to share your photos! Remember to stay safe and know that we'll be thinking about you. We'll miss you very much.

We hope you have a great time away this year! What an adventure – a whole year off to experience lots of new places, sights and sounds. You've worked very hard to deserve this trip, so make the most of it. And remember that we're only a phone call away. Stay safe!

We hope you have a fabulous journey! We're so excited that you'll have the chance to see all of the places you've dreamt of. Here's hoping this trip is everything you desire. Remember to stay in touch and we can't wait till you return and share all the travel stories.

Quotations to Use

'A vacation is like love – anticipated with pleasure, experienced with discomfort, and remembered with nostalgia.' – Author unknown

'Wandering re-establishes the original harmony which once existed between man and the universe.' – Anatole France

'When preparing to travel, lay out all your clothes and all your money. Then take half the clothes and twice the money.' – Susan Heller

SAYING WELL DONE

To say, 'well done'
to any bit of
good work is
to take hold of
the powers which
have made the effort
and strengthen
them beyond our
knowledge.

Phillips Brooks

General

Isn't it great when a loved one achieves something? If you know the person well, feelings of pride may mingle with relief that there was a successful outcome! Such an event is an excuse for friends and family to get together and celebrate.

In this section, you'll find examples of speeches you can use at an occasion when you say well done. You will also find some quotations that you might like to include in your speech. A toast can be a fitting way to say well done, so for more information about toasts, see pages 108–112.

Graduations

Today, the term 'graduation' isn't only applied to getting a university degree, but also to the end of primary and secondary school, and getting an apprenticeship. Proud parents often combine a party for an eighteenth birthday with a celebration for the end of formal schooling. Remember to name the achievement in your speech, and focus on the exciting future to come.

I'd like you to join with me in saying 'well done' to our magnificent student, [name]. As you all know, this is the end of school for [name]. Next year, she will join the ranks of students at [name]. We've watched as you've grown and applied yourself to your studies, and we couldn't be prouder of the efforts you've made and your achievement. Well done!

Well done on your graduation from [name of course]. We all know how hard you've worked and how dedicated you've been to getting this qualification. Now, you can look forward to a successful career as a [name]. You've made us all very proud of who you are and what you've achieved. Today you can relax and celebrate your achievements!

We're here tonight to say well done to [name], who's just finished [name] and got [name]. We've seen you work really hard and give up lots of things so you can achieve this. We're so proud of you and can't wait to see what the next exciting phase holds for you. Well done!

Quotations to Use

'The tassel's worth the hassle!' – Author unknown

'The fireworks begin today. Each diploma is a lighted match. Each one of you is a fuse.' – Edward Koch

'Don't live down to expectations. Go out there and do something remarkable.' – Wendy Wasserstein

Awards

If it's your job to deliver a speech when someone receives an award, there is no set formula to follow, as with many other speeches. But remember to name the actual award, and if it is an object, ask the recipient if you can hold it up. No doubt your audience will love to see the medal, trophy or plaque. But refrain from handing it around – it's up to the recipient to offer this.

The [name of award] is a special award given to those who [say specifically what the award has been given for]. I'm delighted to say that [name] has received this award. [Name] is an amazing person who has dedicated his life to [name of cause]. We are all so proud of you, [name] – the way you've devoted yourself to this cause is inspirational. We are so honoured that you are our [name of relationship] and are overjoyed to be celebrating this occasion with you.

Well done to [name], who's won an award for [say specifically what the award has been given for]. We're so incredibly proud of you. We've all watched as you've dedicated yourself to [name of subject or activity] and think it's a just reward that you've been honoured in this way. Well done!

Today, we're saying well done to [name], who has just been given an award for [say specifically what the award has been given for]. We're so proud of the great things you've achieved and the difference you've made to people's lives along the way. You richly deserve this great honour.

Quotations to Use

'Shoot for the moon. Even if you miss, you'll land among the stars.' – Les Brown

'The road to success is dotted with many tempting parking places.' – Author unknown

'When the world says, "Give up,"
Hope whispers, "Try it one more time."' – Author unknown

Promotions

Another occasion to say 'well done' is when someone gets a promotion. It's not uncommon for a promotion to be celebrated both at work and at home. If a get-together is being held at work and it's your job to say a few words, be brief as there may be employees present who applied for the job and were unsuccessful. Alternatively, if you're hosting a celebration for a loved one who's received a promotion, you won't need to worry about work colleagues' feelings, unless you've invited them. Either way, it's a good idea to check that you've got the correct title for the promotion.

I'd like to say 'well done' to [name] who has just been promoted from [title of job] to [title of job]. [Name] has been with us for [number of months or years] and has done a great job. We're sure [name] will continue to do a great job as she rises to the challenges of her new role. Well done!

Thank you so much for coming tonight to say 'well done' to [name] on his promotion from [title of job] to [title of job]. As you all know, [name] has worked so hard at [workplace], and we believe he richly deserves this reward. Well done!

Well done on being promoted to [title of job]! You've worked so hard to achieve your dreams and now you can enjoy your success. We're sure you're really going to shine in this new role. Well done!

Quotations to Use

'By working faithfully eight hours a day you may eventually get to be boss and work twelve hours a day.' – Robert Frost

'Hard work spotlights the character of people: some turn up their sleeves, some turn up their noses, and some don't turn up at all.' – Sam Ewing

'Many dream, some try, but only a few achieve. You are an achiever.' – Author unknown

SAYING
CONGRATULATIONS

We offer you a
warm embrace
of congratulations
and wishes of
happiness
for the rest of
your life!

Author unknown

General

Who doesn't love a wedding and all of those occasions that go along with weddings – engagements and anniversaries? Most of us love a happy ending, and all of the ritual and celebration that go with these occasions. They are another perfect opportunity for family and friends to get together and perfect times for speeches as well.

In this section, you'll find examples of speeches you can use at an occasion when you say congratulations. There are also some quotations that you might like to include in your speech. There is information about toasts on pages 108–112, and pointers if you plan to roast a bride and groom at a wedding on pages 124–127.

Toasts

Traditionally, to toast someone, you raised your glass with your right hand straight from the shoulder. It is said that this position evolved from the time when a sword or dagger was hidden in the right hand or sleeve, in case of attack. If you adopted this stance in front of someone, you were indicating your friendship towards them.

Also according to tradition, after raising your glass and saying your toast, you touch glasses with the person or people whom you're toasting – the bride and groom, for example. It's said that the tradition of touching glasses came about because of concerns about poisoning. By touching glasses, what's in their glass spills into your glass, showing that you're not worried about drinking what's in their glass.

These days, a toast is still regarded as a gesture of honour and goodwill by one person to another. Nonetheless, the etiquette about when and how to make a toast has been relaxed. The setting will tell you whether or not you need to follow the old rules. So, if friends are toasting a birthday boy or girl in a bar, no one minds if some people have empty glasses and if the toaster is interrupted and puts his or her glass down during the toast. The same behaviour may not be appreciated at a wedding where the bride and groom want to follow the old protocols. For information about how to make a toast at a wedding, see pages 116–123.

According to the traditional etiquette, a toast should have three parts: the introduction, the oration and the actual toast.

- In the introduction, the toaster will call for attention, say who he or she is and explain his or her relationship to the toastee.

- The oration is the body of the toast, when the toaster mentions the occasion and why he or she is making the toast to the toastee.

- Then, in the actual toast, the toaster raises his or her glass and says, 'To X'.

While giving the toast, the toaster must look at the toastee and touch their glass if within reach. Otherwise, the toaster and toastee may 'air touch' their glasses. Keep in mind when writing your toast that it isn't a speech, so it shouldn't be too long. And a toast is never a roast – it should always be kind to the toastee and show them in a favourable light, unless humour is appropriate for the setting and the company.

Occasionally, depending on the situation, a toast isn't offered to a person, but to a concept, such as 'peace' or 'good health'. And sometimes a specific word replaces the actual toast, such as 'cheers' or the equivalent in another language. Go to pages 155-158 for the equivalent to cheers in different languages.

Ladies and gentlemen, your attention please. I'm [your name], [name]'s [relationship to toastee]. I'd like to propose a toast to [name], who is celebrating [details of the occasion]. So, please, join with me in raising your glasses. To [name].

Everyone, as you know, I'm [name], [name]'s [relationship to toastee]. Here's a toast to you, [name], for [details of the occasion]. We're so proud of you! To [name].

Please raise your glasses to [concept], a worthy ideal! Here's to [concept]. Cheers!

Engagements

An engagement is almost as exciting as a wedding. There is so much to look forward to. If you're asked to give a speech at an engagement, it's a good idea to ask the couple if they'd also like you to propose a toast. Speeches and toasts for engagements don't really follow any formula. The main thing is to wish the couple well.

We couldn't be happier that you are taking this step. In fact, we've all been hoping that we would see this day, as you are such a perfect couple. It gives us great joy to see how happy you are together. There's so much to look forward to and we can't wait for your wedding. Congratulations on your engagement!

Congratulations to [name] and [name] on your engagement! Seeing how happy you are today makes us so happy. We're delighted you're making this commitment to each other and look forward to the big day. We wish you a long and happy life together filled with many blessings.

We're so happy you're engaged and are thrilled to see you setting out together on the journey through life. May your love and respect for each other grow as you grow old together. We wish you all the best that life has to offer. No two people deserve this happiness more than you two. Congratulations on your engagement!

Quotations to Use

'He felt now that he was not simply close to her, but that he did not know where he ended and she began.' – Leo Tolstoy

'The arms of love encompass you with your present, your past, your future, the arms of love gather you together.' – Antoine de Saint-Exupéry

'Love would never be a promise of a rose garden unless it is showered with light of faith, water of sincerity and air of passion.' – Author unknown

Weddings

A number of speeches may be given at different times during a wedding reception. Today, it really is up to the bride and groom to decide how many speeches are given, when and by whom. The bride and groom will also decide whether or not there are to be any toasts, who will give them and when.

If the bridal couple ask you to give a speech at their wedding, it's wise to ask them for details, including the purpose and timing of the speech, and if they would like a toast as well. For example, a bridal couple may ask their parents or a close friend, such as the best man or maid or matron of honour, to give a speech accompanied by a toast.

If, however, the bridal couple is following the traditional wedding speech and toast protocol, this is one formula to follow. In his role as host, the bride's father offers the first speech and toast. He thanks the guests for coming, expresses his love and pride for his daughter, and offers a toast to the happiness of the newlyweds. Next, the best man gives a short speech about the bride and groom in which he may tell a funny but tasteful story about the groom, and praise and compliment the bride before offering a toast to their happiness.

The best man is followed by the maid or matron of honour, who offers a short speech in which she tells a funny but tasteful story about the bride and also compliments her, before offering a toast to the couple's happiness. Finally, the groom will make a speech thanking the bride's parents for hosting the wedding and the guests for coming, before offering a toast to the bridesmaids. The bride's mother, the groom's mother or father, and the bride might also give speeches.

Depending on the bride and groom, the best man and the maid or matron of honour may use their funny story as an opportunity to roast the bride and groom. See pages 124–127 for more information about roasting at a wedding.

Examples of wedding speeches and toasts are provided on the following pages.

Father of the bride: I'd like to thank you all for coming today to the wedding of [name] and [name]. We're so proud of [name], our daughter. We've watched her grow from a clever, funny, engaging girl to the beautiful, accomplished woman she is today. We couldn't love her any more than today on her wedding day. So, I'd like to propose a toast to our daughter and her wonderful new husband, [name]. May they know nothing but happiness, health and good fortune in their new life together. To [name] and [name].

Best man: Congratulations to [name] and [name] on this – their wedding day. I remember when they met! [Name of groom] was [provide funny but tasteful story]. But here he is today, married to the beautiful [name of bride]. Doesn't she look stunning and don't they make a wonderful couple! So, I'd like to propose a toast to their happiness always. To [name] and [name].

Maid or matron of honour: I'd like to offer my congratulations to my beautiful friend, [name], and her wonderful new husband, [name]. I've known [name of bride] for [number of months or years] now and have seen [provide funny but tasteful story]. Yet, look at her now – happy and in love! I'd like to propose a toast to a long and happy life together filled with many blessings. To [name] and [name].

Groom: First, I'd like to offer our thanks to [name of bride]'s parents for this truly wonderful day. It's everything we hoped for – so thank you from the bottom of our hearts. And thank you to all of you for coming today. This special day wouldn't be the same if all of you weren't here to share it with us. And, finally, I'd like to propose a toast to the bridesmaid/s, [name/s]. They look stunning and have looked after my beautiful wife, [name], so well. To [name/s].

Of course, it's up to the bridal couple to decide whether or not to follow this formula. They may decide to do their own thing. If this is the case and you're asked to give a speech either with or without a toast, ask the couple for some direction. Here are some examples you can adapt for your own speech.

Congratulations to [name] and [name] on your wedding day. We all wish you a long and happy future together filled with everything life has to offer. Enjoy this special day, and treasure always the love you share. We're so proud of you both!

Best wishes on your special day, [name] and [name]. We look forward to watching the two of you make a life together, and we'll be here to love and support you every step of the way. We feel truly blessed to be sharing this day with you. Thank you for all of the joy you have brought into our lives.

Congratulations on your wedding, [name] and [name]. We hope that today is the start of a long and happy life together, filled with every blessing. Enjoy every moment of this special day, and always treasure the love you share.

Quotations to Use

'True love stories never have endings.' – Richard Bach

'Love one another and you will be happy. It's as simple and as difficult as that.' – Michael Leunig

'Grow old with me! The best is yet to be.' – Robert Browning

'The highest happiness on earth is marriage.' – William Lyon Phelps

'It's so great to find that one special person you want to annoy for the rest of your life.' – Rita Rudner

Roasting at a Wedding

Whether or not to roast at a wedding is a decision that must be made with the bride and groom, because a 'surprise' roast may offend. Even if you're given the go-ahead to roast at wedding, it's a good idea to clear what you plan to say with the bride and groom. They will let you know whether you're going too far or not far enough.

At a wedding where the traditional speech and toast protocol is followed, the two people who have the chance to roast are the best man and the maid or matron of honour. In both cases, follow the speech examples provided earlier and insert your roast where indicated.

Best man: Congratulations to [name] and [name] on this – their wedding day. I remember when they met! [Name of groom] was [insert roast here instead of funny but tasteful story].** But here he is today, married to the beautiful [name of bride]. Doesn't she look stunning and don't they make a wonderful couple! So, I'd like to propose a toast to their happiness always. To [name] and [name].

Maid or matron of honour: I'd like to offer my congratulations to my beautiful friend, [name], and her wonderful new husband, [name]. I've known [name of bride] for [number of months or years] now and have seen [insert roast here instead of funny but tasteful story].** Yet, look at her now – happy and in love! I'd like to propose a toast to a long and happy life together filled with many blessings. To [name] and [name].

If the bride and groom are doing their own thing for speeches and toasts on their big day, work together if you're going to roast them. You could use one of the earlier speeches and insert your roast where appropriate, using one of the opening comments.

**Now, I don't know how many people know this about [name] and [name], but one day they [describe activity]. In fact, I remember a time when [tell what happened].

**Does anyone remember when [name] and [name] did [describe activity]? Well, you probably don't know that they also did [tell what happened].

**I know something about [name] and [name] that no one else knows, and I don't think they knew that I know! So, let me tell you what happened [describe activity].

**Have you ever heard that [name] and [name] did [describe activity]? Well, allow me to tell you all about it [tell what happened].

Anniversaries

Anniversaries are another happy event that bring family and friends together to celebrate. Often, couples will bring their bridal party back together to help them celebrate. The wedding anniversaries that are traditionally celebrated in a big way are the tenth, twenty-fifth or silver anniversary, followed by the thirtieth or pearl, fortieth or ruby, fiftieth or golden and the really big one – sixtieth or diamond anniversary. The alternative name for each anniversary is a guide for an appropriate gift for the couple.

Whatever the form of the celebration, it's usual for a speech accompanied by a toast to be made, traditionally by the child or children of the couple, if they are old enough. A wedding anniversary is a very happy occasion when thanks is given for the loving relationship from which children and grandchildren – even great-grandchildren – have come.

Congratulations on your wedding anniversary! It's still a joy to see the two of you together after [number of years]. On this special day, we wish you love, happiness and laughter for the rest of your life together. And thank you for all of the blessings that have come our way since your wedding day.

Congratulations on your [number] anniversary, [Mum and Dad/Grandma and Grandpa]. Your marriage is the foundation on which our whole family rests. We have grown up surrounded by the love, stability and support that your wonderful relationship provides. Here's to many more happy years together.

Happy [number] wedding anniversary to a wonderful couple. On this special day, we wish you continued love, happiness, good health and long life. Thank you for all the joy you've brought into our lives. Congratulations!

Quotations to Use

'Our wedding was many years ago. The celebration continues to this day.' – Gene Perret

'A wedding anniversary is the celebration of love, trust, partnership, tolerance and tenacity. The order varies for any given year.' – Paul Sweeney

'An anniversary is a time to celebrate the joys of today, the memories of yesterday, and the hopes of tomorrow.' – Author unknown

Saying Happy Holiday

Let us cherish
the gift
of family
and
friends this
holiday season.

Author unknown

General

While the Christmas–New Year holiday over December and January is perhaps the most well-known holiday, people celebrate significant festivals and holidays throughout the whole year. At these times, families and friends get together to share a special meal and engage in rituals that add meaning and richness to their lives.

In this section, you'll find examples of speeches you can use for holidays and festivals. There is also some quotations you can use in your speech. It's a lovely idea to offer a toast during the holiday season, so for more information about toasts, see pages 108–112. And see pages 153–154 for appropriate greetings for different holidays and festivals.

Thanksgiving Day

Thanksgiving Day is celebrated on the second Monday of October in Canada and on the fourth Thursday in November in the United States of America. It's a holiday celebrated largely in Canada and the US, and began as a special day to give thanks for the harvest. Today, it's a day to give thanks for the blessings of the year past.

At this special time, let's give thanks for our happy home, our family and friends, and this table piled high with good food. Let's always remember how lucky we are and to be thankful. Happy Thanksgiving!

Happy Thanksgiving to everyone here today. Let's always be thankful for all of the good things we have.

Thanksgiving is a reminder to us all to give thanks for our family and friends, and our good fortune. Thank you to everyone here for contributing to this day and enriching our lives. Happy Thanksgiving!

Quotations to Use

'If the only prayer you said in your whole life was, "thank you," that would suffice.' – Meister Eckhart

'Thanksgiving Day is a jewel, to set in the hearts of honest men; but be careful that you do not take the day, and leave out the gratitude.' – E.P. Powell

'As we express our gratitude, we must never forget that the highest appreciation is not to utter words, but to live by them.' – John Fitzgerald Kennedy

Christmas and New Year

Christmas commemorates the birth of Jesus Christ and is held around the world on 25 December. Millions of people around the world celebrate Christmas, both Christians and non-Christians. New Year is then celebrated one week later, with New Year's Eve on 31 December being the night for parties to see in the New Year and displays of fireworks in cities around the world. Christmas and New Year are called the festive season and are a time when most people have a few days off to spend time with family and friends.

Wishing you and your family a happy and holy Christmas filled with many blessings. And here's to a very Happy New Year!

Merry Christmas and Happy New Year! Wishing you and yours all the love, peace and joy in the world this festive season.

May your holiday season be filled with the joy and love of family and friends. We hope that the coming year is one of peace, joy and love for you and yours.

May the New Year bring you and your loved ones prosperity and peace. May you realise your ambitions, and enjoy longevity and happiness.

Here's hoping you will be blessed with happiness without limit in this New Year. May you also experience security, good health and prosperity.

Quotations to Use

'The best of all gifts around any Christmas tree: the presence of a happy family all wrapped up in each other.' – Burton Hillis

'May Peace be your gift at Christmas and your blessing all year through!' – Author unknown

'Cheers to a new year and another chance for us to get it right.' – Oprah Winfrey

'We will open the book. Its pages are blank. We are going to put words on them ourselves. The book is called Opportunity and its first chapter is New Year's Day.' – Edith Lovejoy Pierce

Other New Year Celebrations

In Western cultures, New Year, when one year ends and another begins, is celebrated on 31 December – 1 January. Combined with Christmas, it's the biggest festival of the year in most Western countries. In other cultures, New Year is celebrated at other times during the year. Here's a list of some other celebrations of New Year around the world.

Chinese New Year

Chinese New Year is the most important Chinese celebration of the year. It takes place each year on the new moon of the first lunar month, so it can occur any day between 21 January and 21 February.

I would like to take this opportunity to extend to you my New Year greetings and wish all of you a happy life in the 'Year of the [name animal]'!

Wishing everyone here today New Year greetings in this auspicious Year of the [name animal]! May you and yours experience good fortune, happiness and good health in this New Year.

Kung Hei Fat Choi to everyone – wishing you and yours prosperity and wealth. May this New Year bring you all continued good health and happiness as well.

Rosh Hashanah

Hebrew for 'Head of the Year', Rosh Hashanah is the Jewish New Year and is celebrated in September. It is a two-day festival that begins on the first day of *Tishrei*, which is the first month of the Jewish calendar. Apple slices are dipped in honey to symbolise a sweet new year.

New beginnings, new hopes, new starts and new chances! May you all be inscribed in the Book of Life for the coming year. May your new beginnings welcome through your doors the richest blessings.

As we dip our apples in honey, may we experience blessings in the year ahead. Also let us hope that the world will become a sweeter place for all of our children.

Tet

Tet is the Vietnamese New Year, which is celebrated at the same time as Chinese New Year, because Vietnam uses the Chinese calendar. It is the most important and popular holiday for the Vietnamese.

Wishing a New Year of health, success and especially happiness to you and yours. We hope the coming year is a good one.

Congratulations and may you prosper this New Year. May money flow in like water and may you have plenty of good health.

Islamic New Year

The Islamic New Year takes place on 1 Muharram, which is the first month of the Islamic calendar. The date of the month of Muharram moves each year, because the Islamic calendar is a lunar one. It is considered to be the most sacred of all Islamic months, except for Ramadan.

On these last days of the lunar year, let us pray that it will be a year of peace, happiness and abundance. May Allah bless you throughout the New Year.

Gujarati New Year

Celebrated the day after the Indian festival of Diwali, Gujarati New Year takes place in either October or November, depending on the lunar calendar. The festival is called *Bestu Varas* or Happy New Year. Most other Hindus celebrate the New Year earlier.

Saal Mubarak (Happy New Year). Put your worries behind you and welcome a new beginning.

Easter

Easter is a Christian festival celebrating the resurrection of Jesus Christ after his crucifixion. It is preceded by Good Friday, which is the day commemorating Jesus's crucifixion. It takes place at a different time each year, but usually on a Sunday between 22 March and 25 April. Easter is celebrated around the world by both Christians and non-Christians with egg hunting and family get-togethers.

May this Easter season find you with friends and family. Wishing you all joy and happiness over this holiday period.

Easter is a special time to come together and celebrate life's blessings. Let's always be thankful for all we have. Happy Easter!

Quotations to Use

'For I remember it is Easter morn,
And life and love and peace are all new born.' – Alice
Freeman Palmer

'Easter is the demonstration of God that life is
essentially spiritual and timeless.' – Charles M. Crowe

Kwanzaa

Kwanzaa is a celebration of family, community and culture. It is celebrated between 26 December and 1 January in the United States and honours African heritage in African-American culture. The festival has seven core principles, including unity and collective work and responsibility. It was first celebrated in 1966–1967 and was created by Maulana Karenga.

Wishing you and yours a joyous Kwanzaa. May you be with your family and friends at this time and come together in unity.

Quotations to Use

'Sticks in a bundle are unbreakable.' – Kenyan proverb

'Service to others is the rent you pay for your room here on earth.' – Muhammad Ali

'Unity to be real must stand the severest strain without breaking.' – Mahatma Gandhi

'In all things that are purely social we can be as separate as the fingers, yet one as the hand in all things essential to mutual progress.' – Booker T. Washington

Diwali

Diwali is a five-day Hindu festival between October and November known as the 'Festival of Lights'. It is an official holiday in India and is celebrated in Nepal, Fiji, Singapore, Sri Lanka, Malaysia, Myanmar, Mauritius, Guyana, Trinidad and Tobago, and Suriname.

Diwali night is full of lights. May your life be filled with the colours and lights of happiness. Happy Diwali!

Vesak

Buddhists commemorate the birth, enlightenment and death of Buddha on Vesak. Often called 'Buddha's birthday', it falls in April or May. The festivities may include offerings, songs, meditation and candlelit processions through streets decorated with lanterns.

Happy Vesak Day! May the teaching of the Buddha guide you and give you peace. We hope that this Vesak is a time of reflection, harmony and happiness.

Yom Kippur

Yom Kippur is also known as the 'Day of Atonement' and is the holiest of days for Jewish people. Many people fast on this day, praying and thinking about atonement and repentance. Yom Kippur is held on the tenth day of the month *Tishrei*, which usually falls in September or October. According to tradition, Rosh Hashanah is the day when God inscribes each person's fate into the Book of Life, and Yom Kippur is the day when God seals the verdict.

May you be written and sealed for a good and sweet year. May you have many years.

May you be sealed in the Book of Life. May you have an easy fast.

Hanukkah

Hanukkah is an eight-day Jewish festival also known as the 'Feast of Lights'. It commemorates the re-dedication of the Holy Temple in Jerusalem in the 2nd century BC. It usually occurs any time from late November to late December. Hanukkah is celebrated by lighting the branches of a candelabra called a Menorah, which has nine branches. Each night, one more branch of the Menorah is lit.

Happy Hanukkah to you and your family.

Quotations to Use

'I ask not for a lighter burden, but for broader shoulders.' – Jewish proverb

'Kindle the taper like the steadfast star
Ablaze on evening's forehead o'er the earth,
And add each night a lustre till afar
An eightfold splendour shine above thy
hearth.' – Emma Lazarus, The Feast of Lights

'May the lights of Hanukkah usher in a better world for all humankind.' – Author unknown

Eid al-Fitr

Eid al-Fitr is an important festival celebrated by Muslims around the world. It is also known as 'Feast of Breaking the Fast' and ends Ramadan, which is the Islamic holy month of fasting. Eid al-Fitr usually takes place in August each year. It occurs over one, two or three days, and people celebrate the end of fasting with a sweet breakfast, good deeds and prayers.

May your Eid be blessed. May peace, happiness and faith be yours on Eid.

Wishing you all the joys and wonders of Eid al-Fitr. May this Eid be a special one for you and may it bring you many happy moments to cherish forever.

Chuseok

Chuseok is a harvest festival celebrated in Korea on the 15th day of the eighth month of the lunar calendar. It usually occurs in September on a different date each year. It is a three-day festival when Koreans visit their home towns and share a feast of traditional Korean food and rice wines with their family. It is celebrated in both North and South Korea.

Happy Chuseok! Let's all look at the full moon tonight and make a wish. May you spend Chuseok well with family.

APPROPRIATE GREETINGS FOR FESTIVALS

Here's how to greet people on their special festival.

Gujarati New Year – *Saal Mubarak* (Happy New Year) (say 'saal moo-bah-rak')

Chinese New Year *'Kung Hei Fat Choi'* (Congratulations and be prosperous) (say 'koong hi fat choy')

Christmas – 'Merry Christmas'

Chuseok (Korean Harvest Festival) – *'Chuseok chahl bo-nay-say-yo'* (Have a happy Chuseok) (say 'choos-e-ock chaal bo-nay-say-yo); *'Jeul-geo-oon Chuseok Doi-se-yo'* (Have a joyous Chuseok) (say 'jool-ge-oon choos-e-ock doi-se-yo')

Diwali – 'Happy Diwali' (say 'divali')

Easter – 'Happy Easter'

Eid al-Fitr – '*Eid Mubārak*' (Blessed Eid) (say 'id moo-bah-rak); '*Eid Sa'id*' (Happy Eid) (say 'id said')

Hanukkah (Jewish Festival of Lights) – '*Chag Chanukah Sameach*' (Happy Chanukah Holiday) (say 'charg chan-oo-kah sam-ich')

Kwanzaa – 'Joyous Kwanzaa'

New Year – 'Happy New Year'

Rosh Hashanah (Jewish New Year) – '*L'Shana Tova*' (For a good year) (say 'la-shannah to-vah')

Tet (Vietnamese New Year) – '*chúc mừng năm mới*' (Happy New Year) (say 'chook moong nam moy'); '*cung chúc tân xuân*' (Gracious wishes of the new spring) (say 'koong chook tarn shjarn')

Thanksgiving – 'Happy Thanksgiving'

Vesak (celebration of Buddha's birth, enlightenment and death) – 'Happy Vesak Day!'

Yom Kippur (Jewish Day of Atonement) – '*G'mar Hatimah Tovah*' (May you be sealed for a good year) (say 'ge-mah hat-ee-mah to-vah')

CHEERS IN OTHER LANGUAGES

Occasionally, a toaster will use a specific word, such as cheers, to replace the actual toast. And, depending on your company, you may like to use the equivalent word to cheers in another language.

Albanian – '*Gëzuar*' (enjoy) (say 'geh-zoo-ah')

Arabic – '*Sahtak*' (for your health) (say 'sah-e-tek')

Australian – 'Scull' (to finish your drink quickly)

Belarusian – '*Budzma*' (may we live!) (say 'bood-zz-mah')

Bosnian – '*Živjeli*' (live!) (say 'zhee-vi-lee')

Bulgarian – '*Nazdrave*' (to health) (say 'naz-dra-vey')

Chinese – '*Gānbēi*' (empty cup) (say 'gan-bay')

Czech – '*Na zdraví*' (to health) (say 'naz-drah-vi')

Danish – '*Skål*' (bowl) (say 'skoal')

Dutch – '*Proost*' (may it be good) (say 'prohst')

Estonian – '*Terviseks*' (for the health)
(say 'ter-vih-seks')

Filipino – '*Mabuhay*' (to life) (say 'mah-boo-hay')

French – '*Santé*' (health) (say 'sahn-tay')

German – '*Prost*' (may it be good) (say 'prohst')

Greek – '*γειά*' (for health) (say 'ya-mas')

Hebrew – '*L'Chayyim*' (to life) (say 'l'chaim')

Italian – '*Salute*' (health) (say 'saw-lu-tay')

Japanese – '*Kanpai*' (dry the glass) (say 'kan-pie')

Korean – '*Gunbae*' (empty cup) (say 'gun-bae')

Norwegian – '*Skål*' (bowl) (say 'skawl')

Polish – '*Na zdrowie*' (to health)
(say 'naz-droh-vee-ay')

Portuguese – '*Saúde*' (health) (say 'saw-oo-de')

Romanian – 'Noroc' (good luck) (say 'no-rock');
'*Sănătate*' (health) (say 'sahn-a-tate')

Serbian – '*Živeli*' (live!) (say 'zhee-ve-lee')

Slovak – '*Na zdravie*' (to health)
(say 'naz-drah-vee-ay')

Spanish – '*Salud*' (health) (say 'sah-lud')

Swedish – '*Skål*' (bowl) (say 'skawl')

Thai – '*Chai-yo!*' (hurrah!) (say 'cho-do')

Turkish – '*Serefe*' (to honour) (say 'sher-i-feh')

Ukrainian – '*Budmo*' (let us be!) (say 'bood-mo')

Vietnamese – '*Một hai ba, yo*' (one, two, three, yo!) (say 'moat hi bah, yo')

Welsh – '*Iechyd Dda*' (good health)
(say 'yeh-chid dah')

Index